EPIC GEOGRAPHY

EPIC GEOGRAPHY

James Joyce's
Ulysses

BY

MICHAEL SEIDEL

MAPS DRAWN BY
THOMAS CRAWFORD

PRINCETON UNIVERSITY PRESS

FOR MARIA

*La tua benignità non pur soccorre
a chi domanda, ma molte fïate
liberamente al dimandar precorre.*

"If that fellow was dropped in the middle of the Sahara, he'd sit, be God, and make a map of it."

(John Joyce of his son, James, at seven [Ellmann, *JJ*, p. 28])

PREFACE

KANT has written that the human mind appeals to geography for spatial orientation as readily as it appeals to history for temporal orientation. This is a book about epic geography and narrative design in James Joyce's *Ulysses*. *Ulysses*, among other things, is a novel of carefully recorded movements over carefully mapped spaces. Geography tells part of its story. Places and directions are not only implicated in the texture of the novel; they contribute to Joyce's rediscovery of epic-narrative potential.

In a notesheet entry for the *Nestor* episode of *Ulysses*, Joyce writes of both place and time as inspirational: "nature develops the spirit in place, history in time."[1] In another note for *Ulysses*, this for *Ithaca*, Joyce defines a related land science, geology, as "embedded storia"[2] (embedded history *or* narrative). Geography is to geology what space is to time: extended *storia*. My approach in this book traces Joyce's development of the narrative spirit in place through his extension or "translation" of a Homeric geography to Dublin. I am not interested in rehearsing the Homeric correspondences in *Ulysses* in the way they have been rehearsed in the past. Instead, I will begin by asking how a longer, and perhaps different, look at the geographical structure of the *Odyssey* might initiate a fuller understanding of the ways in which Joyce accommodates and continues his narrative model.

Twenty years ago Hugh Kenner cast a small but penetrating beacon of light through the fog surrounding Joyce's use of Homer. Kenner argued that the "fundamental correspondence is not between incident and incident, but between situation and situation."[3] If one takes Kenner more literally than he may have meant to be taken at the time, the movement from physical "situation" to narrative "situation" is at the heart of both the Homeric epic and Joyce's *Ulysses*. Kenner views Joyce's re-situation of the *Odyssey* as essentially ironic,

[1] Joyce, *Scribbledehobble: The Ur-Workbook for "Finnegans Wake,"* ed. Thomas E. Connolly (Evanston, Ill., 1961), p. 87. This notebook contains some material intended for *Ulysses*.

[2] Herring, p. 455.

[3] Hugh Kenner, *Dublin's Joyce* (Boston: Beacon Press, 1956, rpt., 1962), p. 181.

but he allows the epic correspondences an important potential: where some see what Pound called Joyce's "poached epic," Kenner sees a narrative layering, a multiple plot. In his recent *The Pound Era*, Kenner himself literalizes his conception of the Homeric Joyce; he writes that Joyce's Homer "was the archaeologist's Homer."[4] Schliemann's and Dörpfeld's excavations, Victor Bérard's Phoenician navigational theories, and Samuel Butler's reconstruction of the *Odyssey* in the city of Trapani on Sicily directly fed Joyce's imagination, concerned as all were "with maps and *periploi*, with stickpins and headgear, with lost coins, broken dishes, cutlery, kitchen debris."[5] Butler's treatment of Homer's epic in *The Authoress of the Odyssey* is especially revealing. Kenner speculates that as a novelist working on the *Odyssey* in novelistic ways, Butler provides a model for Joyce's epic translation. Just as Butler conflates the *Odyssey*'s spatial boundaries in and around one city on one island, the home of the poem's putative narrator, the princess Nausicaa, Joyce reduces the scope of the Homeric action to one city on another island, the home of the novel's actual narrator or narrators.

When Samuel Butler finds a new place for the *Odyssey*, he moves it west by matching local Homeric descriptions with the Greek island settlement, Sicily. When Joyce moves the *Odyssey* to Dublin, he, too, continues it—he follows through on its directional potential. All movement recalls historical movement, a geographical relocation in time. Stephen Dedalus thinks about the manifestation of history in *Ulysses*, and he concludes, with some help from Aristotle and Giambattista Vico, that it "must be a movement then, an actuality of the possible as possible" (25). Joyce's Homeric scheme is, in part, a movement that actualizes a range of possibilities for Dublin as an epic or counter-epic domain. Ireland, as Joyce puts it in *Finnegans Wake*, is a nation where the "possible is the improbable and the improbable the inevitable" (*FW*, 110).

As its name has come to imply, the *Odyssey* is a poem of plotted movement. Joyce was more interested in epics of migration than he was in epics of cross-cultural strife. It is fitting that he writes his own migratory epic of small Greek heroes in Dublin while the strife "epic" of World War I raged in Europe. Migration in the *Odyssey* is a drift to the west. According to the one Homeric scholar

[4] Kenner, *The Pound Era* (Berkeley, 1971), p. 44. See also, Kenner, "Homer's Sticks and Stones," *JJQ*, 6 (1969), 285-298.
[5] *The Pound Era*, p. 45.

Joyce admired above all others, Victor Bérard, the narrative theme of exile is but a version of the historical migration of early Greek settlements to western Mediterranean coasts. This is a feature of the epic that Virgil well understands when he adapts the Odyssean pattern in the *Aeneid*. Dante, of course, pulls the Greek hero further west along a danger axis that takes him to the edge of the world beyond the Mediterranean. If the "Ulysses" canto of the *Inferno* exits at the Straits of Gibraltar, Joyce draws the epic line across the Atlantic to Ireland, the Green Erin of the West. Epic geography depends upon the principle of extension where the new or the remote becomes a version of the old or the familiar. Time extends space. The line of transmission is emphasized in *Ulysses*. Following Molly Bloom's brass bed, which she at least tells Bloom has traveled "All the way from Gibraltar" (56), the novel risks the seas beyond the Pillars of Hercules even though Joyce's hero, Bloom, like many exiles, imagines only the return. In *Calypso*, the opening episode of the *Wanderings*, Bloom thinks of the fruits vended by Dublin's Jews: "Coming all that way: Spain, Gibraltar, Mediterranean, the Levant" (60).

Joyce's fictional temperament is not so serious that he issues a certificate of solemnity against the comic wit of his novel's odyssey. The very translated and reduced spaces of Dublin provide a commentary, often parodic, on the larger and longer movements of the Homeric original. But the counter-epic strain in *Ulysses* is rarely a full debasement of mimicked structures. Joyce's parodic design mediates between remembered and potential conditions. It is not his way to structure a narrative joke for nearly eight hundred pages without letting the joke itself assume a sustaining energy. The very title of *Ulysses* parodies the epic in Dublin, but titles for Joyce are also prescriptions. *Ulysses* prescribes Odyssean spaces for a new time and a new place.

This book began as a study of narrative movement over real and imagined terrain in the *Odyssey* and in *Ulysses*. But there were attendant concerns almost immediately. Geography in narrative is an encompassing system; it generates more than one set of imaginative principles. Spatially, imagination "has a body to it," as Joyce writes in his *Ulysses* notesheets;[6] and that body is geodetic and

[6] Herring, p. 256.

gynotropic at the same time. Molly Bloom in *Ulysses* and Anna Livia Plurabelle in *Finnegans Wake* absorb space. Temporally, Joyce conceives of narrative space as historical conflation—Irish, Scandinavian, Greek, Semitic. He enters a quick note for *Ulysses* which he borrows as much from Charles Vallancey's discredited theory of Irish migrations as from Victor Bérard's accounts of Phoenician *periploi*: "Topical History: places remember events."[7] Vallancey writes of a people's migrational memory.

> It will not be surprising to find a people, at length fixed in a sequestered corner of the Globe, whose history by their frequent migrations must consequently depend much on tradition, work up the events of their ancestors in Armenia, Persia, Assyria, Spain, etc. into one history of the country they at present possess: nay, even to borrow events of their other colonies, which never were transacted by themselves: it is a foible common to all other nations . . . when Colonies went abroad and made anywhere a settlement, they ingrafted upon their *antecedent history* the subsequent events of the place.[8]

For Joyce, the hubs of all civilizations converge on Ireland, and produce what are some of the more complex turns of the geographical imagination. Racial and national types, habits, climates, and myths jostle for fictional localization; and much of the tension and much of the wit in *Ulysses* or, later, in *Finnegans Wake*, derive from national displacements or superimpositions. Geography is, finally, part of a cultural, myth-producing process. Apollo, Hermes, Hercules, Cadmus, Odysseus, Aeneas, Odin, Finn MacCool are migrating gods and heroes—they follow the sun. Movement over spaces is geopoetic: new lands are founded in the west, herds of cattle are stolen by the gods to mark spots of migrational extension, journeys to the land of the dead and back are taken to revitalize domain.

The first part of this book deals generally with epic geography and narrative structure. An introduction sets the larger spatial contours of the *Odyssey* as Joyce would have understood them from Victor Bérard's *Les Phéniciens et l'Odyssée* (Paris, 1902-1903). The five subsequent chapters in part one introduce material with which Joyce

[7] Herring, p. 119.

[8] Charles Vallancey, "A Vindication of the Ancient History of Ireland," in *Collectanea de rebus hibernicis* (Dublin, 1786-1804), IV, xi-xii.

worked in plotting *Ulysses*. Each of these chapters describes a separate logic of epic geography: chapter one proposes a theory of directional and migrational movement for the Mediterranean and for Ireland; chapter two focuses on Giambattista Vico's theory of *Poetic Geography*, treating body-worlds, astrological projections, narrative micro- and macrocosms; chapter three tests the validities and ironies of climate theory and geographical locale; chapter four treats varieties of fictional domain—epics in large and small spaces; and chapter five considers the legend of Proteus in the *Odyssey* as a myth of spatial extension and return.

The second part of the book is more detailed and concentrated. It maps the sequence and significance of the movements in the decade of the *Odyssey* and in the day of *Ulysses*, and its chapters conform to the ordering of the Homeric episodes in Joyce's novel. Richard Ellmann calls *Ulysses* a "multiterritorial pun,"[9] but territory for Ellmann, like temporality, serves only as a stand-in for one of the Homeric gods who reconcile talismanic and dialectical contraries. Ultimately, perhaps even necessarily, there is a real texture to the spaces of *Ulysses* that always precedes dialectic. Harry Levin describes the narrative parallels in the novel as a kind of metonymic cartography: "the myth of the *Odyssey* is superimposed upon the map of Dublin."[10] The second part of this book takes Levin's observation at face value: the spaces of the *Odyssey* are literally superimposed upon the territory Joyce maps in *Ulysses*.[11] By looking at the novel this way, I hope to provide some answers to basic and important questions about the Dublin day: what does it mean to be placed or moving at given times in *Ulysses*? what is the significance of Joyce's alteration in the sequence of Homeric adventures? what effects do the periods of lost time in *Ulysses* have on the meaning of the novel's action?

My treatment of Joyce's geographical superimpositions in *Ulysses*, or, more accurately, the layering of Irish and Mediterranean spaces, will involve some detailed plotting of movements in the Homeric

[9] Richard Ellmann, *Ulysses on the Liffey* (New York, 1972), p. 2.

[10] Harry Levin, *James Joyce: A Critical Introduction* (Norfolk, Va., 1960), p. 76.

[11] There is, perhaps, a sociological basis for the particular areas of Dublin Joyce maps during the day. See J. C. C. Mays, "Some Comments on the Dublin of 'Ulysses,'" in *Ulysses Cinquante Ans Après*, ed. Louis Bonnerot (Paris, 1974), pp. 83-98.

Odyssey. I have not included the researches of scholars on this issue other than those of Victor Bérard, although scholarship on Homeric geography continues throughout this century. The *Annual of the British School at Athens* has been reporting on excavations in Ithaca since the 1930's. In the 1950's Louis Moulinier's "Quelques hypothèses relatives à la Géographie d'Homère dans l'Odyssée" appeared in the *Annales de la Faculté des Lettres, Aix-en-Provence,* XXIII (1958). Even more recently, A. Rousseau-Liessens published a much longer (and less interesting) four-volume work, *Géographie de l'Odyssée* (Brussels, 1961). Italian scholars have contributed their own local flavor to the pursuit: Gaetano Baglió's *Odisseo nel mare mediterraneo centrale* (Rome, 1958), and Luigi Ferrari, *Realtà e fantasia nella geografia dell'Odisseo* (Palermo, 1968). One version of the Odyssean *Wanderings,* Gilbert Pillot's, *Le Code Secret de l'Odyssée* (Paris, 1969), argues that Homer's epic maps Atlantic and northern seas—the *Lestrygonian* episode even takes place in Ireland near Galway. The more standard and useful Alan J. B. Wace and Frank H. Stubbings, *A Companion to Homer* (London, 1962), contains a chapter on the *Odyssey*'s "Principal Homeric Sites" (pp. 398-421). These works to some extent disagree among themselves and with Bérard. In his own time Bérard was admired when his researches remained close to Ithaca, and thought obsessed when he began to range the Phoenician Mediterranean. The bulk of Homeric scholarship at the turn of the century, just as now, was less convinced that the "fantasy" adventures of Odysseus could be precisely localized than that the home or Ithacan adventure had a factual basis. Schliemann and Dörpfeld were busy excavating on Ithaca for the remains of the Odyssean home city. Dörpfeld soon convinced himself, primarily from internal evidence in the poem, that the home island must have been Leucas rather than Ithaca. Bérard may have disagreed with Schliemann on Ithacan locations, but Dörpfeld, over the years, drove him to despair. I am certain the feeling was mutual. Bérard's reputation as an eccentric Homeric scholar must have appealed to Joyce. As a toponymist Bérard is often more ingenious than convincing. As an epic cartographer, he is superb at mapping out real places on what many considered the barest shreds of mythic evidence.

My exclusive use of Bérard's findings in both parts of this book has to do only with Joyce's almost exclusive reliance on those same findings. He may have checked on matters of general mythology, Homeric and otherwise, in various sources, especially Wilhelm Roscher's

Ausführliches Lexikon der Griechischen und Römischen Mythologie (Leipzig, 1886-1937). But Joyce owes his real debt in the matter of Homeric scholarship to Bérard. Even the names of other classicists, Homeric toponymists, and Egyptologists appearing in Joyce's notebooks and notesheets derive from *Les Phéniciens et l'Odyssée*. If Bérard mentions a name, Joyce, more often than not, would write it down. It is unlikely his researches progressed much further. Joyce knew an economy of time in absorbing material. If he liked particular facts, it did not matter how thoroughly he researched them.

One final matter ought to be addressed in prefatory remarks. Joyce's habit of composition—his refined exercise of the mnemotechnic, as Virag, the mock lord of language (*basilcogrammate*), puts it in *Circe*—manifests a strange craving for seemingly irrelevant detail. Many have complained loudly and often that *Ulysses* gets lost in the paraphernalia included in its own narrative—the maps, the atlases, the address directories, the almanacs, the guide books, the scribbled notes on library slips, the colored notational pencils, the various *schemata*, the notebooks, and the notesheets. Proliferation kills the king, as the *Odyssey* itself should tell us.

But Joyce is crafty, in every sense of the word. It is difficult to write on *Ulysses*, or think about it seriously, and avoid the battle that has raged for over fifty years since Ezra Pound's remark on Joyce's "mediaevalism" as a scaffold "chiefly his own affair."[12] A scaffold is a dispensable structure once the building is built. But if the process of building is as important as the result, the scaffold never disappears. Joyce toys with Pound's phrasing when in *Finnegans Wake* he has Anna Livia remind her Humpty-Dumpty hero,

[12] Ezra Pound, "Paris Letter" (June 1922), in *Pound/Joyce: The Letters of Ezra Pound to James Joyce*, ed. Forrest Read (New York, 1967), p. 197. In another context, Read argues that Pound later came to see the epic texture of *Ulysses* as something more crucial to the novel. See Read's essay, "Pound, Joyce, and Flaubert: The Odysseans," in *New Approaches to Ezra Pound*, ed. Eva Hesse (Berkeley, 1969), pp. 125-144. A. Walton Litz acknowledges Pound's changing position on *Ulysses*, but differs from Read in the extent to which he thinks Pound ever abandoned his earlier emphasis on the novel's realism. See Litz, "Pound and Eliot on *Ulysses*: The Critical Tradition," in *Ulysses: Fifty Years*, ed. Thomas F. Staley (Bloomington, Ind., 1972), pp. 5-18.

Earwicker: "And people thinks you missed the scaffold. Of fell design" (*FW*, 621). Some fine critics such as S. L. Goldberg are still
taken aback by Joyce's elaborate fictional structures, and find many
of the chapters of *Ulysses* in which Joyce was over-activated, over-
ingenious, and over-encyclopedic, basically unacceptable. Perhaps un-
deservedly, Stuart Gilbert, the bag-man for Joyce's esoterica, has
taken the brunt of the attack in this respect. Many blame Gilbert's
book, *James Joyce's Ulysses* (1930), for making public Joyce's arcane
schemes, arguing that Joyce used Gilbert's book to establish his
novel's credentials at a time when *Ulysses* itself was under attack
for obscenity. Gilbert is seen as a dummy who moves his lips in
synchronization with his master's trickster voice. This is an easy
but inaccurate solution to the extravagances of Joyce's mind. To
some it may be an unpleasant thought that Gilbert often erred in
the opposite direction. He did not take Joyce's schemes far enough
to reveal the extent to which some of them informed the narrative
design of the novel.

My aim is to recover an epic pattern in an encyclopedic, comic
narrative. *Ulysses* is an immensely complex and, in one way or another, an immensely human document. Its best critics admire its
complexity and value its humanity. My hope is that what I have to
say about the novel will prove of use to those who are willing to
entertain the full range of *Ulysses*—its details, its wit, its narrative
scope, and its human substance.

ACKNOWLEDGMENTS

THOSE who have no part in a book look to the acknowledgments to find the smoking pistol of complicity. I will make my acknowledgments as brief as I can to save all concerned undue embarrassment. Many have helped me. My greatest debt is to my wife, Maria DiBattista of Princeton University. No one has put in more time on this book and been a more selfless victim of my chatter about it. I have dedicated this book to her, and I thank her deeply. At about the time I had completed a draft of this study I met Michael Groden of Princeton, who was working on Joyce's composition and revisions of *Ulysses* from early in 1918 on. His help has meant a great deal to the final form of this book.

Many colleagues at Yale have read chapters in draft, and much of their advice has been incorporated. I thank Jim Price, Edward Mendelson, Stephen Barney, and Bartlett Giamatti. The completed manuscript, in one or another version, was read by colleagues at Yale and elsewhere: Professors James Nohrnberg, Heinrich von Staden, John Hodgson, Charles Feidelson, Hugh Kenner, Earl Miner, and Walton Litz. I am grateful to all of them for their time and for their patience.

I owe special debts to three of those who read the full manuscript. Professor Heinrich von Staden of the Classics Department at Yale again and again provided invaluable information about Homer. There were times when he no doubt felt that he was conducting a private seminar with me as his only student. Over the last two years he has made unfamiliar territory more familiar to me, and I owe him more than I can repay. Similarly, Professor James Nohrnberg of the University of Virginia, whose knowledge of the Renaissance epic is prodigious, and who displays a modest willingness to encroach upon Joyce's terrain, has shared dozens of his ideas with me. If he recognizes parts of this book above others, it is doubtless because he inspired them. And I thank Professor Walton Litz of Princeton University for the continued interest he has shown in this project and for the countless suggestions and "leads" he has provided (all of which proved fruitful).

Victor Bérard's volumes on the *Odyssey* have not been translated. I am afraid that those translations from *Les Phéniciens et l'Odyssée* which appear in the body of this book represent my own efforts. I had a great deal of help from Barbara Axelrod of Yale University, often asking her to translate material at some distance from the full context of Bérard's text. I could not have done the translations without her help, but those that seem most awkward are my own. Thomas Crawford, who has rendered the maps and diagrams for the book, is a Joycean of recent but special distinction. His sense of Dublin is akin to that of a native's. For many months his dedication to this project has been thorough; he has put a tremendous amount of work into it; and I am glad he can share credit for all he has done. Many of my students at Yale in the past several years have contributed to the ideas in this book, but I extend a special thanks to one recent student, William Pease, who has written on the migratory patterns in *Finnegans Wake*. For editorial assistance, I thank Rita Stern, Claire Pettengill, and Susanna Freed; for a grant providing me some of the time to work on the book, I thank the National Endowment for the Humanities.

Finally, I owe a great deal to my editor at Princeton University Press, Marjorie Sherwood, whose learning and intelligence made me rely on her from the start. Her help and her support have been unflagging.

Los Angeles—New Haven
1975

TABLE OF CONTENTS

CONTENTS

LIST OF MAPS

LIST OF ABBREVIATIONS

Bérard	Victor Bérard, *Les Phéniciens et l'Odyssée* (Paris, 1902-1903)
Budgen	Frank Budgen, *James Joyce and the Making of Ulysses* (Bloomington, Ind., 1934, rpt., 1960)
CW	*Critical Writings of James Joyce*, ed., Ellsworth Mason and Richard Ellmann (New York, 1964)
D	James Joyce, *Dubliners* (New York: Viking Press, 1967)
FW	James Joyce, *Finnegans Wake* (New York: Viking Press, 1958)
Fitzgerald	*The Odyssey: Homer*, trans. Robert Fitzgerald (New York: Anchor, 1961)
Gilbert	Stuart Gilbert, *James Joyce's Ulysses* (New York, 2nd ed. rev., 1952)
Hart and Hayman	*James Joyce's Ulysses: Critical Essays*, ed. Clive Hart and David Hayman (Berkeley, 1974)
Hart and Knuth	Clive Hart and Leo Knuth, *A Topographical Guide to James Joyce's Ulysses* (Colchester, Eng., 1975)
Herring	*Joyce's Ulysses Notesheets in the British Museum*, ed. Phillip F. Herring (Charlottesville, Va., 1972)
JJ	Richard Ellmann, *James Joyce* (New York, 1959)
JJQ	*James Joyce Quarterly*
Letters	*The Letters of James Joyce*, ed. Stuart Gilbert (Vol. I) and Richard Ellmann (Vols. II and III) (New York, 1957-1966)
New Science	Giambattista Vico, *The New Science of Giambattista Vico*, trans. Thomas Goddard Bergin and Max Harold Fisch (Ithaca, New York, 1970)
P	James Joyce, *Portrait of the Artist as a Young Man* (New York: Viking Press, 1964)

Ulysses James Joyce, *Ulysses* (New York: Vintage Press, 1961)

VIII.A.5 Phillip F. Herring, "*Ulysses* Notebook VIII.A.5 at Buffalo," *Studies in Bibliography*, xxii (1969), 287-310.

PART ONE

INTRODUCTION

In his *James Joyce's Ulysses*, the much maligned Stuart Gilbert provides considerable information from Victor Bérard's *Les Phéniciens et l'Odyssée*. Bérard called himself a toponymist or, in his own coinage, a *topologist*, and Gilbert was willing enough to follow Joyce's lead on Bérard's importance for *Ulysses*.

"Have you read Victor Bérard's *Les Phéniciens et l'Odyssée?*" Joyce asked me when I mentioned my reading of the *Odyssey*. (This interrogative method of suggestion was characteristic, as I soon came to learn.) I at once procured a copy of that bulky work, and found it fascinating reading. While immensely erudite, Bérard is no pedant, and his reconstruction of the Mediterranean scene in the age of the rhapsodists is not only a triumph of scholarship but also a work of art.[1]

Gilbert's understanding of *Les Phéniciens* centers on what has come down as Bérard's generative insight, particularly appealing to Joyce, that the *Odyssey* is a Semitic-Greek poem. Joyce, who looked at a Jew in Dublin and saw a wandering Greek, naturally relished Bérard's sense of Homeric origins. According to Bérard, the *Odyssey* is filled with Phoenician sea-dogs, Levantine versions of Joyce's Murphy the sailor in *Eumaeus*. Phoenician accounts of island and

---

[1] Gilbert, p. vii. William Schutte sees this passage as evidence of a hoax (*Joyce and Shakespeare: A Study in the Meaning of Ulysses* [New Haven, 1957], p. 3). For Schutte the key word is bulky, and he imagines Joyce making needless work for Gilbert. Bérard's volumes are large, but they are also substantive. Joyce was right about their importance to his understanding of the *Odyssey*, and Gilbert was right to pursue them as far as he did. Stanislaus Joyce claimed that his brother read, to his recollection, only two critical-scholarly books on the *Odyssey*: Samuel Butler's *The Authoress of the Odyssey* (1897), and Victor Bérard's *Les Phéniciens et l'Odyssée* (Paris, 1902-1903). See W. B. Stanford, *The Ulysses Theme: A Study in the Adaptability of a Traditional Hero* (Ann Arbor, 2nd ed., 1968), p. 276, n. 6. Mary and Padraic Colum, *Our Friend James Joyce* (New York, 1958), describe Joyce's reverence for Bérard. He was "deeply impressed" by Bérard's work, he attended Bérard's funeral, and he gave Bérard's translation of the *Odyssey* as gifts to his friends, including a copy to Padraic Colum (p. 89).

3

coastal voyages (*periploi*) filter through the Homeric rhapsodist's ear to the tip of his Greek tongue. Hence Bérard sees the *Odyssey* as a Greek poem with a Semitic intelligence behind it: "Le poète—Homère, si l'on veut,—était Grec; le navigateur—Ulysse, pour lui donner un nom,—était Phénicien" (The poet—Homer, if one wishes—is Greek; the mariner—Ulysses, to give him a name—is Phoenician) [Bérard, ii, 557]. Geographical facts, far-away places, and local mappings, at times anthropomorphic in detail, at times buried under layers of etymological clues, fill the *Odyssey*. The poem's geology or "topology" of place names (Egyptian, Semitic, and Greek) marks the appearance of an easterner in western waters.

Gilbert does not take Bérard's findings much further. If he had, he might have uncovered in *Les Phéniciens* a comprehensive theory of epic geography. For Joyce, Bérard offers more than a series of Semitic-Greco coincidences—he opens an entirely new range of possibilities for his own epic of migration. The *Odyssey*'s Semitic inheritance explains the significance of placement and direction. Bérard conceives of the *Odyssey* as a poem of a special kind of movement. He believes that the Phoenician waters in the west tested by Odysseus represent a Greek colonial expansion from the Ionian coast off the Peloponnese to the boot of Italy, where early settlements had begun to appear. The *Odyssey* is an etiological travelogue, but of a unique narrative variety that embodies history in narrative: "Les descriptions odysséennes furent la première vision qui s'offrit aux yeux des Hellènes quand pour la première fois leurs flottes pénétraient en ces parages occidentaux" (The Odyssean descriptions were the first vision offered to the eyes of the Greeks when for the first time their ships penetrated western regions) [Bérard, ii, 558]. Bérard accounts for the attractions of certain narrative forms. Greek voyagers are, in a sense, inexperienced. When they are out on the seas they think of little but home. Phoenicians, on the other hand, are at home only on the sea—they revel in long journeys to the islands, capes, and peninsulas of the extended Mediterranean. These characteristics come together in the structure of the *Odyssey*: wanderings and homecomings. Bérard draws together the narrative strands: "Les Hellènes avaient leurs *nostoi*; les Sémites avaient leurs périples" (The Greeks have their *nostoi*; the Semites have their *periploi*) [Bérard, ii, 577].

The *Odyssey* for Bérard is a two-part poem that conforms to the character of the Mediterranean races that contribute to it. It is an extension and a return, a commerce in the unknown and the familiar. Bérard sees the structure of the narrative in its place names, all of which are migrations, after a fashion, from original roots. The root-route pun is not so facile as it might seem. Almost all the action in the *Odyssey* takes place along an axis of adventure or an axis of origin. Odysseus experiences trials in unknown waters, and Telemachus travels back along a familiar Phoenician trade route over land. At Sparta he even hears a tale of Proteus in the Nile. Proteus is a great original—in a Greek variant of the legend he is the first man, a man of the sea. Telemachus travels toward the height of the sun, toward the point of origin, the east.

Bérard's volumes on the Homeric poem treat the *Telemachiad*, the *Wanderings*, and the *Nostos*. These divisions map three geographical areas and three narrative theaters: the Peloponnese and the Levantine southeastern axis, the Mediterranean *couchant*, mostly around the boot of Italy, and the home island of Ithaca off the coast of western Greece. At the beginning of the poem Telemachus moves along the southeastern axis and Odysseus finds himself exiled at the end of the world in the northwest (relative to a Phoenician geographical system). The action of the *Odyssey* returns father and son to an Ithacan center from geographically opposite directions. Homer, who retells his tale in different versions throughout the narrative, even miniaturizes the directional scheme on Ithaca. The same axis, southeast and northwest, is set up in the *Nostos* by the detailed home island positionings described in the poem. According to Bérard, Telemachus beaches at Point Andri in the southeast and joins the disguised Odysseus at Eumaeus' hut down-island; both proceed, on parallel routes, homeward to the palace in the northwest of Ithaca near present-day Stavros and Port Polis.

Joyce, who provides the episodes in *Ulysses* with the same Homeric names as the chapters in Bérard's *Les Phéniciens*, also maps Dublin in accord with the major structural divisions of the *Odyssey*: *Telemachiad, Wanderings*, and *Nostos*. Joyce, of course, is forced to overlap the separate spaces of the three Homeric theaters in Dublin (which he often does by lapses or *trous* in the narrative time of the novel), but he organizes the day's movements to mirror the larger directional scheme of the *Odyssey*. *Ulysses* is a novel of movement. Miles are logged on June 16, 1904, and a good portion of them are precisely recorded. Characters appear and reappear in their city. Men and boys take long walks. Urban eccentrics walk nowhere in

5

circles. But important patterns of positioning and movement keep repeating the Homeric elliptical exile and return along a southeast-northwest axis. Twice in the course of the day Dedalus and Bloom begin at the same time from points southeast and northwest respectively and converge at the same time in the same place: Sandymount around 11:00 A.M. and the Newspaper offices after 12:00 P.M. (Hart and Knuth, p. 24). Throughout the day the movements of Dedalus and Bloom, with almost thirty miles between them, continue to inform the meaning of the narrative. Between 8:45 A.M. on June 16 and 1:00 A.M. the next day, Leopold Bloom journeys twice from Sandymount in the southeast of Dublin to two locations in the northwest: the Prospect cemetery in Glasnevin, and, long after midnight, to his own home at 7 Eccles street near the *Mater Misericordiae*, death-ward for incurables. Stephen Dedalus, who arrives from outside Dublin even farther southeast from Sandycove, spends most of his day in the southeast quadrant of the city before connecting with Bloom at the Holles street hospital, birth-ward. From that point southeast the two "heroes" move along the northwest route eventually to 7 Eccles: *Nostos* (see maps pp. 136-37).

Joyce has already reduced the scope of the *Odyssey*'s full range from the Mediterranean to Dublin's city limits, but just like Bérard's Homer, he makes an important conversion that mirrors the narrative transition in the *Odyssey* from *Wanderings* to *Nostos*, from the sea map to the land map. Odysseus and Telemachus reposition themselves approximately half-way through the narrative, after the drop-off by the Phaeacians on the Ithacan home island and the return from Pylos. Bérard's scheme for the *Nostos* on Ithaca and the arrangement of Bloom's and Stephen's progress in *Ulysses* from *Nausicaa* on are strikingly similar. Joyce labeled his *Nostos* from *Eumaeus*, but, in a sense, he may have kept pace with the *Odyssey* by remapping his city where we would expect *Nostos* to occur, that is after the Phaeacian (*Nausicaa*) adventure. The Holles street hospital, Nighttown, the Cabman's shelter (Eumaeus' hut), and 7 Eccles (palace) replicate, point for point, the sequence Bérard projects for the orientations and directions of places on Ithaca (see maps pp. 248-49).

Spatial details and neatly plotted movements are not alien to Joyce's imagination. Dublin, a point of origin for some in his fiction, is always a sea of western troubles for others. In his earlier collection of stories, *Dubliners*, Joyce had already begun to work out the rudiments of a directional theory of narrative value, possibly with the *Odyssey* in mind.[2] Two early stories in *Dubliners* have young Irish lads following the pattern of Telemachus by making what for them are considerable eastern voyages in Dublin. At the end of *Dubliners* Joyce turns his directional focus toward the northwest gloom of Galway where the last flicker of life succumbs to the dark in the cold night of the west. One of the earlier stories is called "Araby," the name of an eastern bazaar in Ballsbridge. The last story, at the extension, is simply "The Dead." To renew the land, insofar as it is renewable, Joyce has to go outside it. *Portrait of the Artist* records the beginnings of a cisatlantic connection, and *Ulysses* returns to an epic original in Mediterranean waters. In *Finnegans Wake* Joyce is still absorbed with the axis of epic origins and extensions. Translated into its French version, the "Wake" of the title is simply "Sillage," the path of an object through the waters. *Finnegans Wake* returns Dublin's Phoenix Park to Levantine seas ("Phoenician wakes," *FW*, 608) and extends its full length across the greater ocean northwest: Sir Tristram "had passencore rearrived from North Armorica" (*FW*, 3). Joyce's notesheets for *Eumaeus*, the episode of "Navigation" in *Ulysses*, reveal another possibility: "New York = New Jerus. New Dublin" (Herring, p. 396). *Finnegans Wake* improves on the migration with its American "doublin" (Dublin) in "Laurens County's gorgios" (*FW*, 3). As for Joyce's personal odyssey, his European progress and return mimics the movements of Telemachus and Odysseus: southeast and northwest. His final migration is on the northwest axis, but endstopped before *Nostos*. The last page of *Ulysses* records the relevant segment of his journey: "*Trieste-Zürich-Paris*, 1914-1921" (783).

FOUR PILLARS OF THE EARTH:
MEDITERRANEAN GEOGRAPHY

The *Odyssey* narrates the geography of actual and mythic spaces—spaces localized in and extended beyond familiar Greek waters. Ho-

[2] The original projected title for *Dubliners* was "Ulysses in Dublin," and the many parallels in the stories to the *Odyssey* are worked out by Richard Levin and Charles Shattuck, "First Flight to Ithaca: A New Reading of Joyce's *Dubliners*," first printed in *Accent*, Winter, 1944 and reprinted in *James Joyce: Two Decades of Criticism*, ed. Seon Givens (New York, 1948), pp. 47-94.

meric geography sweeps the coasts of a Mediterranean world: Asia Minor, Phoenicia, Mauritania, Hesperia, Thesprotia, and the Peloponnese. Eventually the contours of that world are extended to the ocean's very bourne, to the domain of Poseidon and, beyond, to the regions of death.

There is considerable evidence both inside and outside *Ulysses* that Joyce concerned himself with the details of the *Odyssey*'s geography. In the early months of 1918, while he was working on the beginning chapters of Bloom's wanderings, Joyce transcribed considerable material in his Zürich notebook (VIII.A.5) from Bérard's *Les Phéniciens*. He later copied much of this material, and added more, to his notesheets now in the British Museum. Phillip Herring, who has made the Zürich and British Museum notes, including those on Bérard, available, is the first to admit that there is more in Bérard than readily meets the eye. Bérard's contribution to *Ulysses* is a "typical example of an important influence on Joyce which has never been properly explored" (VIII.A.5, p. 290).

At one point in his Zürich notebook Joyce even sketched a geographical scheme for the Mediterranean. In a long explanation on why Odysseus heads toward the dawn after his escape from the Lestrygonians, Bérard explains, and Joyce diagrams, the implications of the flight toward Circe's hawk isle. Direction conforms to the sun's path through the four quadrants of the pillared earth [Bérard, ii, 261-263]. Later in *Les Phéniciens*, Bérard explains the origins of the scheme.

A chaque pas, nous avons dû recourir aux vocabulaire, notions et théories des Sémites ou de leurs maîtres égyptiens, pour comprendre les formules et métaphores de cette navigation. "Devant" et "derrière" désignant le Levant et l'Occident; "maisons" de l'aurore, du soleil, du couchant et du *zophos*, "pilier" du monde: les Sémites et Égyptiens parlaient ainsi.

(At each step, we must retrace the vocabulary, the notions, and the theories of the Semites or their Egyptian masters in order to understand the formulas and metaphors of this [Odyssean] navigation. "Before" and "behind" designate the east and west, "houses" of the dawn, of the sun, of the sunset, and of the *zophos* [gloom], "pillars" of the world: the Semites and Egyptians spoke this way.) [Bérard, ii, 561]

Joyce offers two diagrammatic perspectives in his notesheets:

Egyptian

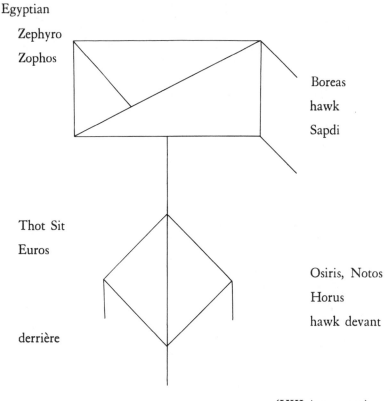

Zephyro
Zophos

Boreas
hawk
Sapdi

Thot Sit
Euros

Osiris, Notos
Horus
hawk devant

derrière

(VIII.A.5, p. 302)

The earth in this system rests between the four pillars of the world, extending from Asia to the Straits at Gibraltar. In a later notesheet entry, Joyce simply describes the grid: "Egyptian 4 suns for seasons (4 maids)" (Herring, p. 281). Not only did Joyce record the scheme of the *Odyssey*'s space from primitive geographical theories of direction, but his decision to end *Ulysses* with the rotating hulk of a slightly worn Dublin earth-goddess, Molly Bloom, may owe something to the Egyptian earth-body, an earth-body now rounded, having had the temerity to move beyond Gibraltar.

9

In his study of the *Odyssey* Bérard makes a special use of the Egyptian-Semitic-Greek grid. He adjusts the myth of the Mediterranean to geographical fact. What Bérard sees when he looks at the adventures is worth citing in full because his premises lead to an integrated sense of the poem's spatial structure.

De Kalypso chez Alkinoos, du détroit de Gibraltar à l'entrée de l'Adriatique, on voit que le récit d'Ulysse nous fournit cinq ou six grandes étapes. Il est à noter que la plupart de ces étapes sont à quelque porte de la Mer Occidentale: les Phéaciens gardent le Canal d'Otrante; les Lotophages ouvrent le passage entre la Sicile et l'Afrique; Charybde et Skylla veillent au Fare de Messine, les Sirènes aux Bouches de Capri, les Kyklopes au détroit de Nisida, les Lestrygons aux Bouches de Bonifacio et Kalypso aux Colonnes d'Hercule. Dans la mer redoutable, qui s'ouvre au delà d'Ithaque, le poète connaît en résumé *sept* grandes portes, qui toutes présentent quelques risques aux navigateurs (je reviendrai longuement à ce sujet, quand nous traiterons la *Composition de l'Odysseia*). Dans les mers civilisées, d'autre part, sur les routes achéennes qui rejoignent Ithaque à l'Archipel et aux côtes d'Asie Mineure, le poète connaît trois autres portes dangereuses: l'îlot et les guetteurs d'Astéris barrent le canal d'Ithaque; les Roches Pointues encombrent le canal de Zante; les coups de vent, les courants et la houle ferment le plus souvent les Bouches de Cérigo. En résumé, il semblerait que depuis les côtes d'Asie Mineure, où le poète est installé, jusqu'aux extrémités de la Grande Mer, où demeure Kalypso, la *Télémakheia* et le *Nostos* nous décrivent *dix* portes redoutées. Nous savons comment la Méditerranée phénicienne avait *sept* grandes îles et comment la Méditerranée grecque en eut *dix*. Nous connaissons les *sept* sages de la Grèce primitive et les *dix* orateurs de l'Athènes classique.

(From Calypso to the home of Alcinous, from the Straits of Gibraltar to the entrance of the Adriatic, one sees that the narration of Ulysses provides us with five or six great stages. It is worth noting that most of these stages are in one or another port of the Western sea: the Phaeacians guard the Straits of Otranto; the Lotuseaters open the passage between Sicily and Africa; Charybdis and Scylla guard the Straits of Messina, the Sirens the Mouths of Capri, the Cyclopes the Straits of Nisida, the Lestrygonians the Mouths of Bonifacio, and Calypso the Pillars of Hercules. In the

dangerous seas that open beyond Ithaca, the poet recognizes, in review, seven great ports, all presenting some risks to navigators. . . . In the civilized seas, on the other hand, along the Greek routes which join Ithaca to the Archipelago and to the coasts of Asia Minor, the poet recognizes three other dangerous ports: the islet and the ambuscades of Asteris blocking the Ithacan channel; the Pointed Rocks encumbering the canal of Zante; the gusts of wind, the currents, and the surging waves shutting off, most of the time, the mouths of Cerigo. In review it would seem that from the coasts of Asia Minor, where the poet is located, to the extremities of the greater Mediterranean, where Calypso resides, the *Telemachiad* and the *Nostos* describe for us *ten* formidable ports. We know that the Phoenician Mediterranean had *seven* great isles and that the Greek Mediterranean had *ten*. We know the *seven* sages of primitive Greece and the *ten* orators of classical Athens.)
[Bérard, II, 400-401]

Bérard's Greco-Semitic conception of the *Odyssey* counts partly on a vast numerological game of migration in time. He compares the seven-year wanderings of Menelaus in eastern seas to the Semitic predisposition to see things in sevens, and he compares the decade of Odysseus' *Wanderings* to the Greek tendency to think in multiples of five. For Bérard, the seventeen days it takes Odysseus to return from the end of the world at Calypso's *couchant* island confirms his Phoenician and Greek reading of the epic. Seventeen (seven plus ten) days is in itself a geographical fable. Moreover, Bérard sets Menelaus' seventh-year adventure with Proteus on the isle of Pharos, in the western Nile Basin off the eastern coast of Libya. Odysseus' first adventure in western seas takes place, according to Bérard, in the land of the Lotophagoi on Djerba off the Libyan coast. In the east-west, Semitic-Greek, design of the *Odyssey*, Odysseus, in effect, takes over from Menelaus—he moves with the narrative to western domains.

If Odysseus spends most of his wandering years in the west, trying himself in troubled waters, another geographical fable is taking place over eastern seas and upon eastern lands. At the beginning of the *Odyssey* Telemachus leaves Ithaca along the normal trade-route axis to the Peloponnese. He moves southeast in search of news of his father. He moves toward a point of origin and orientation in order to assure himself that his own origin is, in fact, the substantive one of king's son. Telemachus not only does not know whether his father is alive, but he has only Penelope's word that Odysseus is his father. Once father and son return, from different directions, to the home island, the grid contracts but the issues stay the same. Together Odysseus and Telemachus establish a new northwest axis, marked carefully by Bérard in the place names of the *Nostos*, to take revenge on the suitors in the gloom of Ithaca.

Narrative Space and Epic Alternation

At a crucial point in the *Lotuseaters* episode of *Ulysses*, Bloom has his view of a woman's well-turned calf blocked by a cross-cutting tram: "Paradise and the peri. Always happening like that" (74). Peri are angels blocked from entering paradise. In narrative terms, paradise and the peri reconstruct a good deal of *Ulysses'* action: paradise is a version of homecoming, and peri experience the involuntary commitment to exile. The peri establish the novel's vertical axis—if not up to paradise then down to where angels fall. In *Ulysses* the mock-epic plunge counters the epic sublime. Dublin's pigeons are always overhead to deposit their modern commentary on the bowlers of Joyce's reincarnated homecomers. But there is another way to look at the idea of fulfillment and blocking in *Ulysses* that conforms to a much larger narrative pattern in the *Odyssey*.

One of Odysseus' tasks in the western seas over which he wanders is to mediate between strange versions of paradisaical enchantment and versions of hellish barbarism. The Mediterranean offers the Greek hero lands of light and warmth, full of ease, and dark lands of sheer physical torture. Odysseus tests extremes in the western oceans, and then returns home to a microcosmic version of the Mediterranean. The suitors are both easefully indolent and ravenous —they parody hospitality and make Odysseus' homecoming another trial. All Odysseus' adventures are set in lands with either too little civilized form or too little human substance. On Ithaca the suitors' form is bad and their substance not their own.

The essential rhythm of the *Odyssey* is set up in the spatial alternation of its episodes. Various lands and places extend invitations or make threats. Lotusland is paradise to the Cyclops' hellish cave. Aeolus' is an easeful kingdom to the Lestrygonians' treacherous domain. Circe lives on a double isle, at first nightmarish then paradisaical. Between Odysseus' two visits to Circe he actually voyages to the realm of Hades to summon the shades. The pattern picks up again in alternating lands. Scylla is a violent threat, and Trinacria a verdant paradise. Charybdis is a dark whirlpool, and Calypso's island a preview of immortality. After Calypso, Odysseus once again tests the rough sea of troubles before he lands on Phaeacian shores, the "desirable life" (187) as the poet Russell calls it in *Ulysses*.

These alternations are deliberate and reinforce two potential diffi- culties for wanderers: the desire to stop and the risks upon stopping. Odysseus and his men are continually lured to places they discover they would rather not be. Bérard sees this as characteristic of the various Phoenician *periploi* he records, but the process has narrative significance in an epic of migration. Wanderers sometimes create new homes, better than the ones they remember. But to do so they must test unknown territories, risk unknown encounters. The Greek hero of the *Odyssey*, even before the Latin hero of the *Aeneid*, pushes back certain western borders—he overcomes the trials of displace- ment. Much of the action of the narrative connects place and process for Odysseus. Even the active gods of the poem represent the alter- nating conditions of its territories. Poseidon is the adversary god of the western oceans and deeper realms. His domain is elemental and formless. Athena is the goddess of the hearth, the eastern landfall. Her arts are formal and stable. Images of the *Odyssey*'s space double as images of the hero's transformative process: sea to land or ele- mental to civilized.[3] In light of the Odyssean mediation, Joyce's well known remarks to Budgen on Ulysses as "allroundman" make con- siderable sense. Odysseus defines himself by relations that draw him toward a civilized, perhaps even a recivilized center. Joyce's sense of Odysseus covers the expanse of the eastern and western Mediter- ranean, while drawing the hero to a new spatial center: "Ulysses is son to Laertes, but he is father to Telemachus, husband to Penel- ope, lover of Calypso, companion in arms of the Greek warriors around Troy and King of Ithaca." Joyce continued, as Budgen re- counts, laughing: "he was the first gentleman in Europe. When he advanced, naked, to meet the young princess he hid from her maidenly eyes the parts that mattered of his brine-soaked, barnacle- encrusted body" (Budgen, pp. 16-17). The scene Joyce recalls here

---

[3] I am much indebted to the chapters on the *Odyssey* (and on the *Iliad*) in Thomas Greene's *Descent from Heaven* (New Haven, 1963), and to an essay by George E. Dimock, Jr., "The Name of Odysseus," *The Hudson Re- view*, IX (1956), 52-70.

from the Phaeacian encounter with Nausicaa conflates the extremes of the poem: Athena's decorous ways imaged in Poseidon's primal state. Odysseus cannot help his appearance—he spends much of the poem in the element of his adversary. Athena, as she is wont to do, soon provides the gentleman with a shining suit of clothes. Odysseus has moved east to Scheria, nearing his civilized, or supposedly civilized, native territory.

The extremes that Odysseus faces and the direction the *Odyssey* takes are reflected throughout the narrative in its boundaries and in its local details. In many ways, the *Odyssey* makes its lands speak. Nowhere is this so apparent as in the spatial allegory of the neighbor kingdoms, the former Phaeacians and the present Cyclopes. The subtle Phaeacians, to whose new home Odysseus sails east, used to live as neighbors of the Cyclopes on the plains of Hypereia, which Bérard places off the Neopolitan Bay in Italy. The Phaeacians, as westerners, could not live in proximity with brutal giants. They migrated east as a nation to Scheria, back toward the civilized world. But the retrogressive path of the Phaeacian *translatio* is a feeble effort to stop time by moving back space. The *ethos* of the *Odyssey* demands the western confrontation before the eastern *Nostos*. Odysseus encounters one of these very barbaric Cyclopes on the same Hypereian plain. And he does what an entire race of people would not do: he bests barbarity with guile and measured force. Leopold Bloom, the Dubliner, has the right to remember, as he does in *Eumaeus* of *Ulysses*, the same western triumph of the eastern voyager. The citizen-Cyclops thinks all space belongs to Ireland—but Bloom, the Semite, the mythic Brightdayler, takes some of that space back along the Semitic axis.

> At the same time he inwardly chuckled over his repartee to the blood and ouns champion about his God being a jew. People could put up with being bitten by a wolf but what properly riled them was a bite from a sheep. The most vulnerable point too of tender Achilles, your God was a jew, because mostly they appeared to imagine he came from Carrick-on-Shannon or somewhere about in the county Sligo. (658)

If in *Ulysses* Joyce settles for small cultural victories, the larger *Odyssey* depicts a culture's coming of age in the Mediterranean. Extremes are endured, from cannibalism to oblivion, and the home kingdom, Ithaca, is renewed.

14

EPIC ALTERNATION

↑
N

MEDITERRANEAN

Poseidon: Athena:
{Elemental   {Civilization
{unknown   {known

Lestrygonians   Ismarus
\
Circe
\
ITALY   Hades   GREECE
\
Cyclops   Troy
\
Phaeacia — — — — — — → Phaeacia
\   \
Sirens   Ithaca
\   \
← W   Scylla & Charybdis   Pylos   E →
\   \
Aeolus   Sparta
\   \
Oxen of Sun   Crete
(Sicily)   \
\   \
↖ to   Lotusland   \
Calypso   \
\
\
\
Egypt
(Proteus)

S
↓

ZOPHOS: TOWARD THE GLOOM
MIGRATIONS, ORIENTATIONS, DIRECTIONS

MASTERS OF THE MEDITERRANEAN

In the *Aeolus* episode of *Ulysses*, an Irish blowhard, Professor Mac-Hugh, comments on the passing of empires: "The sack of windy Troy. Kingdoms of this world. The masters of the Mediterranean are fellaheen today" (144). MacHugh's implosive turn is one of the day's endless epitomes for Joyce's Irish epic. The Greeks are "fellaheen" in that the Mediterranean is a Semitic sea, and "fellaheen" in that they are fallen—are parodically grounded in the meager domain of contemporary Dublin.

Just after the professor's remarks, Dedalus requests the floor: "I have a vision too" (144): *A Pisgah Sight of Palestine or the Parable of the Plums*. The migratory *Nostos* of the Israelites is reduced, in this instance, to another Hellenic pun, a *periplous* or a voyage around an island.[1] The Semitic world of Moses is fellaheen as the Dublin matrons drop their plum pits from Nelson's Pillar at "thirtytwo feet per sec" according to the novel's law of comic gravity. But the movement of civilizations is not simply a migratory plunge for Joyce. There are some cultural drifts that he takes seriously. The fellaheen or Semitic connection places the Irish back where they began—with the Phoenician navigators of the Mediterranean. In a lecture delivered in Trieste in 1907, *Ireland, Island of Saints and Sages*, Joyce speaks of the origins of the Irish language and people.

> This language is oriental in origin, and has been identified by many philologists with the ancient language of the Phoenicians, the originators of trade and navigation, according to historians. This adventurous people, who had a monopoly of the sea, established in Ireland a civilization that had decayed and almost disappeared before the first Greek historian took his pen in hand. It jealously preserved the secrets of its knowledge, and the first mention of the island of Ireland in foreign literature is found in a Greek poem of the fifth century before Christ, where the historian repeats the Phoenician tradition. (*CW*, 156)

[1] See J. G. Keogh, "*Ulysses*' 'Parable of the Plums' as Parable and Periplum," *JJQ*, 7 (1970), 377-378.

The historical and philological connections, borrowed from the Irish scholar, Charles Vallancey, are suspect, but the fellaheen path extends from Scythia to Greece to Phoenicia to North Africa to Spain to Ireland. The fulminating hero of *Cyclops*, Joyce's citizen loyal to a forgotten cause, honors the flag of "three crowns on a blue field, the three sons of Milesius" (328). The chronicles of the tenth to twelfth centuries hold that the ancestors of the original Irish, following the Jews out of Egypt, inhabited Scythia and the Euxine, settling under Mile in what are now Slavic regions. Later they migrated across the Mediterranean, and from the Straits of Gibraltar eventually sailed to Ireland.[2] Stuart Gilbert refers to these mythic migrations in a short chapter, "Dubliners—Vikings—Achaeans" (Gilbert, 65-76), and Victor Bérard treats a chord of the full line in *Les Phéniciens et l'Odyssée*: "Aux débuts de l'histoire écrite, ce sont les Milésiens qui, les premiers des Hellènes, entreprennent l'exploitation commerciale du Pont-Euxin" (The Milesians appear at the beginning of written history, the first Greeks undertaking commercial exploitation of the Euxine) [Bérard, 1, 74]. When the citizen in *Ulysses* remembers the drift of chronicled Irish migrations, he plays on a well-known Homeric epithet, *epi oinopa ponton*, the wine-dark sea: "We had our trade with Spain and the French and with the Flemings before those mongrels were pupped, Spanish ale in Galway, the winebark on the winedark waterway" (327).

The progress is legendary, and Joyce recognizes it as such, but the legend substantiates an important fictional axis. In *Ulysses* Joyce draws back to origins; the novel displays what Gilbert calls *Drang nach Osten*, an eastern stress, and indeed Joyce first stops in Greece for a Homeric hero, detours to Scythian regions for a citizen of Hungarian extraction, Virag-Bloom, and pauses at the Straits of Gibraltar on the way to Ireland for an ample chanteuse with Spanish blood in her veins. For Joyce the east-west migration extends further in time, especially in the context of the massive Irish emigration in the nineteenth century to America. In a notesheet entry for the *Cyclops* episode he charts the progress: "Milesian (Argos) exp. Euxine, America" (Herring, p. 106).

[2] M. H. D'Ambois de Jubainville, *The Irish Mythological Cycle*, trans. Richard Best (Dublin, 1903), writes that "the sons of Mile came out of Spain, and not from the land of the Dead; and Christian scholars, preoccupied with etymological questions, held that the ancestors of the Irish, when they left the Asiatic cradle of the human race, wandered about the world for many years, sojourning for a time in divers places, such as Egypt, and particularly Scythia" (p. 127).

Departures and arrivals make up the racial-epic drifts of Joyce's fiction. The riddles of migration harbor hundreds of coincidences, coincidences Joyce noticed early in his life and later embedded in the polyglot spaces of *Finnegans Wake*. In the Trieste lecture on Ireland, Joyce asks a question, a variant of which was to appear on Buck Mulligan's darting tongue in the first chapter of *Ulysses*: "Is this country destined to resume its ancient position as the Hellas of the north some day?" (*CW*, 172). Joyce answers his question with a series of antecedent questions. Failing to arrive at a satisfactory answer, he at least establishes a significant direction.

> Is the Celtic mind, like the Slavic mind which it resembles in many ways, destined to enrich the civil conscience with new discoveries and new insights in the future? Or must the Celtic world, the five Celtic nations, driven by stronger nations to the edge of the continent, to the outermost islands of Europe, finally be cast into the ocean after a struggle of centuries?
>
> (*CW*, 172-173)

The western progress to Ireland haunted Joyce's imagination for years. *Ulysses* and then *Finnegans Wake* are ghost stories, ancestral, epic, and comic, about the complexities of multiple migrations. Kingdoms of past worlds return for a space of time. The falls and resurrections of a *mélange* of Phoenicians, Semites, Greeks, Slavs, Norsemen, and Celts inhabit Joyce's fictional vision of Ireland. Joyce wrote to Carlo Linati that *Ulysses* is an epic of essentially two races, Israelite and Irish (*Letters*, 1, 146-147). In another notesheet entry for *Cyclops* Joyce jots down: "Jews & Irish remember past" (Herring, p. 82). But a third culture edges between the Israelites and the Irish. In a passage from *Circe,* long recognized as crucial to *Ulysses*, Lynch's talking cap mocks the fellaheen or Semitic conceit of Joyce's migrating *homo mediterraneus*: "Jewgreek is greekjew. Extremes meet. Death is the highest form of life. Bah!" (504). Joyce notes the mysterious appearance of a dark stranger, a Jew, on the strand at Sandymount in an entry for *Nausicaa*. The Semitic Odysseus is the western wandering Jew.

$$\text{Jew} \longrightarrow \text{West}$$
$$\text{East} \longleftarrow \text{Zion}$$

(Herring, p. 128)

When Joyce was living in Zürich after the conclusion of World War I, he conversed regularly with his friend Frank Budgen. Budgen noticed the mass of modern Greeks in Zürich and commented to Joyce how strangely like Jews they were. "Not so strangely," Joyce replied. "Anyway, they are Greeks. And there's a lot to be said for the theory that the *Odyssey* is a Semitic poem" (Budgen, pp. 169-170). Such a theory, of course, makes its detailed way into *Ulysses* through Victor Bérard's *Les Phéniciens et l'Odyssée*. Bérard saw the Semitic-Greek connections of the Homeric *Odyssey*, and he also commented on the nature of migrating Greek populations of the present day. In his 1918 Zürich notebook Joyce records the phrase "odyssey v emigration" (VIII.A.5, 297) in reference to Bérard's remarks on the migration of modern Ithacans and Ionians to Britain [Bérard, ii, 526-527]. Late in *Les Phéniciens*, Bérard even indulges in an appropriate bit of transportational slang. After Odysseus' tales of wandering narrated in the assembly of the Phaeacians, Bérard writes that Alcinous "lui donne un 'transatlantique' pour revenir dans son royaume" (gives him a "transatlantic" in order to return to his kingdom) [Bérard, ii, 401]. Bérard's French pun becomes a narrative progress for Joyce who moves one modest wandering Odysseus from Ithaca to Europe and slips him through the Pillars of Hercules on a "transatlantic" to Ireland. In so doing, he answers a question the citizen poses in *Cyclops*, although the answer is one the citizen would consider inadequate: "Where are the Greek merchants that came through the Pillars of Hercules . . . ?" (326).

Joyce was always delighted to find the "wishmarks" of his imagination corroborated by classicists and mythologists. In 1938 he wrote Louis Gillet about Heinrich Zimmer's study of Scandinavian and Irish mythology. Joyce remarked that Zimmer confirmed the migrating myths in *Finnegans Wake* much as Bérard had done for *Ulysses* years before. Both scholars provided evidence for basing systems of language and myth on the flow of historical movement. Of the revelations of Zimmer Joyce writes in French: "Il est arrivé un étrange parallèle avec le cas Ulysse—Victor Bérard. Son étude homérique est venue confirmer ma théorie du sémitisme de l'Odyssée quand j'avais déjà écrit trois quarts du livre" (A strange parallel occurred with Victor Bérard's Ulysses. His Homeric study confirmed my theory of semitism in the *Odyssey* when I had already written three-quarters of the book) [*Letters*, i, 401].

Joyce had read or re-read Bérard early in 1918, as dozens of entries in his Zürich notebook suggest. At that time he had completed the *Telemachiad*, drafted part of the *Nostos*, and was in the midst of the early chapters of the *Wanderings*: *Calypso, Lotuseaters, Hades, Aeolus*, and *Lestrygonians*. Of course, he later revised all of *Ulysses* using the notebooks and notesheets upon which he had transcribed extensively from *Les Phéniciens*.[3] Even if Joyce exaggerates slightly and was not precisely three-quarters done with *Ulysses* when he discovered Bérard, the Semitic idea is manifest early, just as he says. The second chapter of *Ulysses, Nestor*, opens with a disappointed Greek in the Mediterranean, Pyrrhus, and concludes with Mr. Deasy's shout in the street exiling the wandering Semite from Nestor's western gate.

> —I just wanted to say, he said. Ireland, they say, has the honour of being the only country which never persecuted the jews. Do you know that? No. And do you know why?
> He frowned sternly on the bright air.
> —Why sir? Stephen asked, beginning to smile.
> —Because she never let them in, Mr Deasy said solemnly.
>
> (36)

Rebels against the spirit of the Semitic Mediterranean, the Irish are cut off from one source of cultural sustenance. Joyce had always wondered about the Mediterranean and its fellaheen, Greek, and Roman masters. In May of 1905, around the time he began thinking of adapting the Homeric *Odyssey* for his own fiction, he wrote his brother Stanislaus from Trieste: "Have you ever reflected what an important sea the Mediterranean is? . . . Perhaps the Baltic will replace the Mediterranean but till now importance seems to have been in the direct ratio of nearness to the Mediterranean" (*Letters*, II, 90). The Mediterranean unites and divides continents. Its climates are similar along its coastal regions; various in its deserts, islands, and peninsulas. It supports a heterogeneous mixture of races from

[3] See Michael Groden, *The Growth of James Joyce's Ulysses* (Ph.D. Dissertation, Princeton, 1975), pp. 36-60. Joyce wrote Harriet Weaver in October of 1921, "*Eolus* is recast. *Hades* and the *Lotuseaters* much amplified and the other episodes retouched a good deal" (*Letters*, I, 172). Part of the amplification and retouching involved working in specific information gleaned from Bérard, or, more simply, following a hint from Bérard and expanding it. This is the case, for instance, with the array of flowers added to *Lotuseaters*. When he learned that the lotus plant was not a narcotic but an edible variety of water-lily, Joyce virtually "enflowered" the episode.

Asia to North Africa. Its sea routes were known to the most ancient navigators from the beginning of recorded history. Joyce's fascination with this great Phoenician sea was a constant fascination. In his last work, *Finnegans Wake*, he returns back along a navigable line in time and space from northern seas "to the atlantic and Phenitia Proper" (*FW*, 85). One of the many metamorphoses of the *Wake*'s collapsing Scandinavian-Irish-Semitic hero, Earwicker, is "the gran Phenician rover" (*FW*, 197).[4] And the great Norseman, Shaun, describes his artist brother, Shem, as a "semi-semitic serendipitist," a connoisseur of literature's migrational axis through the Mediterranean and westward: "Europasianised Afferyank!" (*FW*, 191).

THE PHOENICIAN ODYSSEY

In his *Scienza Nuova*, Giambattista Vico, one of Joyce's favorite Italians, describes the Homeric *Odyssey*'s reliance on the storehouse of Phoenician Mediterranean lore.

> . . . the Greeks, as appears from numerous passages particularly in the *Odyssey*, had long since opened their own country to commerce with the Phoenicians, whose tales no less than their merchandise the Greek peoples had come to delight in, just as Europeans do now in those of the Indies. There is thus no contradiction between these two facts: on the one hand that Homer never saw Egypt, and on the other that he recounts so many things of Egypt and Libya, of Phoenicia and Asia, and above all of Italy and Sicily; for these things had been related to the Greeks by the Phoenicians. (*New Science*, 253-254)

Victor Bérard begins his *Les Phéniciens* with a similar observation by the Greek geographer Strabo: "L'ensemble des études qui vont suivre n'est guère que le développement d'une ou deux phrases de Strabon: 'Si Homère décrivit exactement les contrées, tant de la mer Intérieure que de la mer Extérieure, c'est qu'il tenait sa science des Phéniciens'" (The following comprehensive study is merely the development of only one or two remarks of Strabo: 'If Homer described lands exactly, as much the interior as the exterior seas, it is because he derived his knowledge from the Phoenicians') [Bérard,

[4] For a treatment of the eastern influences on *Finnegans Wake*, see Dounia Christiani, "H. C. Earwicker the Ostman," *JJQ*, 2 (1965), 150-157.

I, 3].[5] Strabo believes in the traceable locations of Homer's epic topography. In his *Geography* he writes of the *Odyssey*: "the story cannot with plausibility be called wholly a fiction."[6] More important, Strabo argues for the necessity of localization as part of the very fabric of epic literature. Events and places must have tangible significance for the imagination of a culture to absorb them. Strabo's Homer is

> the founder of the science of geography; for Homer has surpassed all men, both of ancient and modern times, not only in the excellence of his poetry, but also, I might say, in his acquaintance with all that pertains to public life. And this acquaintance made him busy himself not only about public activities, to the end that he might learn of as many of them as possible and give an account of them to posterity, but also about the geography both of the individual countries and of the inhabited world at large, both land and sea; for otherwise he would not have gone to the uttermost bounds of the inhabited world, encompassing the whole of it in his description.[7]

When Victor Bérard follows Strabo in pursuit of the Phoenician Homer, he refines a method suited to both archaeology and narrative: "*la topologie*" or the "géologie des sites" [Bérard, I, 26]. At the conclusion of his long study, Bérard writes that the Homeric *Odyssey* realizes locale: "Chaque Aventure même n'a pour ressort que la mise en action de la toponymie" (Indeed, the initial impulse of each adventure is the realization of place names) [Bérard, II, 563]. Bérard traces Homer to the limits of the Mediterranean by plotting migratory expansions in the temporal layering of local names. Of the poem's adventures Bérard asserts: "1° Ils sont localisés dans l'espace; ils appartiennent sûrement à tel pays, à tel site; 2° Ils sont presque toujours localisés dans le temps; ils peuvent être sériés et datés avec

[5] Strabo was not Bérard's only source for Homer and his eastern connections: "Suivant Hérodote, Thucydide et Strabon, suivant tous les Anciens qui eurent une renommée d'érudition ou de critique, les Orientaux avaient été les maîtres et les initiateurs des Grecs" (According to Herodotus, Thucydides, and Strabo, as well as all the ancients who were renowned for erudition and for critical judgment, the easterners were the masters and teachers of the Greeks) [Bérard, I, 24].

[6] *The Geography of Strabo*, trans. Horace Leonard Jones (London, 1917), I, 163.

[7] Strabo, *Geography*, I, 5.

quelque approximation" (1: They are localized in space; they surely belong to a definite country, a definite site; 2: They are almost always localized in time; they can be arranged and dated with some approximation) [Bérard, 1, 26].

Geography records the history of the *Odyssey*'s range just as geology records the history of its timing. For Bérard the *Odyssey* is not

l'assemblage de contes à dormir debout que les vains littérateurs nous présentent. C'est un document géographique. C'est la peinture poétique, mais non déformée, d'une certaine Méditerranée avec ses habitudes de navigation, ses théories du monde et de la vie navale, sa langue, ses Instructions Nautiques et son commerce. . . . Ulysse ne navigue plus dans une brume de légende en des pays imaginaires. De cap en cap, d'île en île, il cabote sur les côtes italiennes ou espagnoles que fréquentait déjà le commerce phénicien.

([The *Odyssey* is not] a collection of silly tales that the literati present to us. It is a geographical document. It is a poetic painting, but in no way deformed, of a definite Mediterranean with its navigational customs, its theories of the world and of the ocean world, its language, its log books, and its commerce. . . . Ulysses no longer navigates in a legendary fog in imaginary countries. From cape to cape, from isle to isle, he traffics over the Italian or Spanish coasts already frequented by Phoenician commerce)

[Bérard, 1, 52].

Bérard confirms the narrative perspective on double worlds that Joyce re-envisages with a fervor all his own in *Ulysses*: "cette Méditerranée odysséenne est aussi la Méditerrannée des doublets gréco-sémitiques, car l'*Ulysséide* n'est qu'un tissu de ces doublets" (this Odyssean Mediterranean is also the Mediterranean of Greco-Semitic doublets, because the *Ulysseiad* is but a texture of these doublets) [Bérard, 1, 52]. Jewgreek is indeed Greekjew. A culture documents its movements, and remembers its places. For Joyce, as for Bérard, the processes of narrative are directly related to the recording processes of civilization. And the topological records of a race, even those buried under dump heaps like the litter-letter of *Finnegans Wake*, tell the encompassing story of a land's local, comic, and sublime history.

Bérard's understanding of the *Odyssey* is keyed to a system of

23

geographical orientation. The sun is the axis upon which the Odyssean migratory epic turns. Bérard speaks of the *Odyssey* as a poem of "tours et retours du soleil, cette marche ou danse en rond" (turns and returns of the sun, this march or dance in round) [Bérard, II, 263]. Joyce observes the same diurnal structure in *Ulysses*, whose episodes dance to the tune of the hours, Ponchielli's and Dublin's.[8] The day moves along what Dante had called—appropriately, in the "Ulysses" canto of the *Inferno—di retro al sol*, the track of the sun. Leopold Bloom speaks of setting off at dawn, somewhere in the east to "travel round in front of the sun" (57). His early morning revery is fulfilled in the evening catalogue of his library: Fredrick Diodati Thompson's *In the Track of the Sun: Diary of a Globe Trotter* (London, 1893).

The solar process is not limited to the Odyssean version of the epic. In *Finnegans Wake* Joyce writes of all things as "solarsystemised, seriolcosmically, in a more and more almightily expanding universe under one, there is rhymeless reason to believe, original sun" (*FW*, 263). The sun's daily path across the sky marks what Jean Richer sees in *La Géographie Sacrée du Monde Grec* (Paris, 1967) as the earth's orienting itself under the superimposed structure of the heavens. For the Greeks, as for other ancient Mediterranean cultures, "le soleil, chaque soir semble mourir à l'ouest" (the sun, each evening, seems to die in the west). In medieval and Renaissance Europe the track of the sun still measures and values space. Cathedral architecture, for instance, not only plans the shape of the church to image Christ on the cross, but situates it to repeat the hierarchy of cosmic direction. The cathedral tells the tale of its compass points. Emile Mâle describes the gothic design of the medieval church as "oriented from the rising to the setting sun." He cites a rule of Gulielmus Durandus that "The foundations must be disposed in such a manner that the head of the church lies exactly to the east, that is to the part of the sky in which the sun rises at the equinox." Mâle continues.

> Each cardinal point has its significance in churches . . . the north, region of cold and darkness, is usually consecrated to the Old Testament, and the south, bathed in warm sunlight, is devoted to

[8] Many make the point about the hourly dance of *Ulysses*, but Edward L. Epstein makes it best in his chapter, "Stephen's Dance," in *The Ordeal of Stephen Dedalus* (Carbondale, Ill., 1971), pp. 156-173.

the New . . . the western facade—where the setting sun lights up the great scene of the evening of the world's history . . . became for them the region of death.[9]

From the eastern head, the point of orientation, to the western extension, the region of gloom—"gonemost west" says the undertaker in *Finnegans Wake*—the rise and fall of the sun replicates the image of man's universe. The movement from east to west is a movement from birth to death. Orientation in a geographical sense, however, is dependent upon a relative system of positioning. When in the *Odyssey* Eumaeus tells his sad tale of kidnapping to Odysseus, he speaks of a small triadic island group in eastern seas near an early Greek *omphalos* at Delos (Ortygia).

> A certain island, Syriê by name—
> you may have heard the name—lies off Ortýgia
> due west, and holds the sunsets of the year.
>
> (Book xv, Fitzgerald, pp. 280-281)

Syriê (Syros) is indeed west in the group, but the setting of the sun is conceived on a very small grid. According to Bérard, that grid expands to include the whole of the *Odyssey*. Odysseus wanders for the most part in the direction of the sunset, the gloom, what Homer calls the *zophos*. Homer uses the term, *zophos*, selectively. He means by it either the darkening northwest or the underworld, as when Odysseus asks Elpenor in Book xi how he came down to the murky darkness (*ēeroenta zophon*). To come out of the darkness in the *Odyssey* means to return to life. Orientation is always relative, but it also always carries with it a set of attendant values. In *Les Phéniciens* Bérard digresses to explain why Odysseus, in full flight from the man-eaters of Lamos, seeks the region of Circe's dawn for ready salvation. His eastern turn reveals a system shared by the Egyptians, the Chaldeans, the Phoenicians, and the Greeks. Joyce, as already mentioned, transcribed Bérard's explanation in his Zürich notebook and his British Museum notesheets (VIII.A.5, 302-303; Herring, p. 281, see diagram on my p. 9). The passage from Bérard is crucial.

---

[9] Emile Mâle, *Religious Art in France of the Thirteenth Century* (New York, 1972), pp. 5-6. For a more general essay on the theory of directional significance, especially in Renaissance Europe, see Loren Baritz, "The Idea of the West," *American Historical Review*, LXVI (1961), 618-640.

Pour les Égyptiens, le ciel reposait sur quatre piliers. A la con-
servation de chacun d'eux, un dieu était attaché: Osiris ou Horus,
l'épervier, présidait au pilier méridional, Sit au pilier septentrional,
Thot à celui de l'Ouest, et Sapdi, l'auteur de la lumière zodiacale,
à celui de l'Est. Ils partageaient le monde en quatre régions ou
plutôt en quatre *maisons*, délimitées par les montagnes qui bordent
le ciel et par les diamètres qui se croisent entre les piliers.

(For the Egyptians, the sky reposes on four pillars. A god is re-
sponsible for the protection of each of them: Osiris or Horus, the
sparrow-hawk, presides at the meridional pillar, Set at the septentrional pillar, Thoth at the western one, and Sept, the inventor of
the zodiacal dial, at the eastern one. They parcel the world in four
regions or, rather, four houses, marked by the mountains which
border the sky and by the diagonal lines which cross between
the pillars) [Bérard, ii, 261].

As the sun progresses across the domed heavens, from the dawn
and toward the gloom, space is given directional value.

La valeur de ces différents termes apparaît clairement si nous
imaginons la terre sous la forme d'un édifice carré, dont les quatre
angles seraient au Nord, à l'Est, au Sud et à l'Ouest: les quatre
façades seraient donc Nord-Est, Est-Sud, Sud-Ouest, Ouest-Nord.
La façade Nord-Est verrait le soleil à son lever: c'est le côté, la
maison de l'aurore et du levant. La façade Est-Sud recevrait les
rayons du soleil pendant presque toute la journée: c'est le midi,
le jour, la *maison* du soleil. La façade Sud-Ouest verrait le soleil
à son coucher: c'est la *maison* du soir, du couchant, ἕσπερος. Enfin
la façade Ouest-Nord ne reçoit jamais le soleil: c'est le côté, la
maison de l'ombre, ce que le poète odysséen appelle *zophos*, ζόφος,
et ce que les commentateurs classiques traduisent par σκία, l'*ombre*,
σκότος, l'*obscurité* . . . pour s'orienter, l'homme se tourne vers
le levant et vers le soleil: il a donc une moitié du ciel, soit deux
maisons, *devant* soi, et l'autre moitié du ciel, deux maisons, *der-*
rière. Nous avons vu que le poète odysséen connaît ces termes
et les emploie. Pour lui, tout ce qui est *devant* est l'aurore et la
lumière; tout ce qui est *derrière* est le couchant et l'ombre. Les
peuples habitent soit *devant*, vers l'aurore et le soleil, soit *derrière*,
vers l'obscurité, vers le *zophos*; ces deux groupes constituent
l'humanité tout entière.

(The value of these different terms appears clearly if we imagine
the earth under the form of a square edifice, whose four corners
would be in the north, in the east, in the south, and in the west:
the four facades, therefore, would be north-east, east-south, southwest, west-north. The north-east facade would witness the rising of
the sun: it is the side, the house, of dawn and sunrise. The east-
south facade would receive the rays of the sun during the entire
day: it is noontime, the full day, the house of the sun. The southwest facade would see the sunset: it is the house of evening, of
sunset, ἕσπερος. Finally, the west-north facade never receives the
sun: it is the side, the house, of shade, that the Odyssean poet calls
zophos, ζόφος and that classical scholars translate by σκία, the
shade, σκότος, the obscurity . . . in order to orient himself, man
turns toward the sunrise and toward the sun: he has, then, half
the sky, that is, two houses, in front of him, and the other half
of the sky, two houses, behind. We have seen that the Odyssean
poet knows these terms and uses them. For him, all that is in front
is the dawn and the light; all that is behind is the sunset and the
shade. People live either in front, toward the dawn and the sun,
or behind, toward the obscurity, toward the zophos; these two
groups constitute the whole of humanity)   [Bérard, II, 262-263].

At the center of the narrative action in the *Odyssey* for Bérard is
the struggle for geographical reorientation. The Mediterranean *Wanderings* plot a westward exile toward the dark regions of death and
a return toward the sustenance of the sun. Bérard sees other Greek
myths implicated in a similar process. The founding of Europe on
Greek soil, for instance, is literally the westward pursuit of Europe
by Asia. For Bérard, Cadmus, the founder of Europe, is the Semitic
Kadam or *Kedem*, signifying the Orient. And Europa derives from
the participle form *'arab* of the substantive *'eroba*, meaning sunset,
or the Occident [Bérard, I, 224-225]. Moreover, the migrational pattern translates place names. Old borders become new centers. Cadmus establishes Europe in Greece (Boeotia), and later the Greeks
extend the borders of Europe to the Straits of Gibraltar at the Pillars
of Hercules. In his chapter on the Homeric Calypso, Bérard points
out that the geographical terminology for the supposed end of the
world is similar to that of an earlier migration near the Saronic sea
where Cadmus settled in Boeotia. Variants of the same Semitic place
names appear, including the mysterious Ogygia, Calypso's isle. Ogy-

ges was a son of Cadmus, whose name became a common epithet for the seacoast around Megara. At the time, the area off the Saronic and across to the Corinthian straits marked the end of the world for the Greeks. Calypso's Ogygia, Bérard suggests, is a generic name —it simply means at the ocean's bourne. Later, the line continues when Plutarch identifies Calypso's Ogygia with an isle west of Britain where Kronos was imprisoned (*Moralia*, 941a).

The migratory expansion of the geographical grid does not cease with classical civilizations. Toward the end of his study of Greek geographical orientation, Jean Richer plots the path of extensions, which, in time, become new centers. Eastern *omphaloi* like Delos and Delphi become western *omphaloi* like Sicily, Cumae, and Calypso's isle at Gibraltar. Once beyond the Mediterranean, Richer imagines the extension carrying to the Isle of Man between Great Britain and Ireland. This isle would make an excellent candidate for the *omphalos* of the northwest, a Celtic center.[10] We remember Joyce's running joke in *Ulysses* about the "homerule sun," associated with the Manx Parliament on the Isle of Man, "rising in the northwest" (57).[11]

One task of the bard of migrations, even of comic migrations, is to re-illumine domain, to make ends meet in the track of the sun. In the geography lesson of *Finnegans Wake*, Joyce superimposes the Greek *omphalos* at Delphi, the most important of classical times, onto tenebrous Dublin.

4. What Irish capitol city (a dea o dea!) of two syllables and six letters, with a deltic origin and a nuinous end, (ah dust oh dust!) can boost of having *a*) the most extensive public park in

[10] A. W. Moore, *A History of the Isle of Man* (London, 1900), explains that the isle's insignia (three legs in a circle) was originally Sicilian (pp. 136-137). A Mediterranean *omphalos*, in this case, lends a Celtic island its symbolic configuration.

[11] One extreme version of the western transmission would have delighted Joyce. Gilbert Pillot's *Le Code Secret de l'Odyssée* (Paris, 1969) argues that Odysseus' *Wanderings* took place almost entirely in the North Atlantic. Odysseus, in Pillot's version, even put in a port of call near Galway in Ireland, the land of the Lestrygonians. The thought of Irish *anthropophagi* harks back to Swift's *Modest Proposal*. Of course, Pillot's northern theory is not exactly new. The Theosophist Madame Blavatsky, whom Stephen and Joyce so ridicule throughout *Ulysses*' day, asserts with her customary authority that Odysseus voyaged to Lestrygonian territory far beyond the Atlantic to the North Sea (*Isis Unveiled: A Master-Key to the Mysteries of Ancient and Modern Science and Theology* [New York, 1877], I, 549).

the world, *b*) the most expensive brewing industry in the world, *c*) the most expansive peopling thoroughfare in the world, *d*) the most phillohippuc theobibbous paùpulation in the world: and harmonise your abecedeed responses?

Answer: *a*) Delfas . . . *b*) Dorhqk . . . *c*) Nublid . . . *d*) Dalway . . . .   *(FW,* 140)

The translation is from a Greek center to versions of Celtic centers —Joyce even continues the axis past Dublin to Galway in the west. When the twins of *Finnegans Wake*, the men of western brawn and eastern brain, unite in a climactic passage to renew epic spaces, the migrational mission is made comically sublime. Dublin's Phoenix Park becomes its Phoenician original.

Eftsoon so too will our own sphoenix spark spirt his spyre and sunward stride the rampante flambe. Ay, already the sombrer opacities of the gloom are sphanished! Brave footsore Haun! Work your progress! Hold to! Now! Win out, ye divil ye! The silent cock shall crow at last. The west shall shake the east awake. Walk while ye have the night for morn, lightbreakfastbringer, morroweth whereon every past shall full fost sleep. Amain.

(FW, 473)

The allusion here is to *Malachi*, the last Book of the Old Testament, but the passage recalls a variant of epic migration, the Renaissance paean to the new world in Samuel Purchas' *Pilgrimes*: "thus hath God given opportunity by Navigation into all parts, that in the Sun-set and Evening of the World, the Sunne of righteousnesse might arise out of our West to illuminate the east."[12] *Finnegans Wake* was titled *Work in Progress* before Joyce revealed that it had a title. Fiction *is* a progress for Joyce. The last mock-epithet we have for Leopold Bloom in *Ulysses* is the western hero *redivivus*: "Darkinbad the Brightdayler" (737). Earlier in *Ulysses*, another Malachi, Malachi Mulligan, the mocking messenger of *Telemachus* ironically delivered the enlightening injunction at the beginning of the day: "God Kinch, if you and I could only work together we might do

---

[12] *Purchas, His Pilgrimes, in Hakluytus Posthumus* (Glasgow, 1905-1907), I, 173. The Biblical text closes the Old Testament and reads: *Malachi*, 4:2: "But unto you that fear my name shall the Sun of righteousness arise with healing in his wings; and ye shall go forth, and grow up as calves of the stall." For a fine essay on this and related topics, see Geoffrey Hartman, "Romantic Poetry and the Genius Loci," in *Beyond Formalism* (New Haven, 1970), pp. 311-336.

something for the island. Hellenise it" (7). The progress is west-ward: Hellas to Hibernia in the Heart of the Dublin metropolis. And it recalls the mission of another pair of strange northern *Übermenschen*, Mephisto and Faust, one the mocker and the other the purist, as they move to and from the Gothic north and the clear light of southern Greece. Like *Faust, Ulysses* partly mocks and partly re-illumines the darkened paths of the epic tradition. Goethe travels to Greece for a radiant heroine, Helen of Troy, and Joyce returns to Ireland with a *bona fide* solar hero, a Semitic Odysseus.

THE HOME ISLANDS: ITHACA AND DUBLIN

Odysseus travels east toward the light of the sun when he returns from Calypso's isle to the Greek half of the Mediterranean sea, but relative to an older conception of Greek borders even his native Ithaca lies off the western coast of the Peloponnese where the sun leaves the day in obscurity. Odysseus is precise about the location of his home, and this has created something of a crux in Homeric scholarship. He describes his island archipelago kingdom to Alcinous and specifies that his own island is furthest northwest toward the gloom or *zophos*. Butcher and Lang maintain the Homeric meta-phor: "Now Ithaca lies low, furthest up the sea-line towards the darkness, but those others face the dawning and the sun" (IX, 21-26). Robert Fitzgerald's verse translation substitutes directions for meta-phors.

> My home is on the peaked sea-mark of Ithaka
> under Mount Neion's wind-blown robe of leaves,
> in sight of other islands—Doulíkhion,
> Samê, wooded Zakynthos—Ithaka
> being most lofty in that coastal sea,
> and northwest, while the rest lie east and south.
>
> (Book IX, Fitzgerald, p. 146)

Classical scholars differ as to exactly what island of the western group Odysseus means. Bérard is certain he means present-day Ithaca, and Dörpfeld suspects Leucas.[13] Bérard insists that geogra-phy can account for Ithaca's positioning.

---

[13] Dörpfeld developed his theory in time for Bérard to attack it in *Les Phéniciens*, but its fullest statement is in *Alt-Ithaka* (Munich, 1927). The dispute between Bérard and Dörpfeld has its lighter moments. Bérard writes

Je légitimerai mot par mot la traduction que j'en donne ici: πανυπερτάτη est l'exact équivalent du latin *suprema*, avec le double sens de *hauteur* et d'*extrémité*: ζόφος est le côté de l'ombre, la partie Ouest-Nord-Ouest, que le soleil ne visite jamais. Ithaque est "la suprême île vers le Nord-Ouest," parce que le poète odyséen emploie, comme toujours, le langage des marins.

(I will justify word by word the translation that I have provided here: πανυπερτάτη is the exact equivalent of the Latin, *suprema*, with the double sense of height and extremity: ζόφος is the side of the shade, the region west-north-west, that the sun never visits. Ithaca is "the extreme isle toward the north-west," because the Odyssean poet uses, as always, the terminology of mariners)
[Bérard, 1, 486-487].

Situated where it was, Ithaca was one of the last outposts of civilization for the Homeric Greek world. Even as king, on his island, Odysseus is a border hero. Bérard locates the suitor-infested palace in the extreme northwest quadrant of the island near the modern city of Stavros.[14] Since Odysseus moves from Eumaeus' hut in the south of the island, he essentially replicates the drift of his larger movements in the Mediterranean. Ithaca divides the civilized nations toward the dawn from the mysterious regions of the Mediterranean *couchant*. Beyond the straits between Ithaca and Samê (Cephalonia) are the unfamiliar seas of Poseidon's domain. In a later study, *Les Navigations d'Ulysse* (Paris, 1927-1929), Bérard writes that Ithaca halves the life-death regions of the Mediterranean grid: "Le monde est ainsi partagé en deux moitiés; Ithaque est sur le tranchant qui les sépare" (The world is therefore divided in half; Ithaca is on the edge which separates them) [1, 72]. It is no coincidence that the Homeric word *zophos* occurs in the *Odyssey* in ref-

---

that Dörpfeld takes figures of speech literally. When Telemachus asks Odysseus whether he walked to Ithaca, Dörpfeld thinks that Telemachus means what he says. Therefore there must have been a land route to Ithaca, which would be almost true if Ithaca were present-day Leucas. Bérard suggests that for Dörpfeld if someone dropped from heaven, it would prove the existence of Jacob's ladder [Bérard, II, 411].

[14] See Alan J. B. Wace and Frank H. Stubbings, *A Companion to Homer* (London, 1962). In a chapter devoted to "Principal Homeric Sites: Ithaca," Wace and Stubbings agree with Bérard over Schliemann, who placed the palace near the city of Aetos (pp. 398-421).

erence to Ithaca and to the darkness of the mythic, western underworld.

In the Homeric epic directional bearings have narrative implications. A general logic of the epic's geography is possible because
within its own structure the *Odyssey* offers provisional and realized
examples of what *Nostos* or the reorientation homeward means.
Odysseus returns from one or another version of death. The spatial
outlines of the poem indicate a simple structure—out and back—
but the epic process treats more than the movement of heroes: it
treats the conditions associated with location. In the *Iliad* the Tro-
jans fight on their own eastern territory for values the Greek warriors, long separated from their homes, do not understand. Part of
the power of that strife epic arises from the realization that the
Trojan War measures one civilization that is more refined against
another that has come east to assert the growing strength of its
previously isolated tribal kingdoms from the barbarous west. Joyce
sees the Greek invasion of the east as an attempt to force the Levantine trading world out of its older Phoenician pockets. Georges
Borach recorded Joyce's reaction to the Iliadic conflict in his 1917
journal: "Ulysses didn't want to go off to Troy; he knew that the
official reason for the war, the dissemination of the culture of Hellas,
was only a pretext for the Greek merchants, who were seeking new
markets."[15]

When the Greeks return from this war, as the epics and fragments of *nostoi* make clear, it is not new markets they bring back
with them, but problems of readjustment to the western homes they
have deserted for so long. In essence, the Greeks are no longer marginal in the Mediterranean world, and some find the reorientation
difficult. As the *Odyssey* reveals again and again, King Agamem-
non's murder at homecoming is the nightmare of new Achaean history from which Odysseus tries to awake. In order to do so, the Homeric poet sets a geographical trial. Ten years of the Trojan War in
the east are balanced by ten years of wanderings over greater expanses in the west. Odysseus is his race's scapegoat. He takes upon
himself the burdens of the gloom to enlighten his land. The *Odyssey*
is not only a border epic placing its Greek hero in the uncharted seas
of the *couchant* Mediterranean, but an epic eventually recivilizing

[15] Ellmann, *JJ*, p. 430.

the very hero whose mission it is to recivilize his land.[16] Geography is a significant trial in the poem, for beyond the Straits of Ithaca, beyond the White Rock of Leucas, Odysseus disappears from "des mers grecques, des mers 'farinières,' pour entrer dans les ténèbres de la barbarie anthropophage" (Greek seas, seas of "breadeaters," in order to enter the dark regions of man-eating barbarity) [Bérard, II, 435].

Part of the narrative design of the *Odyssey* familiarizes the remote. Bérard sees the poem as enculturating. It teaches the Greeks something of what they might want to know about their Mediterranean expanse. It opens a discourse between myth and fact: "L'histoire des origines terrestres, ayant repris contact avec la réalité contemporaine, fut moins miraculeuse, moins héroïque et divine: elle devint plus vraisemblable, plus proche de l'humble, mais certaine vérité" (The account of earthly origins, having remade contact with contemporary reality, was less miraculous, less heroic and divine: it became more truthful, approaching the commonplace, but certainly true) [Bérard, I, 17].

The exchange between mythic extensions and local returns is as important for Joyce as it was for Bérard's Homer. Joyce merely reduces the local scope and expands the historical-mythic range. In the *Proteus* episode of *Ulysses*, at high noon in the extreme southeast of Dublin, Stephen Dedalus watches two "Egyptian" cockle-pickers "westering" with the tide along the sands of Sandymount. He remembers Shelley's lyrical drama *Hellas*: "Across the sands of all the world, followed by the sun's flaming sword, to the west, trekking to evening lands" (47). In *Hellas* Shelley complains that the modern Turks, vying with the Greeks for supremacy, have turned out the original light of civilization's dawn. Shelley's *Semichorus* II speaks after the desolation.

> If Greece must be
> A wreck, yet shall its fragments reassemble,
> And build themselves again impregnably
> In a diviner clime. . . .   (1002-1005)

[16] See Cedric H. Whitman, "The *Odyssey* and Change," in *Homer and the Heroic Tradition* (New York, 1965), pp. 285-309. See also George deF. Lord, "The Odyssey and the Western World," *Sewanee Review*, LXIII (1954), 406-427.

The migration is, as usual, westward: *translatio imperii*. Shelley's
Semichorus I picks up the progress.

> Darkness has dawned in the East
> On the noon of time:
> The death-birds descend to their feast
> From the hungry clime.
> Let Freedom and Peace flee far
> To a sunnier strand,
> And follow Love's folding-star
> To the Evening land! (1023-1030)

The concluding chorus of *Hellas* contains the couplet: "A new
Ulysses leaves once more / Calypso for his native shore" (1076-
1077). Like Dante's heroic but false counsellor, Shelley's Ulysses
breaks beyond the Straits of Gibralter. Dante's victim is cast south
at the rim of the world—Shelley's voyager seeks the northwest passage. Civilizations migrate, centers migrate, and in *Ulysses* Joyce records the extension of the *zophos* to the very local shores of Ireland's
evening lands.

In *Finnegans Wake* Joyce called *Ulysses* his "usylessly unreadable
Blue Book of Eccles, *édition de ténèbres*" (*FW*, 179). But toward
the end of the novel the modern Odysseus stands in his yard, in his
tenebrous regions, and contemplates remaining for the "diffusion
of daybreak, the apparition of a new solar disk" (705). Bloom had
done so before, turning his gaze in the direction of Mizrach, the
east. Directional associations in *Ulysses* are as precise as those in
the *Odyssey*. Northwest is a danger zone; southeast is renewal. In
the *Oxen of the Sun*, the tortured ersatz Anglo-Saxon tells us that
Bloom "was living with dear wife and lovesome daughter that then
over land and seafloor nine year had long outwandered" (385). This
seems one of the few *direct* parallels to the time-space scheme of the
Odyssey, but it also refers to the fact that Bloom used to live on
Holles street in the southeast quadrant of Dublin near the maternity
ward, and by 1904 has wandered to his 7 Eccles street home in the
northwest quadrant of his city. Those years have not been fertile ones
for the much-buffeted Bloom. The northwest is death's region. When
Odysseus is instructed to summon the shades from Hades, he must
travel toward Oceanus in the northwest where Helios' eye never
shines. Beyond Bloom's home at 7 Eccles street in Dublin, and on the
continuation of the northwest axis, is the Prospect cemetery at Glas-

nevin, the farthest extension toward the gloom in the course of day. At the beginning of *Ulysses* Bloom orients himself from 7 Eccles or Calypso's boundary isle. That 7 Eccles street is at once Calypso's island at the supposed Mediterranean extension and, later, Penelope's Ithaca, tells us that Calypso's Ogygia is a border island toward the *zophos* between known and unknown worlds, just as Ithaca is the northwest border island between the known Levantine and the death-defying *couchant* Mediterranean. Homer duplicates the trial axis in the *Odyssey*, and Joyce, by re-situating the epic action, does the same in the Dublin of *Ulysses*.

Many other details of the day's action reinforce the novel's directional associations. As the funeral entourage of *Hades* makes its way from Sandymount to the northwest site of the Glasnevin cemetery, Bloom notes his own street near the hospital for the dying: "The *Mater Misericordiae*. Eccles street. My house down there. Big place. Ward for incurables there. Very encouraging. Our Lady's Hospice for the dying. Deadhouse handy underneath" (97). Molly all the while lies listlessly on her brass bed from Gibraltar, both, so Bloom thinks, having traveled northwest along life's solar-declining axis. When Blazes Boylan later has a basket of fruit sent to Dublin's Calypso of 7 Eccles street, he lies to speed the delivery: "It's for an invalid" (227). Perhaps he also tells the truth about Joyce's Mediterranean nymph transplanted to Dublin's *zophos*.

The south and east in Dublin are the haunts of memory's better days and warmer places. Bloom's childhood was spent on Clanbrassil street in the heart of Dublin's small Jewish section in the city's southern quadrant. And the happier years of his marriage were spent, for the most part, on Pleasants street and Lombard street west, south of the Liffey and south or southeast of the Old City center.[17] Life had been different: "I was happier then. Or was that I? Or am I now I? Twentyeight I was. She twentythree when we left Lombard street west something changed" (168). The memory turns Bloom's mind further back to another Jewish quarter, to his racial source in the fruitful east.

---

[17] For information on Dublin's Jewish quarter, see John Henry Raleigh, "Afoot in Dublin in Search of the Habitations of Some Shades," *JJQ*, 8 (1971), 129-141. In discussing the chronology of Bloom's many address changes in Dublin, Clive Hart and Leo Knuth point out that Bloom oversimplifies his many urban trials by linking them all with Rudy's death and his move from Lombard street west (Hart and Knuth, p. 17).

Useless to go back. Had to be. Tell me all.

High voices. Sunwarm silk. Jingling harnesses. All for a woman,
home and houses, silk webs, silver, rich fruits, spicy from Jaffa.
Agendath Netaim. Wealth of the world.   (168)

Bloom's and Molly's marriage has been stagnant during their
many moves since the death of their infant son while they were
living in Dublin's extreme northwest at the City Arms Hotel off the
North Circular road. "Me. And me now," Bloom thinks (176). His
ten-year *Wanderings* are as long, in one sense, as Odysseus' in
gloomy western seas. Bloom's involuntary exile is migration's trial.
He is affected culturally, temperamentally, and physically as he is
wrenched from the southeast to the northwest. Bloom, the

> new exponent of morals and healer of ills is at his best an exotic
> tree which, when rooted in its native orient, throve and flourished
> and was abundant in balm but, transplanted to a clime more tem-
> perate, its roots have lost their quondam vigour while the stuff
> that comes away from it is stagnant, acid and inoperative. (410)

Joyce offers an interesting gloss on this passage in his *Cyclops*
notes: "LB. Sexual impulse only the root of tree" (Herring, p. 86).
Here Joyce refers specifically to a section in *Cyclops* where heroes
pursue maidens to the temperate clime of Elbana, or Ireland. For
Bloom, his present life is but a parody of Odyssean virility. Molly
Bloom, as Joyce tells us and as she demonstrates, is "fertilisable"
(*Letters*, I, 170), but Bloom, out of his clime, seeks release only on
her plump melonous hemispheres.[18] Molly's rump becomes the "melonfields north of Jaffa" (60), much too far north for Bloom in his
dormant state.

Late in the novel, Bloom recapitulates his travels "from Sandymount in the south to Glasnevin in the north" (704). He had followed a corpse over Dublin's treacherous terrain. At 12:00 noon he
returns from Dublin's *zophos*, southeast toward the center of his
city for the *Aeolus* episode. At 8:00 P.M. he returns again southeast
to Sandymount for the beginning of another sweep northwest, a nocturnal homecoming. "In the midst of death we are in life" (108),
Bloom thinks in *Hades*, misappropriating the phrase from the Burial

---

[18] See Adaline Glasheen, "Calypso," in Hart and Hayman, pp. 51-70, for
an extremely witty and intelligent essay on Bloom's and Molly's sexual peculi-
arities.

Service for the Dead. Given his "New lease of life" (109), Bloom always turns in the direction of the eastern sun. It is the "new I want" (377), he says later on the Sandymount strand. In the evening hours of *Nausicaa* he silently thanks a young girl who activated his libido by displaying her lace panties. Earlier in the day, the morning sun from the east made Bloom feel the heat of youth: "Makes you feel young" (57). "Sun's heat it is," Bloom repeats in *Lestrygonians*: "Seems to a secret touch telling me memory" (175). The renewal of *Nausicaa* provides a similar pleasure: "Made me feel so young" (382). If the extending compass points in epic geography insist that Ireland's sun rise in the northwest, the process has its corollary for Bloom, physically in Dublin's southeast at sunset: "Homerule sun setting in the southeast. My native land, goodnight" (376).

After the *Nausicaa* nocturne it is as if the Odyssean hero has landed. And, for reasons I will elaborate in Part II of this book, Joyce scales his narrative down from the larger Mediterranean map at this point to image the home island of Ithaca. Bloom moves northwest to the Holles street maternity ward where he attends another renewal, the birth of Mina Purefoy's son. At the hospital he takes an interest in another man's son, an oddly named, twenty-two-year-old drunken aesthete. After the pursuit to Nighttown and the respite at the Cabman's shelter, buying sobriety as Odysseus buys time, Bloom and Dedalus continue the island path northwest to 7 Eccles. Late evening finds itself, as Stephen Dedalus had predicted much earlier in the day: "My cockle hat and staff and his my sandal shoon. Where? To evening lands. Evening will find itself" (50). Dedalus leaves the house of the Jew before daybreak, and *Ithaca* concludes with the lone commercial traveler bedding down in anticipation of the returning day. Eccles street, with its nominal *Ecclesiastes* ring, is the center where one small home-rule sun also rises near daybreak for another June morning.

At the conclusion of *Ithaca*, Joyce, seemingly mistaken, describes the earth as rotating westward when it should be, by all the laws of the universe, rotating eastward.[19] But if we have attended to the

[19] William S. Doxey, "Ithaca's Westward-turning Earth: A New Portal of Discovery," *JJQ*, 7 (1970), 371-373. Doxey is forced to guess that Joyce's mistake is one of those portals of discovery that artists make from error. Doxey thinks that Bloom gets the motion wrong (although it is not Bloom who "writes" or "speaks" this passage) and that Molly comes along in the next earth-turning chapter to get it right. Perhaps so, but since the entire

37

geographical plot of the novel, with all its comic variations, the movement rounds out the day in the direction Joyce has taken it. Bloom, the narrator, extends northwest and west; Molly, the listener, lies southeast and east.

In what directions did listener and narrator lie?
Listener, S.E. by E.; Narrator, N.W. by W.: on the 53rd parallel of latitude, N. and 6th meridian of longitude, W.: at an angle of 45° to the terrestrial equator.

In what state of rest or motion?
At rest relatively to themselves and to each other. In motion being each and both carried westward, forward and rereward respectively, by the proper perpetual motion of the earth through everchanging tracks of neverchanging space.

In what posture?
Listener: reclined semilaterally, left, left hand under head, right leg extended in a straight line and resting on left leg, flexed, in the attitude of Gea-Tellus, fulfilled, recumbent, big with seed. Narrator: reclined laterally, left, with right and left legs flexed, the indexfinger and thumb of the right hand resting on the bridge of the nose, in the attitude depicted on a snapshot photograph made by Percy Apjohn, the childman weary, the manchild in the womb.

Womb? Weary?
He rests. He has travelled.   (736-737)

When Molly Bloom assumes the narrative voice in the final episode of *Ulysses*, she travels in her mind's eye back along the solar-axis to her native Gibraltar home where Homer's Mediterranean had left off. Her monologue and her vision are cyclic. Even her proof of the existence of God sustains the axis of epic geography: the sun comes up every morning after setting every evening. Or, as Samuel Beckett, writing his first novel under the influence of Joyce, will put it in *Murphy*: "The sun shone, having no alternative."

---

epic moves westward, and since the special *Ulysses* sun "rises" in the northwest, it is fitting to close the *Nostos* with the world rotating in the direction of home.

GEOGRAPHICAL PROJECTIONS
MACROANTHROPOS, HEAVENTREE, CIRCLE SQUARED

Mundus Muliebris

EPIC geography for Joyce is more than the translation of a Mediterranean grid along a northwest axis to Ireland. It is also part of a natural and very basic verbal process. Joyce understands language as lending another dimension to imaged forms. As language becomes more complex, the dimension it lends becomes more encompassing. If one were to write that Joyce begins with images "immediately at hand," he would be providing an example of the process I am describing. "At hand" is a metaphor defining a relationship by an extended image, a hand, which is part of the human body. "Immediately" at hand says what we would expect it to say—it measures the extension, it defines proximity. If we merely translate the words back into an image, the phrase "immediately at hand" explains its own origin. For his larger narratives, Joyce begins with the most immediate image available to him, the human body, and proceeds to dress it in the language of space and time. In *Finnegans Wake*, Shem the Penman, in the guise of William Blake and with the voice of Giambattista Vico, explains how "the first till last alshemist wrote over every square inch of the only foolscap available, his own body, till by its corrosive sublimation one continuous present tense integument slowly unfolded all marryvoising moodmoulded cyclewheeling history" (*FW*, 185-186). This is hardly a new idea,[1] and Joyce admits as much in a conversation with Frank Budgen about his version of *Ulysses*. Joyce merely thinks his solutions to old problems are more ingenious than anyone else's.

[1] See Leonard Barkan, *Nature's Work of Art: The Human Body as Image of the World* (New Haven, 1975). Joyce's friend, Ezra Pound, had long been interested in body-word-world systems from his interest in ancient Chinese character writing. In his essay, *L'uomo nel Ideogramma*, he sees in Chinese radicals representations of the human body that gain in complexity as they image relationships with extending and surrounding forms. See Hugh Kenner's chapter, "The Invention of Language," in *The Pound Era* (Berkeley, 1971), pp. 94-120.

39

"Among other things," he said, "my book is the epic of the human body. The only man I know who has attempted the same thing is Phineas Fletcher. But then his *Purple Island* is purely descriptive, a kind of coloured anatomical chart of the human body. In my book the body lives in and moves through space and is the home of a full human personality. The words I write are adapted to express first one of its functions then another."

(Budgen, p. 21)

Budgen remembers another conversation with Joyce, this one about the bodies of women, in which Budgen began, "you always fell back upon the fact that the woman's body was desirable and provoking, whatever else was objectionable about her." Joyce reacted, " '*Ma che!*' . . . 'Perhaps I did. But now I don't care a damn about their bodies. I am only interested in their clothes' " (Budgen, p. 319). Actually, he was interested in both. An unusually lucid passage from *Finnegans Wake* pieces together the litter-letter of the dump heap, a "mamafesta" for her "Mosthighest" husband by Anna Livia Plurabelle, body, woman, wife, mother, and river.

Yet to concentrate solely on the literal sense or even the psychological content of any document to the sore neglect of the enveloping facts themselves circumstantiating it is just as hurtful to sound sense (and let it be added to the truest taste) as were some fellow in the act of perhaps getting an intro from another fellow turning out to be a friend in need of his, say, to a lady of the latter's acquaintance, engaged in performing the elaborative antecistral ceremony of upstheres, straightaway to run off and vision her plump and plain in her natural altogether, preferring to close his blinkhard's eye to the ethiquethical fact that she was, after all, wearing for the space of time being some definite articles of evolutionary clothing, inharmonious creations, a captious critic might describe them as, or not strictly necessary or a trifle irritating here and there, but for all that suddenly full of local colour and personal perfume and suggestive, too, of so very much more and capable of being stretched, filled out, if need or wish were, of having their surprisingly like coincidental parts separated don't they now, for better survey by the deft hand of an expert, don't you know?   (*FW*, 109)

As in many of his partial reflections on the processes of his own fiction, there is more than a touch of irony here. But there is also more than a touch of accuracy. For Joyce the configuration of narrative is personal for the "space of time being," but finally dresses the body in its evolutionary clothing, an "evolution increasingly vaster" as he had put it in *Ulysses*. Space is "suddenly full of local colour." The letter in *Finnegans Wake* needs and gets its informing envelope—the extension defines the object. Joyce's commentary on Anna Livia's testament concludes with homage to the body-world, a feminine fiction, clothed and unclothed: "Who in his heart doubts either that the facts of feminine clothiering are there all the time or that the feminine fiction, stranger than the facts, is there also at the same time, only a little to the rere?" (*FW*, 109). We are reminded of what Joyce calls Molly Bloom's "gynomorphic" (Herring, p. 499) presence at the conclusion of *Ulysses*. And as Joyce explains in a famous letter to Budgen, Molly holds the cardinal points of the earth in bodily orbit, a little to the "rere" as "each plump melonous hemisphere" (734) rounds out the day. The form of *Penelope* turns as a "huge earthball" on its axis of renewal: "*Weib. Ich bin das Fleisch das stets bejaht*" (*Letters*, I, 170). Molly Bloom, born on Gibraltar, builds her narration on the rotating rock of her own body. She, like Anna Livia, adorns the spaces of the world in which she appears.

A powerful description of the bodily world of nature that may have influenced Joyce's vision of Molly Bloom and Anna Livia appears in Giambattista Vico's *Scienza Nuova*. In his second Book, *Poetic Wisdom*, Vico considers what he calls *Poetic Cosmography*. He writes of the linguistic progress from one visual form to another, from the geographical contours of the earth to the curves of a woman's body. Language accommodates the shapes of nature.

> Finally, beginning with the idea by which every slight slope was called *mundus* (whence the phrases *in mundo est, in proclivi est*, for it is easy; and later everything for the embellishment of a woman came to be called *mundus muliebris*), when they came to understand that the earth and the sky were spherical in form, and that from every point of the circumference there is a slope toward every other, and that the ocean bathes the land on every shore, and that the whole of things is adorned with countless varied and diverse sensible forms, the poets called this universe *mundus* as being that with which, by a beautifully sublime metaphor, nature adorns herself. (*New Science*, p. 226)

Whether Joyce remembers this extraordinary passage for *Ulysses* or *Finnegans Wake* is uncertain. But clearly he approaches its essence. In a letter to Claud Sykes he describes Molly as "amplitudinously curvilinear" (*Letters*, I, 164), and when Bloom thinks of the shapely Greek goddesses in the Museum he concludes: "curves, curves are beauty" (176). Shem the Penman in *Finnegans Wake* invokes a similar cosmic and cosmetic world-forming feminine conceit. The portrait of the artist is one of adornment through time in space, ample, fulfilling, and marvelously comic: "In the beginning was the gest he jousstly says, for the end is with woman, flesh-without-word, while the man to be is in a worse case after than before since she on the supine satisfies the verg to him!" (*FW*, 468).

For Joyce, Viconian adornment and the turns of feminine fiction "circumstantiate" narrative geography. Joyce presents the Anna Liffey, like Pope's Belinda, all bedecked, serpentining her way to the greater ocean east beyond Earwicker's Howth Hill.

First she let her hair fal and down it flussed to her feet its teviots winding coils. Then, mothernaked, she sampood herself with galawater and fraguant pistania mud, wupper and lauar, from crown to sole. Next she greesed the groove of her keel, warthes and wears and mole and itcher, with antifouling butterscatch and turfentide and serpenthyme and with leafmould she ushered round prunella isles and eslats dun, quincecunct, allover her little mary. Peeld gold of waxwork her jellybelly and her grains of incense anguille bronze. And after that she wove a garland for her hair. She pleated it. She plaited it. Of meadowgrass and riverflags, the bulrush and waterweed, and of fallen griefs of weeping willow. Then she made her bracelets and her anklets and her armlets and a jetty amulet for necklace of clicking cobbles and pattering pebbles and rumbledown rubble, richmond and rehr, of Irish rhunerhinerstones and shellmarble bangles. That done, a dawk of smut to her airy ey, Annushka Lutetiavitch Pufflovah, and the lellipos cream to her lippeleens and the pick of the paintbox for her pommettes, from strawbirry reds to extra violates, and she sendred her boudeloire maids to His Affluence, Ciliegia Grande and Kirschie Real, the two chirsines, with respecks from his missus, seepy and sewery, and a request might she passe of him for a minnikin. A call to pay and light a taper, in Brie-on-Arrosa, back in a sprizzling. The cock striking mine, the stalls bridely sign, there's Zambosy waiting for Me! She said she wouldn't be half her length away. Then, then, as soon as the lump his back was turned, with her mealiebag slang over her shulder, Anna Livia, oysterface, forth of her bassein came.

(*FW*, 206-207)

Massive (and beautiful) bodily curves bring the world to the city in Joyce's fiction. As he writes in *Circe* of *Ulysses*: "*womancity, nude, white, still, cool, in luxury*" (477). In its geographical forms, the body mediates between formation and fulfillment. In its human form, the body tells the cyclic story of renewal. Joyce had worked through a series of models to his geodetic sense of human narrative. Samuel Beckett leads off the 1929 tribute to Joyce, *Our Exagmination Round his Factification for Incamination of Work in Progress*, with an essay on Joyce's major Italian influences, one dot per century: "Dante . . . Bruno . Vico . . Joyce."[2] These Italians had arrived on Joyce's doorstep before the publication of *Ulysses* in 1922.[3] Dante writes the vernacular epic of civic particulars and bounded forms, what Shaun will call in a marginal note of *Finnegans Wake* the "IMAGINABLE ITINERARY THROUGH THE PARTIC-ULAR UNIVERSAL" (*FW*, 260). Bruno provides the hermetic conceit of the micro- and macrocosmic worlds, what Beckett calls in his own fiction the microcosmopolitan universe. And Vico? Vico offers Joyce a theory of language and the human imagination, the mind traveling through itself to reveal the bodily forms outside itself.

Richard Ellmann thinks that Joyce's interest in Vico was stimulated, or restimulated, by his reading in 1914 of Benedetto Croce's *Estetica*, with its short chapter on Vico (*JJ*, p. 351). Ellmann neglects to mention that the drift of Croce's chapter is polemical. Croce argues that Vico was as much a theorist of poetic forms as a philosopher of history: "The importance of Vico's new poetic theory in

[2] Samuel Beckett, "Dante . . . Bruno . Vico . . Joyce," in *Our Exagmination Round his Factification for Incamination of Work in Progress* (New York: New Directions, 1972), pp. 3-22.

[3] Joyce's interest in the *Divine Comedy* as a literary model is apparent from the structure of the short story, "Grace," in *Dubliners*. He had written on Bruno in 1901, beginning his essay on the Abbey Theatre, *The Day of the Rabblement*, with a cryptic reference to Giordano Bruno of Nola: "No man, said the Nolan, can be a lover of the true or the good unless he abhors the multitude" (*CW*, 69); and in 1903 he wrote a little piece for the Dublin *Daily Express* on *The Bruno Philosophy* (*CW*, 132-134). Richard Ellmann dates Joyce's interest in Vico at least from 1911 when he discussed "this Neapolitan philosopher" with his pupil, Paolo Cuzzi, in Trieste (*JJ*, p. 351).

his thought as a whole as well as in the organism of his *Scienza nuova* has never been fully appreciated, and the Neapolitan philosopher
is still commonly regarded as the inventor of the Philosophy of History."[4] Croce insists upon revaluation for an important reason. He
writes that Vico's theory of the evolution of language and poetic
language has a relation to reality that his historical theory does not.
Poetry absorbs the immediate in an expanding factual narration.
Croce writes of Vico's theory, "poetry precedes intellect, but follows
sense" (222). In time, "primitive history was poetry, its plot was
the narration of fact" (224). And among all the poets of history,
Vico saw one as the *strongest* poet, the poet who made sense co-
existent with intellect, the poet who created a "natural meaning"
from the "natural origin" of words and extensions. Needless to say,
that poet was Homer.

THE LANGUAGE OF EXTENSION

Giambattista Vico's *Principi di Scienza Nuova di Giambattista
Vico d'Intorno alla Comune Natura delle Nazioni* (expanded
3rd edition, 1744) is one of the Enlightenment's massive syntheses
of myth, ethics, law, and geography. It treats of the human order
from burial customs to class struggles. Vico's work is a document
of etymological history—as much an experiment in verbal expansion as a theory of historical repetition. From the stutter of the
godhead to the fixed grammar of democracy, Vico's system fills
space with linguistic expansions. The idiom of Joyce's own fiction,
from body-word to body-word, acknowledges the grammar of Vico's
linguistic theories.

All language for Vico is a fable of the mind's perception of bodily
forms, what Joyce calls the "mappamund" in *Finnegans Wake*. Vico
writes of metaphor and the human mind in a subsection, *Poetic
Logic*, of his second Book, *Poetic Wisdom*.

It is noteworthy that in all languages the greater part of the
expressions relating to inanimate things are formed by metaphor
from the human body and its parts and from the human senses

[4] Benedetto Croce, *Aesthetic as Science of Expression and General Linguistic*, trans. Douglas Ainslie (London, 2nd ed., 1922), p. 231. Subsequent
references to Croce's *Aesthetic* will be to this edition and page numbers will
be cited in the body of the text.

and passions. Thus, head for top or beginning; the brow and shoulders of a hill; the eyes of needles and of potatoes; mouth for any opening; the lip of a cup or pitcher; the teeth of a rake, a saw, a comb; the beard of wheat; the tongue of a shoe; the gorge of a river; a neck of land; an arm of the sea; the hands of a clock; heart for center (the Latins used *umbilicus*, navel, in this sense). . . . All of which is a consequence of our axiom that man in his ignorance makes himself the rule of the universe, for in the examples cited he has made of himself an entire world. So that, as rational metaphysics teaches that man becomes all things by understanding them (*homo intelligendo fit omnia*), this imaginative metaphysics shows that man becomes all things by *not* understanding them (*homo non intelligendo fit omnia*); and perhaps the latter proposition is truer than the former, for when man understands he extends his mind and takes in the things, but when he does not understand he makes the things out of himself and becomes them by transforming himself into them.

(*New Science*, p. 88)

Vico's axiom is a "mistake" of the intellect, but a find for the imagination. Joyce certainly sees it this way. In a later subsection, specifically entitled, *Poetic Geography*, Vico continues the conceit of bodily extension to the physical landscape. He provides an etymological confirmation of the translation of places. This is an instance in which Vico and Victor Bérard overlap.

It remains for us now to cleanse the other eye of poetic history, namely poetic geography. By the property of human nature that in describing unknown or distant things, in respect of which they either have not had the true idea themselves or wish to explain it to others who do not have it, men make use of the semblances of things known or near at hand, poetic geography, in all its parts and as a whole, began with restricted ideas within the confines of Greece. Then, as the Greeks went abroad into the world, it was gradually amplified until it reached the form in which it has come down to us. The ancient geographers agree on this truth although they were unable to avail themselves of it, for they affirm that the ancient nations, emigrating to strange and distant lands, gave their own native names to the [new-found] cities, mountains, rivers, hills, straits, isles, and promontories.

(*New Science*, p. 234)

45

Vico argues that all extended grounds are etymological grounds. Within "Greece itself, accordingly, lay the original East called Asia or India, the West called Europe or Hesperia, the North called Thrace or Scythia, and the South called Libya or Mauretania" (*New Science*, p. 234). The "names for the regions of the little world of Greece were [later] applied to those of the world [at large] in virtue of the correspondence which the Greeks observed between the two" (*New Science*, p. 234). Like Bérard's Homer, Vico reconstructs the expanded Mediterranean on its westward axis.

On these principles, the great peninsula to the east of Greece came to be called Asia Minor when the name Asia was extended to that great eastern part of the world which has continued to be called Asia without qualification. On the other hand, Greece itself, which was to the west of Asia, was called Europe, the Europe which Jove, in the form of a bull, abducted. Later the name was extended to embrace this other great continent as far as the western ocean. They gave the name Hesperia to the western part of Greece, where the evening star Hesperus comes out in the fourth quarter of the horizon. Later they saw Italy in the same quarter much larger than the Hesperia of Greece, and they called it Hesperia Magna. And finally when they reached Spain in the same direction, they called it Hesperia Ultima.

(*New Science*, p. 235)

With the idea of spatial familiarity as an "immense projection" upon the unknown, the familiar and the alien, the localized and the foreign, are bound in poetic geography. The *Odyssey*, a migratory epic, pits Odysseus against the god of the western oceans, Poseidon, and Vico offers a gloss on the poem's potential range.

Finally, when the Greeks reached the Ocean, they expanded the narrow idea of any sea with an unobstructed prospect (in virtue of which Homer said the isle of Aeolia was girt by the Ocean), and along with the idea the name Ocean was also extended to signify the sea that girds the whole earth, which was conceived as a great island. The power of Neptune was thus immensely enlarged, so that from the abyss of the waters, which Plato placed in the very bowels of the earth, he could shake it with his great trident.   (*New Science*, p. 236)

Once the whole world is an island, all islands are, after a meta-phoric fashion, the same island. And all parables of wandering are Homeric *periploi*. The process expands and contracts. Ireland is an extended Greece, Hesperia Hibernia beyond the Straits, and Dublin an extended Ithaca. Joyce's epic turns the process around and Dublin, "Hesperia Minima," becomes the larger Mediterranean in the narrative superimposition of *Ulysses*. The virtue of a linguistic conception of space is that it both enlarges and diminishes. We know from the testimony of his brother Stanislaus that Joyce read with keen interest Samuel Butler's bizarre book, *The Authoress of the Odyssey*. In support of an argument that the epic could have been composed by a young girl on Sicily, Butler suggests that the absorption of familiar but fantastic stories from remote to local places is as much a childhood habit as its reverse, the extension of immediate experience to parts remote. Double places and trans-lated names explain the Homeric poem for Butler. The process is Viconian.

> Young people when transferring familiar stories to their own neighborhood, as almost all young people do, never stick at in-consistencies. They are like eminent Homeric scholars, and when they mean to have things in any given way they will not let the native hue of resolution be balked by thought; and will find it equally easy to have an Ithaca in one place and also in another, and to see the voyages of Columbus to the tropics in their own sliding over a frozen pool.[5]

If this were but a childhood game, Joyce, for one, never tired of playing it. His two lads in the short story, "An Encounter," conjure visions of the American west in Dublin while walking toward the Pigeonhouse strand. In *Ulysses*, of course, Joyce does exactly what Butler suggests, he has "an Ithaca in one place and also in another." Leopold Bloom's frustrated remark to the citizen in *Cyclops* is fic-tionally prescriptive: "A nation is the same people living in the same place. . . . Or also living in different places" (331). By the time of *Finnegans Wake* Dublin's Chapelizod is a veritable gazetteer of the world's places and fables. The curves of the Anna Liffey form the human "geoglyphy" in motion, and the bulk of Earwicker, like

[5] Samuel Butler, *The Authoress of the Odyssey* (Chicago, rept. of 2nd ed., 1922; 1967), p. 172.

Blake's Albion, spreads over all space from zenith to nadir: "Your heart is in the system of the Shewolf and your crested head is in the tropic of Copricapron. Your feet are in the cloister of Virgo. Your olala is in the region of sahuls. And that's ashore as you were born" (*FW*, 26).[6]

Generally, Vico's theory of history, not geography, attracts Joyce commentators, especially commentators on *Finnegans Wake*. Civilization originates in the stuttered imitations of godspeech, thunder. The suppressed fear and shame over acts of bestiality committed by men and witnessed by God result in ritual burial, marriage, religion, and law. Phases of divine, heroic, and human orders circle back in the course of time. But Viconian process in *Ulysses* is as much geographical as temporal. This has created something of a problem. In 1948 Ellsworth Mason proposed that, like *Finnegans Wake*, *Ulysses* aligned its chapters with Vico's ages of man. Richard Ellmann, who most recently has waded into these troubled waters, confesses that he loses Mr. Mason on the Viconian parallels after the *Hades* chapter: "I find the relation of Vico's ages to Joyce's book to be different, after the first six chapters, from that which Mr Mason urges."[7] Unfortunately, Mason and Ellmann also differ on two of the first six chapters,[8] which suggests that the application of Vico's ages is arbitrary at best. A. M. Klein, in his usual way, has gone to far greater pains to prove that Vico overwhelmed at least the chapter in *Ulysses* whose schematic art is history, *Nestor*. But Klein paves the way for the true skeptic. We learn that in the thirty-second Viconian cycle of *Nestor* the heroic age is represented by Koch's preparation for foot and mouth disease. Why? Klein is ready with the answer: "Koch—cook. Homer, says Vico, describes his heroes as always eating roast meat."[9]

[6] See Northrop Frye, "Quest and Cycle in *Finnegans Wake*," *James Joyce Review*, 1 (1957), 39-47, for a comparison of the giant figures of Blake and Joyce.

[7] Richard Ellmann, *Ulysses on the Liffey* (New York, 1972), p. 52n. See Ellsworth A. Mason, "James Joyce's Ulysses and Vico's Cycle" (Ph.D. Dissertation, Yale University, 1948).

[8] Mason records *Lotuseaters* and *Hades* as theocratic chapters in Vico's cycle, and Ellmann finds them aristocratic and democratic respectively.

[9] A. M. Klein, "A Shout in the Street," in *New Directions*, 13 (New York, 1951), p. 343. Klein cites Harriet Weaver's letter from Joyce in which he told her not to pay overmuch attention to Bruno and Vico "beyond using them for all they are worth" (*Letters*, 1, 241). But Klein does not mention that Joyce was writing about *Finnegans Wake* in this instance, not *Ulysses*. For a much more tempered view on the "ambiguous part" played by Viconian

Joyce is always ready to absorb external structures into his fiction, and I am certain that Klein is generally right about Vico and *Nestor*. But the Vico of historical cycles only works for aspects of *Ulysses*. The idea of *ricorso*, or return, is obvious in the progression of hours —morning, evening, and morning again; and *Oxen of the Sun, Circe*, parts of *Ithaca*, and *Penelope* are undoubtedly Viconian in their time schemes. Joyce, however, works with a clearly marked Homeric structure that exists independently from Viconian cycles. In fact, Vico's understanding of the *Odyssey* as a clash between aristocratic and plebeian orders is not one that is particularly useful to Joyce. Furthermore, literal time is more important to *Ulysses* than to *Finnegans Wake*, where Viconian cycles work because the night of the book is almost all metaphor. We might for a moment recall Croce, who insisted that Vico was a better aesthetician than historian. What Joyce required in *Ulysses* was a rationale for the translation of the *Odyssey*'s form and its terrain: language and poetic geography provide that rationale. The human mind creates a vocabulary to unfold over real spaces where positioning is as important as sequence. In *Ulysses* Joyce adapts the Viconian theory that self-imagining, territorial extension, and narrative expand from a human center.

Joyce plots his course in the smaller and larger spaces of the novel. The day begins for Leopold Bloom with the fine tang of faintly scented inner organs, and it ends with the affirming flesh of a translated nymph and wife, splendid in her turns and orbits. In a related excursus on the poetics of space, Stephen Dedalus ponders the octave in *Circe*: "If I could only find out about octaves. Reduplication of personality" (518). Personality is, for the novel, extension. A few pages earlier, Stephen parried with Lynch's talking cap.

STEPHEN

Here's another for you. (*He frowns.*) The reason is because the fundamental and the dominant are separated by the greatest possible interval which . . .

---

ideas in *Ulysses*, see A. Walton Litz, "Vico and Joyce," in *Giambattista Vico: An International Symposium*, ed. Giorgio Tagliacozzo (Baltimore, 1969), pp. 245-255. Litz writes that most of the "Vichian cycles that have been discovered in *Ulysses* since the publication of *Finnegans Wake* would seem to lie on the borderline between the private imagination of the author and the public structure of the novel" (p. 248).

THE CAP

Which? Finish. You can't.

STEPHEN

(*With an effort.*) Interval which. Is the greatest possible ellipse. Consistent with. The ultimate return. The octave. Which.

THE CAP

Which?

(*Outside the gramophone begins to blare* The Holy City.)

STEPHEN

(*Abruptly.*) What went forth to the ends of the world to traverse not itself. God, the sun, Shakespeare, a commercial traveller, having itself traversed in reality itself, becomes that self. Wait a moment. Wait a second. Damn that fellow's noise in the street. Self which it itself was ineluctably preconditioned to become. *Ecco!*

(504-505)

Expanded personality is analogous to musical space and, finally, to epic and mythic space. That damned fellow's "noise in the street" is the Viconian manifestation of God's voice we first heard in *Nestor*. But, more important, the track of time is elliptical—an extension and a return. Odysseus towards the *zophos*, Shakespeare from London to Stratford, Bloom from Sandymount to 7 Eccles all follow the elliptical path of the sun. Stephen's "*Ecco!*" (Here it is!) gives us homonymous pause: echo—the eighth tone of the octave repeats a tone with twice (or half) as many vibrations. In *Ulysses*, as Stuart Gilbert long ago recognized, Bloom returns to Molly's eight-sentence monologue an octave removed from her first appearance as Calypso in the morning. And when Bloom returns to Molly's "spaces" he brings the octave back to a feminine fundamental. *Ecco* is the Italian philosopher's *ricorso*. The Homeric Odysseus wanders across an ocean of troubles to a body of land. "The rite is the poet's rest" (503), as Dedalus puts it; and the rest is the hero's right at the end of *Ulysses*: "He rests. He has travelled" (737). The body comes full circle.

The reciprocity between the image of man and his spatial surroundings is an ancient idea, almost elemental, as Vico records. Followers of Pythagoras, as early as the 5th century B.C., saw the four cosmic elements, air, fire, water, and earth, made manifest in man's breath, blood, heart, and genitalia. These elements and these organs controlled intellect, movement, desire, and gestation. In the occult sciences of the Middle Ages and early Renaissance, the conceit of elemental reciprocity served the alchemical and hermetic philosophies as another system of microcosmic and macrocosmic correspondences. The greatest of the Renaissance alchemists, Paracelsus, even "boxed" the cosmic compass. He argued that the four elements extended beyond the body, beyond the physical components of the world, to emanations from the stars positioned at geographical corners of the firmament. In his *Vulgar Errors* (*Pseudodoxia Epidemica*), Sir Thomas Browne parodies the body-world conceit and Paracelsus in particular.

> It is also improbable and something singular what some conceive, and Eusebius Nierembergius, a learned Jesuit of Spain delivers, that the body of man is magnetical, and being placed in a Boat, the Vessel will never rest until the head respecteth the North. If this be true, the bodies of Christians do lye unnaturally in their Graves. King Cheopos in his Tomb, and the jews in their beds have fallen upon the natural position: who reverentially declining the situation of their Temple, nor willing to lye as that stood, do place their Beds from North to South, and delight to sleep Meridionally. This Opinion confirmed would much advance the Microcosmical conceit, and commend the Geography of Paracelsus, who according to the Cardinal points of the World, divideth the body of man; and therefore working upon humane ordure, and by long preparation rendering it odiferous, he terms it *Zibeta Occidentalis*, Western Civet; making the face the East, but the posteriors the America or Western part of his Microcosm.[10]

Browne's diverting remarks beckon the ghosts of Rabelais' giants and look forward to Swift's. (Swift even cites this passage in the scatological *potpourri* of *A Tale of A Tub*.) And in another context we remember Leopold Bloom, a man most interested in his wife's posterior region, poised at Aphrodite's orifice in the Dublin Na-

---

[10] Sir Thomas Browne, *Enquiries into Vulgar and Common Errors*, in *Works*, ed. Geoffrey Keynes (Chicago, 1964), Book II, chapter 3, p. 119.

tional Museum, trying to learn something of the enduring quality of *Zibeta Occidentalis*. Phillip Herring points out that the infinity sign (∞) of Joyce's notesheets, connoting among other things, Molly's infinite pleasures, bears a striking resemblance to a fine pair of buttocks. Herring even implicates the geography of Joyce's Dublin: "A glance at a map of Dublin will show that the city proper is circumscribed by canals and the North and South Circular Roads, and, with a little imagination one can picture a reclining posterior" (Hart and Hayman, p. 73n). Whether true or not, this is a wonderful thought: we return to image, body, woman, city, and sloping world, and *in mundo est, in proclivi est*, for it is now easy.

THE MAP OF THE HEAVENS

In *Portrait of the Artist*, as a lad at Clongowes Wood, Stephen Dedalus inscribed on the flyleaf of his geography book.

> *Stephen Dedalus*
> *Class of Elements*
> *Clongowes Wood College*
> *Salins*
> *County Kildare*
> *Ireland*
> *Europe*
> *The World*
> *The Universe* (P, 15)

"Why not endless to the farthest star?" (48) Stephen thinks of his shadow, his hermetic form of forms, this time on the strand in the *Proteus* episode of *Ulysses*. We have Joyce's own testimony in a letter to Budgen how in *Ithaca* Stephen and Bloom "become heavenly bodies, wanderers like the stars at which they gaze" (*Letters*, I, 160). Their orbits are elliptical—they are comets plotting their paths around the cardinal points of the novel's last chapter. The circle is squared just as in *Finnegans Wake*, the four old men, the novel's enveloping Hebrew apostles of Chapelizod, Mamalujo, image the boundaries of space as the elliptical "four hoarsemen on their apolkaloops, Norreys, Soothbys, Yates and Welks" (*FW*, 557). In *Finnegans Wake* the macro-anthropomorphic conceit is picked up where Joyce had left it in *Ulysses*—with the turns and returns of language and worlds. Joyce says of H.C.E.'s range in Anna Livia's testament: "it has its cardinal points for all that. . . . It is seriously believed by some that the intention may have been geodetic" (*FW*, 114).

The geodetic fiction is soon interstellar in Joyce's "setting of a starchart" (*FW*, 96), and both *Ulysses* and *Finnegans Wake* parodically adapt a system common to ancient Mediterranean cultures: the idea of geographical extension was incomplete without the spatial theater of the heavens. The skies are readable, and the zodiac and its heavenly projections are national resources. An entry in the *Encyclopedia of Religion and Ethics*, explains the zodiacal horoscope: "The scheme of the horoscope, accordingly, became a comprehensive map of the world . . . in the center was the navel of the world, which every nation sought to claim for its own territory, and as the site of a national sanctuary."[11] Vico writes that the Greeks learned how to map the land from the stars. And Michel Butor puts it very simply in the introduction to Jean Richer's *La Géographie Sacrée du Monde Grec*: "Ainsi toute la religion greque pourrait s'inscrire dans une immense metaphore: la terre devenant semblable au ciel" (Therefore all Greek religion can be inscribed in an immense metaphor: the earth likening itself to the heavens).[12] Richer repeats Butor's observation when he comes to his specific study of the Greek *omphaloi, Delphes, Delos, et Cumes* (Paris, 1970), in which the configurations of the zodiac actually map territory around one or another sacred center of an extended Greece.

Once orientation is determined, the sky is a ready map. Joyce plots the heavens in *Finnegans Wake*: "Ers, Mores and Merkery are surgents below the rim of the Zenith Part while Arctura, Anatolia, Hesper and Mesembria weep in their mansions over Noth, Haste, Soot and Waste" (*FW*, 494). It is predictable that in the macrocosm the heavenly projection would also take bodily form. The zodiac is a giant walking through starry domains. Aries, the first sign on the dial, begins as the head, Taurus the neck, Gemini the arms, Cancer the breast, Leo the sides and back, Virgo the loins, Libra the buttocks, Scorpio the genitals, Sagittarius the thighs, Capricorn the knees, Aquarius the legs, and Pisces the feet. In *Ulysses*, a novel whose episodes correspond to some of these bodily parts, one

[11] *Encyclopedia of Religion and Ethics*, ed. James Hastings (New York, 1922), XII, 55-56.

[12] Jean Richer, *La Géographie Sacrée du Monde Grec* (Paris, 1967), p. 18.

of Leopold Bloom's early projects was a kaleidoscope of the greater heavens "exhibiting the twelve constellations of the zodiac from Aries to Pisces" (683).[13]

There are many indications in *Ulysses* that Joyce provides his novel with its own tantalizing zodiac in which Dublin is set as *omphalos*. But we must proceed with caution here. If Joyce was capable of parodying the epic, he was more than capable of taking a dim view of the stars. In its way, zodiacal astrology is the novel's bastard form of epic destiny. As the province of modern day Theosophists, it is at once suggestive and suspect, another in Madame Blavatsky's bag of tricks, herself "a nice old bag of tricks" (140). The Theosophist Æ (Russell) appears in *Circe* as Mananaan MacLir, the Irish Old Man of the Sea. He is in the company of the zodiac and the "Occult pimander of Hermes Trismegistos."[14]

> (*He smites with his bicycle pump the crayfish in his left hand. On its co-operative dial glow the twelve signs of the zodiac. He wails with the vehemence of the ocean.*) Aum! Baum! Pyjaum! I am the light of the homestead, I am the dreamery creamery butter. (510)

In this context it is difficult to take anything astrological very seriously. Astrological reading is as suspicious as the occultic hand-reading which also takes place in *Circe*. Similarly, when Paddy Dignam reappears in *Cyclops* for his astrological forecast, marking devanic circles with all the conveniences of modern technology ("tālāfānā, ālāvātār, hātākāldā, wātāklāsāt," 301), we descend from the stars with esoteric haste. Reading the day from the heavens presents even more obstacles when in *Ithaca*, the most discriminating episode, the matter of stellar projection is left very much where the narrator finds it, up in the air. Bloom is questioned on the panoramic

---

[13] This system is a standard one, see Robert Fludd, *De Supernaturali, naturali, praetnaturali et contranaturali microsmi historia* (London, 1619), p. 113. Joyce makes an entry for Bloom's kaleidoscopic zodiac in his *Ithaca* notesheets: " ♈ ♉ ♊ ♋ ♌ ♍ ♎ ♏ ♐ ♑ ♒ ♓ " (Herring, p. 455).

[14] See William York Tindall, "James Joyce and the Hermetic Tradition," *Journal of the History of Ideas*, xv (1954), 23-39. Usually the least reluctant of Joyce's commentators to seek and find symbolic configurations, Tindall shies away from the novel's astrology. But he was tempted: "promising as this looks, no systematic correspondences between sign and action or character seems intended. Most of the zodiacal concentrations, moreover, occur in the ironic passages about Theosophy" (p. 37).

accessibility of the stars. He is not impressed. The questioner tries again.

Was he more convinced of the esthetic value of the spectacle?
Indubitably in consequence of the reiterated examples of poets in the delirium of the frenzy of attachment or in the abasement of rejection invoking ardent sympathetic constellations or the frigidity of the satellite of their planet.

Did he then accept as an article of belief the theory of astrological influences upon sublunary disasters?
It seemed to him as possible of proof as of confutation and the nomenclature employed in its selenographical charts as attributable to verifiable intuition as to fallacious analogy: the lake of dreams, the sea of rains, the gulf of dews, the ocean of fecundity. (701)

Fallacious analogy may be a risk in Joyce's fiction, but in its way fallacious analogy is also the very substance of *Ulysses*. Despite the Theosophic drivel in astrology there is one astrological work in the hermetic tradition that influences Joyce to a degree that possibly no one has yet suspected: Giordano Bruno's *Spaccio della bestia trionfante* (1584). In *Spaccio* Bruno employs the constellations as a spatial allegory of degenerate time. His allegory has a familiar plot —wandering and return. The structure of *Spaccio* is similar in its import and directional significance to that of the *Odyssey* or of *Ulysses*. Bruno proposes the regeneration of a debased cosmos, a return to origins, specifically Semitic origins. The corrupt constellations are purged by their pure originals so that justice replaces inequity in the northern regions of the sign of the Bear and a guided despotism replaces the Lion's tyranny in the south. Stephen Dedalus may allude to the allegory in Bruno's *Spaccio della bestia trionfante* while walking along Sandymount strand in *Proteus*: "Me sits there with his augur's rod of ash, in borrowed sandals, by day beside a livid sea, unbeheld, in violet night walking beneath a reign of uncouth stars" (48). The rod and the sandals are magical (Hermes: hence hermetic) and the uncouth stars belong to Bruno's astrological system in *Spaccio*. Later, in *Scylla and Charybdis*, Stephen associates Shakespeare with the Cassiopeian *W* he had first mentioned in *Proteus*: "the signature of his initial among the stars" (210). The allusions make sense when we learn that in Bruno's allegory Cas-

55

siopeia signifies vanity in its corrupted allegorical state. Stephen, of course, considers Shakespeare's dramatic career a purge of his vanity-plagued soul from "scortatory love and its foul pleasures" (201). Shakespeare studied the role of the redeeming ghost in *Hamlet* "all the years of his life which were vanity in order to play the part of the spectre" (188). In *Ithaca*, before the heavens over Cassiopeia are purged by a shooting star, Bloom is asked whether the problem of racial redemption would be solved any more easily in an interstellar world. No, he answers, because there as here all would probably "remain inalterably and inalienably attached to vanities, to vanities of vanities and all that is vanity" (700).

Bruno's vision of the corrupted heavens is important in *Proteus* and in *Ithaca*, but perhaps more important in *Oxen of the Sun* where the ironic embryonic structure of the episode involves the birth of a child named Purefoy during the drink-corrupted carousing of the young medicals. Corruption and purification are the extremes of the chapter. In the style of Thomas De Quincey a visionary voice imagines the debased host of night moving across the heavens in pursuit of the original sun northwest to the land of the dead, *Lacus Mortis* (Dead Sea and *Lucrinus*).

Ominous, revengeful zodiacal host! They moan, passing upon the clouds, horned and capricorned, the trumpeted with the tusked, the lionmaned the giantantlered, snouter and crawler, rodent, ruminant and pachyderm, all their moving moaning multitude, murderers of the sun.

Onward to the dead sea they tramp to drink, unslaked and with horrible gulpings, the salt somnolent inexhaustible flood. And the equine portent grows again, magnified in the deserted heavens, nay to heaven's own magnitude, till it looms, vast, over the house of Virgo. And, lo, wonder of metempsychosis, it is she, the everlasting bride, harbinger of the daystar, the bride, ever virgin. It is she, Martha, thou lost one, Millicent, the young, the dear, the radiant. How serene does she now arise, a queen among the Pleiades, in the pentultimate antelucan hour, shod in sandals of bright gold, coifed with a veil of what do you call it gossamer! It floats, it flows about her starborn flesh and loose it streams emerald, sapphire, mauve and heliotrope, sustained on currents of cold interstellar wind, winding, coiling, simply swirling, writhing in the skies a mysterious writing till after a myriad metamorphoses

of symbol, it blazes, Alpha, a ruby and triangled sign upon the
forehead of Taurus. (414)

Beneath this reign of uncouth stars and their revitalizing eastern
purifiers, a number of things are happening.[15] The Odyssean parallel
to the murderers of the cattle of Helios on Trinacria is obvious. So,
too, is the anthropomorphic fiction. The vision has a plot—gathering
phrases, snatches of the day's lyrics, memories of the day's hours, it
augurs the return of the day from the depths of night. An un-
regenerate zodiacal host are murderers of the sun, proliferous killers
of the king. In migration myths, whether of Europa and Cadmus
or Hercules and the herds of Geryon, cattle often lead the way
as symbols of sustenance. To kill the kine is to limit mythical and
literal movement. But, as happens often in *Ulysses*, vision is reconstitutive along the sun's axis. In *Calypso* the eastern sun renews the
Dead Sea of the Holy Lands, "grey sunken cunt of the world" (61):
"Quick warm sunlight came running from Berkeley Road, swiftly,
in slim sandals, along the brightening footpath. Runs, she runs to
meet me, a girl with gold hair on the wind" (61). Venus, "harbinger
of the day," reappears in the panoramic heavens still shod in sandals
of bright gold and still ushering in the sun.

This much is simple in the passage. But the larger pattern is
recurrent and insistent in *Ulysses*. Whenever Bloom dwells on corruption he demands renewal. In *Hades* he despairs of corpses and
returns to live bodies: "Plenty to see and hear and feel yet. Feel
live warm beings near you. Let them sleep in their maggoty beds.
They are not going to get me this innings. Warm beds: warm full-
blooded life" (115). As the constellations pursue the sun across
the night sky, the morning stars, Venus and Alpha-Tauri (Aldebaran), rise in the deserted heavens. Venus is feminine, Aldebaran is
masculine: daughters and sons (Millicent and Stephen). The meta-
morphosed star finally blazes "Alpha, a ruby and triangled sign upon
the forehead of Taurus." Earlier, the self-torturing Dedalus reads
the stars for the image of the crowned cow, but the cold bard finds
himself unloved by feminine warmth: "Read the skies. *Autontimer-
umenos. Bous Stephanoumenos*. Where's your configuration? Ste-

---

[15] For a detailed review of the astronomy of the passage, see Mark E. Litt-
mann and Charles A. Schweighauser, "Astronomical Allusions, Their Meaning
and Purpose, in *Ulysses*," *JJQ*, 2 (1965), 238-246. I am in debt to their ex-
pertise in these matters.

phen, Stephen, cut the bread even. S.D.: *sua donna. Già: di lui. Gelindo risolve di non amar.* S.D." (210).

The *Oxen of the Sun* configuration weaves several strands—Stephen's aspirations, his confusion, even his drunkenness, and the Odyssean violation and renewal. Trinacria, the isle of the sacred oxen in the *Odyssey*, is a triangular island, but in *Ulysses* the astrological epiphany settles on the triangular insignia of a bottle of Bass propped on the table. We are fallen from the firmament, as so often occurs in Joyce's "fallacious analogies," but we need not immediately abandon the larger projection. Parody thrives between worlds—it may not affirm, but it does not always deny. The progress of the zodiacal host purges the heavens of the proliferous brood. Bass's emblem shines forth after the drunken medicals mock the light of the day. Before Aledebaran rises, the morning star Venus passes over the house of Virgo. Virgo is the sign of the *Odyssey*'s Athena and of *Ulysses*' Molly Bloom, born on September 8, the day of the Virgin Mary. Joyce is not over-solemn about all this—there is a joke of sorts implied. But even though far from virgin, Molly is inviolable in her way. The narrative correspondence has her as Penelope, supposedly chaste when pursued; the symbolic correspondence in *Ithaca* has her as "a visible splendid sign" (702), Dante's Mary in her paradisaical lighted window.[16]

The zodiac is so infinitely adjustable that it is provisional. But its projections do pique curiosity. If Molly is a Virgo (8 September), Bloom is a Taurus. He may have associations with the zodiacal sign Leo (and the people's prince of the Northern Crown), but his birth sign is clearly Taurus. In *Eumaeus* Bloom remembers the Invincibles affair of 6 May 1882: "early in the eighties, eightyone to be correct, when he was just turned fifteen" (629). To be correct, someone (either Bloom or the wearied narrator) gets the Invincibles year wrong, but the month is still May.[17] Bloom had a birthday in early May—he has one every May. *Ithaca* provides corroboration when we learn that a "star (2nd magnitude) . . . had appeared in and disappeared from the constellation of the Corono Septentrionalis about the period of the birth of Leopold Bloom" (700-701). Joyce

[16] The scene in *Ithaca* continues a pattern of Dantesque allusion. See Walton Litz, "Ithaca," in Hart and Hayman, pp. 399-401, and William York Tindall, *A Reader's Guide to James Joyce* (New York, 1959), p. 225.

[17] Robert Martin Adams, in *Surface and Symbol: The Consistency of James Joyce's Ulysses* (New York, 1962), discusses this incident and this error, p. 162.

enters the date of the star in his *Ithaca* notesheets: "in Northern Crown 1866 new star" (Herring, p. 454). And Don Gifford dates the star, T. Coronae Borealis, from May of 1866.[18] Joyce has gone to some trouble to make Bloom a Taurus. Taurus is a sun sign, a sign of productivity, a money sign. Feminine in nature (Athena in one manifestation is ox-headed), Taurus combines with the masculine bull, the sign of the godhead in most eastern religions. Bloom is the new womanly man of *Circe*. When Taurus incorporates the Alpha in its forehead it parturates like the bullock-mocking Mulligan of *Scylla and Charybdis*. Joyce notes that Stephen is the Aquarian son by birth: "Birth SD Acquarius" (Herring, p. 297). Aquarius is a masculine sign, representative of national goals and marked for the collective good of the people. Aquarius is also the sign of letters, *alpha* or *aleph*, the beginning ox-letter in a Semitic-Greek doublet. Superimposed on the Taurus triangle, Dedalus ends up as Stephen *Bous Stephanoumenos*, the crowned ox on the bull's forehead. The configuration places the young man of letters, the Daedalian artist, at the center of the labyrinth, near the bull-god. Either Stephen is temporarily steeped in Bass's stout or he has found a bullock to befriend him. The choice, insofar as the novel offers choices, is ambiguous but the heavenly projection later fulfills itself.

In *Ithaca* Stephen and Bloom see a shooting star "precipitated with great apparent velocity across the firmament from Vega in the Lyre above the zenith beyond the stargroup of the Tress of Berenice towards the zodiacal sign of Leo" (703). These are northern skies now purified. The lyre is the instrument invented by Hermes, the patron of artists and young men. Bloom is clearly "in" Leo, and Molly as Berenice is another faithful Penelope. Joyce called this the "starry milky" chapter in the Linati *schema*. Odysseus has his regenerative mission, Bruno has his purifying mission, and in the zodiacal projections of *Ulysses* Joyce works out a comic design that allows his wandering Jew to extend his potential range far enough to purge the home skies. His notesheets for *Ithaca* suggest the projection: "comet wandering jew" (Herring, p. 460). The novel plots the epic and comic orbits.

Would the departed never nowhere nohow reappear?
Ever he would wander, selfcompelled, to the extreme limit of

---

[18] Don Gifford with Robert J. Seidman, *Notes for Joyce* (New York, 1974), p. 479.

his cometary orbit, beyond the fixed stars and variable suns and telescopic planets, astronomical waifs and strays, to the extreme boundary of space, passing from land to land, among peoples, amid events. Somewhere imperceptibly he would hear and somehow reluctantly, suncompelled, obey the summons of recall. Whence, disappearing from the constellation of the Northern Crown he would somehow reappear reborn above the delta in the constellation of Cassiopeia and after incalculable eons of peregrination return an estranged avenger, a wreaker of justice on malefactors, a dark crusader, a sleeper awakened, with financial resources (by supposition) surpassing those of Rothschild or of the silver king. (727-728)

Ithaca offers the celestial version of the self-imaged Odyssean wanderer in Bloom. But Bloom's common sense tells him to remain in bed because modern science cannot guarantee the return. We must settle for a rebirth beneath rather than "above the delta in the constellation of Cassiopeia." Cassiopeia is Shakespeare's configuration, and another bard, Dedalus, adapts its deltic insignia. Delta also serves as Joyce's sign for Anna Livia in *Finnegans Wake*; and we wonder, finally, if delta is not Joyce's Dublin with its "deltic origin" and Delphic northwest extension.

Zenith to Nadir the End of the World: Joyce and Blake

In 1912 Joyce lectured on two writers in Trieste, Daniel Defoe and William Blake. If Defoe's most famous wanderer, Robinson Crusoe, reduces English civilization to life on an uninhabited island in remote South American seas, Blake spreads the visionary body of England's Albion to the four corners of the hermetic expanse. It is a critical commonplace by now that the Trieste lectures represent the poles of Joyce's own fiction, Defoe's objective "factification" and Blake's visionary expansiveness.[19] Blake's narrative system is indeed hermetic—it progresses by balancing contraries and organizing micro- and macrosystems. The visions arising out of hermeticism have been important to philosophers and imaginative writers for whom

---

[19] See A. Walton Litz, "Ithaca" in Hart and Hayman, pp. 387-391. See also Joseph Prescott's introduction to Joyce's Defoe lecture, *Daniel Defoe*, in *Buffalo Studies*, 1 (Buffalo, New York, 1964).

Joyce had great respect, and in whom he had great interest: Bruno, Blake, Coleridge, Yeats. Joyce insists that hermetic mysticism serve an aesthetic end. Although the modern-day representatives of hermetic philosophy, the Theosophists, amused him as much as they interested him, Joyce was even capable of borrowing narrative material from mystics like Russell,[20] or from Theosophy's whore, as Joyce called her, Madame Blavatsky: "fundamentially theosophagusted over the whorse proceedings" (*FW*, 610).[21] As for one older hermeticist, Giordano Bruno, Joyce's interest was life-long. Samuel Beckett writes of Bruno and the structure of Joyce's fiction: "There is no difference, says Bruno, between the smallest possible chord and the smallest possible arc, no difference between the infinite circle and the straight line."[22]

Coleridge perhaps provides the clearest statement of the hermetic aesthetic in a letter to his friend Cottle.

> The common end of all *narrative*, nay, of *all* Poems is to convert series into a *Whole*: to make those events, which in real or imagined History move on a *strait* Line, assume to our Understandings a *circular* motion—the snake with its Tail in its Mouth.[23]

The hermetic curve is, as Stephen Dedalus puts it, "the greatest possible ellipse. Consistent with. The ultimate return" (504). Narrative projection makes the entire cosmos adjustable to varieties of plot.

---

[20] Richard Ellmann describes a late-night meeting in August of 1902 between Joyce and Æ (Russell) on the subject of the new hermeticism, modern Theosophy. Joyce was skeptical but nevertheless "he was genuinely interested in such Theosophical themes as cycles, reincarnation, the succession of gods, and the eternal mother-faith that underlies all transitory religions" (*JJ*, 103). Ellmann dismisses the account circulated among Joyce's friends that he was merely pulling Russell's Theosophic leg on the occasion.

[21] It has been noticed that when Bloom defines metempsychosis for Molly, he lifts the definition right out of Madame Blavatsky's *Key to Theosophy* (London, 1889). Bloom explains: "Some people believe, he said, that we go on living in another body after death, that we lived before. They call it reincarnation. That we all lived before on the earth thousands of years ago or some other planet" (65). Madame Blavatsky's *Key* phrases the same question: "You mean, then, that we have all lived on earth before, in many past reincarnations, and shall go on so living?" Her Theosophic answer is a definitive yes (p. 197). For a general review of Joyce's reading on mysticism and hermeticism, see Stuart Gilbert, pp. 41-50.

[22] Beckett, "Dante . . . Bruno . Vico . . Joyce," *op. cit.*, p. 6.

[23] Coleridge, *Collected Letters*, ed. Earl Leslie Griggs (Oxford, 1959), IV, 545.

The *Odyssey*, for instance, activates the *zophos* on a linear grid, but re-mythifies Ithaca, circling its hero back with the sun. Dante's *Divine Comedy* sets its hero in errant woods, descendent *bolgia*, and ascendent mountains, but seeks that hermetic center which is all circumference. When Joyce read Yeats's *A Vision*, a hermetic scheme keyed to spatial and temporal extensions, projections of the phases of the moon, the range of the compass points, the parts of the human body, the zodiacal influences, the essences of the human spirit, he commented to Eugene Jolas on what a pity it was that Yeats had not incorporated his vast conic-like scheme into a major imaginative work.[24] For this very reason Joyce admires Blake's mystical epics. "In him," writes Joyce, "the visionary faculty is directly connected with the artistic faculty" (*CW*, 221).

At one point in the *Circe* episode, Joyce conjures up Blake by parodying the modern Theosophists, but also recalls in that mad English poet the prophet of regeneration so important to *Ulysses*, Elijah: "*Along an infinite invisible tightrope taut from zenith to nadir the End of the World*" (507). As a mythographer, Blake sets up a massive directional grid for his visionary domain, a domain with its four corners, its heights and depths, and its cyclical movements: turns and returns. The *Four Zoas, Milton,* and *Jerusalem* share epic and mythic boundaries. Joyce is not so skeptical as to be uninterested. Time is degenerate and potentially regenerate for Blake; space is usurped and potentially reintegrated. Primal unity—the parent power Tharmas—departs upon the loss of his emanations to the darkening West. The movement to the limits leaves a void at the center as the body of the giant Albion loses its orientation—its head is turned westward, its feet to the east. Eden, the high place of unity, has descended in the *Four Zoas* "beneath Albion's / Death Couch, in the caverns of death, in the corner of / the Atlantic." Blake's refashioners, his creators, his poets come to fill the void. Blake's scheme is strange, but it is little different from the life-death axis we have seen in the *Odyssey* and in *Ulysses*. The map of Blake's cosmography is predominantly mythic, but he, too, will touch local ground, adapting Near-Eastern and English place names along the axis of his reintegrating vision.

In the *Four Zoas* refashioning the void signals an end of darkness

---

[24] Eugene Jolas, "My Friend James Joyce," in *James Joyce: Two Decades of Criticism*, ed. Seon Givens (New York, 1948), p. 15.

and cold northern blasts. In *Milton* Blake seeks to renew real and mythic spaces—he looks to origins of two kinds, ancestral and poetic.

> I will not cease from Mental Fight,
> Nor shall my Sword sleep in my hand:
> Till we have built Jerusalem,
> In Englands green & pleasant Land.   (1, 13-16)

Joyce's New Bloomusalem in *Circe* is partly a parody of this process and partly an indication of what is going on seriously in Joyce's literary prescriptions for Ireland: the infusion of eastern spirit into western domains: "Our homerole poet to Ostelinda" (*FW*, 445), as Shaun says of Shem. In his poem called *Jerusalem* Blake adapts an orienting grid, one we have come to recognize. North is nadir, fallen below the frozen wastes. West is circumference as it always has been. South is zenith—its heat rising. And East is origin or *omphalos*. If we understand the projection, we have come a long way in understanding the vision. Blake will awaken and reorient his sleeping giant just as Joyce expects Bloom as "Brightdayler" or Finnegan as revivified hero to get up in the morning and attend their daily wakes. We can even see something of the same process when Shelley unbinds his version of the cosmic giant, Prometheus, to spread love from the Ganges to Atlantis in the room-world of closet drama. Time takes its spatial course back to the first days of creation when "the Celt knew the Indian" (II, iv, 94). Molly Bloom as a spinning giantess in *Ulysses* is more modest. She only introduces the Semite to the Irishman, passing through the Straits of Gibraltar to do so.

INFLUENCE OF THE CLIMATE
GEOGRAPHY AND NATIONAL TEMPERAMENT

The Climatic Compass

ONE of the traditional tasks of the writer of epics is to mark the qualities of a land in the narrative events of a race. The epic is and always has been regionally and nationally determined. Theorists from Georg Lukács to Northrop Frye insist that the epic is a bounded document before it is boundless, locally immanent before it is transcendent.[1] For Joyce this is as much a fact of history as a basis for narrative. He writes of his own land in his lecture, *Ireland, Island of Saints and Sages.*

> Nationality (if it really is not a convenient fiction like so many others to which the scalpels of present-day scientists have given the coup de grâce) must find its reason for being rooted in something that surpasses and transcends and informs changing things like blood and the human word. The mystic theologian who assumed the pseudonym of Dionysius, the pseudo-Areopagite, says somewhere, "God has disposed the limits of nations according to his angels", and this probably is not a purely mystical concept. Do we not see that in Ireland the Danes, the Firbolgs, the Milesians from Spain, the Norman invaders, and the Anglo-Saxon settlers have united to form a new entity, one might say under the influence of a local deity? And, although the present race in Ireland is backward and inferior, it is worth taking into account the fact that it is the only race of the entire Celtic family that has not been willing to sell its birthright for a mess of pottage.

> (*CW*, 166)

According to Richard Ellmann, in 1915 Joyce became acquainted with Ottocaro Weiss, a student of political economy at the Univer-

---

[1] See Georg Lukács, *The Theory of the Novel*, trans. Anna Bostock (Cambridge, Mass., 1971): "[the epic] can never, while remaining epic, transcend the breadth and depth, the rounded, sensual, richly ordered nature of life as historically given" (p. 46). Also, Northrop Frye, *Anatomy of Criticism* (Princeton, 1957): "The cyclical form of the Classical epic is based on the natural cycle, a mediterranean known world in the middle of a boundlessness (*apeiron*) and between the upper and the lower gods" (p. 318).

sity of Zürich. Ellmann mentions the substance, as Weiss remembers it, of one of their many conversations.

> Their talk often turned to political science and literature. Weiss told Joyce of Montesquieu's theory that political institutions were inevitably the special product of local conditions. Joyce was uniformly skeptical and ironical about all such theories, although some of them made an appearance in *Ulysses* and *Finnegans Wake*. (*JJ*, p. 406)

As politically skeptical as Joyce may have been, he was intrigued with the idea of national determinants. He may have learned from Montesquieu (via Weiss) or from Guglielmo Ferrero's *L'Europa giovane*, to which he alludes in an early letter to Stanislaus (*Letters*, II, p. 190), that national temperament is, in part, a regional, climatic condition. In *Ulysses* Joyce works with a climatically displaced hero. If the Semitic Bloom has a difficult time of it in Ireland, a northwestern nation, he also has his difficulties with the Mediterranean sun-culture, the climate in which the prototypical Odysseus sails. Late in the day while Bloom tries to keep up both ends of a conversation with Stephen Dedalus, the desultory talk of *Eumaeus* turns to Dublin's Little Italy and Molly's Spain. Bloom chatters away and Stephen recalls the Italians near the Cabman's shelter haggling over money. The indecorous "*Putana madonna*" strikes Bloom's ears as "*Bella Poetria*." Bloom persists.

> —Spaniards, for instance, he continued, passionate temperaments like that, impetuous as Old Nick, are given to taking the law into their own hands and give you your quietus double quick with those poignards they carry in the abdomen. It comes from the great heat, climate generally. My wife is, so to speak, Spanish, half, that is. Point of fact she could actually claim Spanish nationality if she wanted, having been born in (technically) Spain, i.e. Gibraltar. She has the Spanish type. Quite dark, regular brunette, black. I, for one, certainly believe climate accounts for character. That's why I asked you if you wrote your poetry in Italian.
> (637)

Stephen undercuts his companion and his companion's theories: "The temperaments at the door, Stephen interposed with, were very passionate about ten shillings" (637). But Bloom continues at cross purposes.

—It's in the blood, Mr Bloom acceded at once. All are washed in the blood of the sun. Coincidence, I just happened to be in the Kildare street Museum today, shortly prior to our meeting, if I can so call it, and I was just looking at those antique statues there. The splendid proportions of hips, bosom. You simply don't knock against those kind of women here. An exception here and there. Handsome, yes, pretty in a way you find, but what I'm talking about is the female form. Besides, they have so little taste in dress, most of them, which greatly enhances a woman's natural beauty, no matter what you say. (637)

Bloom, like Joyce,[2] honors the ample and adorned feminine form; he joins Vico in the land of Mediterranean substance: *mundus muliebris*. His thoughts on the meaning of particular Mediterranean words, although erroneous, are based on traditional climate theory. Bloom gets the sound quality right, if not the sense. Tommaso Campanella, author of the well-known *City of the Sun*, argues in his *De sensu rerum* that the relationship of hot climates to vowel sounds produces the fiery or languid tones of Mediterranean tongues, and the relationship of cold to consonants produces the guttural sounds of the north. "Influence of the climate" (71), Bloom thinks earlier when he ponders eastern and southern ease ("*dolce far niente*"). Wherever we look in the day of *Ulysses*, the novel's major themes— fertility, sterility, love, music, politics, sustenance, drunkenness, renewal—touch in one way or another upon climate.

Just as in Giambattista Vico's and Victor Bérard's conceptions of topographical extension in the naming of places, climate theory works on a contracted or expanded grid. Depending on where we choose to center and how far we choose to extend, the climatic winds blow warmer or colder by degrees. In the Greek Mediterranean epic the known world was limited, but the differences in climates were great enough, at least in mythic regions, to encompass a fairly various narrative terrain. The *Iliad* and the *Odyssey* describe the Mediterranean from the coasts of eastern Troy to the desert lands of the Lotophagoi in the south, to the barbaric straits of the northern Lestrygonian giants, to the temperate climes of the far west near the isle of Calypso.

In the *Odyssey* the adventures alternate between excesses of prof-

[2] According to Stanislaus Joyce, *My Brother's Keeper* (New York, 1958), his brother "likes them sizable" (p. 113).

fered ease and excesses of violent barbarism. These adventures have
climatic bases. Life is either languorous or death-defying depending,
very literally, on where Odysseus is placed: in the sun or in the
gloom. The Greek hero, as always, mediates. For the Mediterranean
epic, of course, the hero faces severe tests when he is forced by
circumstances, or by his men, to rebel against the nature that usually sustains him. The most egregious crime in the world of the
Odyssey is perpetrated not by the suitors on Ithaca who abuse, and
badly abuse, custom, but by Odysseus' crew on Trinacria when they
slaughter the cattle of the sun king. Violation of the principle of
life in the Mediterranean is simply unthinkable. And the narrative
places a strain upon Odysseus for a crime he himself did not commit,
but merely witnessed too late to control. After his crew slay and
feast upon the kine of Helios—the initiator of sun-produced perception and articulation "by whom all things are seen, all speech is
known"—Odysseus is cast adrift at sea for a second pass at Scylla
and Charybdis. To avoid the Charybdian whirlpool, Odysseus seizes
the branch of a fig tree extending over Scylla's rock, swinging like
a bat on a bough. There he remains, hanging, for most of the day
until Charybdis subsides. The fig, a staple and symbolic fruit in the
Mediterranean, has from ancient times been fertilized by draping
male flowers with their pollen-producing caprifigs over branches of
the female receptacles. Odysseus, in effect, initiates a process of refertilization after his men have silenced the articulation of life on
Helios' isle. He is unaware of the particular significance of what
happens to him, but in the narrative action of the *Odyssey* he is reborn into the greater Mediterranean. It is no coincidence that later,
in the Virgilian Latin epic, supposedly measured by a pious new
civic rigor, Romulus and Remus, the originators of it all, were born
beneath a fig tree. The glory that will be Rome in the vision of the
Aeneid has characteristically fertile Mediterranean roots.

Aristotle was the first to systematize climate theory, and it is clear
from the relevant passage in his *Politics* that Greek civilization serves
as his middle terrain.

The nations inhabiting the cold places and those of Europe are
full of spirit but somewhat deficient in intelligence and skill, so
that they continue comparatively free, but lacking in political or-
ganization and capacity to rule their neighbours. The peoples of
Asia on the other hand are intelligent and skillful in tempera-

ment, but lack spirit, so that they are in continuous subjection and slavery. But the Greek race participates in both characters, just as it occupies the middle position geographically, for it is both spirited and intelligent; hence it continues to be free and to have very good political institutions, and to be capable of ruling all mankind if it attains constitutional unity.

(*Politics*, VII, vi, 1327b)

The Aristotelian theory was popularized by Jean Bodin in the Renaissance; worked into poetic theory by Sir William Temple in England; expanded into a system of political, economic, and cultural determinants by the Baron de Montesquieu;[3] and given comic literary form before Joyce by Byron in his great epic of climatic drift, *Don Juan*. In an interesting note for the *Penelope* episode in *Ulysses*, Joyce summarizes one of the assumptions of climate theory: "sea = distance. distinctions of personality. . . ." (Herring, p. 499). Such distinctions, of course, are regionally relative. The values of any climatic direction go two ways. For the west, the clarity and precision of the east seems time-bound, decadent. In *Ulysses*, as a small cloud covers the eastern sun, Leopold Bloom turns in his mind from the sun-drenched orange groves of the original land—from his home, his "native place," as J. J. O'Molloy puts it in *Circe*—to the desolate and decadent version of the east under western eyes. The "immense melonfields north of Jaffa" (60)—Jaffa, or Haifa, literally means east in Hebrew—become a "barren land, bare waste. . . . Sodom, Gomorrah, Edom. All dead names. A dead sea in a dead land, grey and old" (61). The place is the same, but the associations alter with the rays of the sun and the mood of the day. The same is true for the west. Those extended regions toward the gloom are either eternally temperate or eternally bleak. In *Finnegans Wake* Joyce conveys the possibilities in the pun: "Osman glory, ebbing wasteward" (*FW*, 235). It is all here: east man (original, oriental) glory migrating to western wastes. In *Ulysses* the west is either the new land or the dead land. For the citizen in *Cyclops* whose race is his memory, Galway, Ireland's western port, bustles with the renewable promise of past Atlantic vigor. In *Nestor*, Galway is the seat of an

[3] See Book 1 of Jean Bodin's *Six Bookes of the Commonweale*, trans. Richard Knolles (London, 1606); William Temple's *Of Poetry* (London, 1692); and Montesquieu's *Esprit des Lois* (Paris, 1748), Books XIV, XV, XVI, XVII, XVIII.

ancient, primitive, and dying grace, always in the empty gloom of another nation's imperial domain.

North and south carry directional values of their own. Precisely because of climate and terrain, the Mediterranean world expanded equatorially before meridionally. The north was simply Scythia for the Greeks, a massive region deprived of the light of the sun. Only above and beyond Scythia did the Greeks conceive of a mythic hyperborean land more suited to their temperate tastes. That leap of the imagination over the expanse of northern terrain tells us something of the isolation of Northern Europe before the tribal invasions of the first millennium. The north, which only subsequently became the hardy *vagina gentium* of Europe, was conceived of as a barbarian waste.[4] And after the Gothic invasions, a profound terror was associated with the north that has not yet left it. In a fascinating narrative adaptation of climate theory, Mary Shelley constructs a Gothic tale around climatic extremes: the processes of life's creation are reversed in its destruction at the polar regions in the north. The possessed Doctor Frankenstein pursues his doppelgänger monster to frozen icecaps of the arctic, the antidote to the animating energy that produced the creature in the first place. The tale is a fable of interior and exterior extremes. When in *Finnegans Wake* Joyce turns to the north, we can see how domain measures his conception of narrative structure. The cold rigor of Scandinavian and Germanic regions produces what he sees as tight tribal and familial bonds, pressures as great as the elemental extreme of the climate. Icelandic, Scandinavian, and Germanic sagas are great family struggles. Even in *Ulysses* Stephen parodies the plight of the northern son when he smashes the chandelier in *Circe*'s *Götterdämmerung* sequence. Edward Epstein sees this scene as the great divide between the Hebraic-Greco and Germanic cultures, and I think he is right.[5] Bloom is the dark-backed "enlightener" from warmer regions; Stephen the anxiety-ridden rebel against both the light and the gloom, against the warmth and the cold.

The equatorial south is the last region to open up for climate theory and for narrative. Heliodorus touches on Ethiopia, Ariosto sends his space-maddened hero to Africa, the Portuguese *Lusiad*

[4] See Thor J. Beck, *Northern Antiquities in French Learning and Literature* (New York, 1934).

[5] Edward Epstein, "Stephen's Dance," in *The Ordeal of Stephen Dedalus* (Carbondale, 1971), pp. 156-173.

follows da Gama around the Cape of Good Hope, Defoe sends Crusoe both to the slave-trade coast of Africa and the mouth of the Orinoco, and Blake leaves Albion's dark satanic mills in his *Song of Los* to dip into "heart-shaped" Africa. But only Lawrence and Conrad, perhaps Melville in America, treat the sub-continents or southern seas with the ranging climatic compass employed for the east, west, and north. Lawrence's treatment is the most striking. Influenced by Pryse's theory of erogenous zones and Spengler's theory of a rising Africa, Lawrence discovered a microcosmic climatic world in man and predicted a macrocosmic climatic apocalypse for the world. The passage is from *Women in Love*, and two cultures, one ice-bound, the other sun-scorched, meet their doom.

> The white races, having the Arctic north behind them, the vast abstraction of ice and snow, would fulfil a mystery of ice-destructive knowledge, snow-abstract annihilation. Whereas the West Africans, controlled by the burning death-abstraction of the Sahara, had been fulfilled in sun-destruction, the putrescent mystery of sunrays.[6]

Northmen's thing made southfolk's place

Joyce's climatic regions were not nearly so frightening as Lawrence's. He was given to the pun before the apocalypse: "If he spice east he seethes in sooth and if he pierce north he wilts in the waist" (*FW*, 251). Nonetheless, Joyce's fiction explores those territories where regional temperaments meet and sometimes clash. We know that Bloom and Molly in Dublin strain their eastern and southern connections. In *Finnegans Wake* Shem the Penman has an "iberborealic imagination" (*FW*, 487)—that is, Iberian, Hibernian, and Hyperborean—and we see the northwest passage again, from the Mediterranean Straits to the land Joyce calls "Scandiknavery" (*FW*, 47). (Significantly, Victor Bérard derives the place name *Iberia* from the Semitic root meaning isle of passage [Bérard, 1, 287].) In the Ireland of *Ulysses*, Leopold Bloom has a climatic problem. He needs more warmth than he gets. Only in his wily imagination can he forge a northern city with just a dash of southern ease. He dreams of a house in the suburbs with a "southerly aspect" (712). The house itself might well be on either side of Dublin. All that matters to

[6] D. H. Lawrence, *Women in Love* (New York, 1960), p. 246.

Bloom is that it face south for the warmth of the sun—he is philotropic, as we learn in *Ithaca*.

Dublin is a city, like New Bloomusalem, confused in its origins. History says the Danes founded it from the north; myth says the Milesians settled it from southeast.[7] *Finnegans Wake* says both: "Northmen's thing made southfolk's place" (*FW*, 215). The Norsemen of Joyce's world are the stage Irishmen—Mulligan, Boylan, the Citizen, even Finnegan. These are men of northern and western brawn, the Irish mockers, the Sir Louts whose very size, as Joyce points out to Budgen, makes them weak reproductively (Budgen, p. 52). Dublin's Norsemen, red-faced from drink, embody the associations of their territory. Garrett Deasy of the "Black north" rides the favorite, "*Cock of the North*," to a dead last finish in *Circe*'s re-running of the day's Goldcup race (573). Buck Mulligan, the king's son—the "*Fertiliser and Incubator, Lambay Island*" (402)—is really Dublin's expert on the "causes of sterility" (402). Paddy Dignam, whose death has put Bloom in mourning clothes for the day, is moved with his casket from his home in Sandymount to his grave in Glasnevin, from the warmth of the Gulf Stream touching the bay to the cold of the Prospect cemetery in the northwest of Dublin: "Washing child, washing corpse. Dignam" (373). Blazes Boylan, the "man of brawn in possession" (541) of 7 Eccles street for the afternoon, is a typical Sir Lout—Molly says he has little spunk in him.

Joyce distrusts the native, blustering Irish and what he described to his brother Stanislaus as their "asexual intellect."[8] Boylan, as his name suggests, and Mulligan, as his role suggests, are the devils in an Irish land that supposedly has no hell. "Worst man in Dublin" (92), Bloom thinks as Boylan passes in *Hades*, and in the same chapter Simon Dedalus says of his son's *fidus Achates*, Mulligan: "That Mulligan is a contaminated bloody doubledyed ruffian by all accounts. His name stinks all over Dublin" (88). The northern usurpers are powerful and guileful at the same time. Molly comments on Boylan's weapon, "that tremendous big red brute of a thing he has" (742), and Dedalus parries Mulligan's weapon, his cold steel pen, with one of his own. Mulligan pretends to be Greek, his name having "a Hellenic ring, hasn't it? Tripping and sunny like the buck

---

[7] See Stuart Gilbert's chapter, "Dubliners-Vikings-Achaeans," in Gilbert, pp. 65-76.

[8] Stanislaus Joyce, *My Brother's Keeper*, p. 158.

himself" (4). But he is as Norse Irish as they come, a king's son, a great pretender: "I'm hyperborean as much as you" (5), he says to Dedalus. The allusion is to another sexless northern superman, Nietzsche's *Übermensch*.

Mulligan, in a way, tries to usurp all Dedalus' space, from his Greek name to his hyperborean temperament—above the crowd. Blazes Boylan, the other usurping Antinous of *Ulysses*, tries to usurp Bloom's space. He leads his own mission to Bloom's southern exposure, his wife Molly. Perhaps for one day Boylan enjoys a Mediterranean woman's warmth, but all he can muster for the future is a singing-tour for Molly in the north of Ireland. Joyce, like Dante, packs his local devil in ice. Molly, who knows the sunsets and fig trees of Gibraltar, is washed in the blood of the sun—she is of a different order from Irish home-made beauties, and Bloom, the Jew, senses it.

> That's where Molly can knock spots off them. It is the blood of the south. Moorish. Also the form, the figure. Hands felt for the opulent. Just compare for instance those others. Wife locked up at home, skeleton in the cupboard. Allow me to introduce my. Then they trot you out some kind of a nondescript, wouldn't know what to call her. (373)

If Bloom "wouldn't know what to call her," Molly does. She labels the Irish home-growns: "a lot of sparrowfarts" (762). Her allegiance, finally, is to her own, to her invented lover on Gibraltar, Don Miguel de la Flora, to Don Poldo de la Flora of Howth Hill and environs. "Why me?" wonders Bloom, remembering Molly's, "Because you were so foreign from the others" (380). Bloom, in many ways, is a foreigner, out of his "native orient" and "transplanted to a clime" where his "roots have lost their quondam vigour" (410). He does not belong in a city that murders life and love by mocking both. And Molly, much as she suffers from the sterility of her marriage, transplants Bloom in her memories back and forth from the Mediterranean Sea in which the Semitic originals sailed. Mulvey of the H.M.S. *Calypso* in Gibraltar is Bloom of Howth Hill. First Molly recalls the day Bloom proposed.

> . . . the sun shines for you he said the day we were lying among the rhododendrons on Howth head in the grey tweed suit and his straw hat the day I got him to propose to me yes first I have him the bit of seedcake out of my mouth and it was leapyear like

now yes 16 years ago my God after that long kiss I near lost my
breath yes he said I was a flower of the mountain yes so we are
flowers all a womans body yes. . . .   (782)

And then the novel backtracks along its axis. Molly turns to the
south but, in her memory and in her language, conflates two lovers,
two days, and two regions.

> . . . and Gibraltar as a girl where I was a Flower of the mountain
> yes when I put the rose in my hair like the Andalusian girls used
> or shall I wear a red yes and how he kissed me under the Moorish
> wall and I thought well as well him as another and then I asked
> him with my eyes to ask again yes and then he asked me would
> I yes to say yes my mountain flower. . . .   (783)

No matter how we view Molly and no matter how we read
Ulysses, Dublin alone cannot match this Mediterranean vision. The
antithesis of northern and southern values in *Ulysses* is generally
reminiscent of another comic epic in which a Mediterranean hero
tests life in the British Isles, Byron's *Don Juan*. A young and vital
stranger from Spain travels to England, and the closest approach he
makes to human contact is when he is beaten and robbed in Britain's
"independent" clime. Like Joyce's vision of Odysseus in Dublin,
Byron's narrative deals with the pathos and comedy of warmth
meeting cold, with the Mediterranean soul enmeshed in northwestern terrain. Don Juan shares territorial ancestry with Molly Bloom,
and with Bloom's Spanish avatar, Don Poldo de la Flora. All attempt
the translation of the resurgent breath of the south to the northwest
gloom, and all bog down in the great "moral" wastes of the English-
speaking nations.

The mock-epic imagination can even pull Mediterranean voyagers in beyond Ireland, north. Vincent Cosgrave, the Lynch of
Portrait and *Ulysses*, wrote Joyce about Oliver St. John Gogarty's
(or Mulligan's) version of Sinbad the Sailor. The same letter included Gogarty's "Song of the Cheerful (but slightly sarcastic)
Jesus," three stanzas of which appear in the opening chapter of
Ulysses. Cosgrave explains that Gogarty's Mediterranean Sinbad
is chucked overboard in northern seas, which belong, more properly,
to Coleridge's Ancient Mariner. Sinbad, the transformed hero of
the pantomime stage, of course resurfaces for Joyce, squaring the
compass in *Ithaca*. Cosgrave writes.

His sailor is going further still. Last time I met him he had almost reached the North Pole, but he complained of the weather,

The sailor feels	Oh whales that swim & snort & blow!
The climatic rigor	O Walruses whose front-teeth show!
	Oh Seals that still select a floe
	To cool desire!
	I don't know how the Hell you go
	Without a fire.

The judgment of Providence overtook the crew captain for so ruthlessly chucking Sinbad overboard. They were driving on death but before the final disaster

The Sailors hear	Where weighed Atlantic's lift and power
The Syren Voices	And thunder down on Labrador
	They heard beyond a din & roar
	Like Thor's great mallet
	The calling of the Coal-Quay Whore
	Which has no palate.

(*Letters*, II, 126)

The effort is sorry Coleridge, but the directional drift is remembered in *Ulysses*. Mulligan still has a polar, hyperborean attraction. In *Finnegans Wake* the Mulligan prototype is filled by Shaun, the thoroughly Irish twin. Shaun is not only Stanislaus, Joyce's brother, but Gogarty, his "everdevoting fiend" (*FW*, 408). "Brawn is my name" (*FW*, 187), boasts Shaun, and with his "mac Frieze o'coat of far suparior ruggedness" (*FW*, 404), Shaun is the "picture primitive" (*FW*, 405) of Ireland's northern domains.

IRELAND SOBER IS IRELAND STIFF

The Baron de Montesquieu's five chapters on climate and geography in *Esprit des Lois* (1748) touch on matters of comic importance to *Ulysses*. The subjects are general enough: love, politics, music, drink. Although Joyce offers no slavish reproduction of Montesquieu—he may not, for that matter, even have read him firsthand—Montesquieu's theories on such topics as the geography of love have a bearing on the action of *Ulysses*.

From this delicacy of organs peculiar to warm climates it follows that the soul is most sensibly moved by whatever relates to the union of the two sexes: here everything leads to this object.

In northern climates scarcely has the animal part of love a power of making itself felt. In temperate climates, love, attended by a thousand appendages, endeavors to please by things that have at first the appearance, though not the reality, of this passion. In warmer climates it is liked for its own sake, it is the only cause of happiness, it is life itself.[9]

Yet again, warmth articulates love and life. In Montesquieu's scheme, Ireland is northern-temperate, but Joyce conceives of it as northern-"animal"—his nation is left out in the cold. Bloom, the Jew, is the only citizen radiating much in the way of warmth, and he gets himself into difficulty doing so. Love is at least better than hate, Bloom pleads to the citizen in Barney Kiernan's north-westerly pub shortly before the citizen nearly brains Joyce's loving easterner with a biscuit tin. In *Cyclops*, of course, "Jumbo, the elephant, loves Alice, the elephant" (333), but love's "happiness" makes itself felt for few others in this city of paralytics. Like Joyce's Mrs. Sinico from the short story, "A Painful Case," Dubliners die over and again from a "sudden failure of the heart's action" (*D*, 114). At 7 Eccles street the home-ground lies fallow since the death of the Blooms' infant son: "it was we were never the same since O Im not going to think myself into the glooms about that any more" (778). Of course, that is precisely where Molly thinks herself whenever she thinks of life and love in present-day Dublin: "youve no chances at all in this place like you used long ago I wish somebody would write me a loveletter" (758).

Molly gets no love-letters—just appointments for afternoon trysts. Bloom, on the other hand, does get a love-letter, from Martha Clifford, typist. But, in a version of Montesquieu's formulation, Bloom "endeavors to please by things that have at first the appearance, though not the reality" of love's emotion. His organ lies like a languid floating flower in the Turkish baths of *Lotuseaters*, the "limp father of thousands" (86). He knows that Boylan's "big red brute of a thing" will perform its animal task later in the day. Love for Bloom is merely an Odyssean false homecoming, what Stephen Dedalus would call "almosting it." Early in the day Bloom

[9] Montesquieu, *The Spirit of the Laws*, trans. Thomas Nugent (New York, 1949), p. 223. Subsequent citations will be from this translation and pages noted in the body of the text.

tries to catch a glimpse of an elegant lady's calf as she boards a
tram. No luck. M'Coy's talking head distracts Bloom's concentration
just as another tram blocks his view. The incident parodies Odysseus' southern turn in the sea lanes around Cape Malea, but for
Bloom a geographical mishap is a sexual one.

> Proud: rich: silk stockings.
> —Yes, Mr Bloom said.
> He moved a little to the side of M'Coy's talking head. Getting
> up in a minute.
> —*What's wrong with him?* he said. *He's dead,* he said. And,
> faith, he filled up. *Is it Paddy Dignam?* I said. I couldn't believe
> it when I heard it. I was with him no later than Friday last or
> Thursday was it in the Arch. *Yes,* he said. *He's gone. He died on
> Monday, poor fellow.*
> Watch! Watch! Silk flash rich stockings white. Watch!
> A heavy tramcar honking its gong slewed between.
> Lost it. Curse your noisy pugnose. Feels locked out of it. Para-
> dise and the peri. Always happening like that. The very moment.
> Girl in Eustace street hallway. Monday was it settling her garter.
> Her friend covering the display of. *Esprit de corps.* Well, what
> are you gaping at?
> —Yes, yes, Mr Bloom said after a dull sigh. Another gone.
>
> (74)

Another gone, and not Dignam: Bloom's day is a southern "dream
of wellfilled hose" (368) in the reality of Dublin's lifelessness. In
the *Sirens* episode, the love theme in *Ulysses* modulates into a musical key. Montesquieu makes distinctions between climates on the
basis of musical tastes similar to those he makes on the basis of
amatory habits. Ireland is but a nation of musical pretenders. Bloom
settles for the strains of a tune he himself will not sing.

> Flood of warm jimjam lickitup secretness flowed to flow in
> music out, in desire, dark to lick flow, invading. Tipping her tep-
> ping her tapping her topping her. Tup. Pores to dilate dilating.
> Tup. The joy the feel the warm the. Tup. To pour o'er sluices
> pouring gushes. Flood, gush, flow, joygush, tupthrop. Now! Lan-
> guage of love. (274)

He conjures up the south and Idolores of southern seas: "Spanishy
eyes. Under a peartree alone patio this hour in old Madrid one side

in shadow Dolores shedolores. At me. Luring. Ah, alluring" (275). Simon Dedalus sings from Flotow's *Martha*, and Bloom continues to hear the Sirens, as limited an experience for him as his epistolary flirtation with Martha Clifford.

> Quitting all languor Lionel cried in grief, in cry of passion domi-nant to love to return with deepening yet with rising chords of harmony. In cry of lionel loneliness that she should know, must Martha feel. For only her he waited. Where? Here there try there here all try where. Somewhere.
> —*Co-me, thou lost one!*
> *Co-me thou dear one!*
> Alone. One love. One hope. One comfort me. Martha, chest-note, return.
> —*Come!*   (275)

The musical consummation includes Martha, Molly, Flotow's Martha and Lionel, Simon Dedalus (later "Siopold"), and Bloom (Leo the Lionel). But love's song is another gone: "Thou lost one. All songs on that theme. Yet more Bloom stretched his string. Cruel it seems. Let people get fond of each other: lure them on. Then tear asunder" (277). Passion to dominant to love to return is the minia-ture epic of the octave, in Stephen's later rendering of it, but music's loss is not love's gain in Dublin. While Bloom thinks of Montes-quieu's only "cause of happiness," Blazes Boylan, the "conquering hero" (264), moves on towards Molly as the "Cock of the North" with "a loud proud knocker, with a cock carracarracarra cock. Cock-cock" (282). If Blazes is scarcely anything but the northern "ani-mal part of love," brutal and inconsiderate, Bloom does not exactly know what to do with his own "delicacy of organs peculiar to warm climates." Only Molly seems to sense the south in the many things Bloom knows "especially about the body and the insides" (743). Boylan, with "no manners nor no refinement" (776) is no match for Molly's memories of "the great Suggester Don Poldo de la Flora" (778) who understands and feels "what a woman is" (782). And Bloom's mind, too, even in *Sirens*, turns to more than a mock con-summation: "I, too, last of my race. Milly young student. Well, my fault perhaps. No son. Rudy. Too late now. Or if not? If not? If still?" (285).

But there are other climatic problems in Ireland's gloom. Montes-quieu argues that not only the human emotions and human arts are tied to the effects of climate, but so too are systems of human law. Peoples in warm climates, by turns lethargic and volatile, require stringent controls; those in colder climates, hardy and insulated, insist on political liberty. In *Aeolus* and *Cyclops* we see a little of what this means for the Irish. Ireland is a land in bondage, with predictable northern pretensions to independence. But Joyce sees Ireland's patriots paying only a curious lip service to liberty in their land; the reaction to bondage is to tip the glass, to drown political woes in drink. This much is consistent with Montesquieu's sense of the north.

In warm countries the aqueous part of the blood loses itself greatly by perspiration; it must, therefore, be supplied by a like liquid. Water is there of admirable use; strong liquors would congeal the globules of blood that remain after the transuding of the aqueous humor.

In cold countries the aqueous part of the blood is very little evacuated by perspiration. They may, therefore, make use of spirituous liquors, without which the blood would congeal. They are full of humors; consequently strong liquors, which give a motion to the blood, are proper for those countries.

The law of Mohammed, which prohibits the drinking of wine, is, therefore, fitted to the climate of Arabia: and, indeed, before Mohammed's time, water was the common drink of the Arabs. The law which forbade the Carthaginians to drink wine was a law of the climate; and, indeed, the climate of those two countries is pretty nearly the same.

Such a law would be improper for cold countries, where the climate seems to force them to a kind of national intemperance, very different from personal ebriety. Drunkenness predominates throughout the world, in proportion to the coldness and humidity of the climate. Go from the equator to the north pole, and you will find this vice increasing together with the degree of latitude. Go from the equator again to the south pole, and you will find the same vice travelling south, exactly in the same proportion. (228)

Bloom is an eastern teetotaler. Most of the Irish male population in *Ulysses*, excessively intemperate, lose the will to whatever freedom they think themselves heir to. It is always high tide at Dublin's bars. "Ireland sober is Ireland stiff," as Joyce puts it in *Finnegans Wake*. Dublin is as stupefied by alcohol as it is by political indolence: "isle of dreadful thirst" (41), Dedalus calls it. As a child, he had told himself: "You prayed to the Blessed Virgin that you might not have a red nose" (40). For Paddy Dignam, drinking up what life he had left in a local pub, a Dubliner's home is indeed his coffin. The "red-faced one," Elpenor in the Homeric parallel, Dignam dies of a literal failure of the heart's action.

> —Breakdown, Martin Cunningham said. Heart.
> He tapped his chest sadly.
> Blazing face: redhot. Too much John Barleycorn. Cure for a red nose. Drink like the devil till it turns adelite. A lot of money he spent colouring it. (95)

Northern women, Montesquieu writes, are better off than their men in respect to drink because they "have a natural restraint" being "always on the defensive" (252). In Dublin that is not much consolation. The city's husbands, fathers, and friends are petty tyrants, from Master Dignam's "poor pa" to Gerty MacDowell's father deep in "the clutches of demon drink" (354) to Simon Dedalus hustling pence in the gutters of O'Connell street while berating his pitiful daughter for asking for money on which to feed the family.

> —Wait awhile, Mr Dedalus said threateningly. You're like the rest of them, are you? An insolent pack of little bitches since your poor mother died. But wait awhile. You'll all get a short shrift and a long day from me. Low blackguardism! I'm going to get rid of you. Wouldn't care if I was stretched out stiff. He's dead. The man upstairs is dead. (238)

In the *Odyssey* if fathers were dead, the narrative would have no subject. But in *Ulysses* Simon the drinker is "stiff" like another Irish father, Paddy Dignam. Master Dignam remembers an Irish night in the regions of the dead—dead drunk.

> The last night pa was boosed he was standing on the landing there bawling out for his boots to go out to Tunney's for to boose more and he looked butty and short in his shirt. Never see him again. Death, that is. Pa is dead. My father is dead. He told me to be a good son to ma. I couldn't hear the other things he said but I saw his tongue and his teeth trying to say it better. Poor pa. That was Mr Dignam, my father. (251)

The litany of the day's wanderings even for the dispossessed son is a list of pubs and drinking stops. Stephen as Philip Sober accosts himself as Philip Drunk: "Mooney's en ville, Mooney's sur mer, the Moira, Larchet's, Holles street hospital, Burke's. Eh? I am watching you" (518). Philip Drunk offers the Dubliner's response: "Ah, bosh man. Go to hell! I paid my way" (518). The new woman-ly man, Bloom, sharing with Montesquieu's woman "a natural restraint," spends his time at the beginning of the *Nostos* of *Ulysses* trying to sober Stephen up. Earlier in the day, Dublin's drunks had put him on the defensive in ways he would rather have avoided. He encounters the drunken citizen in *Cyclops* and is fortunate enough to escape injury, receiving a little support from the abstemious east: "Christ was a jew like me" (342). The riled citizen giant, his aim skewed by drink, just misses recrucifying Bloom, bearer of light to the northern gentiles: "By Jesus, I'll crucify him so I will. Give us that biscuitbox here" (342).

Earlier in his *Wanderings*, Bloom had an idea for an unsolvable puzzle: "cross Dublin without passing a pub" (58). *Thom's Directory* for Dublin lists over four hundred licensed public houses within the city's limits. In *Finnegans Wake*, Joyce's Dublin Everyman, Earwicker, runs one of them in Chapelizod. And he falls into a stupor from having drunk the dregs of his customers' glasses. The plight of his nation is of such proportions that Joyce finds himself amused in his notesheets for *Ithaca* with another possibility: "If Earth got drunk!" (Herring, p. 483). One of Joyce's students at the Berlitz school in Trieste recorded a tirade against Dublin delivered by Joyce during lessons in English. Richard Ellmann repeats it.

Dubliners, strictly speaking, are my fellow-countrymen, but I don't care to speak of our "dear, dirty Dublin" as they do. Dubliners are the most hopeless, useless, and inconsistent race of charlatans I have ever come across, on the island or the continent. This is why the English Parliament is full of the greatest windbags in the world. The Dubliner passes his time gabbing and making the rounds in bars or taverns or cathouses, without ever getting 'fed up' with the double doses of whisky and Home Rule, and at night, when he can hold no more and is swollen up with poison like a toad, he staggers from the side-door and, guided by an instinctive desire for stability along the straight line of the houses, he goes slithering his backside against all walls and cor-

ners. He goes "arsing along" as we say in English. There's the
Dubliner for you.   (*JJ*, pp. 225-226)

The tempting home-rule sun that Bloom contemplates rising in
the northwest over the Bank of Ireland can neither rise nor set at
the bottom of a glass of Guinness. For Joyce to offer Bloom, the
eastern man of restraint, as an epic resource for his inebriated land
is at once a liberating dream and a latitudinal joke. But what
Ulysses will not presume on the level of naturalism, it activates on
the level of symbolic renewal. Montesquieu's observation that in
warm countries water rather than spirituous liquor "is there of
admirable use" provides one of the lost keys to Dublin's day. Water
is a comic and cosmic antidote to Ireland's northern hangover. Bloom
in *Ithaca* becomes the water-carrier for Dedalus, a hydrophobe born
under the sign of Aquarius whose last bath had "taken place
in the month of October" (673). For an island civilization, water
is its sustenance. The serpentine Liffey moves through Dublin to
Dublin Bay from its southern origin in county Wicklow. In the
directional scheme of the novel, Dublin Bay is the antithesis to death's
country, the Glasnevin cemetery. The waters look to the southeast,
to the place of origins. Only Dedalus, the hydrophobe, sees death
in water. On June 16, 1904, it rains, relieving the summer drought:
"Wanted for the country" (90), Mr. Power says of the rainfall.
Ithaca provides one of the most extraordinary passages of *Ulysses*
in a homage to water. It is no longer alcohol that is ironically the
"Elixir of life" (98) as it was in the death chapter of *Hades*, but
admirable water. The passage is one of those Joyce greatly expanded
from an earlier draft, and it merits full citation.

> What in water did Bloom, waterlover, drawer of water, water-
> carrier returning to the range, admire?
> Its universality: its democratic equality and constancy to its
> nature in seeking its own level: its vastness in the ocean of Mer-
> cator's projection: its unplumbed profundity in the Sundam
> trench of the Pacific exceeding 8,000 fathoms: the restlessness of
> its waves and surface particles visiting in turn all points of its
> seaboard: the independence of its units: the variability of states
> of sea: its hydrostatic quiescence in calm: its hydrokinetic turgid-
> ity in neap and spring tides: its subsidence after devastation: its
> sterility in the circumpolar icecaps, arctic and antarctic: its climatic
> and commercial significance: its preponderance of 3 to 1 over the

dry land of the globe: its indisputable hegemony extending in square leagues over all the region below the subequatorial tropic of Capricorn: the multisecular stability of its primeval basin: its luteofulvous bed: its capacity to dissolve and hold in solution all soluble substances including millions of tons of the most precious metals: its slow erosions of peninsulas and downwardtending promontories: its alluvial deposits: its weight and volume and density: its imperturbability in lagoons and highland tarns: its gradation of colours in the torrid and temperate and frigid zones: its vehicular ramifications in continental lakecontained streams and confluent ocean flowing rivers with their tributaries and transoceanic currents: gulfstream, north and south equatorial courses: its violence in seaquakes, waterspouts, artesian wells, eruptions, torrents, eddies, freshets, spates, groundswells, watersheds, waterpartings, geysers, cataracts, whirlpools, maelstroms, inundations, deluges, cloudbursts: its vast circumterrestrial ahorizontal curve: its secrecy in springs, and latent humidity, revealed by rhabdomantic or hygrometric instruments and exemplified by the hole in the wall at Ashtown gate, saturation of air, distillation of dew: the simplicity of its composition, two constituent parts of hydrogen with one constituent part of oxygen: its healing virtues: its buoyancy in the waters of the Dead Sea: its persevering penetrativeness in runnels, gullies, inadequate dams, leaks on shipboard: its properties for cleansing, quenching thirst and fire, nourishing vegetation: its infallibility as paradigm and paragon: its metamorphoses as vapour, mist, cloud, rain, sleet, snow, hail: its strength in rigid hydrants: its variety of forms in loughs and bays and gulfs and bights and guts and lagoons and atolls and archipelagos and sounds and fjords and minches and tidal estuaries and arms of sea: its solidity in glaciers, icebergs, icefloes: its docility in working hydraulic millwheels, turbines, dynamos, electric power stations, bleachworks, tanneries, scutchmills: its utility in canals, rivers, if navigable, floating and graving docks: its potentiality derivable from harnessed tides or watercourses falling from level to level: its submarine fauna and flora (anacoustic, photophobe) numerically, if not literally, the inhabitants of the globe: its ubiquity as constituting 90% of the human body: the noxiousness of its effluvia in lacustrine marshes, pestilential fens, faded flowerwater, stagnant pools in the waning moon.

(671-672)

Water is the fully migrated hero in an expanded Mediterranean world, and certainly a material hero of *Ulysses*. It seeks its own level, from Odysseus to Bloom. It reveals the secrets of Proteus in serving life and art. It is sterile at the poles and abundant in the tropics, conforming to the climatic axis of warmth and cold. It nourishes and renews. It is paradigmatic and it reincarnates. All Dublin's water flows from the south, from "Roundwood reservoir in county Wicklow" (671). The day of *Ulysses* begins with the water of the bay, snotgreen as Mulligan calls it, and, for mockers, "a bowl of bitter waters." But the novel ends with the "deepdown torrent" and the crimson sea of Gibraltar. Calypso of Gibraltar's Straits lives on an island, Ogygia, whose name means, among other things, ocean. Victor Bérard traces the etymology to the "grand fleuve qui d'un cours ininterrompu entoure la masse terrestre: c'est l'Océan homérique" (the great river that in an uninterrupted course belts the entire earth: it is the Homeric ocean) [Bérard, 1, 292]. Water is both the source and the final shaping form. In *Ulysses*, Molly of Eccles street ends her own drought for the day. If the forecast is ambiguous, the climate is ripe.

THE EPIC'S NOVEL GEOGRAPHY
HOMER, JOYCE, DEFOE

EPIC AND FICTIONAL DOMAIN: MISSIONS AND OBSTACLES

WHEN an epic teaches a culture or people a version of its own history, it tests the *ethos* of the forming events it records. But the epic imagination, partly because it so often extends its scope to the very borders of a nation's territory, finds itself ranging spaces where an *ethos* is either severely challenged or broken down. Border and boundary narratives deal with the risk of territorial disorientation. One of the reasons that the Homeric *Odyssey* is a "novelist's" epic above all others is that it not only defines its local nature by defining its extended hero, but also positions its hero as an adversary at home. Nearly half the poem is set in Ithaca, its hero-king disguised as a beggar. For the most part, alien citizens, the suitors, run the home front. They virtually control the hero's domain, defining its *ethos*, its use and misuse. Odysseus is placed in what for him, as a man, is a precarious situation. If he were not almost mythically endowed as king, and if he had not the assistance of a goddess, he would be but a victim on his native ground.

Joyce may reposition the *Odyssey* in Dublin, but his hero is not a king, has not the assistance of a goddess, and is not mythically endowed. Epic resolution in *Ulysses* is more a hope than a promise, and Joyce emphasizes the local contingencies of the day before the full resolution of his novel's plot. Samuel Butler's curious reading of Homer in *The Authoress of the Odyssey* is comparable to *Ulysses* in this respect. With a set of Homeric theories resembling those of Stephen Dedalus' on Shakespeare, Butler combines a few narrative facts, many local and topographical details, and a great deal of raw wit to place the authoress of the *Odyssey*, the young Nausicaa, in a small town on the west coast of Sicily.[1] That which occurs in the poem is an elaboration of local fears and aspirations. Butler's is an important work for Joyce because its strategies treat the Homeric epic *as if it were a novel*. The poem works out the experiences of a young woman confined near her home. Whether Butler actually

[1] See Hugh Kenner's "Homer's Sticks and Stones," *JJQ* 6 (1969), 285-298.

believes his theory or not is unimportant. What matters is the fictional material out of which Butler builds his reconstruction.

No artist can reach an ideal higher than his own best actual environment. Trying to materially improve upon that which he or she is fairly familiar invariably ends in failure. It is only adjunct that may be arranged and varied, the essence may be taken or left, but it must not be bettered.[2]

Commenting on the locale to which his brother's ranging narrative imagination always returned, Stanislaus Joyce remarks on Joyce's allegiance to his home territory.

The dominant passions of my brother's life were to be love of father and of fatherland. The latter was not the love of a patriot, which is an emotion for the market-place, part hatred of some other country, part falsehood. It was the comprehending love of an artist for his subject.[3]

Stanislaus' observation, if a little blurred in its fervor, is clear in its implications. Joyce's fascination with Ireland was a fascination both for its local detail, and for its artistic epic potential. The patrimonial voices of Dublin range from Simon Dedalus' songs in *Ulysses* to a shout in the city streets. These are voices that echo and bounce off the stuff of Dublin's world—pubs, monuments, bridges, houses, shelters for the night—echo beyond Dublin Bay to the Straits of Gibraltar, to the Milesian Euxine, to the Greek Mediterranean. *Ulysses* is an expanding human document, but it begins in closed spaces.

When Samuel Butler adjusts the plot of the *Odyssey*, he does much the same thing: he closes its spaces. If things occur as they do, it is because an idiosyncratic personality behind the larger narrative movements in the poem fits the *Wanderings* into a reduced grid. Butler's book is both serious and sophistic; serious in that it provides an artist's rationale for the scope and subject matter of an Homeric original, and sophistic in that Butler has his foils to help him, just as Stephen has Russell, Best, and Eglinton for his Shakespearean reconstruction. When a friend argues that Butler's thesis is ridiculous because a woman author would never have included the

<hr>

[2] Samuel Butler, *The Authoress of the Odyssey* (Chicago, rept. 1922 ed., 1967), p. 208.

[3] Stanislaus Joyce, *My Brother's Keeper* (New York, 1958), p. 238.

carnage scene in the palace at Ithaca, Butler replies that the scene is, in fact, directed to a more appropriate climax. A woman would want the floors cleaned of bloodstains, and "Lo and behold, this is exactly what Odysseus does."

Joyce at twelve read the *Odyssey* in Charles Lamb's prose version and was pleased with its mysticism.[4] Butler's version of the poem, ultimately more important for the mature Joyce, reduces the mystic and mythic proportions of the *Odyssey* and increases the motivational, psychological, naturalistic bases of its design. Where the traditional Homeric poet might look at the gift-giving rituals in the poem and see them as part of the myth of cultural substance, Butler sees a parody of accumulation from the ironic viewpoint of a stay-at-home youngster with only her imagination as her wealth. Athena induces a dream that encourages Telemachus to come home immediately from Sparta. Penelope is about to declare on marriage.

> Telemachus does indeed wake up (xv. 43) in great distress, but it is about his property, not his mother. "Who steals my mother steals trash, but whoso filches from me my family heirlooms" etc. He kicks poor Pisistratus to wake him, and says they must harness the horses and be off home at once. Pisistratus rejoins that it is pitch dark; come what may they must really wait till morning. . . . Besides, they ought to say good bye to Menelaus and get a present out of him; he will be sure to give them one, if Telemachus will not be in such an unreasonable hurry.[5]

This is witty, but Butler takes both the narrative and transcendent qualities out of the episode. Joyce will do the same with his somewhat questionable young hero, Dedalus. Stephen calls his mother a ghoul when she appears to him in a hallucination in *Circe*. Telemachus in the *Odyssey* is also returning from a search for a father to a northwest island, where he will find one. This, too, is something of a problem in Dublin's gloom, where the dead (or drunken) do not easily awake, and where, to paraphrase Butler on the Odyssean suitors, the Dublin citizenry include a mixture of imperfect lovers and perfect spongers.

The beginnings of the *Odyssey* and of *Ulysses* suggest something of the important differences between the approaches to narrative

---

[4] See W. B. Stanford, "The Mysticism that Pleased Him," *Envoi*, v (1951), 62-69.

[5] Butler, *Authoress of the Odyssey, op. cit.*, pp. 134-135.

domain. Homer's *Telemachiad* opens out; Joyce's closes in. Telemachus leaves his city; Dedalus enters into its labyrinth. Not knowing if his father is alive, Telamachus voyages to the Peloponnese for news of Odysseus. In a way, he tries to bring a ghost back from the dead, to revitalize the king. When he reaches the court of Nestor at Pylos, he is recognized as resembling Odysseus, and he begins to sense his connection to origins—in effect, he is lent substance. All who disbelieve in the potential return of Odysseus disbelieve in the process of remythification, the turn away from darkness (*zophos*) so necessary in the poem. Telemachus travels even farther toward origins (across the Peloponnese) to learn from Menelaus what Menelaus learned from Proteus: Odysseus is alive at the world's end just *before* the regions of death in the west. Proteus, who has the gift of prophetic sight, reports that Odysseus is Calypso's captive. The suitors, rooted on Ithaca, all think as does Melanthios, the disloyal goatherd, that "Odysseus died at sea; no coming home for him" (Book XVII, Fitzgerald, p. 318). In the *Odyssey*, spatial limitations are prophetic limitations. Those who deny a certain kind of spatial range mock the very idea of homecoming—symbolically, a rebirth. Odysseus, as the nurse Euyklia says in the famous scar episode, is mocked in his land as he was mocked by circumstance far away from it. Mockery in the *Odyssey* is the ultimate incivility, the last word in disbelief. Telemachus' east-west journey allows for his initiation and return. The suitors who stay in one place are those for whom death is a real end, as we will learn in the last book of the *Odyssey* when the suitors end up where they thought Odysseus had been—at the wastes of Asphodel "beyond" the edge of the world.

In *Ulysses*, mockery and disbelief are as dangerous to the idea of epic (or artistic) *Nostos* as they were in the *Odyssey*. But Joyce complicates the process by making his characters ignorant of the parallel plot and places that the novel they are in depicts. For Joyce, everyone literally stays in one place, and this affects the nature of his characters' commitment to action. The connection between mission (movement) and belief is intentionally ambiguous. Joyce's parody of the Odyssean situation does not so much undercut the *Odyssey* as contract its range and slow its narrative pulse. In *Telemachus* Haines asks Dedalus if he is a believer, "I mean, a believer in the narrow sense of the word. Creation from nothing and miracles and a personal God" (19). Stephen tells him, "There's only one sense of the word" (19). Belief puts a strain on Dedalus. He calls himself an example of "free thought" (20), and although the phrase means an atheist, the words themselves are equivocal. Free thought has a range that atheism does not. Similarly, Dedalus does not know whether to believe or disbelieve his own ghost-theory of *Hamlet* and Shakespeare: "I believe, O Lord, help my unbelief. That is, help me to believe or help me to unbelieve?" (214). This is a crucially unmade decision that affects the action of the day and also affects Stephen's later meeting with the paternally inclined Bloom. In the *Odyssey* Telemachus has the decision made for him—in Dublin there is no Menelaus to tell Proteus' story, no Egyptian prophet to define the extension and the return.

Joyce does not, however, spare us the *Odyssey*'s mockery, and here, too, Stephen is implicated more than exonerated. Mulligan, like Antinous the suitor and Claudius the king, offends against the living as much as against the dead. He plays the satirist priest officiating at the Martello mass in the opening pages of the novel. Stanislaus Joyce argued with his brother that the mass was a meager revival of cannibalistic practice, but he explains James's more artistic (and paranoid) reaction to the mass "as the drama of a man who has a perilous mission to fulfil, which he must fulfil even though he knows beforehand that those nearest to his heart will betray him."[6] The mass is a drama of mythic reinvigoration, even artistic reinvigoration, and its mockers are no better than the usurpers and betrayers of the *Odyssey* or *Hamlet*. Mulligan sees only white corpuscles in the consecrated host, just as he sees in Dedalus' Irish art its new color: "snotgreen." The Irish Buck even kills the king and gets drunk at the renewing coronation: "*O, won't we have a merry time / Drinking whisky, beer and wine, / On coronation, / Coronation day?*" (11). For Mulligan the king's two bodies are what they are for all usurpers: dead ones. And when Mulligan refers to the death of Stephen's mother as "a beastly thing and nothing else" (8), all Dedalus can do in Dublin is take personal offense.

The closed spaces of *Ulysses* emphasize the shift in scope from an epic of resolved *Wanderings* to a novel of urban dilemma.[7] Although the sterility of Bloom's life at 7 Eccles street draws him to Stephen Dedalus for reasons that we can understand more fully than Bloom or Stephen, we must also recognize that the man who

[6] Stanislaus Joyce, *My Brother's Keeper, op. cit.*, p. 105.

[7] Perhaps the best book still on this aspect of *Ulysses* is S. L. Goldberg's *The Classical Temper: A Study of James Joyce's Ulysses* (London, 1961).

presumably brings the day its epic renewal is a suspicious and foreign soul in Dublin. As much as Odysseus, Bloom is a stranger in his land, only in his case he has never left it. The tension in the *Odyssey* builds in the strategic motions of its *Nostos* and resolution, but as the day of *Ulysses* draws on, Joyce's reader begins to suspect the novel's homecoming. In the epic, return validates wandering. In *Ulysses,* Dublin's *Nostos* depicts the real and metaphoric parting of the ways in *Ithaca.* If the design of the *Odyssey* brings a father and son together from the ends of a Mediterranean world, the design of *Ulysses* immobilizes a Semite in a city where even potential "sons" do not grasp the range of the day. The catechismic voice asks of Stephen and Bloom:

> In what common study did their mutual reflections merge?
> The increasing simplification traceable from the Egyptian epi-graphic hieroglyphs to the Greek and Roman alphabets and the anticipation of modern stenography and telegraphic code in the cuneiform inscriptions (Semitic) and the virgular quinquecostate ogham writing (Celtic).
>
> Did the guest comply with his host's request?
> Doubly, by appending his signature in Irish and Roman char-acters.
>
> What was Stephen's auditive sensation?
> He heard in a profound ancient male unfamiliar melody the accumulation of the past.
>
> What was Bloom's visual sensation?
> He saw in a quick young male familiar form the predestination of a future. (689)

Dublin's range allows for the epic convergence of Hebraic, Greek, Roman, and Irish cultures, but *Ithaca* also insists on the novelistic divergence of individual natures. There is something so different about the unfamiliar Jew of Eccles street for Stephen Dedalus that he cannot remain under his roof for one night of shelter. Many of the novel's commentators worry needlessly about the exigency of Stephen's departure. Disregarding for a moment the biographical explanation for his leaving (Joyce as young artist on the lapwing axis to productive exile), we can look to Dublin to see some of the counter-epic pressures on Dedalus and Bloom. These pressures not only reveal fissures in the Odyssean plot, but limit the epic expectations of the day. On the strand in *Proteus*, Dedalus remembers his prophetic dream of the evening before. His memory is a bit murkier than Proteus' revelation to Menelaus of the living Odysseus, but the dream still images an exiled king, an eastern savior for Dublin's Nighttown.

> After he woke me up last night same dream or was it? Wait. Open hallway. Street of harlots. Remember. Haroun al Raschid. I am almosting it. That man led me, spoke. I was not afraid. The melon he had he held against my face. Smiled: creamfruit smell. That was the rule, said. In. Come. Red carpet spread. You will see who. (47)

In *Scylla and Charybdis* Bloom himself appears as the eastern caliph, more Greek than the Greeks, hence the Semitic wanderer. Mulligan warns Dedalus about the dark-backed Jew's seeming perversity. Any warning coming from Mulligan is, by its nature, mockery, but in *Cyclops* even Bloom's one friend of the day, Martin Cunningham, contributes to the ambiguity of this very issue. He calls the Irishman, Bloom, a "perverted jew" (337), meaning a Jew turned away from his culture and religion. "Perverted," however, cannot help but carry with it a more sinister suggestion. Before warning Stephen, Mulligan had seen Bloom under suspicious circumstances in the Kildare street Museum examining Aphrodite's posterior: "His Pale Galilean eyes were upon her mesial groove. Venus Kallipyge. O, the thunder of those loins! *The god pursuing the maiden hid*" (201). Stephen remembers his dream later in the same episode.

> Here I watched the birds for augury. Ængus of the birds. They go, they come. Last night I flew. Easily flew. Men wondered. Street of harlots after. A creamfruit melon he held to me. In. You will see.
> —The wandering jew, Buck Mulligan whispered with clown's awe. Did you see his eye? He looked upon you to lust after you. I fear thee, ancient mariner. O, Kinch, thou art in peril. Get thee a breechpad. (217)

When Dedalus finally does meet Bloom, and, later, when he is sober enough to understand what is happening, the result is predictable. In *Eumaeus* the unwashed, asexual aesthete is shaky at the prospect of Bloom's foreign and eastern touch.

Accordingly he passed his left arm in Stephen's right and led him on accordingly.

—Yes, Stephen said uncertainly, because he thought he felt a strange kind of flesh of a different man approach him, sinewless and wobbly and all that. (660)

After admitting in *Eumaeus* to Lord John Corley that he has "no place to sleep myself" (617), Dedalus at Bloom's home in *Ithaca* "Promptly, inexplicably, with amicability, gratefully" (695) declines the offer of at least one night's rest from urban trials. But if his departure is odd, so is his presence. Joyce's *Nostos* is imperfect. For instance, why, in the home of a man he knows to be a Jew, would Dedalus chant a ballad of Jewish ritual murder (690-691)? Even if Stephen's ballad is accidentally, not designedly, offensive, he is always part mocker in Dublin. What he had no way of knowing was that Bloom's thoughts had turned to Jewish ritual murder in *Hades*' death chapter. A medieval tradition holds that Jews sought victims because they needed blood for the seder meal. Bloom enlivens the formula: "It's the blood sinking in the earth gives new life. Same idea those jews they said killed the christian boy" (108). Dedalus, "the christian boy," sees no sustenance in any Dublin locale. He shakes Bloom's strange eastern hand once again, and upon leaving he hears in the chimes of St. George's the echo of the prayer for the dead. And that is the way Joyce ends the day for Dedalus—still between death and rebirth, himself mocked by the tolling of the hour. Dedalus steps out into the gloom, and Bloom still does not know what part of his racial and epic heritage belongs to him in his city. Only the mythic voice in *Ithaca*, a narrator's voice, will re-establish the axis that leads back to *Penelope* and the wider Mediterranean homecoming.

PARODIC SPACES: DUBLIN

Samuel Beckett saw life itself as but a figure and a ground. Narrative, by implication, is a problem of dimension. In *Ulysses* Joyce does not have Homer's spaces at his disposal, but he has an angle of vision on Homer's plot that can open up another kind of narrative space—a comic overlap. The *Odyssey* is so designed that it informs its participants at the end how sequences of events circle around to epic destiny. *Ulysses* is so designed that its participants never learn very much about the plot they are in. Bloom, the comic hero, occa-

sionally senses something about the day's destiny. When he hands
Bantom Lyons the morning paper, mentioning, out of politeness,
that he was about to throw it away, Lyons takes this as a cryptic
reference to *Throwaway*, the eventual long-shot winner of that
afternoon's Goldcup horse race. A horse that had not "an earthly"
chance wins. Bloom is the prophet of a ghost who returned a handsome profit at the payoff window. But in Dublin's confused world
the prophetic touch, "the secret of the race, graven in the language
of prediction" (676), gets Bloom, himself a Dublin throwaway, in
trouble. The louts at Barney Kiernan's think he has won money
on the race and is too cheap to go a round of drinks. Later Bloom
ponders the phenomenon of prediction and fulfillment. It unsettles
him at first.

What qualifying considerations allayed his perturbations?
The difficulties of interpretation since the significance of any
event followed its occurrence as variably as the acoustic report followed the electrical discharge and of counterestimating against an
actual loss by failure to interpret the total sum of all possible losses
proceeding originally from a successful interpretation.   (676)

In *Ithaca*, where this passage occurs, we are fully immersed in the
novel's precarious vision. Especially in its forms that surprise epic
expectations, the comic novel has, traditionally, broken the letter, if
not the spirit, of what Georg Lukács would call the laws of epic
immanence. From Defoe through Sterne and Dickens to Joyce, the
novel's world sets dilemmas as obstacles to certainties. Fictional characters stumble through a treacherous terrain, an urban "chaosmos,"
as Joyce calls it in *Finnegans Wake*. Joyce is well aware of the disjunction between the destiny of the Odyssean plot and the fabric of
accidents that make up the realistic world of his fiction. In *Oxen of
the Sun*, we hear the skeptic's Victorian voice pose the questions for
which there are no answers.

. . . both natality and mortality, as well as all other phenomena
of evolution, tidal movements, lunar phases, blood temperatures,
diseases in general, everything, in fine, in nature's vast workshop
from the extinction of some remote sun to the blossoming of one
of the countless flowers which beautify our public parks, is subject
to a law of numeration as yet unascertained.   (419)

In *Ulysses*, events arising from peculiar and unpredictable circumstances counter the normative structures of epic narrative. Departure is not necessarily the first step in the direction of arrival, and return is not a guarantee of renewal. Movement on a spatial grid may well replicate the epic path of cyclic return, but the action of the day also takes its almost pathological urban plunge. If Bloom should lose all his money, what lay in store for him?

> Reduce Bloom by cross multiplication of reverses of fortune, from which these supports protected him, and by elimination of all positive values to a negligible negative irrational unreal quantity.
>
> Successively, in descending helotic order: Poverty: that of the outdoor hawker of imitation jewellery, the dun for the recovery of bad and doubtful debts, the poor rate and deputy cess collector. Mendicancy: that of the fraudulent bankrupt with negligible assets paying 1s. 4d. in the £, sandwichman, distributor of throwaways, nocturnal vagrant, insinuating sycophant, maimed sailor, blind stripling, superannuated bailiff's man, marfeast, lickplate, spoilsport, pickthank, eccentric public laughingstock seated on bench of public park under discarded perforated umbrella. Destitution: the inmate of Old Man's House (Royal Hospital), Kilmainham, the inmate of Simpson's Hospital for reduced but respectable men permanently disabled by gout or want of sight. Nadir of misery: the aged impotent disfranchised ratesupported moribund lunatic pauper. (725)

This is the social equivalent of the novel's parodic fall from the realm of the epic—its "Law of falling bodies: per second, per second. They all fall to the ground" (72). The catalogue of Bloom's woebegone potential fate is funny in spite of itself. At every turn, good to bad and bad to worse, *Ithaca* offers a commentary on the descent from myth to an almost atomistic realism, from the expanded to the contracted world.[8] Bloom is asked by the questioner about the perfectibility of human life. The question comes after it is explained that Bloom had once marked a florin for its own odyssey "on the

---

[8] A. Walton Litz writes of *Ithaca*: "If *Ulysses* is a crucial testing ground for theories of the novel, as it seems to have become, then the 'Ithaca' episode must be a *locus classicus* for every critic interested in the traditions of English and European fiction" ("Ithaca," in Hart and Hayman, p. 385).

waters of civic finance" (696) hoping that it would return to him. This is Dublin, not Ithaca. The florin did not return.

Why would a recurrent frustration the more depress him?

Because at the critical turningpoint of human existence he desired to amend many social conditions, the product of inequality and avarice and international animosity.

He believed then that human life was infinitely perfectible, eliminating these conditions?

There remained the generic conditions imposed by natural, as distinct from human law, as integral parts of the human whole: the necessity of destruction to procure alimentary sustenance: the painful character of the ultimate functions of separate existence, the agonies of birth and death: the monotonous menstruation of simian and (particularly) human females extending from the age of puberty to the menopause: inevitable accidents at sea, in mines and factories: certain very painful maladies and their resultant surgical operations, innate lunacy and congenital criminality, decimating epidemics: catastrophic cataclysms which make terror the basis of human mentality: seismic upheavals the epicentres of which are located in densely populated regions: the fact of vital growth, through convulsions of metamorphosis from infancy through maturity to decay.

Why did he desist from speculation?

Because it was a task for a superior intelligence to substitute other more acceptable phenomena in place of the less acceptable phenomena to be removed.   (696-697)

When terror is made the basis of human mentality, we cannot count on epic paradigms to see us through. The conditions Joyce refers to here are "generic conditions" in more than one sense of the phrase. Only an artist, as a "superior intelligence," can introduce "more acceptable phenomena" into the world in which his characters move. For Dedalus, Bloom, and Molly, Dublin remains the haunt of the urban-conditioned victim. During the day Bloom wanders the streets because, short of direct confrontation with Molly about her plans for the afternoon, he has little choice. "Make hay while the sun shines," he tells himself as he begins his day hurrying out of Dlugacz the butcher's to catch a glimpse of a servant girl's "moving hams" (59). What hay he makes will be far from local fields because, as *Finnegans Wake* tells us, there is none at home: "Ninny, there is no hay in Eccles's hostel" (*FW*, 514).

Samuel Beckett calls the modern city world of the novel that "howling fiasco" of material pursuits. Odysseus circles widely, sometimes to return to where he had been before, but Bloom, in a much shorter span of time, consistently returns to where he has just been, consistently stumbles into the same snares that have trapped him before. The city is redundant in its buffetings. *Wandering Rocks*, the most methodically urban episode of the novel, is described by Joyce as labyrinthine. Bloom calls the night version of the city, *Circe*, a "chapter of accidents." The parodic voice of *Ulysses* is the urban voice of Dublin: loud, insistent, hyperbolic, and depersonalized. As the city takes over the characters recede. The first manifestation of the city voice are the headlines in *Aeolus*, a late addition on Joyce's part, which, as the text now stands, hint at the full-blown newspaper parodies of *Cyclops*. *Aeolus* is set at the center of Dublin—it is the first chapter not filtered through the consciousness of Stephen or Bloom. It belongs to the city alone.[9] The first headline reads: "IN THE HEART OF THE HIBERNIAN METROPOLIS" (116). Newspapers record Dublin's image as the city would like to see itself, not as Joyce sees it. We get more than the comic world of a novel pretending to be an epic—we get the parodic world of a sad city trying to be a great city. Joyce knows precisely where to go when he wants obstacles to the fulfillment of epic form. He goes to the streets.

Dublin is all plot and no resolution. Its meaning is in its slogans: *"What is home without / Plumtree's Potted Meat? / Incomplete"* (75). Any city, ancient or modern, ought to represent a *fait accompli* of civilization, a battle well waged and well won within the limitations of an environment. But in *Ulysses* the rewards of urbanity are suppressed by windbags and drunks. The city chokes on its own sewer gas. Its urban biology circulates trams that stop in the middle of nowhere and newscopy that has nothing to say. Its spaces are filled with pubs and the seedy streets of the Liberties or Nighttown. At one point in *Circe*, Dedalus alters the old romance formula, *thou art in perilous ways*, with the appropriate Dublin pun: "Steve, thou art in a parlous way" (517). Dublin articulates only hopeless

[9] See Michael Groden, *The Growth of James Joyce's Ulysses* (Ph.D. Dissertation, Princeton, 1975), *passim*, for the development of the parodic style in the composition of *Ulysses*.

palaver. Like the talented waif in Dickens' *Our Mutual Friend* who can do the police in different voices, the parodic voices of *Ulysses* do the punning "polis in plain clothes" (442). The loudest city chapter is set in Kiernan's pub, northwest, filled with retired or semi-retired men of Irish brawn, ex-members of the DMP.

In the apocryphal episode of the day, *Wandering Rocks*, the prophetic voice of narrative is reduced to cityscape emblems of the day's varying significance. Cashel Boyle O'Connor Fitzmaurice Tisdall Farrell, who not only walks on the outside of lampposts in the street, but has been wandering in aimless circles south of Merrion square, stares at a poster bearing the name of Elijah, messenger of the Old Testament, and mutters with rats' teeth, "*Coactus volui*" (250). After buffeting the "thewless body" of the blind stripling, Tisdall Farrell is himself cursed by another prophet, blind and Tiresian: "God's curse on you, he said sourly, whoever you are! You're blinder nor I am, you bitch's bastard!" (250). Dublin's parody, the city's crazy Endymion, meets the prophets. He curses the light, is cursed by the dark, and continues to walk in circles.

Ulysses is filled with a brood of mockers who do not know where they are going, and cannot see through to what they are doing. The city robs its citizens of their very souls in Bloom's urban version of metempsychosis.

> Cityful passing away, other cityful coming, passing away too: other coming on, passing on. Houses, lines of houses, streets, miles of pavements, piledup bricks, stones. Changing hands. This owner, that. Landlord never dies they say. Other steps into his shoes when he gets his notice to quit. They buy the place up with gold and still they have all the gold. Swindle in it somewhere. Piled up in cities, worn away age after age. Pyramids in sand. Built on bread and onions. Slaves. Chinese wall. Babylon. Big stones left. Round towers. Rest rubble, sprawling suburbs, jerry-built, Kerwan's mushroom houses, built of breeze. Shelter for the night.
>
> No one is anything. (164)

In *Circe*—Dublin's Nighttown—the novel reincarnates its urban scene yet again. The citizenry is unsteady, unsure, suffering, as the whore Zoe says, from locomotor ataxy. Early in the episode, an unseemly night wanderer, a deaf mute with Saint Vitus' dance, walks by, mocked by a gaggle of children. Pathology is a dance of death, and all ceremony becomes mockery. *Circe* is taken out of Homeric order in *Ulysses*, and occurs just before the *Nostos* proper. Joyce wants the night city, the Nighttown scene, as a capstone to the wandering day. Bloom, exhausted, is almost run down by a monstrous sand-strewer on the tram tracks: "Hey, shitbreeches, are you doing the hattrick?" (435). In this chapter of no accounts and lost balances, Bella Cohen taunts Bloom: "I'll make you remember me for the balance of your natural life" (532). Every dream in these spaces has a worse nightmare—every up a worse down. "All Ireland versus one!" (543). Only Bloom's exertion of reserve energy turns epic destiny into *Circe*'s "Kismet," and only the novelist's last-minute imposition of "more acceptable phenomena" allows for the homeward path of the urban ellipsis, the return of Irish wild geese (or exiles).

BLOOM

Wildgoose chase this. Disorderly houses. Lord knows where they are gone. Drunks cover distance double quick. Nice mixup. Scene at Westland row. Then jump in first class with third ticket. Then too far. Train with engine behind. Might have taken me to Malahide or a siding for the night or collision. Second drink does it. Once is a dose. What am I following him for? Still, he's the best of that lot. If I hadn't heard about Mrs Beaufoy Purefoy I wouldn't have gone and wouldn't have met. Kismet. . . . (452)

Poor Robinson Crusoe: Defoe

In addition to his lecture on William Blake, Joyce lectured on Defoe in Trieste, 1912: *idealismo* and *verismo*, as Joyce titled the series. Defoe is a novelist, although even today some of his books, pure fabrications, are catalogued in libraries as journals, memoirs, and biographies. Frank Budgen has written: "Joyce was a great admirer of Defoe. He possessed his complete works, and had read every line of them" (Budgen, p. 181). Budgen must mean his major works, because Defoe's canon contains over five hundred separate titles. Defoe was a prodigious writer on politics, political theory, religion, casuistry, history, economics, travel, and trade; but Joyce admired him for his mastery of the compacted form of the narrative journal, the fiction of material fact.

Continental and French fiction of the seventeenth century tries to accommodate the world of romance in the closed spaces of the salons of the *savantes*. The result is what the English call "novel." In England itself, an insular civilization, what we now call the novel was first called "Lives and Adventures," "Memoirs," "True Journals," and the like. Fiction has its bedrock in an adaptation, and in many cases a parody, of historical and biographical forms. One of the more popular of these is the shipboard journey to remote lands across the seas. In his expanded study of Homeric geography, *Les Navigations d'Ulysse*, Victor Bérard includes a sub-section on Defoe's *Robinson Crusoe*. He does so in a long chapter on Calypso and the Atlantic Ocean because he sees the Crusoe legend as a western extension of the *Odyssey* beyond the Mediterranean. For Bérard, Spain, or *Ispania*, means island of hidden treasure. The Spanish myth of the city of gold, El Dorado, near the mouth of the Orinoco River, is but the translation of an old Phoenician treasure myth from the extension at Spain to the new world across the Atlantic to South America. Defoe takes Crusoe from the Straits of Gibraltar near *Ispania*, but the treasure that brings him to the Orinoco, quite by accident, is a modern treasure indeed: the slave trade from the African coast. As time passes, the world widens, and narrative readjusts different sets of values to different boundaries, different accidents to different ends.

Defoe could reach from the Orinoco to the wolf-infested forests of Spain to the back alleys of London, and transform space in accord with the texture of the English merchant mind. In his Trieste lecture Joyce makes the same obvious connection Bérard would make in *Les Navigations*. Robinson Crusoe is the English Ulysses. This is not an idle observation for Joyce who had been gathering momentum for his own Irish *Ulysses*. Much later, in *Finnegans Wake*, Joyce works Crusoe into the mold of an eastern original, Semite to savior: "Rabbisohn Crucis." Crusoe is another westering hero, a commercial traveler wandering to the limits of the expanse that measures him. Defoe invents a fictional exile out of a scrap of new-world legend, the account of the Scotsman Selkirk's abandonment on the isle of Juan Fernandez. And in his novel Defoe deliberately moves Crusoe from the narrower circle of the Mediterranean, from North Africa, where he begins as a prisoner of the Moors, to the larger circle of the commercial trade world in the seventeenth century. The expanded domain of Calypso's ocean becomes the frame for Defoe's novel of material isolation. Characteristically, the novel closes up space before it opens it. Crusoe's island is not merely another adventure in wandering—it is another kind of homecoming. Defoe makes the remote as familiar as home when his man of property makes his island the domain of his reconstructed civilization.

Defoe is not a conscious myth-maker like Blake, but he can refashion substance out of that great icon of British civilization, the fact. For Defoe, and for writers in the tradition of post-Renaissance fiction, the material surrounding an individual defines his extended world. Behavior is linked to place and property. (Property and propriety even carry the same meaning through the earlier eighteenth century.) Robinson Crusoe's island becomes more and more real to him as he designs a rudimentary material order, a system of measured priorities and relationships. After many years, Crusoe, the squire, even has his town and country estates. Near the end of his stay he proclaims himself king and practices his transformative powers—he is once again like other famous exiled kings in narrative, Homer's Odysseus or Shakespeare's Prospero. Defoe moves his hero from a twenty-eight year factual exile back to a tradition-long image of the island king.

Joyce speaks in his lecture of the substantiating qualities in Defoe's narratives that encourage the layering of local strata whether or not the fiction ever achieves mythic status. He compares Defoe's fabrications to the placeless, timeless lyrical surge in Joyce's own time that appears as "the emotional revolt of modern man against human or superhuman inequity." These are large, even heroic, themes, but Joyce turns back to works such as Defoe's *Journal of the Plague Year*, and it is obvious what Defoe offers him that his own contemporaries do not.

> In Defoe there is nothing of the kind: neither lyricism nor art for art's sake nor social consciousness. The saddler walks through the deserted street, listens to the cries of anguish, keeps his distance from the sick, reads the orders of the Lord Mayor, chats with the sextons, who chew garlic and rue, discusses matters with a waterman at Blackwall, faithfully compiles his statistics, takes an interest in the price of bread, complains of the watchmen,

walks up to the top of the hill above Greenwich and estimates how many people have taken refuge on the ships anchored in the Thames.[10]

Joyce sees in Defoe's citizens versions of Bloom in Dublin. Although Molly was unimpressed when Bloom gave her Defoe's appropriately titled *Moll Flanders*, Defoe and Joyce depict similar struggles in their urban narratives. They pit the city against its citizens, and observe as indignities begin to pile up. "*O, poor Robinson Crusoe, | How could you possibly do so?*" (109) goes the refrain in *Ulysses*, and the answer to that riddle is one of the answers to the novel's form for over two hundred years. Crusoe creates a semi-permanent home in exile. Citizens are bounded and limited by the worlds created around them. On his island Crusoe keeps a free man's journal—on his, Leopold Bloom works for a newspaper calling itself the *Freeman's Journal*.

The echoes of *Robinson Crusoe* in the Irish *Ulysses* are not extensive nor terribly profound, but they are clever. Crusoe and Bloom, like their creators, Defoe and Joyce, are great projectors. In the narrative design, Crusoe is another returned ghost like Odysseus, King Hamlet, Christ, Shakespeare, and Rip Van Winkle. Both literary sons, Robinson and Stephen Dedalus, leave their "father's house" to "seek misfortune" (619), as Stephen puts it in *Eumeaus*. The lying sailor of *Eumaeus*, Murphy, is something like Odysseus and Telemachus, sailing the seas "to fly in the face of providence" (630). This very decision is the major action and the major theological issue in Defoe's narrative. Crusoe flies in the face of his father's warning and leaves England by sea. Joyce enters a teasing note for *Eumaeus* in reference to Odysseus' irritation that Telemachus is not on Ithaca when he arrives: "didn't want son go to sea" (Herring, p. 403). Bloom's rambling observations on Murphy in *Eumaeus* are funny in themselves, and are also a wonderful commentary on the fate of the "true adventurer" in the comic urban novel. Murphy is a mock culture hero, an Irish navigator with the flexible features of a Greek tattooed on his chest. But he returns on the merchant ship "*Rosevean* from Bridgwater with bricks" (249). Defoe, of course, made his fortune by fabricating bricks at Tilbury. Bloom on Murphy:

[10] Joyce, "Robinson Crusoe," *Buffalo Studies*, 1 (1964), p. 17. Subsequent reference will include page numbers from this text.

Possibly he had tried to find out the secret for himself, floundering up and down the antipodes and all that sort of thing and over and under—well, not exactly under, tempting the fates. And the odds were twenty to nil there was really no secret about it at all. Nevertheless, without going into the minutiae of the business, the eloquent fact remained that the sea was there in all its glory and in the natural course of things somebody or other had to sail on it and fly in the face of providence though it merely went to show how people usually contrived to load that sort of onus on to the other fellow like the hell idea. . . . (630)

The middle-class citizen talks about the sea adventurer—the glory of the structure of *Robinson Crusoe* and the comic structure of *Ulysses* is that the middle-class citizen *is* the sea adventurer. Crusoe is also the trader, the grower, the builder, the projector who, through an accident, enters a world of remote exile, a world usually reserved for romance heroes. He is neither the actual exile, Selkirk, upon whom he was modeled, nor is he a seventeenth-century Odysseus merely because his exile expands the western wanderings of the hero beyond Calypso's border isle. But *Robinson Crusoe* reveals that the fabrication of "truth" is the novelist's authority to employ forms as old as epic or romance in the service of modern narrative. Similarly, in *Ulysses*, it is precisely the effectiveness of Bloom as an imitation of a real Dubliner in a real Dublin that allows the epic and romance trappings he wears some legitimacy. Joyce fills the gap between the "allround" citizen Bloom and the mythic renewer, Darkinbad the Brightdayler, with the stuff of local places and times. Bloom strains against as many roles as he fulfills, and he does so because he is *real* in the novel's terms. The most obvious reincarnations of Bloom for Bloom are the anagram spellings of that which belongs only to him, his citizen's name.

Leopold Bloom
Ellpodbomool
Molldopeloob
Bollopedoom
Old Ollebo, M. P. (678)

Bloom, like Crusoe, is to myth what the microscope is to the telescope. Joyce notes with some pleasure that in Defoe's *History of the Devil* even Milton's magnificent Satan falls into civic straits.

Defoe's devil has few things in common with the strange son
of Chaos who enters upon eternal war against the purposes of
the Supreme Being. He resembles rather a hose-factor who has
suffered a calamitous financial upset. Defoe puts himself in the
Devil's place with a realism which seems at first disconcerting.
He boldly quarrels with the conception of the majestic protagonist
of *Paradise Lost*. He wonders how many days it took the Devil
to fall from heaven into the abyss, how many spirits fell with
him, when he became aware of the creation of the world, how
he beguiled Eve, where he prefers to live, why and how he made
himself wings. This attitude in the presence of the supernatural,
which follows his literary principles as a logical corollary, is the
attitude of a sensible barbarian.   (Trieste Lecture, p. 18)

Joyce's vision of the Devil as hose factor in financial difficulties
is an allusion to Defoe's bankruptcy in 1692. Perhaps Joyce gets the
details wrong—it was civet cats, diving engines, and ship insur-
ance rather than hosiery—but no matter. Not only does myth turn
into material anxiety for Defoe, it builds from personal experience.
Defoe's serious literary career began with his *Essay Upon Projects*,
a work conceived and partly executed while he was in hiding from
his creditors, and a work designed to procure for his nation whatever
securities in a precarious world he felt had been denied to him.
Joyce could well understand the impulse. He designed such schemes
as the hawking of Irish tweeds on the continent while virtually
destitute in self-imposed exile. Joyce's vision of Shakespeare, on
whom he also lectured in 1912, is much the same. The artist in
exile weaves the myth of himself into the material fabric of his
land.[11] Shakespeare's Globe Theater is the equivalent of Defoe's
brick factory at Tilbury or Joyce's project for film theaters in Ireland. Personal trials work their way through regional exile to sustaining ventures. Exile for Homer's Odysseus is the result of mythic
dissonances in his, and in his nation's, character. Exile for Shakespeare in London after his flight from Stratford, for Defoe on the

[11] See William H. Quillian, "Shakespeare in Trieste: Joyce's 1912 *Hamlet*
Lectures," *JJQ*, 12 (Fall 1974/Winter 1975), 7-63. Joyce's notes for his lecture
series on Shakespeare and *Hamlet* indicate that he was as absorbed with
local detail as was Stephen Dedalus in the library episode of *Ulysses*. Quillian
writes that the Shakespeare lectures suggest that Joyce's "method was founded
firmly on the idea of 'verismo' as he defined it in the Defoe-Blake dichotomy"
(p. 15).

outskirts of London after his financial ruin, and for Joyce on the continent after his lapwing escape from Irish paralysis, is the result of a material dissonance in private lives. Shakespeare's late romances in Joyce's (and Stephen's) theory, Defoe's *Robinson Crusoe*, and *Ulysses* put strangers in strange lands, but from the Bermudas to the Orinoco to Dublin's gloom, space is as privately textured as it is geographically remote.

Joyce suggests at one point in his lecture that Defoe is often dull because he takes such pains with local detail. If so, he is dull for the same reason that Joyce is sometimes dull. Joyce's remarks on Defoe's *Storm* are grudgingly admiring. Like so many writers on other writers, Joyce says of Defoe what he probably thinks of himself: "The book succeeds in being, needless to say, phenomenally boring. The Modern reader does a good deal of groaning before he reaches the conclusion, but in the end the object of the chronicles has been achieved. By dint of repetitions, contradictions, details, figures, noises, the storm has come alive, the ruin is visible" (Trieste Lecture, p. 16).

Joyce writes of the domain of Defoe's fiction as that place where one finds the "strange solitary, Crusoe, and so many other solitaries lost in the great sea of social irony." The modern novel resides in Defoe "like the soul that slumbers in an imperfect and amorphous organism" (Trieste Lecture, p. 14). Defoe seeks a remote island for Crusoe to prove a local case. Two hundred years later, Joyce releases Leopold Bloom on a local island to substantiate what is left of a remote myth. Bloom is transformed as Crusoe transforms. The novel reproduces the material shape of its civilizations, be it in the texture of personalities and places or the signate form of a footprint in the sand. Joyce concludes his lecture on Defoe with high praise for *Crusoe*, high praise indeed from a novelist whose own work will contain an all-around citizen with the heroic instincts of the rational animal and a young artist who reads the signature of all things from markings on the beach, Sandymount strand, Dublin.

The story of the shipwrecked sailor who lived on the desert island for four years[12] reveals, as perhaps no other book throughout the long history of English literature does, the wary and heroic instinct of the rational animal and the prophecy of the empire. . . .

---

[12] Joyce here refers to Selkirk who was stranded for four years; Crusoe was exiled for twenty-eight.

The true symbol of the British conquest is Robinson Crusoe, who, cast away on a desert island, in his pocket a knife and a pipe, becomes an architect, a carpenter, a knifegrinder, an astronomer, a baker, a shipwright, a potter, a saddler, a farmer, a tailor, an umbrella-maker, and a clergyman. He is the true prototype of the British colonist, as Friday (the trusty savage who arrives on an unlucky day) is the symbol of the subject races. The whole Anglo-Saxon spirit is in Crusoe: the manly independence; the unconscious cruelty; the persistence; the slow yet efficient intelligence; the sexual apathy; the practical, well-balanced religiousness; the calculating taciturnity. Whoever rereads this simple, moving book in the light of subsequent history cannot help but fall under its prophetic spell.

Saint John the Evangelist saw on the island of Patmos the apocalyptic ruin of the universe and the building of the walls of the eternal city sparkling with beryl and emerald, with onyx and jasper, with sapphire and ruby. Crusoe saw only one marvel in all the fertile creation around him, the print of a naked foot in the virgin sand. And who knows if the latter is not more significant than the former? (Trieste Lecture, pp. 24-25)

THE MYTH OF PROTEUS

MASTERPLOTS AND MASTERBILKERS

An Oriental Tale of Origins and Ends:
Proteus, Thoth, Hermes

AFTER a brief indication in the beginning that the gods are about to free Odysseus from his space-bound trial on Calypso's western isle, the Homeric *Odyssey* moves east. The *Telemachiad* transfers its younger hero to the Peloponnese, first to Pylos and then to Menelaus' Sparta, where Telemachus is told an original tale, one of the oldest Egyptian tales, a tale of the Ancient of the Salt Sea, Proteus. The structure of Menelaus' adventure is a miniature *Odyssey*. He had wandered for seven years along Levantine coasts and in Levantine ports. Odysseus had wandered for ten years mainly in *couchant* waters. Victor Bérard is convinced that both accounts relate to Mediterranean geographical history, to *periploi* around the seven larger isles of the eastern seas and the ten isles of the greater western Mediterranean. That Odysseus takes seventeen days to return from Calypso's island to Scheria, near his home seas, indicates to Bérard that the Homeric poet has combined an eastern and a western odyssey into one major epic.

When his adventures come to an end Menelaus is literally bogged down in the Nile, rendered immobile. Odysseus, who began from the same place, Troy, experiences his first adventure at about the same latitude as Menelaus' last: off the Libyan coast but much further west in the land of the Lotuseaters. Odysseus' last adventure finds him bogged down on Calypso's Ogygia, he, too, rendered immobile. We therefore have two Greek heroes awaiting *Nostos*, one in the Nile Basin near the mythic source, the mythic point of entrance to the Egyptian Mediterranean, and the other at the Straits of Gibraltar, the mythic point of egress from the Mediterranean. When Proteus, once pinned down in the Nile Basin, relays to Menelaus the western whereabouts of Odysseus, we can see the *Odyssey*'s full geographical range. Eventually, both heroes engage in an elemental struggle merely to move toward home. Menelaus encounters the minor sea god, Proteus; Odysseus, as always, encounters the major god, Poseidon, the god of the world's greater oceans.

On Pharos Isle Menelaus succeeds in snaring Proteus into submission. After his capture, the sea god speaks of western extensions; he projects in time as well as space and tells Menelaus of his future life beyond the end of the world in the Elysian Fields. Menelaus returns home after overcoming Proteus. The situation for Odysseus is different; Poseidon is never really overcome, merely appeased. In this sense, the *Proteus* episode finds a more appropriate analogue in Odysseus' domination of Circe, another magus-goddess who controls elemental shapes. Circe, once mastered, directs Odysseus to Hades and instructs him on *Nostos*, just as Proteus takes Menelaus on a visionary tour of the afterworld.

For the *Odyssey*, the Proteus legend is paradigmatic in many ways. The land the episode covers and the time it takes are, according to Bérard, elements in an important migration myth. Bérard begins his treatment of Proteus by discussing the ancient transmissions of myths from Egypt to Greece. In the Egyptian versions of the Proteus legend, the possession of and control over matter is magical. Proteus derives his name from "certaines formules protocolaires," certain periphrastic references to the sacred magician-king on earth, the Pharaoh: "Il est le *Double-Palais: paroui-aoui.* . . . Il est *Sa Majesté* ou *Sa Sainteté, le Soleil des Deux Terres, l'Horus Maître du Pays.* Il est encore *la Sublime-Porte: Prouiti, Prouti*, disaient les Égyptiens" (He is *the Double-Palace, paroui-aoui* . . . He is *His Blessedness, the Sun of Two Earths, Great Master of the Land.* He is also the *Sublime Entrance: Prouiti, Prouti*, say the Egyptians) [Bérard, II, 49]. The Odyssean Proteus is only remotely connected to Bérard's original who, in fact, was the Pharaoh himself: "*Proutis* de la réalité, c'est-à-dire les Pharaons authentiques" (*Proutis* in reality, that is to say, actual Pharaohs) [Bérard, II, 56]. The legendary sea god Proteus and the Pharaoh-priest both practice magical arts. For Bérard, magic is the transformative element in a myth-based culture. Magic not only explains, but controls, the unknown. *Prouiti-proutis* guard the Nile basin because the river is the source of secrets. In an interesting Greek version of the myth, Nereus, the Old Man of the River, the first man, guards access to the final land, the Hyperborean otherworld. Nereus, also a shape-shifter, lives in the waters of the Po in northern Italy. The Hyperborean land is mythically if not directionally equivalent to the Elysian Fields. Since death is the ultimate secret, the earliest of the Proteus legends inscribed on papyrus dealt, according to Bérard, with one or another digression to the world's end.

Bérard tries to trace important features of the Proteus myth back through layers of Egyptian lore. He thinks the myth appears in Greek variations only after traveling from Egypt through Crete. The transmissions get especially complicated when the Egyptians begin borrowing back. Stesichorus, Herodotus, Diodorus of Sicily, Euripides, Apollodorus, and Servius all report, for example, a version of the Proteus story, the civic Proteus, in which King Proteus of Memphis kidnapped the real Helen of Troy and substituted a false image when Paris, who had stopped in Egypt, continued his journey to his homeland.[1] Menelaus returns to Egypt after the Trojan War to exchange the image for the real woman. Joyce is aware of this variant when he has Stephen think in *Proteus*: "Old Father Ocean. *Prix de Paris*: beware of imitations" (50), and when he writes in his *Cyclops* notesheets: "Herodotus opens hist with Phen. version of rape of Helen" (Herring, p. 106). Bérard is certain that the civic Proteus of Memphis is merely a modern version of the Pharaoh, and that the sea god and the king are two versions of the same original. That the Egyptians themselves speak of the King Proteus story is no problem. The Sphinx was chasing its tail here, so to speak. The Egyptians created the original Proteus legend and periodically took it back. In this case, they "adaptèrent la légende grecque aux romans d'Égypte. Il faut aller plus loin, je crois. L'histoire de Proteus dans Hérodote est sans doute la réadaptation égyptienne d'une légende homérique; mais cette légende homérique elle-même n'avait été que l'adaptation grecque d'un conte égyptien" ([they] adapted the Greek legend to Egyptian tales. It is, I believe, necessary to go further. The account of Proteus in Herodotus is undoubtedly the Egyptian readaptation of a Homeric legend; but this legend itself was only the Greek adaptation of an Egyptian tale) [Bérard, II, 50]. The reappearance of the legend many centuries later in the *Arabian Nights* story of Sinbad the Sailor is yet another adaptation from the Greek adaptation. Joyce doubles back here as well, having Stephen identify in the *Proteus* episode the mystery man

[1] See Frank Grotten, Jr., *The Traditions of the Helen Legend in Greek Literature* (Ph.D. Dissertation, Princeton, 1955), for a full rundown of the sources of the civic Proteus myth. Not all are as willing as Bérard to link the sea god and the Protean king.

from his dream of the night before as Haroun al Raschid, caliph at the time of Sinbad's encounter with Proteus. This was a later addition to *Proteus* after he had read Bérard's theory of the civic Proteus: "Proteus odysséen n'est pas une invention grecque. Ce n'est que le Pharaon, le *Prouti*, ou, si l'on veut, le khalife, l'Haroun-al-Raschid, d'une des vieilles *Mille et une Nuits* égyptiennes" (The Odyssean Proteus is not a Greek invention. It is only the Pharaoh, the *Prouti*, or, if one wishes, the Caliph, Haroun al Raschid, of the *Thousand and One Arabian Nights*) [Bérard, II, 51]. A Joycean civic Proteus appears again as the head of the household, H. C. Earwicker, in *Finnegans Wake*: "Haroun Childeric Eggeberth" (*FW*, 4). The eggbirth, of course, is another origin, and H.C.E. (Here Comes Everybody) another protean migration to western extensions.

For the narrative artist, the myth of Proteus has often meant encountering and out-devising the frightening shapelessness of temporal and spatial form. As an adversary figure Proteus bars access to controlled illusion; once pinned down, he becomes an ally in comprehending process and prophetic design. His control is over the most restless and powerful of elements: water. Stephen Dedalus (the hydrophobe of *Ulysses*—a fledgling artist, hence a bathetic Icarus) fears drowning. Daedalus, the father-artificer, a master of forms, flies over water east to west, from Crete to Sicily. Stephen, like Icarus, fears the vertical plunge. Joyce's partly ironic narration in the *Proteus* episode of *Ulysses* details what Stephen *does not* learn from Proteus. The Proteus figure has range as well as depth—something Stephen can barely understand. In a fine essay titled "Proteus Unbound," A. Bartlett Giamatti discusses the many shapes of the shape-shifter in the progress of western history.[2] The protean figure is not only artist, but hero and king. He possesses coded knowledge and provides essential laws. He is a craftsman and a visionary. He is also a conjurer and a counterfeiter—artist as trickster or Joyce's "masterbilker" and "ambitrickster" from "Wimmegame's Fake." From the Greek Phidias to the twentieth-century Felix Krull, the protean artist keeps surfacing from the Nile in different shapes. As Joyce puts it in *Finnegans Wake*: "He prophets most who bilks the best" (*FW*, 305).

[2] A. Bartlett Giamatti, "Proteus Unbound: Some Versions of the Sea-God in the Renaissance," in *The Disciplines of Criticism*, ed. Peter Demetz, Thomas Greene, and Lowry Nelson, Jr. (New Haven, 1968), pp. 437-475.

Proteus is old, very old. In occult systems he is the symbol of first matter. As such, Proteus contains all the unified and diverse elements of the universe within himself—he is the microcosm and the macrocosm, the hermetic first man, even first god (*Pro-theus*, in one derivation), thus the hermetic final extension. One of the traditional functions of Proteus is to reveal forms in time and space. When the secrets of the material universe are unveiled, how long and how far are, in a sense, identical questions. The Proteus myth, of course, has a plot we have seen before—one of Joyce's favorite plots. It is a ghost story of exile and return. It is a legend of revived substance from the world of the dead, imparted information, transforming action, and reconciliation. *Proteus* is a narration of double worlds, real and mythic, departures, delays, blockings, multiple identities, multiple *loci*. It is an initiatory fable, a tale of impasse, and a comedy of revivified form. At the heart of the legend is the revelation and transfer of both practical and prophetic knowledge. The legend is engaging because its mechanisms are ambiguous. It mirrors the struggle it is about. Mastery of shapeless forms can never be simple. The artist, like the hero, must lie, cheat, and distort merely to gain access to the secrets of illusion that themselves lie, cheat, and distort. As a hero in the *Odyssey*, Menelaus is fortunate. He has to trick Proteus only once. Artists have to confront the shape-shifter for each of their substantial efforts. Even if successful, the artist still faces the prospect that he has merely learned how to lie. The return from the other world, as Virgil tells us, is through the deceiving gates of ivory, not the gates of horn.

In his chapter on Proteus, which he calls *Les Contes Égyptiennes*, Bérard argues that the Proteus legend is very closely connected to the Egyptian myth of the secrets of Thoth passed down to the court astrologers (magi) and Pharaohs of Egypt, themselves magi. "Thoth, god of libraries, a birdgod, moonycrowned" (193) is no stranger to Joyce's Stephen Dedalus. In *Portrait of the Artist* Dedalus feared what he did not know. Thoth, the god of language, is linked with a mythic Greek, Daedalus the artificer, the father-artist.

> A sense of fear of the unknown moved in the heart of his weariness, a fear of symbols and portents, of the hawklike man whose name he bore soaring out of his captivity on oiserwoven wings, of Thoth, the god of writers, writing with a reed upon a tablet and bearing on his narrow ibis head the cusped moon.   (*P*, 225)

As an Aristotelian who finds comfort in moving from the known to the unknown, Stephen fears the mystery of gods and fathers. Bérard's association of the Proteus myth with the magical god Thoth is important. Like Stephen's god of writers, Proteus also possesses formulaic secrets, including the power to conjure up visions of the world beyond.[3] Bérard discusses the Proteus figure as one "qui possédait tous les secrets de la divinité au ciel, sur la terre et dans l'enfer" (who possessed all the secrets of the heavens, of the earth, and of the underworld) [Bérard, II, 54]. He recounts one version of the legend in which Noferkephtah, the son of Pharaoh, recovers the Book of Thoth from beneath the waters of the Nile. As a magician-*prouti*, a model for Proteus, Noferkephtah enlists the support of his wife in fashioning a hole in the middle of the river to retrieve the secrets of Thoth and charm "le ciel, la terre, le monde de la nuit, les montagnes, les eaux" (the heavens, the earth, the world of the night, the mountains, the waters) [Bérard, II, 52]. Bérard sees this legend as a parallel to Menelaus' seeking the aid of Proteus' daughter, Eidothea. This makes Noferkephtah a version of both Proteus and the stymied hero-king. Noferkephtah, a young man, does not fare much better than does Stephen Dedalus in Sandymount. Ra, the sun god, is so disgruntled at Noferkephtah's arrogance that he banishes him to Memphis. Bérard, naturally, sees the beginnings of the civic Proteus legend here. The later King Proteus of Memphis is still up to old tricks.

The introduction of Thoth into the Proteus tale, of course, is more an issue for Bérard and Joyce than for the Homeric poet. Thoth is, and always has been, an extraordinary figure in the east and the west. He is the general factotum of the Egyptian gods, a messenger, a scribe, a secretary to Osiris, a magician, a "name to conjure with" as Frances Yates puts it.[4] In hermetic lore, the many keys to theologies identified Thoth, thrice great as a philosopher, prophet, and typological king, with another Egyptian, the patriarchal Moses.[5] The Semitic

[3] See the *Book of the Dead, The Papyrus of Ari*, trans. E. A. Wallis Budge (London, 1895). Thoth uttered the words of the creation and had the power to "grant life to the dead," p. cxviii.

[4] Frances Yates, *Giordano Bruno and the Hermetic Tradition* (Chicago, 1964), p. 48.

[5] Ficino, *Theologia Platonica*, VIII, i, *Opera omnia* (Basel, 1576), I, 400. See Wayne Shumaker, *The Occult Sciences in the Renaissance* (Berkeley, 1972), for the east-west connections in hermetic lore: "Hermeticism was basically a Greek contemplative mysticism developed on Egyptian soil," p. 211.

Thoth becomes the Greek Hermes, hence their name for the original Egyptian, Hermes Trismegistos, Hermes thrice great. The two gods cross at several roads. Thoth-Hermes is an east to west migration: Jewgreek is greekjew. Both gods are magicians, gods of language, of landmarks ("signs on a white field"), patrons of artists and travellers, messengers, wayfinders. Thoth bears his reed and tablet, Hermes his staff and wide-brimmed hat. Both are inventors and, if need be, connivers.

In Book XXIV of the *Odyssey* Hermes guides the souls of the slain suitors to the land of the dead at the Fields of Asphodel. Hermes possesses Thoth-like powers over these regions as well. Thoth had conceived of the zodiac, partly to measure limits in the heavens and on earth, and Hermes is the Greek god of limits. He assists in Cadmus' migration to Europe from Asia by pilfering a herd of cattle, a specialty of his, and moving them shoreward for Europa to follow. Cadmus brings the alphabet with him, supposedly blocked out by Hermes. Hermes is an originator who follows through to the extensions. Bérard tells us that in their Semitic roots Cadmus means east and Europa west. He also tells us that the star of Venus, the Semitic *Delephat-Telephassa*, has a stellar son and daughter: the morning star from the east is *Delephat-Kadem* the evening star in the west is *Delephat-Erobe* [Bérard, I, 225]. The westward migration is masculine-feminine.

When Hermes was barely a few minutes old, he had stolen another herd of cattle, his first. These belonged to Apollo. In an act of almost immediate contrition, he leads the cattle to the river Alpheus at Elis. The Alpheus is a source (a.l.p.: aleph, alpha, or ox river); there he initiates sacrifices to the twelve Olympian gods, each associated with a sign of the zodiac. The zodiac maps all space around any given point. Jean Richer makes clear the orientation and the range of Hermes. He is the beginning who circles around to the end: "Les historiens des religions sont d'accord pour voir en Hermès un antique dieu du tas de pierres, des bornes et des limites. Mettre le dieu en relation avec le point initial de l'année, c'est en somme lui assigner dans le zodiaque un rôle analogue" (Historians of religion agree in viewing Hermes as an ancient god of signposts [literally, stone heaps], boundaries and limits. To place the god in relation to the beginning of the year is, in short, to assign him an analogous role in the zodiac).[6]

[6] Jean Richer, *La Geographie Sacrée du Monde Grec* (Paris, 1967), p. 91.

Joyce was aware of this young god, and of the older, greater Thoth. And he saw in the nexus of Proteus, Thoth, Hermes, Egypt-Greece the control of matter, the knowledge of time and space, all the ingredients for a tale he could not yet tell about Stephen Dedalus. From his *Circe* notesheets, we know that Joyce had stored information. Of Hermes, for instance, he records the details: the zodiacal connection, the attributes, the functions, the powers. But he will not let Dedalus become a Hermes to Bloom's greater Thoth in *Ulysses*. Phillip Herring records, as best he can, Joyce's notes. We only need point out for the following list that the "shepherd crioforo" means ram-carrier, hence Aries or the initial Spring sign of the zodiac.

Hermes, S of Maia, babe
1st day robs Apollo's cows, troop
    back, Iris
He (?Od) ?wind herald
Guide, to & from Hereafter
wakes souls with caduceus
stick 2 serpents, god of dreams (nightcap) speed
gymn. eloqu sacrif. tongue
Trismegistos   streets, crossways
fingerposts (?erme) travellers
commerce, thieves, ?good ?nunnery
shepherd crioforo   (Herring, p. 304)

Hermes, Thoth, Proteus, even Hermes' early adversary, Apollo, all have power and range to share. But neither their power nor their range is easy to come by. It is obvious why artists over the centuries identify with gods of this nature. Ezra Pound has written that the "Apollo at Villa Giulia gives tip to Mediterranean gods; startling, sudden, none of that washy late stuff done by sculpting slave models, nor afternoon-tea Xtian piety. Gods tricky as nature."[7] Pound was writing to W. D. Rouse, who was then working on his translation of the *Odyssey*. It is significant that the hero of Homer's epic is descended from one of those tricky gods. Joyce's note on Hermes picks this up: "He (?Od)." Odysseus—the teller of tales that range from Asia to the edge of Europe, the guileful liar, the inventor, the author of false lives and adventures, the wanderer—

[7] Ezra Pound, *The Letters of Ezra Pound*, ed. D. D. Paige (New York, 1950), p. 273.

is related on his maternal side to Hermes. His grandfather, Autolycus the thief (another version of whom is adapted for Shakespeare's *Winter's Tale* as the fastest-talking itinerant thief in all Bohemia), was the son of Hermes, the patron of thieves.[8] W. B. Stanford has this to say about Odysseus' origins.

> In a sense, indeed, he was something of a half-breed—not in the racial or social sense, like the poet Archilochus, but as the grandson of a nobleman, on the one side, and of a professional trickster on the other. Since children often inherit features more markedly from their grandparents than from their parents, it is not surprising that the grandchild had an unusually complex personality.[9]

Joyce enters in his *Cyclops* notesheets: "Grandfather Autolycus" (Herring, p. 120). The Autolycus of *Ulysses*, of course, is Virag, Bloom's paternal grandfather. *Ulysses* is turned around in that its hero has a daughter and no son—its son has a father and no mother. So the hero of Joyce's novel can have a paternal rather than maternal grandfather. Virag appears in *Circe* as *basilicogrammate*, the lord of language (in Robert Martin Adams' transliteration). He is a gadfly like Autolycus and a bird-lord like Thoth, Hermes Trismegistos. Thoth discovered hieroglyphs just as Hermes blocked out the alphabet. Both are lords of language. In *Ulysses*, Bloom as Odysseus is descended from a Hermes figure; as a solar hero he even has connections to Apollo, the "Brightdayler." Stephen, with his Telemachian great-great-grandfather as Hermes, wears his mercurial insignia, his "sandal shoon" and his Latin-quarter hat, and carries his staff-like ash plant. He is set up, as the artist figure, to benefit most from magician-gods. But he does not, and therein lies a story of missed eastern and western connections, of struggles with all the forces in his material world and with all Joyce's versions of Protean tricksters: Simon Dedalus, Buck Mulligan, the poet AE, even Bloom.

ADVERSARIES—ALLIES: VARIANT FORMS

In myth, the means by which power and knowledge are made manifest or transferred to another, is the secret of material process. Hermes,

---

[8] See Norman O. Brown, *Hermes the Thief* (New York, 1947).

[9] W. B. Stanford, *The Ulysses Theme, A Study in the Adaptability of the Traditional Hero* (New York, 2nd ed., 1968), p. 12.

at odds with Apollo from the first moment of his life, makes up with the sun god before the day is over, and the two, in Joyce's idiom, become bullock-befriending godbards, allies in form's cause against matter. The joining of like talents is also at issue in the aborted connection between the young *prouti*, Noferkephtah, and the greater god, Thoth. Joyce sees something of the adversary-ally confrontation in all literature, often reflected in the relations between fathers and sons. Telemachus is unconvinced at the beginning of the *Odyssey* that Odysseus is even his father and the plot works itself out only at *Nostos* when father and son reunite to renew their land. Hamlet suspects the ghost of King Hamlet, but eventually takes his word as law. Stephen Dedalus has a visceral distrust of the man he finally joins, not only as father-son, but as artistic double: "Bloom Stoom" and "Stephen Blephen" (682). Wherever Joyce looks in the literary models that interested him, he finds couplings, sometimes adversary, sometimes ally, sometimes both: Adam-God, Christ-Satan, Icarus-Daedalus, Telemachus-Odysseus, Menelaus-Proteus, Dante-Virgil, Hamlet-King Hamlet, Faust-Mephistopheles. On occasion, the spiritual struggle is made physically literal. In the Sinbad story, for instance, Proteus actually climbs on Sinbad's back and refuses to let go until Sinbad's guile turns a parasitic situation into a symbiotic one. In another version of this relationship, Blake's Urizen climbs onto Albion's back after Night IV of the *Four Zoas*. In *Ulysses*, only Mulligan's clothes are on Stephen's back.

Ulysses is a novel in which adversary-ally roles are ultimately more comic than prophetic. No vanquished Proteus provides explanatory tours to the land of the walking dead. Instead, Joyce debases the myth. Bloom's grandfather, Virag, is the most absurd Thoth-Proteus figure of the day. Luckily for Dedalus, only Bloom has to deal with this eastern Jew.

> *Lipoti Virag, basilicogrammate, chutes rapidly down through the chimneyflue and struts two steps to the left on gawky pink stilts. He is sausaged into several overcoats and wears a brown macintosh under which he holds a roll of parchment. In his left eye flashes the monocle of Cashel Boyle O'Connor Fitzmaurice Tisdall Farrell. On his head is perched an Egyptian pshent. Two quills project over his ears.* (511)

Virag is the parodic *prouti*, his *Sublime-porte* is bathetic: "From the sublime to the ridiculous is but a step" (515). He is the Arabian

magician ("Open Sesame!" 516) and the Protean king: "Long ago
I was a king, / Now I do this kind of thing" (517). He is privy to
the most intimate secrets and the most material lore: "I am the
Virag who disclosed the sex secrets of monks and maidens" (519). If
Bloom has to deal with the memory of Virag in his loose-ended
life, Dedalus has to deal with Mananaan MacLir, the Irish Old Man
of the Sea. Mananaan was one of Joyce's minor but telling additions
to the *Proteus* chapter in a later revision: "The whitemaned sea-
horses, champing, brightwindbridled, the steeds of Mananaan" (38).
The reference is first to another older man, Mr. Deasy, but Mananaan will reappear in *Ulysses* as Dedalus's adversary, Æ, who
clutches the "Occult pimander of Hermes Trismegistos" (510) when
he surfaces in *Circe* dripping wet from the ocean.

Mananaan Maclir

(*With a voice of waves.*) Aum! Hek! Wal! Ak! Lub! Mor! Ma!
White yoghin of the Gods. Occult pimander of Hermes Trismegistos. (*With a voice of whistling seawind.*) Punarjanam
patsypunjaub! I won't have my leg pulled. It has been said by
one: beware the left, the cult of Shakti. (*With a cry of stormbirds.*)
Shakti, Shiva! Dark hidden Father! . . .   (510)

Mananaan fits the protean mold and the Ulyssean parody. He
is the word on the waters, the origin of things, and the hermetic
extension. He carries with him in this scene the zodiacal dial and
the twelve constellate signs. As Æ, Mananaan controls formless domain: "I am the light of the homestead, I am the dreamery
creamery butter" (510). This phrase refers to the Theosophic reading of the *Bhagavad-Gita*, and the entire passage from *Circe* refers
to Stephen's earlier parody of Russell in *Scylla and Charybdis*. Dedalus, the Aristotelian, bristles in the presence of the shapeless
magical mysteries of the east.

Formless spiritual. Father. Word and Holy Breath. Allfather,
the heavenly man. Hiesos Kristos, magician of the beautiful, the
Logos who suffers in us at every moment. This verily is that. I
am the fire upon the altar. I am the sacrificial butter.   (185)

The Theosophic Mananaan is also Russell's "Lord of the Ocean"
in the Druid's chant from his play *Deirdre*. Mananaan is the son of
Lir. Russell was to write of Lir in his *Candle of Vision* as "infinite

depth, an invisible divinity, neither dark nor light, in whom were all things past and to be." Lir is all center, all circumference for Russell. His son, Mananaan, is "the most spiritual divinity known to the ancient Gael, being the Gaelic equivalent of that Spirit which breathed on the face of the waters."[10] The Theosophic Lir and Mananaan are something like Blake's visionary Tharmas and Los, less like Homer's ocean-girding Poseidon and his local genie, Proteus, and even less like the elemental anti-type, Virag, and his touch-of-the-artist grandson, Bloom. But there is a comic progression here, all of it making its way into the chronicle of *Ulysses*. In a humbler version, the *Silva Gadelica*, the Irish Mananaan is the typical shape-shifter, the king, the conjurer, the bowman, the servant, the conductor of tours across the waters. He, like many other trickster gods and spiritual allies, is a friend worth having.

Joyce begins *Ulysses* with an eastern voyager—a hero looking for allies in older men. Dedalus moves from Sandycove to Dalkey on the same directional axis as Telemachus moving from Ithaca to Pylos. Neither learns a great deal from the old man at the western gates, Nestor. But Telemachus continues east to Sparta. Dedalus doubles back in the opposite direction to Dublin. When he resumes his eastern progress on Sandymount (north and then east) he gets few answers he can understand. Joyce had followed this route before. Two early stories in *Dubliners*, "An Encounter" and "Araby," have young men seeking initiatory experiences in the east of Dublin. The truants of "An Encounter" traverse Dublin east toward the Pigeonhouse off Sandymount in order to satisfy their lust for a fantasy at the other end of the world, the American west. Proteus has nothing to tell them of temperate lands beyond the seas. Joyce's truants are merely frightened by an old man on the beach, an incipient pederast. The lad in "Araby" is similarly drawn up short. He anticipates an initiatory experience from the Mirus Bazaar in Ballsbridge, near Sandymount, but his day ends in disappointment and an Irish sense of southeastern decadence.

When Dedalus begins his day nine miles southeast of the city, he encounters several versions of Proteus, none of whom are helpful to him, none of whom he even recognizes for the signs he seeks. In *Telemachus* an old man, a priest of the seas, emerges from Dublin Bay at the forty-foot hole: "An elderly man shot up near the spur

[10] George Russell, *A Candle of Vision* (London, 1918), pp. 153 and 155.

of rock a blowing red face. He scrambled up by the stones, water glistening on his pate and on its garland of grey hair, water rilling over his chest and paunch and spilling jets out of his black sagging loincloth" (22). Mulligan, the mocker, crosses himself when the priest walks by. This aged Proteus will not do for Dedalus—in *Portrait* he has already flown by the nets of the Catholic church. Deasy, the old man of historical cliché, is no prophetic ally either. Only "Old Father Ocean" (50) of *Proteus* remains.

Dedalus walks the shores to learn of matter in the signatures of the sand. Perhaps there is some lifeline from Eve's original navel-cord to the put-together-again pieces of Adam Kadmon, the hermetic first man, the eastern man. Stephen plots the path of "eternity along Sandymount strand" (37) in a vision of westward extension: "world without end" (37). The vatic Proteus is not quick to answer Dedalus' questions. Neither does Blake's Los rush to refashion the void left by the disappearing Tharmas. Stephen spares us none of the allusions in the opening of his monologue in *Proteus*. He even closes his eyes just as Pico della Mirandola, to whom he alludes, says all good mystics must do to see real substance. Pico thinks the word mystic means to shut one's eyes—he derives it literally from the Greek.[11] The red-haired king, Menelaus, has his vision through Proteus, and it is specific: a found father, a future ally for Telemachus.

> Laërtês' son, whose home is Ithaka.
> I saw him weeping, weeping on an island.
> The nymph Kalypso has him, in her hall.
> No means of faring home are left him now;
> no ship with oars, and no ship's company
> to pull him on the broad back of the sea.
> As to your own destiny, prince Meneláos,
> you shall not die in the bluegrass land of Argos;
> rather the gods intend you for Elysion
> with golden Rhadamanthos at the world's end,

[11] Joyce perhaps discovered this piece of information in Walter Pater's "Pico della Mirandola," in *The Renaissance* (New York: Library edition, 1912). Pater writes: "The word *mystic* has been usually derived from a Greek word which signifies *to shut*, as if one shut one's lips brooding on what cannot be uttered; but the Platonists themselves derive it rather from the act of *shutting the eyes*, that one may see the more, inwardly" (p. 37). I am grateful to James Nohrnberg for pointing this passage out to me.

where all existence is a dream of ease.
Snowfall is never known there, neither long
frost of winter, nor torrential rain,
but only mild and lulling airs from Ocean
bearing refreshment for the souls of men—
the West Wind always blowing.

(Book IV, Fitzgerald, p. 69)

The vision of Proteus, like all extension myths, is adjustable to the exigencies of local topography. "Across the sands of all the world, followed by the sun's flaming sword, to the west, trekking to evening lands" (47), thinks Dedalus of the cockle-picking gypsies ("Egyptians") on Sandymount strand. Victor Bérard suggests the actual Egyptian extension: "le monde égyptien s'était agrandi vers l'Ouest. Jadis limitée à la vallée du Nil, l'Égypte avait peu à peu débordé sur le désert, et de ce côté aussi le Champ des Bienheureux s'éloigna vers les extrémités de la terre" (the Egyptian world grew toward the west. Once limited by the Nile Valley, Egypt had little by little spilled on to the desert, and from this [the western] side as well, the Fields of Blessedness were extended toward the extremities of the earth) [Bérard, II, 79-80].

Stephen reduces worlds of time and space to the *nacheinander* and *nebeneinander* of his own footsteps. When the Semitic original, the Wandering Jew himself, turns up in a reconstruction of Dedalus' dream, Stephen does not know what to make of the easterner in the west. He distrusts potential allies. The protean metamorphosis is from dog to panther to Haroun al Raschid, the caliph from the *Arabian Nights*. Haroun was a self-transformer—he loved to go among his people disguised, like Odysseus, as a beggar.

His hindpaws then scattered sand: then his forepaws dabbled and delved. Something he buried there, his grandmother. He rooted in the sand, dabbling, delving and stopped to listen to the air, scraped up the sand again with a fury of his claws, soon ceasing, a pard, a panther, got in spouse-breach, vulturing the dead.
 After he woke me up last night same dream or was it? Wait. Open hallway. Street of harlots. Remember. Haroun al Raschid. I am almosting it. That man led me, spoke. I was not afraid. The melon he had he held against my face. Smiled: creamfruit smell. That was the rule, said. In. Come. Red carpet spread. You will see who. (46-47)

We have seen something of the ambiguity of Stephen's dream of an eastern ally, a Semite for Nighttown. The suspicion goes deeper yet. If Haroun al Raschid is the civic Proteus, the sustaining caliph, the panther of this passage is one of Proteus' more ferocious transformations at high noon on Pharos Isle. For the Egyptians, the panther was not a mild beast—it was guileful and ravenous. For *Ulysses*, A. M. Klein sees the panther as the Christ-like contrary of Haines's nightmare in *Telemachus*.[12] In other words, the panther is adversary in one tradition and ally in another. Joyce's phrase "got in spouse-breach" brings the traditions closer together, but does not help Stephen a great deal in his confusion. Spouse-breach is adultery, and in *Circe*, the bird-like Virag alludes to the story of Jesus' having been fathered on Mary by a Roman centurion: "Panther, the Roman centurion, polluted her with his genitories" (521). Christ is a panther, perhaps, but his putative father, like the medieval Proteus, came to be associated with pure lust. Ariosto, for instance, images Proteus as a rapist.[13] *Oxen of the Sun* tries to untangle the allusions, but confuses matters. Memories of Hamlet and King Hamlet from *Scylla and Charybdis* are added for good measure: "The mystery was unveiled. Haines was the third brother. His real name was Childs. The black panther was himself the ghost of his own father" (412).

In Joyce's comic idiom odd pieces of information begin to add up. We have a black panther—Christ in the European bestiaries, but a ravenous Proteus in another tradition. We have a mystery unveiled, but if we look to the work to which that phrase alludes, the indefatigable Madame Blavatsky's *Isis Unveiled*, we will see yet another version of the panther-Christ story in her recounting of a feud in the eighteenth century between the Jesuits and the Masonic orders. Stephen, of course, is a "jejune jesuit" and Bloom (Leopold: lion: *panthera leo*) is thought to be a member of Dublin's Masonic League. Madame Blavatsky's Masons hold that Joseph Ben Panther fathered the illegitimate Jesus who was spirited off to Egypt by a Jew, a rabbi, to study mysticism.[14] We are back where we began, on

[12] A. M. Klein, "The Black Panther (A Study in Technique)," *Accent*, x (1950), p. 141.

[13] See Giamatti, "Proteus Unbound," pp. 462 and 467. Proteus had a reputation as a sexual miscreant as well as a lawbreaker (the contrary, in every way, of his role as lawgiver).

[14] H. P. Blavatsky, *Isis Unveiled: A Master-Key to the Mysteries of Ancient and Modern Science and Theology* (New York, 1877), II, 386.

the shores of Egypt. But we are now in the company of esoteric lore that Joyce finds fictionally amusing. Even Madame Blavatsky's Jesuits protest that the Masonic translation to Egypt's mysteries is nonsense. Madame Blavatsky's Masons protest that only in Egypt was Christ's magic made possible. If Stephen does not know what to make of his dream, if he does not even know when he makes contact with a Protean ally, Bloom, we need not be surprised. He is not a proficient enough hero or artist to mark the range of the shape-shifters in Joyce's *Ulysses*, a book filled with characters, whether they know it or not, as tricky as the gods. Only Joyce carries the fable across the sands of Egypt to the end of the European world: a magical isle, Ireland. The "masterbilker" fixes the migrational shape of the beginnings and ends of the Odyssean epic tradition.

PART TWO

PRELIMINARY MAPPINGS
ORIENTATIONS, WANDERINGS, NOSTOS

NAMES AND PLACES

JOYCE may well have boasted to Frank Budgen that in *Ulysses* he wanted to present "a picture of Dublin so complete that if the city one day suddenly disappeared from the earth it could be reconstructed out of my book,"[1] but his narrative strategy in *Ulysses* touches on more than city planning or civil defense. As Richard Ellmann puts it, Joyce reefs Homer's sails. He reconstructs an epic map as much as he charts the spaces of his native city. It is not only the general pattern of exile and homecoming that Joyce borrows from the Homeric *Odyssey*, but the placing, direction, timing, orientation, disorientation, and repetition of movement within a recognizable grid. Joyce, of course, is precise. According to Budgen, he worked like an engineer, a surveyor, and, most appropriately, a ship's navigator in placing the people of *Ulysses* in and around Dublin.[2] Clive Hart's and Leo Knuth's recent compilation and mapping, *A Topographical Guide to James Joyce's Ulysses*, offers ample evidence that this is so. Why it is so and what Joyce's narrative gains from its precision are important, lingering questions.

In his *Surface and Symbol: The Consistency of James Joyce's Ulysses*, Robert Martin Adams spends a good many fascinating pages prowling around Dublin's spaces. He emphasizes the importance of selecting from more or less positively and negatively charged "facts" when assessing the strata of the novel's local pilings, as he calls them. Adams works with a legitimate critical problem—what constitutes narrative significance in Joyce's urban epic? The problem is compounded by Joyce's own mercurial (or protean) sense of expanded plot, and by what Adams considers the generally unstable ego in modern fiction "threatened alternately with implosion and explosion," and "haunted by a question of dimension" (p. 252). But

---

[1] Budgen, pp. 67-68.

[2] *Ibid.*, p. 125. See also Clive Hart, "Wandering Rocks," in Hart and Hayman, pp. 181-216. Hart clocks the *Wandering Rocks* chapter and provides ample evidence of Joyce's precision.

there are things to learn about *Ulysses* by paying attention to its city.

Following clues, leads, and hunches, Adams tries to separate Dublin's surfaces from its symbols. Surfaces are materials invited into the novel by Joyce without much concern whether they alter or enhance the fictional substance of the day. Symbols are narratively significant details. *Ulysses* contains certain local mistakes, which may be symbolic. Some are the brandishings of Joyce's cold-steel satirical pen against old Dublin enemies.[3] Others are slight changes for exigencies of plot—Dlugacz, the butcher, is placed on Upper Dorset street so that Bloom can either acknowledge or ignore the compatriotism of a Hungarian Jew. Others yet are intentional slips in the service of wit or irony—the poster of Eugene Stratton, a black man, smiles down on the colonialist Viceregal procession from Royal Canal Bridge, which seems to have wandered to the south side of the Liffey from its usual location in the north. These are all fairly minor. Dublin's places, unlike the Homeric *planktoi*, generally do not move without Joyce's feeling the pangs of mnemonic betrayal. Adams, in essence, renders the *prima facie* landscape of *Ulysses* more surface than symbol.

There are, however, other ways of looking at the significance of Dublin's surfaces. Often place names do what places themselves cannot do—expand the world of the narrative. Joyce will direct his novel to given locales and linger on some streets because their names are suggestive. Putting Bloom, for example, on Gardiner place during the *Nostos* "by an inadvertance" (666), conflates Molly's husband and one of Molly's amours, Lieutenant Gardiner. Joyce is not above teasing Dublin's local geography for verbal significance whenever he can. Adams mentions the incident of the drowned man found off Maiden's Rock, a tiny island—literally no more than a rock— near the larger Dalkey island. Joyce invented the drowning, but the rock is real enough. Obviously, the name Maiden's Rock had its appeal for a modern *Odyssey*. Joyce discovers another western nymph's isle, a Gibraltar "watered-down." A sea traveler is victimized near a maiden's island; a "sea-side girl" lures another

[3] Robert Martin Adams, in *Surface and Symbol* (New York, 1962), writes that Joyce pays off an old debt to one Father Darlington (the Father Butt of *Ulysses*) by placing him, as in insult, in the Physics Theatre at 16 Stephen's Green North, which Joyce well knew was the address of the Protestant Archbishop of Dublin (p. 194).

voyager with her deathly attractions. In the actual *Sirens* episode of
Ulysses, Barton James, cabman, lives at number 1 Harmony Avenue,
an amusing address in a chapter of musical counterpoint. Joyce will
even weave place name strands from chapter to chapter. In *Wandering Rocks*, where Dublin's displaced dominion is honored by the
Viceregal procession, the two old ladies of Stephen's *Pisgah Sight
of Palestine* walk through Irishtown on London Bridge road. In
Stephen's parable, they had already paid tribute to the wrong empire by stopping at the north city dining rooms on Marlborough
street and by climbing the pillar of the "onehandled adulterer" (148),
Lord Nelson. Earlier in the day, the same women walked from
Leahy's terrace along the strand. Stephen identified one as "Mrs
Florence MacCabe, relict of the late Patk MacCabe, deeply lamented,
of Bride Street" (37). Joyce relishes the juxtaposition of a "deeply
lamented" death with a Bride street marriage, and Dublin's sterility
and moribundity are issues not easily forgotten through the hours of
the day. In *Proteus*, of course, Stephen imagined that the bag of the
widow of Bride street contained a stillborn child.

   The difficulty with pursuing place names in, around, and over
Dublin is one of priorities. Joyce is often selective and wry about
names, but just as often his attentions are elsewhere. All the place
names of Dublin are not significant for *Ulysses*, and any attempt to
make them so is apt to prove more quixotic than rewarding. Odyssean meaning can be coaxed from Greek street and Tritonville road,
general meaning can be coaxed from Lime street, Bachelor's Walk,
Pleasants street, Westland Row, even Eccles street. But we are hard
pressed to find meaning in Grafton, O'Connell, Holles, Dorset, or
Mecklenburg (Tyrone) streets, locations where much of the novel
takes place. If the geography of the city contributes to the patterning
of the novel, it is going to have to do so in ways more easily adjustable to narrative values. Here is where we get a great deal of
help from the *Odyssey*, especially from its sense of spatial configuration. Homer wove his hero's *Wanderings* upon the loom of hard
geographical fact, according to Joyce's source on these matters,
Victor Bérard. The relations among mythical, legendary, and historical places in the *Odyssey* offer a model particularly suited to Joyce's
need. Where Dubliners are and why repeats the significant movements of the *Odyssey*. All we need do is understand the attendant
values of positioning and direction in Dublin.

Periploi: Around the Mediterranean to Ithaca

The orientations of the epic day in *Ulysses* begin with two periods of lost time. Dedalus moves southeast the short distance from Sandycove to Dalkey. When he leaves Ithaca, Telemachus moves southeast to Pylos, soon continuing in the same direction from Pylos to Sparta. But in *Ulysses* Stephen shows up in Sandymount six miles to the northwest. He probably took a tram to *Proteus* (Hart and Knuth, p. 24). After his reorientation he heads as far east as he will get within the city, out along the strand toward the Pigeonhouse. Stephen's day in *Ulysses* is spent doing precisely what Telemachus had done on the Peloponnese—almost nothing. Telemachus is presented with one artful and complicated task, however, before the purge at *Nostos*. He is told to beach eastward on Ithaca and avoid the ambush of the suitors in the northwest. Joyce is extremely sensitive to the *Odyssey* on this point. Stephen spends a good part of his day avoiding one or another ambush. Joyce offers several versions of this episode from the *Odyssey* because he is faced with the prospect of having his younger hero much more on the scene than Homer's Telemachus, who is safely localized in Sparta.

Another experience of lost time orients Leopold Bloom. This device seemed Joyce's way of adjusting Dublin to the larger Homeric map. After *Calypso*, where we merely see Bloom dash up and down the block, like Odysseus unable to cast too far adrift from the nymph's cave on Ogygia, Bloom suddenly appears in *Lotuseaters* walking in the east of the city "along Sir John Rogerson's quay" (71) just south of the Liffey. Why and how he arrived there from Eccles street near the North Circular road are unexplained. At first it seems likely that Bloom has strolled a mile or so away from his home to a conveniently remote post office on Westland Row where he negotiates his epistolary flirtation with Martha Clifford, typist (Hart and Knuth, p. 25). But if that were solely the case, he would presumably have been placed by Joyce further west than Lime street off the quay. Bloom is located in the east of Dublin relatively early in the day for no immediately obvious reason. The day is pleasant and perhaps Bloom overshoots the post office simply to take a walk.

But if we speculate for a moment on the narrative arrangement of the *Odyssey*, we can find similarities to the way Homer sets up the *Wanderings*. Odysseus is initially exiled on Calypso's island. It is not until he sails all the way across the Mediterranean, west to east with the constellation of the Bear continuously to his left, that we hear any of the details of his initial *Wanderings*. He reaches Nausicaa's land, the home of the Phaeacians, and offers his recapitulative narration, beginning with Troy ten years before. His orientation is at the opposite end of the world from Calypso's Ogygia. He explains to the Phaeacians how his troubles began when he and his crew raided the land of Ismarus in eastern seas. Fleeing the Cicones, Odysseus and his men sailed southwest into the Mediterranean proper, dipped around the cape at Malea, and were blown in a nine-day gale on to the land of the Lotophagoi in the southwestern Mediterranean. Joyce's Bloom, with the east on his mind while exiled on his Calypso homefront ("Somewhere in the east: early morning: set off at dawn, travel round in front of the sun," 57), arrives in Dublin's east at the beginnings of his *Wanderings* proper. He walks as far east as Lime street, and then duplicates the path of Odysseus as he turns south-southwest, and heads to the lethargy of the Turkish baths approximately where we would expect Lotusland to be in the *Odyssey*. Bloom gets his bearings in *Lotuseaters* just as Odysseus gained his in the Mediterranean. As the day progresses Joyce will alter the sequence of several Odyssean episodes and adjust the spatial relationships they bear to each other, but he does so for reasons that are directionally explicable. But at the beginning of the day, in *Lotuseaters*, he clearly adjusts the compass of *Ulysses* to that of its host epic.

Near the end of his first volume, dealing primarily with Phoenician navigations across the Mediterranean, Victor Bérard turns to the *Wanderings* of Odysseus proper. He writes that it is "vers Kumè maintenant que la suite de l'*Odysseia* et la méthode des *Plus Homériques* vont nous conduire" (towards Cumae now that the sequence of *Wanderings* and the supra-Homeric method will take us) [Bérard, 1, 585-586]. The Cumaean episodes, as Bérard sees them, group around the western Italian boot in the middle of the Mediterranean. Odysseus' *Wanderings* are toward the west, but if we imagine the entire ocean, Levantine to extreme *couchant* waters, the Italian peninsula is middle territory. Bérard suspects that when the Homeric poet was composing the *Odyssey*, Greek settlements had begun to range the Italian coast, especially in the Cumae region and in Sicily, both of which became Apollonian shrines or new western *omphaloi*. In other words, Bérard sees the *Odyssey* as a poem extending the western borders of Greece from Odysseus' home island kingdom in the Ionian sea to new centers in or around Italy. He places central adventures in central waters: *Cyclops, Aeolus, Lestrygonians, Circe, Hades, Sirens, Scylla and Charybdis, Oxen of the Sun*. The *Wanderings* of Leopold Bloom conform generally to Bérard's Homeric map. *Hades* seems an exception here, located as it is in the extreme northwest of Dublin in Glasnevin, but this is easily reconciled with Homeric description. The *Odyssey* places Hades' realm at the ocean's bourne, but Bérard simply argues that the Bay of Cumae *was* the ocean's bourne when the *Nekuia*, a much older episode possibly inserted into the poem piecemeal, was conceived. The rest of the *Wanderings* of Bloom take place within a reasonable circle around the city center at Nelson's Pillar. In the *Odyssey* that center is the island of the wind king, Aeolus. Because of the tricky winds and currents around the Lipari group in the Tyrrhenian sea, where Bérard places the episode, the Lipari islands were a central navigational landmark.

When Joyce strays from the Odyssean order of episodes or from the exact Odyssean positioning, he usually offers clues why he has done so and reorienting compensations for the fact that he has done so. *Ulysses* is aware that its version of the *Odyssey* is partly comic. The novel has its moments of frustration and disorientation, but overall it strives to test its hero in conditions and locations similar to those the Homeric poet provided for Odysseus. But as the novel approaches *Nostos* we are seemingly left with an unexplained jumbling of important episodes. *Nausicaa* takes place much too early. In the *Odyssey* the land of the Phaeacians is the last stopover before Odysseus sails one last night to his native Ithaca. In *Ulysses* two of the *Wanderings* proper, *Oxen of the Sun* and *Circe*, occur after *Nausicaa*. Either Joyce did not care about the rearrangement or he had something in mind. It is possible that he thought that Samuel Butler had preempted him in thrusting the burden of the *Odyssey* on Nausicaa; therefore he wanted the episode in a less prominent position. It is also possible that *Oxen of the Sun* and *Circe* are implicated in the *Nostos* more than they might appear to be. In his notesheets Joyce wrote: "nocturnes—all homegoing" (Herring, p. 478). The sun sets in *Nausicaa* as the novel returns Bloom to Sandymount for a second sweep at his city. According to Bérard, the Phaeacians drop Odysseus at the Cave of Phorkys off the inlet on the eastern side of Ithaca near Port Vathi. The inlet extends almost across the breadth of the narrow island. From that point Odysseus turns away from the direction of his timbered palace further to the northwest near Port Polis and heads southwest to the hut of Eumeaus near Arethusa and Raven's Rock. Telemachus, recalled by Athena, is told to beach eastward at a spot that Bérard marks as Point Andri. Telemachus then moves slightly northwest to Eumeaus' hut and joins his father to plan their strategy in approaching the town, a good distance away.

Bérard suggests that the Homeric poet is unique in his accurate recording of navigations in far western seas. When he begins to approach home, however, he shares a common characteristic with other Greek *nostoi* and fragments of *nostoi*: "C'est aux vers du *Nostos* que les premiers périples grecs essayèrent de rapporter, d'ajuster leur géographie" (It is in the direction of *Nostos* that the first Greek voyages tried to accord, to adjust their geography) [Bérard, II, 559]. I think it can be argued that Joyce, after *Nausicaa*, does something similar. He changes the Homeric Mediterranean map to the Homeric map of Ithaca. Or to put it more flexibly, he allows at least the option of looking at *Oxen of the Sun* and *Circe* as part of the post-*Nausicaa*, nocturnal homecoming. Dedalus, following a string of pubs eastward, if not *per* Athena's instructions, *per* his alter ego, Philip Drunk's, ends up beached at the Holles street hospital. The medical crew for Dedalus are the ambushing Ithacan suitors. *Circe* is another *Nostos* orientation. The location of Nighttown in Dublin (adjusted for Ithaca) not only jibes with the approximate location where the Phaeacians deposited Odysseus, but Bloom, by overshooting the Amiens station as he does in the episode (Hart and Knuth, p. 34), approaches Nighttown from the same direction that Odysseus would have approached Port Vathi. When Joyce's *Nostos* proper begins with *Eumeaus*, the positionings and directions replicate the *Odyssey* exactly: southwest to the Cabman's shelter (hut), and northwest to 7 Eccles street (palace).

If this scheme is a possibility for *Ulysses*, the effect is more than random. The *Odyssey* re-establishes the orientation of the wider epic on the home island by preparing to renew a northwest extension in miniature. Joyce's *Circe*, at the interior of Dublin, is a fitting capstone and recapitulation of the day-long, even life-long, *Wanderings* of Bloom in his wider Irish world. *Circe* is the center and circumference. It stands as the last chapter before the section of *Ulysses* Joyce calls the *Nostos*, but in a very literal way it engulfs the entire novel, beginning to end. Joyce provides some clues here. He obviously conceives of the episode as balancing the opening episode of Bloom's day, *Calypso*. When Odysseus returns from Calypso's isle to Phaeacia, he finds himself telling his story all over again—all its horrors and its few joys. And when he returns from Phaeacia the short distance home, he thinks his adventures were happening all over again—he does not know where he was and he expects the worst. In *Ulysses*, *Circe* makes the day tell its story again, and plunges Bloom on one more strange island in the middle of his home city. Home *is* a strange island in this recapitulative episode. Its connections with the rest of the novel are clear throughout, but Joyce goes to special lengths to connect it to the first of the *Wanderings*, *Calypso*. An entry in the notesheets reads simply: "Circe = Calypso" (Herring, p. 393). Joyce wants the two Odyssean nymphs together before coming home to the Odyssean wife. Three islands plot the return path across the full expanse of ocean: Calypso's Ogygia, Circe's Aiaia, and Penelope's Ithaca. Like Calypso, Circe is a minor island goddess, an enchantress, a mistress of Odysseus, a guardian of death's regions, and a boundary figure: Joyce notes that Calypso was "oceanborn (Okeanides)" (VIII.A.5, 297) and that Circe was a child of Perse, herself a child of the ocean stream: "oceanus . . . Helios = Pérse" (Herring, p. 283). And, of course, in the episode itself, Circe, Calypso, Molly Bloom, and Bella Cohen are persistently linked, suggesting that the movement from the morning's 7 Eccles street to Mecklenburg's Nighttown to the nighttime 7 Eccles somehow frames the day from *Wanderings* to *Nostos*. As Adaline Glasheen puts it so well: "Calypso over, Penelope on, Circe under the bed—virgin goddess, earthly wife, hellish whore" ("Calypso," in Hart and Hayman, p. 62). There is a progression here that makes sense for Bloom as it makes sense for Odysseus. Stephen and Bloom walk around Nighttown's block in *Circe*. The episode is the final *periplous* that includes the *periplous* in extension, *Calypso*, and the *periplous* toward home, *Ithaca*.

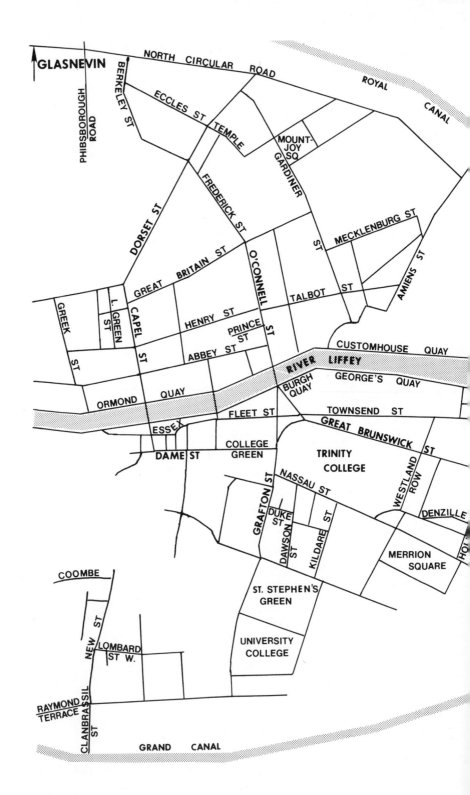

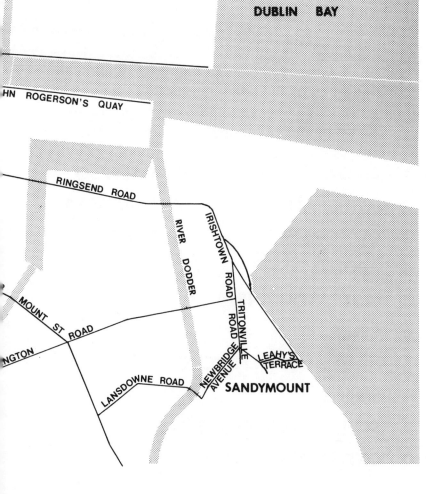

THE DUBLIN OF *ULYSSES*

(Streets of Major Actions)

DUBLIN   BAY

HN   ROGERSON'S   QUAY

RINGSEND   ROAD

RIVER   DODDER

IRISHTOWN ROAD

MOUNT ST ROAD

TRITONVILLE ROAD

NGTON

LEAHY'S
TERRACE

NEWBRIDGE
AVENUE

LANSDOWNE ROAD

SANDYMOUNT

BÉRARD'S ODYSSEY

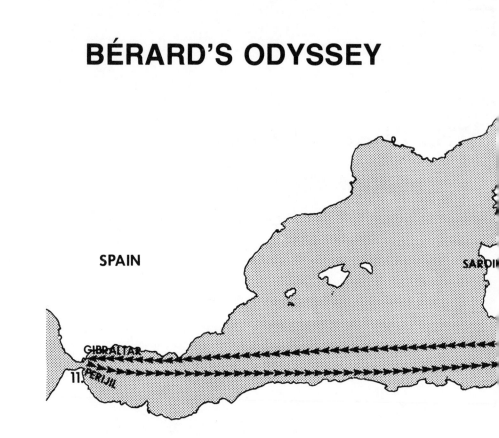

1. CICONES
2. LOTUSEATERS
3. CYCLOPS
4. AEOLUS
5. LESTRYGONIANS
6. CIRCE
7. HADES (RETURN TO CIRCE)
8. SIRENS
9. SCYLLA AND CHARYBDIS
10. OXEN OF THE SUN
11. CALYPSO
12. NAUSICAA
13. NOSTOS

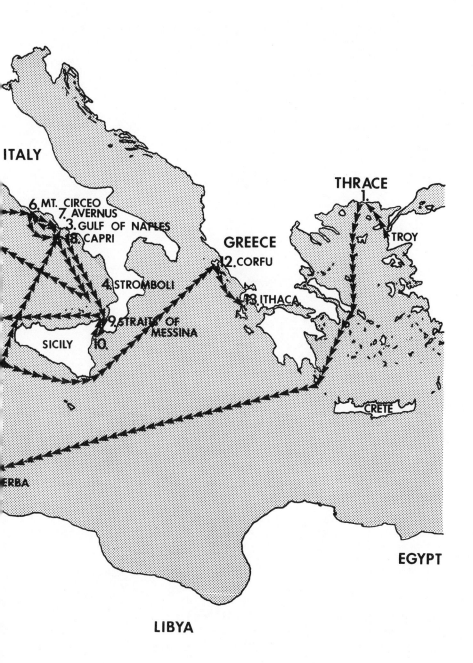

ITALY

6. MT. CIRCEO
7. AVERNUS
3. GULF OF NAPLES
8. CAPRI

4. STROMBOLI

9. STRAITS OF
MESSINA

SICILY

10.

THRACE
1.

TROY

GREECE
12. CORFU

13. ITHACA

CRETE

ERBA

EGYPT

LIBYA

SOUTHEAST-NORTHWEST AXES OF *ULYSSES*

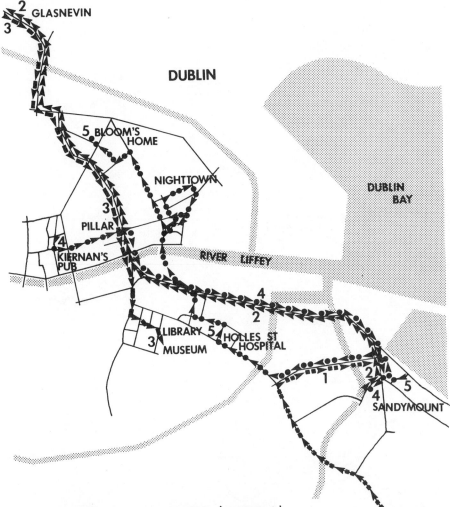

1. **DALKEY–SANDYMOUNT (CHAP. 3)**

2. **SANDYMOUNT–GLASNEVIN (CHAP. 6)**

3. **GLASNEVIN–PILLAR–MUSEUM (CHAP. 7-9)**

4. **KIERNAN'S–(PROJECTED?)–SANDYMOUNT (CHAP. 12-13)**

5. **SANDYMOUNT–HOLLES–NIGHTTOWN–ECCLES (CHAP. 14-17)**

SOUTHEAST-NORTHWEST AXES OF THE *ODYSSEY*

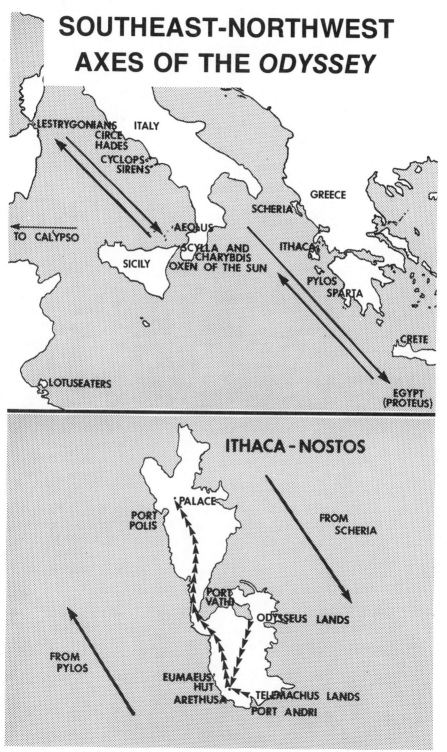

LESTRYGONIANS ITALY
CIRCE
HADES
CYCLOPS
SIRENS

GREECE

SCHERIA

TO CALYPSO

AEOLUS

ITHACA

SCYLLA AND
CHARYBDIS
OXEN OF THE SUN

SICILY

PYLOS
SPARTA

CRETE

LOTUSEATERS

EGYPT
(PROTEUS)

ITHACA - NOSTOS

PALACE

PORT
POLIS

FROM
SCHERIA

PORT
VATHI

ODYSSEUS LANDS

FROM
PYLOS

EUMAEUS'
HUT
ARETHUSA

TELEMACHUS LANDS
PORT ANDRI

TELEMACHIAD

Telemachus

Joyce's *schema* tells us that *Telemachus* does not yet bear a body, but in the opening episode of *Ulysses*, the stately plump epic displays its *omphalos*. The novel begins in one of the many Martello towers dotting the Irish coast as a defense barrier against French invasion set up in the early nineteenth century: "But ours is the *omphalos*" (17), says Mulligan. Stuart Gilbert includes a section on the *omphalos* as the mystical seat of the astral soul (Gilbert, pp. 51-56); if the *omphalos* centers the body, it is also geographically orienting. In *Ulysses* the Martello Tower is poised at the edge of the sea off Dublin Bay, toward the southeast in Sandycove.

In Irish legend, coastal towers have a complicated mythology. They are linked to adventures in death and rebirth.[1] M. H. D'Ambois de Jubainville's study, *The Irish Mythological Cycle and Celtic Mythology* (Dublin, 1903), sees a comparison in the Irish death tower, the Tower of Glass, to the *omphalos* of Calypso's isle on the borders of death's region in a Mediterranean world. The Irish myth recounts how thirty ships from Spain were lured toward the immortal glass tower by the living dead, and all but one were driven to the ocean's floor. The survivors on the remaining ship founded Ireland. De Jubainville compares the positioning and mission of Odysseus on Calypso's Ogygia to this story. Odysseus, too, is storm-tossed, but from an island in which he tests a kind of immortality he returns home to mortal life.[2]

Calypso's Ogygia at one time marked the point dividing the known and unknown worlds at the Straits of Gibraltar. Plutarch, when he came to describe its location, transferred the island west of Britain. Centers move west with civilization, and cultures establish new *omphaloi* as a matter of course. When Mulligan says that the Martello Tower at Sandycove, where Joyce, Gogarty, and Samuel Chenevix Trench, an Englishman, lived for a week in September

---

[1] See Howard Emerson Rogers, "Irish Myth and the Plot of *Ulysses*," *English Literary History*, xv (1948), 306-327.

[2] M. H. D'Ambois de Jubainville, *The Irish Mythological Cycle and Celtic Mythology*, trans. Richard Best (Dublin, 1903), p. 68.

of 1904, is the *omphalos*, he means that it was considered central in the English defense line. For Joyce, the *omphalos* is more paradoxical. The body's navel is the point of origin and the point of sundering, a center that encourages disconnections. The Martello works symbolically the same way; it introduces Dedalus to his daily agonies. Telemachus, who sits idly dreaming of his father in a tower of Ithaca's palace at the beginning of the *Odyssey*, gains a sense of mission under Athena-Mentor's guidance. He is told to seek his origins in the Peloponnese, to return along a traditional southeast-northwest route to learn what he needs to know in order to adjust his life at home. In the *schema*, Joyce labels Dedalus as the dispossessed son in struggle. Stephen's choice, insofar as he really has one in a single day, is between paralysis or substantiation, just as Joyce's surrogate in *Finnegans Wake*, Shem, chooses between Ireland or "a brandnew start for himself to run down his easting" (*FW*, 471). Because Stephen's mother is beastly dead, Joyce lists Penelope as the muse of the chapter in the *schema*. Stephen's drift at the beginning, then, is all potential—from an Odyssean mother as muse to the novel's concluding chapter where the earth's turning, fulfilled body, a "gynomorphic" *Penelope*, assumes the muse's voice.

The spatial vision of the first chapter in Joyce's novel casts beyond the city limits—another connection with the last episode, *Penelope*, which travels back to the original Gibraltar *omphalos*. In the morning sun, the expanse measures "the surrounding country and the awaking mountains" (3). Throughout, Mulligan and Stephen gaze in one direction or another, toward Kingstown or Howth, north; and Bray's head (which actually cannot be seen from Sandycove) or England's territorial waters, the "seas' ruler . . . southward over the bay" (18). To the north are reminders of past invaders, the Danes, and reminders of another literary tower that "beetles o'er his base into the sea," Hamlet's Elsinore, where a disturbed young prince brooded the days away. To the south and east are the imperial British, Jekylls and Hydes, who rage at black panthers at night, and kill with kindness in the light of day. To the west are the "silk of the kine," Old Ireland, an enfeebled race of Celtic originals.

The expanses of the chapter mark the emptiness of its Irish center. Mulligan even goes to Greece to mock the Irish: "The mockery of it, he said gaily" to Dedalus, "Your absurd name, an ancient Greek" (3). And as he does so often in this chapter of usurpation, Mulligan assumes the role that Dedalus ought to play: "My name is absurd too. Malachi Mulligan, two dactyls. But it has a Hellenic ring, hasn't it? Tripping and sunny like the buck himself. We must go to Athens" (4). Stephen's name, of course, is that of the Daedalian artificer and the Christian Saint Stephen, formerly a Jew in Greece. When irritated by Dedalus, Mulligan transposes his double-self to a Nietzschean northern world: "I'm hyperborean as much as you" (5). Mulligan's mockery upsets Stephen by usurping all his space. Mockers are protean parasites—Mulligan takes to the sea of matter and saves men from drowning. Dedalus' reluctance to move only weighs him down in bitter waters. Meanwhile, Mulligan dances over oceans to the limits of time and space. Adri Malachi is a king; Malachi a prophet; Mercury Malachi is the messenger of the gods, Hermes, a god of limits, urbane, articulate, cosmopolitan, daring, tricky. Stephen, who wears Mulligan's pants and shoes, and who carries his own Mercurial accoutrements, his Latin-quarter hat and ash plant, wrestles with his protean friend for dominance. In a touch Joyce added to his opening chapter in late revisions, Mulligan's head bobs like a seal's in the Bay just before Stephen looks toward the sea and thinks: "Usurper" (23). Proteus in the *Odyssey* was a keeper of seals on an island of seals (Bérard, II, 62). Menelaus captured Proteus by disguising himself and his men in seals' hides and taking control of his domain. Part of what Mulligan is, Dedalus needs.

In the beginning of the day, *Telemachus* only opens small spaces. The platform door of the tower lets in the rays of the morning sun. Later, another tower door opens to let in the milk-woman. She is Athena-Mentor in the *schema*, but Ireland herself in the text.

> Old and secret she had entered from a morning world, maybe a messenger. She praised the goodness of the milk, pouring it out. Crouching by a patient cow at daybreak in the lush field, a witch on her toadstool, her wrinkled fingers at the squirting dugs. They lowed about her whom they knew, dewsilky cattle. Silk of the kine and poor old woman, names given her in old times.
>
> (13-14)

The secret names, "silk of the kine" and "poor old woman," were traditional names for Ireland. Western cattle—the initiators in mythic migrations—introduce a half-serious "livestock" theme that will mark its tracks through the dying (and renewing) day of *Ulys-*

ses. At this early hour, the old woman as Ireland climbs to the English-Irish Martello Tower as the two women of Stephen's *Pisgah Sight of Palestine or the Parable of the Plums* will climb to another English-Irish tower, that of the "onehandled adulterer," Nelson's Pillar. "Idle mockery" (21) seems the order of the morning. Dedalus is idle and Mulligan mocks. "Glory be to God" (13) for the morning, says the milk-woman as she enters. "To whom?" asks Mulligan. Stephen, at the episode's end, sends himself something of a message, perhaps more frustrating than reorienting: "I will not sleep here tonight. Home also I cannot go" (23). In the first episode of Bloom's *Wanderings, Calypso*, Bloom, too, will get the message: steer clear of the *omphalos*, at least when Irish men of brawn are in possession.

NESTOR

If the geography of *Telemachus* presents a land with no real center, the geography of *Nestor* seeks a route toward minimal sustenance. Nestor's home, sandy Pylos, was the principal lifeline of the western Peloponnese. Stephen Dedalus at the beginning of *Ulysses* is poised for inaction over spaces of land and sea. In *Nestor* he returns to Greek and Mediterranean spaces. He makes the short southeastern journey from Sandycove to Dalkey. More important, his history lesson at the beginning of the episode is about a Greek in Italy, Pyrrhus, who loses by winning. The result is regrettable, but the effort is at least commendable. Like history itself, the chapter's art in the *schema*, the beginning of movement is the beginning of action. Stephen's formula is Aristotelian and Viconian: "It must be a movement then, an actuality of the possible as possible" (25). Stephen may not have moved a great deal, but he has moved in the right direction. In the *Odyssey* Telemachus leaves his home on Ithaca and sails with the breezes from nightfall to dawn a relatively short distance southeast to the shores of Pylos, the city of the gates to western approaches. Pylos is the last familiar port of consequence at the extension of the Peloponnese for traders along the land and sea routes from the Levantine Mediterranean (Bérard, II, 436). Telemachus in the *Odyssey* moves back in the direction of places the Greeks knew well. His most important discovery abroad is that the memory of his father is still alive.

Partly by recognizing the likeness of Odysseus in Telemachus,

Nestor encourages the young man to fulfill the epic's destiny by connecting past and future. Athena repeats the formula that Nestor will tell history and not lies to those who listen. But it is an all too easy history, hardly worth more than a polite ear. Telemachus listens, leaves, and does not return as asked. Mr. Garrett Deasy of *Ulysses*, Stephen's employer, is garrulous, jingoistic, and blinded by visions of the past that are his alone. He is no less irritating than the *Odyssey*'s Nestor on the face of it. Occasionally, he especially taxes Stephen's indulgence. Deasy believes that the Jews sinned against the light, presumably his own northern lights.[3] "Who has not?" (34) Stephen responds, impatient and irritated.

Nestor's land in the *Odyssey* is in the cattle-rich region of Pylos. If Deasy is the Ulsterman of the "black North" in *Ulysses*, Nestor is of a line of Greek kings from northern Thessaly [Bérard, I, 125]. At the time of the Homeric epics his home territory included the mouth of the famous Alpheus river, although the geographical connections between Nestor's Pylos and the Alpheus are made more explicit in the *Iliad* than in the *Odyssey*. As a mythological river, the Alpheus has its own migrational axis; its waters were said to pass unmixed through the sea, entering west of Olympia and rising again in the fountain of Arethusa in Syracuse on Sicily. Pylos and the Alpheus are points of extension along the trade routes from the eastern world, but points of origin for journeys further west. Bérard places Pylos slightly south of the Alpheus on the western Peloponnese at Samikon, a strongly defended port town capable of protecting its coastal shore from foreign invaders [Bérard, I, 122]. Pylos is associated with the cattle that give the region its distinctiveness, and, in the etymology popularized by Hesychius, give the Alpheus its name. The Semitic *alpha* is the ox, the ox letter, and the beginning of the alphabet. Heracles turns the river at Pylos to clean the stables of Augeas. The Boupraison, the famous ancient Greek cattle market, is located on the Alpheus above Pylos. When Hermes steals Apollo's cattle he takes them to the Alpheus at Elis. There he initiates sacrifices to the Olympian gods, and establishes a bond with Apollo that hints at the possible, but mythically incomplete, relationship between Dedalus, *Bous Stephanoumenos* or crowned ox, and a man with cattle on his mind, a past employee of Dublin's

---

[3] See E. L. Epstein, "Nestor," in Hart and Hayman, p. 25, for some thoughts on the light north's fear of the dark-backed easterner.

cattle market, a Taurus by birth, Leopold Bloom, the Apollonian "Brightdayler" of *Ithaca*.

In *Nestor*, of course, Mr. Deasy wants Stephen to assist him in the printing of a letter on the subject of Dublin's hoof-and-mouth-diseased cattle. Dublin's livestock are infected; Nestor's famous herds in the *Odyssey* are thriving nicely. Therein lies a difference between Joyce's paralytic Dublin (or Telemachus' Ithaca) and the bustling Pylos. Bérard explains: "Le boeuf, qui n'abonde pas dans le reste de la Grèce rocailleuse, a toujours trouvé dans cette plaine maritime des pâturages et des eaux convenables" (Cattle, which do not abound in the rest of rocky Greece, always found enough pasture land and water in this coastal plain) [Bérard, 1, 126]. He elaborates on the supposed origin of the Alpheus's name, an origin that would have interested Joyce as the creator of A. L. P. (Anna Livia Plurabelle and the Liffey river) in *Finnegans Wake*: "Le mot sémitique אלף, *a.l.p.*, qui veut dire *boeuf*, est arrivé aux Hellènes sous la forme emphatique אלפא, *alpha*, nom de leur première lettre" (The Semitic word אלף, *a.l.p.*, that is, cattle, arrives in Greece under the emphatic form אלפא, *alpha*, the name of their first letter) [Bérard, 1, 126].

In the *Odyssey* Telemachus comes upon Nestor at Poseidon's altar sacrificing and feasting upon the beef of the region. Nestor is the historian of generations, his father's, his own, and his son's. Time is always at issue when Nestor is on the scene, and in *Ulysses*, time, more than space, controls the *Nestor* episode. Richard Ellmann argues this point convincingly in his *Ulysses on the Liffey*. Joyce's chapter is historical; it begins with a disappointed Greek general and ends with Mr. Deasy shouting in the street about the history of Ireland's barring the Jews from its western gates. If a new Greek Odysseus is in Dublin, a rather sad Jew also wanders the streets as an exile in his own city. The local and fictional history available in *Nestor* is somewhere between Deasy's jingoism and Stephen's version of history as nightmare. Mid-range is another history—a regeneration of possibilities. *Nestor* does teach its minimal lesson. When Deasy argues that history is the movement toward the one great goal of God's manifestation, he gets the Viconian form correct, though he misses its urban flavor. Stephen supplies the local variant: God is a "shout in the street" (34). For Dublin's day, Stephen's view may be more complex, but it is not inimical to Deasy's. The manifestation of heroes, if not gods, is accompanied in *Ulysses* by street noise. There is a movement in time and across space implied. In *Circe* Stephen will define the paradigmatic elliptical movement of the musical octave as representative of all mythic and actual process. When he does so he is interrupted by a shout on Tyrone street.

Nestor is an early chapter—it offers potential direction but little fulfillment. Not only is Deasy an anti Semite—mocking the novel's southeast/northwest axis—but his specific historical vision is debilitating. Obsessed as he is, like Nestor in the *Odyssey*, with the dangers of feminine endings, Deasy's cold north is antithetical to *Penelope*'s Mediterranean warmth in *Ulysses*. And fearful of homecoming, he is oblivious to the anxieties of exile. Deasy's jingo history eliminates Bloom and Molly before either of them even appears. It will take more than a letter on hoof and mouth disease to reconstitute Ireland. Pyrrhus loses the larger war of Mediterranean hegemony, and Deasy capitulates to the loss of Irish home rule.

PROTEUS

Stephen has moved, probably by tram, about six miles from Dalkey to Sandymount. He appears in Dublin on the strand after crossing from Irishtown near Watery lane, as we later learn when Dignam's funeral procession intersects his path (88). It is 11:00 A.M., and Dedalus heads north on the strand toward Leahy's terrace near the Star of the Sea Church where Bloom will reappear in *Nausicaa*. As the episode progresses, Stephen follows the curve of the Bay until he walks due east paralleling the Pigeonhouse road. He reaches farther east within Dublin's city limits than anyone else in the novel. He then returns and walks back west.

In the *Odyssey* Telemachus leaves Nestor's Pylos for a two-day voyage (with a stopover in Phera) before reaching Menelaus' Sparta. He makes remarkably good time over the Peloponnese to the plains above Argos. Joyce, obviously, does not sustain the southeast movement of Dedalus from Sandycove to Dalkey. If he had, Stephen's *Proteus* monologue would be recited somewhere in the middle of the Irish channel. But Stephen makes good time to Sandymount from Dalkey, even if he is temporarily not travelling in the *Odyssey*'s direction. In another sense, Joyce maintains the axis by having Stephen think of Paris in *Proteus*. Paris is the equivalent, along Bérard's projected axis for the *Odyssey*, not only of Egypt, where the Proteus tale is set, but of Sparta, where it is told. Stephen eventually sets the axis as far as it need go to the southeast when he approaches the mouths of the Nile themselves in requesting that his epiphanies be donated to the great library (defunct) at Alexandria (40). Alexandria is in the Nile Delta near where Bérard places Proteus' isle, Pharos [Bérard, II, 30-31].

There is another interesting aspect to Bérard's projection of Telemachus' route. In the *Odyssey* the Phera stopover is slightly south of the course of the river Alpheus as it bends east through the Peloponnese. Bérard links Phera to the market town Aliphera—which eastern traders set up as a bazaar: "Aliphera est donc le bazar," [Bérard, I, 117]. Stephen's musings in *Proteus* are set in Sandymount near the Mirus Bazaar in Ballsbridge where the Viceregal cavalcade will head later in the afternoon, and where Bloom sees the bazaar fireworks go off in *Nausicaa*. The Mirus Bazaar is in the same locale where another of Joyce's eastern voyagers, the young boy in his short story "Araby," meets with Dublin's version of decadence in evening lands.

The *Proteus* episode in the *Odyssey* is a variant of an Egyptian tale, transported from the east through Crete to Greece, according to Bérard. For most of his stay on Ithaca, Odysseus claims Egyptian or Cretan origins when he lies about his voyages over the seas to western coasts. Telemachus in the *Odyssey*'s version of the Proteus legend receives information about his father's western progress from Menelaus who had received it from Proteus, the material shapeshifter. Hugh Kenner has observed of *Proteus* in *Ulysses* that signate matter is impression and substantial form is intelligibility.[4] The relation between impression and substance is much of what the Proteus legend, the *Odyssey* itself, and *Ulysses* are all about. Intelligible knowledge is often a knowledge of positioning and expansion. Bérard writes of Proteus' knowledge of the west as territorial discovery. The Elysian Fields are only in part mythic.

> Car ces Champs des Bienheureux étaient pour les plus vieux Égyptiens un morceau de notre terre, un pays aussi réel que les régions habitées par les vivants. La situation en était parfaitement déterminée. Ces Champs étaient placés aux extrémitiés de la terre et ils y restèrent toujours. Mais à mesure que les explorations des

[4] Hugh Kenner, *Dublin's Joyce* (Boston: Beacon Press, 1956, rpt., 1962), pp. 138-139.

marchands et les découvertes des navigateurs avaient reculé pour les Égyptiens les extrémités du monde, on avait vu les Champs des Bienheureux se déplacer, et, suivant les progrès des connaissances géographiques, s'éloigner vers le Nord et vers l'Ouest.

(For the Elysian Fields were for the oldest Egyptians a piece of our earth, a country as real as the regions inhabited by the living. Their location had been specifically determined. These fields were placed at the extremity of the earth and they would remain there always. But as the merchants' explorations and the navigators' discoveries extended the ends of the earth, so the Land of the Blessed, following the progress of geographical knowledge, was moved further and further to the north and the west.)

[Bérard, ii, 77]

In order to hear this story of the westward extension from Menelaus, Telemachus, Bérard writes, had only to position himself for the full eastern return: "Étant donnée une route transpéloponnésienne, on peut toujours retrouver la route transégéenne qui lui correspond" (Given a trans-Peloponnesian route, one can always discover the trans-Aegean route that corresponds to it) [Bérard, i, 134]. This, of course, is precisely what Menelaus does for Telemachus. Stranded on Pharos Isle in the Nile Basin, about a day's sail west in the direction of Alexandria, Menelaus pins down Proteus and gains his release and a guarantee of homecoming. A similar Irish tale exchanges the Egyptian Proteus for Mananaan MacLir, the Irish Old Man of the Sea who appears in Joyce's *Proteus* as a late addition to the text. Mananaan leads the hero of the *Voyage of Bran* to an undersea paradise in the extreme west. In the Irish version, as in the Egyptian, the land of the dead is also the land of the living. Knowledge of death at the extension becomes knowledge of rebirth. The Irish paradise on the Mag Mór plain to the west is known as the land of the young, *Tir na n' Og*. Significantly, in a book where the artist finally comprehends all beginnings and all ends, the geography of the full migration is celebrated, from Phoenician origins to western ends: *Finnegans Wake* transforms *Tir na n' Og* to "Tyre-nan-Og" (*FW*, 91).

Dedalus possesses no such confidence in his transforming powers. Menelaus is a sad Kevin Egan in the *schema*, and Egypt at noon is the "fleshpot" of Paris. The eastern axis is there in relation to Dublin, but Stephen is not certain what sustenance it provides. Nor can he know that the homing three-master behind him, the *Rosevean*, with its material cargo of bricks, carries the novel's lying version of Odysseus, the sailor Murphy. The real Odysseus, Bloom, will arrive at the same Sandymount later in the day when the sun goes down.

In *Proteus* Stephen is presented, perhaps unfairly, with the most difficult problem for the hero or artist. He has to read and interpret signs more mysterious than Crusoe's footprint in the sand. When he walks east he thinks of the original unity of matter, of birth, of the beginnings of the alphabet, of first woman, and of first man.[5] The moment he turns around toward the west, he faces the wastes of Ireland. The western turn is death for him at this stage of the day: "Here, I am not walking out to the Kish lightship, am I? He stood suddenly, his feet beginning to sink slowly in the quaking soil. Turn back" (44). He does.

> Turning, he scanned the shore south, his feet sinking again slowly in new sockets. The cold domed room of the tower waits. Through the barbicans the shafts of light are moving ever, slowly ever as my feet are sinking, creeping duskward over the dial floor. Blue dusk, nightfall, deep blue night. In the darkness of the dome they wait, their pushedback chairs, my obelisk valise, around a board of abandoned platters. Who to clear it? He has the key. I will not sleep there when this night comes. A shut door of a silent tower entombing their blind bodies. . . .   (44)

The suitors wait at home in death's tower—a projected vision and another ambush. Ireland, for Dedalus, is the land of western death. It is the region of "Sir Lout's toys," a land of imprisoned giants. Ireland is deprived of the sun as is the realm of giants to the north, the kingdom of Tartarus. Dedalus has not the prophetic or enlivening powers to see the land of darkness as the potential land of rebirth.

Richard Ellmann has pointed to the chapter's dialectical structure, its two-movement turn from primal to terminal.[6] That structure mirrors the geographical directions of the *Odyssey*, and fore-

---

[5] Dedalus alludes to the hermetic first man, Adam Kadmon. In discussing Hermes Trismegistos, or Thoth, connected by Bérard to several versions of the Proteus story, Madame Blavatsky writes: "The Kabalists identify him with Adam *Kadmon*, the first manifestation of Divine Power" (*Isis Unveiled* [New York, 1877], i, xxxiii).

[6] Richard Ellmann, *Ulysses on the Liffey* (New York, 1972), p. 23.

shadows another "turn" in *Ulysses* beginning later in the evening from the strand as Bloom drifts homeward from Sandymount, renewed and soon to be in the company of that lost "son" who had wandered east and returned west to join him. But for Dedalus, *Proteus* is an episode of confused turns. He is a double self, like Telemachus at home and Telemachus abroad: *"Lui, c'est moi"* (41). Stephen vacillates on visiting his aunt, he turns when he might walk on all the way to the Lighthouse, he considers hopping up to the Poolbeg lighthouse road when the tide cuts off his return across the strand at Cock Lake, and he looks around suddenly when he thinks someone is behind him. When he sees the cockle-pickers or "red egyptians" (47), he fuses them into the androgynous primal couple, the wedded Megapenthes of the Spartan marriage celebration in the *Odyssey*. But he has no idea whether the gypsies make a procreative or deathly union, whether they are westering the eastern spirit or engaged in the morose delectation of the coupler's will. Mulligan had called Stephen "dogsbody" in *Telemachus*, and in *Proteus* the confused Dedalus runs into a real live dogsbody sniffing at the carcass of a real dead dogsbody (46). Corpus and corpse or "allwombing tomb" (48)—Stephen has the principles for resurrecting matter at his disposal, but does not know how to control flux. The Proteus legend, shaping matter and shaping space from Pharos Isle to the Blessed Isles, is one model for ordering aesthetic domain, the *nacheinander* and *nebeneinander* of movement or history. *Proteus* is a primal version of the book Dedalus is in. Bloom appears in a dream as Haroun al Raschid, Murphy appears on the *Rosevean*, and the best Stephen can do is scratch out a few words about vampires and south winds on the corner of Garrett Deasy's hoof-and-mouth letter (48).

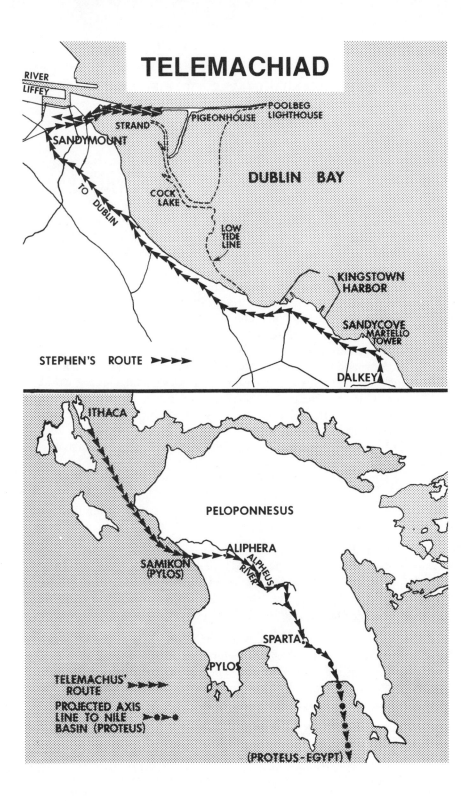

TELEMACHIAD

RIVER LIFFEY

POOLBEG LIGHTHOUSE

PIGEONHOUSE

STRAND

SANDYMOUNT

DUBLIN BAY

COCK LAKE

TO DUBLIN

LOW TIDE LINE

KINGSTOWN HARBOR

SANDYCOVE MARTELLO TOWER

STEPHEN'S ROUTE ▶▶▶▶

DALKEY

ITHACA

PELOPONNESUS

ALIPHERA

SAMIKON (PYLOS)

ALPHEUS RIVER

SPARTA

TELEMACHUS' ROUTE ▶▶▶

PROJECTED AXIS LINE TO NILE BASIN (PROTEUS)

PYLOS

(PROTEUS-EGYPT)

THE WANDERINGS OF ODYSSEUS: I

CALYPSO

BLOOM at 8:00 A.M. is ensconced in the kitchen of his home at 7 Eccles street. *Calypso*'s interior, cramped and below street-level, contrasts with the expanse of the first episode's opening on the parapet overlooking Dublin Bay. Victor Bérard points out that pirates in the Mediterranean often kept prisoners roped or chained in remote island caverns, allowing them some, but not much, leeway to wander [Bérard, I, 159]. After thinking about protecting (and preserving) his daughter's virginity, Bloom says: "Useless: can't move" (67). He is in much the same position with his wife's planned alliance with Boylan. He has a little, but not much, leeway in his own home.

Calypso begins with the citizen's epithet and a particular citizen's interior habits: "Mr Leopold Bloom ate with relish the inner organs of beasts and fowls" (55). Calypso's island in the *Odyssey* is both an enclosure and a mythic extension at the western edge of the world, near Gibraltar. Bérard describes her isle, much like the small isle Perejil at the foot of Mount Atlas-Abila (which Molly later calls Apes Hill), as the Phoenician paradise; "L'île de Kalypso est l'Éden d'un peuple navigateur" (The isle of Calypso is the Eden of a maritime people) [Bérard, I, 150]. The end of the world, guarded by Mount Atlas and the Pillars of Hercules, was a special Phoenician attraction. Significantly, Bérard writes that the Phoenicians later transposed the world's end to the British Isles after sailing through the passage beyond Gibraltar.

Il fut donc un temps où les Phéniciens plaçaient au bout de la Keltique le Pilier du Nord. Mais, dans un âge précédent, de beaucoup antérieur sans doute, leurs premiers navigateurs avaient salué dans notre Mont aux Singes ce Pilier du Couchant, que l'Égypt appelait *Manou*, que les Hellènes nommèrent *Atlas*.

(There was, then, a time when the Phoenicians placed the Pillar of the North at the end of Celtic regions. But at an earlier date, surely much earlier, the first Phoenician navigators had greeted this pillar of the West in our Apes Hill, named *Manou* by the Egyptians and renamed Atlas by the Greeks.)

[Bérard, I, 249]

Joyce records the legend of Phoenician extension from the Mediterranean to Ireland in his 1907 Trieste lecture, *Ireland, Island of Saints and Sages*: "This adventurous people, who had a monopoly of the sea, established in Ireland a civilization that had decayed and almost disappeared before the first Greek historian took his pen in hand" (*CW*, 156). Molly Bloom, daughter of Gibraltar's Major Tweedy, makes the Phoenician connection in *Ulysses*. She was born on Kalpe's rock and later translated to Dublin. In *Calypso's schema*, Joyce lists Molly as the nymph and as Penelope or "wife." If Molly is an Ithacan Penelope, a native of Gibraltar by birth, and an emigrant to 7 Eccles street by marriage, she spans the migratory world of the Odyssean epic as queen, nymph, and wife. Calypso's name means bowl or gulf: the rounded form. Her island, Ogygia, Bérard writes, means ocean: the surrounding form. Joyce sets up in *Calypso* what was parodied in *Telemachus*—forms with ample substance and range. Not only does he begin with the inner organs of the body, but he has Bloom walk down Dorset street and imagine the children in Saint Joseph's National school at their geography lesson. Bloom thinks of the mountain range in southwest Ireland: "At their joggerfry. Mine. Slieve Bloom" (58). Bloom is the mountain to Calypso's ocean bowl. Joyce hints at the possibilities of bodily geography he would explore fully in *Finnegans Wake* with Anna Livia as the river's waters and Earwicker as Howth Hill.

The structural-spatial problem for Joyce in the day of *Ulysses* involves one or another variety of conversion. He must arrange the novel to work through the progress of exile from *Calypso* to *Penelope*. In the Gilbert-Gorman *schema*, exile and family are listed as two of *Calypso's* symbols. Adventure is, in a sense, domestic. If Stephen turns away from his family, Bloom tries in his feeble way to reconstitute the center, nymph and wife. But conversion goes slowly at first. In *Calypso* the home-rule sun is reluctant to rise in the northwest (57); just as in *Proteus* Dedalus talks about his Irish homeland as a ray of darkness in the light, an inversion of the Biblical passage in *John* 1:5.

In the course of *Calypso* Bloom leaves his home only briefly for a short *periplous* down and up the block to purchase a kidney at Dlugacz's on Upper Dorset. Dlugacz's, pork butcher, is one of the few invented shops of *Ulysses*, but Joyce apparently wanted Bloom to reject the "recall" from a fellow Jew as the equivalent of Odysseus' recall to Ithaca. It is not the Jew, nor even Bloom's fond memories of the Jewish section of Dublin, that finally starts the wanderer on his day. Rather, the Mercury-winged delivery of Boylan's letter announcing the afternoon tryst accomplishes the recall. Bloom's short outing in *Calypso* is only a preliminary. The *Odyssey*, too, opens with an invocation and a survey of Odysseus' lot on Calypso's isle. Homer provides a brief resumé of his hero's previous *Wanderings*. Bloom's outing in *Calypso* is a miniaturization of the epic condition: the smaller the spaces, the smaller the journey.

A more important movement in the episode is associational. Place and direction help determine mood. When Bloom walks southeast down Eccles street he thinks of the orienting, recalling sun: "Makes you feel young" (57). At Dlugacz's Bloom picks up a cut sheet of newsprint for wrapping pork and reads of an advertisement for farms in the Holy Land. He thinks of the return to a native paradise until a cloud passes over the sun when he turns northwest on Eccles: "A cloud began to cover the sun wholly slowly wholly. Grey. Far" (61). The only call now is to death, the land of the young morning sun turns to a land ravaged by time, the land of the "oldest people. . . . Now it could bear no more. Dead: an old woman's: the grey sunken cunt of the world" (61). But Bloom, the easterner, unlike the brooding Dedalus, is renewable with the light, even through the northwest gloom. The sun returns and his spirits return along with it: "Quick warm sunlight came running from Berkeley Road, swiftly, in slim sandals, along the brightening foot-path. Runs, she runs to meet me, a girl with gold hair on the wind" (61). The sun's warmth is small consolation for the city exile, but it is reminiscent of the extraordinary simile for homecoming in the *Odyssey* when exile itself becomes the vehicle for the joys of wife and home.

> Now from his breast into his eyes the ache
> of longing mounted, and he wept at last,
> his dear wife, clear and faithful, in his arms, longed for
>   as the sunwarmed earth is longed for by a swimmer
> spent in rough water where his ship went down
> upon Poseidon's blows, gale winds and tons of sea.
>   (Book XXIII, Fitzgerald, p. 436)

Toward the end of the *Calypso* episode, Bloom returns home and prepares for another short trip to the tenebrous regions, the gloom of the jakes: the Odyssean "king was in his counting house" (68). After his morning purge he "pulled back the jerky shaky door of the jakes and came forth from the gloom into the air" (70). Joyce enters a whimsical note in his Zürich notebook comparing Calypso's cave to the grotto of the Naiades on Ithaca at *Nostos*: "Grotto of nymphs WC" (VIII.A.5, p. 296). The *Wanderings* proper are about to begin. In the *Odyssey* the journey is some fifteen hundred miles to Scheria, the land of the Phaeacians, and then overnight to Ithaca. In *Ulysses* the *Wanderings* are set sequentially without the Phaeacian retrospective narration. Joyce begins with an adventure taking place for Odysseus years before in the land of the Lotophagoi.

LOTUSEATERS

If the king emerges from the gloom of his counting-house in *Ca-lypso*, the queen remains behind in *Lotuseaters*: "Mrs Marion Bloom. Not up yet. Queen was in her bedroom eating bread and" (75). Bloom leaves the thought incomplete—he has received the secret message of the morning's winged post. He leaves Eccles street long before Boylan arrives, and he stays out for the day's *Wanderings* until long after Boylan leaves. A converted Jew, Bloom "left the house of his father and left the God of his father" (76). In Dublin he is reduced to leaving his own house for reasons far more de-meaning.

The Linati *schema* for *Lotuseaters* shows Nausicaa with a (2) in parentheses for one of the "persons" of the episode. This is curious, and could mean any of a number of things. Joyce might be explain-ing the sequential change, *Lotuseaters* replacing the landing at Nausicaa's home, Scheria, after *Calypso*. There is also the possible connection between the episodes—both Lotusland and Scheria are false homecomings for Odysseus, formal enjoyment without any substantive effort. Joyce undercuts the narcissism of both episodes in *Ulysses* with the onanistic image of false homecoming: masturba-tion. After the pleasures afforded him by Gerty MacDowell in *Nausicaa*, Bloom thanks his good fortune that he had not wasted his seed in the Turkish baths of *Lotuseaters*: "Damned glad I didn't do it in the bath this morning" (368). In the *Odyssey* both lands of ease open on, but do not fully partake of, the more dangerous western seas. This is of considerable importance in the geographical structure of the *Odyssey*, whose *Wanderings* proper before the

Ithacan *Nostos* begin and end with versions of easeful homecomings. Bérard suggests the comparison when he describes Djerba and Corfu (Scheria) as ports: "les Lotophages sont alors en une situation analogue à celle des Phéaciens: ils ouvrent, eux aussi, l'entrée d'un détroit vers les mers lointaines" (the Lotuseaters are then in an analogous situation to that of the Phaeacians: they also open upon the entrance to a strait toward distant seas) [Bérard, II, 112].

Lotuseaters begins with Bloom walking east along Sir John Rogerson's quay south of the Liffey considerably southeast of 7 Eccles street (Hart and Knuth, p. 25). He passes a post office (18 Rogerson's quay) and notes that he could have given that address too for his flirtatious correspondence with Martha Clifford. His first mission is to the post office at 49-50 Westland Row where he had arranged for an exchange of letters under the name of Henry Flower. After leaving the post office, he walks around the block, east on Great Brunswick street (now Pearse street), south on Cumberland, through the back door and out the front door of All Hallows, to Westland Row again, and, moving southwest, on to the baths at Leinster street. Joyce does not explain why Bloom takes an indirect route to the post office on Westland Row, why he walks as far east as he does along the quay, why he did not go to the baths at Tara as he thought of doing in *Calypso*: "Wonder have I time for a bath this morning. Tara street" (68).

In the *Odyssey*, Odysseus begins his adventures after an ill-advised raid on Ismarus in the land of the Cicones. He moves along the Aegean coasts from Troy, and escapes Ismarus with his fleet luckily intact after the Cicones raid. From that point he is blown south beneath the Cape of Malea, beneath the island of Cythera, and southwest into the wider Mediterranean. He does not touch land until his tempest-driven fleet beaches on the northern coasts of Djerba near Libya. This is the land of the Lotophagoi, so named by the Phoenician voyagers who identified coastal populations on the African sweep of the Mediterranean by what vegetation they ate. Victor Bérard points out that early travelers, using bread-eating populations as a norm, distinguished among cultures by their food: "pour les Anciens, dans l'état de leurs connaissances, c'était la seule manière commode et rationnelle de classer en différents groupes les humanités de même couleur" (for the Ancients, given the state of their knowledge, it was the only easy and rational way of classifying peoples of the same color in different groups) [Bérard, II, 99].

Bérard argues that it is really no more ridiculous to classify the people of various regions by what they ate as to classify them by regional type. For his part, he finds it "moins ridicule que nos 'pan-latinisme,' 'pan-slavisme,' 'pan-germanisme,' 'pan-brittonisme' . . ." (less ridiculous than our panlatinism, panslavism, pangermanism, panbrittonism) [Bérard, II, 100]. Joyce comments in his Zürich notebook: "L.B.—all eat it—all one family" (VIII.A.5, p. 295). In *Ulysses* the wafer of the mass serves to define a religious family: "Hokypoky penny a lump. Then feel all like one family party" (81).

Bérard thinks that the lotus flower of the Odyssean episode derives its name from the Semitic *lot* or plant. The lotus is not a fruit, but an edible variety of water lily common to certain areas along the Libyan coast. Its quality as an opiate is seen by Bérard as Homer's joke long before it became Joyce's. Bérard guesses that the *Odyssey* puns on lotus and *Lethe*, the waters of the mythic oblivion-producing river. Bloom's easy progress through Dublin's southeast quadrant to the botanical oblivion of the bath-waters ("the limp father of thousands, a languid floating flower," 86), maps the urban version of Odysseus' detour from the east to the narcotic south. Bloom is blown past and around a number of interesting capes and islands. Before doubling back to the Westland Row post office, he passes the sailors' chapel on Lombard street, the Wesleyan, Methodist-run *Bethel*. Bloom's associations are with his Jewish origins, *Bethel*, the House of God near Jerusalem, the place of the Ark of the Covenant: "the frowning face of Bethel. El, yes: house of: Aleph, Beth" (71). He passes through the Catholic All Hallows after the post office, and finally "toward the mosque" of the Turkish baths. Bloom's voyage to a port of oblivion tastes of the Jewish, Protestant, Catholic, and Moslem opiates.[1]

In the *Odyssey* the voyage south to Lotusland works to counter the epic homecoming. As the first of the Odyssean marvels, it is also the first of several paradisaical temptations of Odysseus' will. Bérard, who, like Joyce, provides schematic words for each of the Homeric episodes, tags this one as monotony [Bérard, II, 104]. Joyce substitutes a sense of dead weight: "It's the force of gravity of the earth is the weight" (72). Odysseus' men lose the desire to move— *dolce far niente*, as Bloom puts it. This is a crucial loss in a poem of movement. It is sweeter to rest easily in the sun-drenched, lethargic

[1] See Victory Pomeranz, "The Frowning Face of Bethel," *JJQ*, 10 (1973), 342-344.

climate of the flower- and fruit-rich southern Mediterranean. Bloom's mind idles in *Lotuseaters*: "Not doing a hand's turn all day. Sleep six months out of twelve. Too hot to quarrel. Influence of the climate. Lethargy. Flowers of idleness. The air feeds most. Azotes. Hothouse in Botanic gardens. Sensitive plants. Waterlilies. Petals too tired to" (71). Bérard records early descriptions of the coasts of Libya detailing what were, in effect, floral bazaars luring voyagers to particular coastal enclaves. Joyce's later revisions for the chapter add dozens of references to flowers; he literally weighs the episode down with abundant flora.

In the various trials of the *Odyssey*, paradisaical arrivals mark lands that have deceptive formal appeal. But after the easeful Lotusland comes its opposite, the dark caverns of the elemental Cyclopes, sons of Poseidon. Bérard suggests that the first two marvels of the narrative establish a directional and climatic axis. The land of the Cyclopes is due north from Libya: "Les Lotophages sont justement l'opposé des Kyklopes" (The Lotuseaters are the exact opposite of the Cyclopes) [Bérard, II, 106-107]. Opposition in a poem of deliberately located places is both topographical and thematic. In the *Ulysses* version of *Lotuseaters*, Bloom experiences a detached, pleasant hour in a day of potential and real abuses. Instead of facing the Cyclopes next, he merely goes to Hell.

HADES

"I do not like that other world" (77), writes Martha Clifford to Bloom in *Lotuseaters*. In *Hades*, like it or not, we are in that other world, the most renowned of "other worlds."[2] Paddy Dignam's funeral procession makes the first sweep of the day through Dublin from Sandymount to the Glasnevin cemetery in the extreme northwest of the city. Bloom, visiting Dignam's widow later in the evening, will make the second sweep from Sandymount to Eccles street, northwest.

Dignam, a former resident of Newbridge street in Sandymount, precedes the funeral procession in his coffin, the "Descent to Nothing," as the episode's *schema* calls it. Mr. Dignam, dead of a stroke from "too much John Barleycorn," travels stiff as do many Dubliners

[2] See Howard Rollin Patch, *The Other World* (Cambridge, Mass., 1950) for a general description of the classical, Celtic, and European versions of the Land of the Dead.

in the land of western gloom: "The Irishman's house is his coffin" (110). In the *Odyssey* Elpenor reaches the realms of death (*zophos*) before Odysseus journeys to summon the shades in the northwest. All northwest movement is elegiac. Bérard writes of the seas beyond Ithaca: "Après Ithaque, dernière île et dernière ville vers le *zophos*, la Pierre Blanche leur marquait l'entrée véritable de l'océan des ombres et de la nuit" (After Ithaca, last island and last city toward the *zophos*, the White Rock marked for [the Greeks] the true entry into the ocean of shades and night) [Bérard, II, 434-435]. The mythic mind encounters the marvelous in the unknown, and the unknown is associated with a death journey. *Hades* extends the directional metaphor of the *Odyssey*. Odysseus not only challenges the dark waters beyond Ithaca, but to return to a life he knows he travels through death's domains even farther north and went to hold his seance with the shades.

> By night
> our ship ran onward toward the Ocean's bourne,
> the realm and region of the Men of Winter,
> hidden in mist and cloud. Never the flaming
> eye of Hêlios lights on those men
> at morning, when he climbs the sky of stars,
> nor in descending earthward out of heaven;
> ruinous night being rove over those wretches.
>
> (Book XI, Fitzgerald, p. 185)

The *Hades* episode in *Ulysses* is the first to break radically with the order of the Homeric marvels. That Odysseus is narrating his tale retrospectively to the Phaeacians should have little to do with Joyce's decision to take *Hades* out of sequence. In the *Odyssey* the *Cyclops* adventure follows that of *Lotuseaters*. Odysseus sails north to a coastal area, which Bérard marks in the Bay of Naples. Just farther north is the Bay of Cumae. Joyce moves the *Hades* episode several adventures earlier in the sequence, and the *Cyclops* episode several later. The exigencies of the Dublin day account for some obvious shifts. A morning funeral makes more sense than a morning visit to a pub, especially for Bloom. Joyce needs no excuse to juggle the chapters beyond the kind of parallel situations he wishes to set up in his city. But the *Hades* and *Cyclops* adventures are, nonetheless, a likely pair to switch. According to Bérard, Polyphemus lives on the same coastal plain toward which Odysseus must travel on his seaward approach to Avernus, or Hades. Hell, in other words, is summoned in Cyclopean waters. Bérard makes the geographical link explicit in reference to the volcanic, eye-like lakes spread over the Cumaean coasts: "L'Averne n'est qu'un Kyklope, un Oeil Rond, un Oeil rempli de forêts et d'eaux" (Avernus is only a Cyclops, a round eye, an eye filled with trees and water) [Bérard, II, 327]. Joyce may juggle Homeric sequences, but he does not significantly alter Bérard's epic places.

Perhaps even more important for the scheme of the *Odyssey*, Odysseus repeats passively in the *Hades* adventure what he had actively (and hubristically) contrived in *Cyclops*. As a warrior he has to learn restraint. For Joyce the situation, like the order of the episodes, is reversed. His Leopold Bloom, as a humble citizen, has to learn something of assertion. To trick Polyphemus, Odysseus puns on his own name, effacing himself as *Outis*, or nobody, until in a position to taunt the one-eyed creature in ringing tones: "I am Laertes' son, Odysseus." Later in the narrative, the magician Circe tells Odysseus that "no man" has entered the realms of death and pale Persephone and returned to tell about it. Odysseus does just that. In both the *Cyclops* and *Hades* adventures he enters a democrat (a no-man and an everyman) and exits an aristocrat (a named man and a king). If Bloom is less noble than Odysseus, at least by the time of the later *Cyclops* episode, he will shout his identity and his race's name outside the den of the Cyclopean citizen at Barney Kiernan's, again in the northwest of Dublin.

The Celtic depth is like Tartarus—hell for northern giants. In *Hades* our last sight of Bloom is when he passively bests John Henry Menton, listed in the *schema* as Ajax, an Odyssean giant. Bloom turns to the light of day in *Hades*, and he will turn to the greater light of the east in *Cyclops*. In these episodes of *Ulysses* Bloom is at his most durable, his most renewable. Joyce does not distort either the *Odyssey* or the *Odyssey*'s sense in *Ulysses* by reversing *Hades* and *Cyclops*. He does what he will do often in his epic comedy— he readjusts the parent epic for local and domestic trials.

In *Hades* Joyce plots the funeral route carefully across Dublin. The coach in which Bloom, Martin Cunningham, Simon Dedalus, and John Power ride begins its course along Irishtown road paralleling the strand, and passes Stephen Dedalus crossing Watery lane at around 11:00 A.M. Turning from Irishtown road, the coach proceeds northwest to Ringsend road, crosses the Dodder River bridge, crosses the Grand Canal bridge, runs along Great Brunswick street until bearing north in the heart of the Hibernian metropolis at Sackville (O'Connell) street, crosses the Liffey, turns northwest on Berkeley road, catching a glimpse of Bloom's Eccles street and the *Mater* death ward, turns again on the North Circular road, crosses the Royal Canal, and finally arrives at the cemetery on Finglas road. The procession reaches Hades by crossing the four rivers under Lake Avernus, listed in the Gilbert-Gorman *schema* as the rivers and canals of Dublin. In mythological parlance, these rivers are connected to Oceanus at the world's edge. The movement across and towards Dublin's northwest boundary is every citizen's ultimate journey. Dublin's surface, at once the Peloponnese, the Mediterranean, and Ithaca, is now a version of the other world. Even Sackville street has a "Dead side" (95)—its west side, significantly— which Irishmen, in an earlier time, avoided because English soldiers traditionally held to the west side of the street.

In his journey to the regions of the Dead, Odysseus lands with two companions where Circe had explained he must beach. He prepares a votive pit and an offering, and has the shades of the underworld brought to him. Bérard thinks that the Homeric Hades is a "primitif Pays des Morts" (primitive Land of the Dead) [Bérard, II, 313], not literally at Oceanus, or winter's mythic northwest realm, as the narrative tells us. More accurately, Hades in the *Odyssey* was at one time thought to be at the end of the known world in western Italy. Bérard suggests a topographical link between the remote Hades in Homer and the localized Virgilian Lake of Gloom at Avernus off Italy's Cumaean Bay. If this is the case, and if Circe's isle in the *Odyssey*, from which Odysseus had just come, is where toponymists think it is (at the cape off Mount Circeo in the Gulf of Gaeta), then it would make sense that Odysseus sails only a day with the north wind at his back to reach Hades in the coastal plains of Pozzuoli. In effect, Odysseus not only calls the shades to him—he brings the ocean's bourne to him. Bérard sees the ancient legend of the oracle of Acheron in the *Odyssey's Nekuia*, a legend established when Thesprotia was the mythic edge of the world for the Greeks. He orients the progress of the dead from a point beyond Ithaca.

Au delà d'Ithaque et de la Pierre Blanche, les Hellènes eurent à la côte des Thesprotes, dans la vallée de l'Achéron, un Pays des Morts, célèbre dès la première antiquité. Pour les premiers Hellènes, c'était là qu'en vérité les morts, partis sur la route du *zophos* ténébreux, atteignaient la Prairie d'Asphodèle. Avant les Hellènes, il est probable que les premiers thalassocrates déjà fréquentaient en ces parages un oracle des Morts tout semblable à notre oracle de l'Averne.

(Beyond Ithaca and the White Rock, on the coasts of the Thesprotians, in the Valley of Acheron, the Greeks had a Land of the Dead, celebrated since ancient times. For the first Greeks, it was there in fact that the dead, having begun their journey along the route of the tenebrous *zophos*, reached the Meadow of Asphodel. It is probable that before the Greeks, the first thalassocrats had already visited an oracle of the dead in this vicinity, much like our oracle of Avernus)   [Bérard, ii, 435]

The Odyssean *Nekuia* is a perfect example of the migrational history of epic places. One of Odysseus' bogus stories of homecoming that he later tells on his own Ithaca holds that he stopped in Thesprotia before his return as a beggar. In other words, he has returned from what had been an ancient region of death. In the actual narrative, he returns from Calypso's isle *near* the actual ocean stream. Thematically, Odysseus is a returned ghost either way. Bérard marks the full geographical range in his chapter on *Hades*. The underground rivers at the Italian Avernus were supposedly connected with belts of water circling the world at the limits near the Straits of Gibraltar: "Le *golfe* devenait ainsi le *fleuve* circulaire qui doit entourer la terre. Le Golfe de la Richesse ou du Lucre, *Ok-eanos*, désigna désormais le fleuve sans limite qui encercle le monde" (The gulf [Cumae] thus became the circular river that is supposed to encircle the earth. The gulf of riches or wealth, *Okeanos*, is considered an unlimited river that [also] encircles the world) [Bérard, ii, 317]. Moreover, the Roman place name for the gulf near Lake Avernus, *Sinus Lucrinus*, derives, in Bérard's view, from the Semitic original meaning gulf of commerce, similar to the Greek Kolpus Emporikos of the Straits of Gibraltar. The *Proteus* episode of the *Odyssey* provides the western version of the afterworld, the Elysian Fields beyond Gibraltar. Joyce notes the western displacement in *Hades* material from his Zürich notebook: "Od. IV. 563 . . . Rhadamanthys" (VIII.A.5, p. 310).[3]

---

[3] In this context Bérard thinks that Calypso's island refers to the larger ocean (Ogygia = Ocean), but in Hermann Güntert's separate study of *Kalypso* (Halle, 1919), Ogygia is connected to the Stygian underworld as much in the depths as at the end (pp. 167ff).

The myth of the Land of the Dead at the world's end moves across time and space, but the final extension is always a relative one, northwest in the track of the sun—somewhere. In Dublin, Glasnevin will do. Associations remain with locale and direction. Bloom, like Odysseus, always returns from the world's end in one local geographical system or another. The *Odyssey* is an alternation of immortal longings and death trials. The geographical axis of both the *Odyssey* and *Ulysses* is a life-death axis. Joyce continues the metaphor in the very title of his next encyclopedic epic, *Finnegans Wake*, a death and a revivification. Finn MaCool is again awake at the celebration of his death. The revival of the dead, the new life of citizens and places, is at the heart of Joyce's human comedies.

In *Hades* the turn toward the east, toward life, comes late in the episode.[4] Dignam may be *"In paradisum"* (104), but the rest of Dublin merely gravitates toward a votive pit whose oracle is the Irish priest at the cemetery: "Chilly place this. Want to feed well, sitting in there all the morning in the gloom kicking his heels waiting for the next please" (103). Joyce's northwest passage through Dublin had already accumulated shades of the living dead along the way. Even the cattle crossing at the North Circular road are potential ghosts: "Tomorrow is killing day" (97). The episode plots out two patterns—one across the surface of the city toward the *zophos ténébreux*, the other dropping vertically just beneath the ground. In the regions of death the sun falls below the lined horizon only to rise elsewhere: "Red-sinking sun Hades" writes Joyce in his Zürich notebook (VIII.A.5, p. 308). "So much dead weight" (101), thinks Bloom. Death is like the gravitational lethargy of *Lotuseaters*: "Felt heavier myself stepping out of that bath" (101).

In *Hades* dead weight seems at first the last joke of gravity upon mortality: "Once you are dead you are dead" (105). *Hades* is treacherous territory for Bloom. The material traps of his life plague him throughout the episode. In succession, his grievances are manifest on the very Dublin streets: the infidelity of his wife passes in review with the image of Blazes Boylan; the ghost of his race with Reuben Dodd, the skinflint Jew; the memory of his son with the child's coffin; the misery of his father's suicide with the thoughtless palaver in the coach. Dead weight all. But death's counter is, as it was in *Proteus* earlier, re-enlivened form. In the *Odyssey* Tiresias replaces Proteus as tour guide to Hades. The vision of the shades signals

---

[4] See Richard Ellmann's discussion of the life-in-death structure of *Hades* in *Ulysses on the Liffey* (New York, 1972), pp. 47-56.

the possibility of *Nostos*. For Joyce the corpse is potentially the corpus, the gloom the new light. Judging from crumbs on the seat of
their coach, the riders to the funeral conclude that there must have
been a picnic in a previous procession. Life must go on at death's
feast. The chapter is filled with revivifying hints. The rain ends the
drought; Dixon, the intern, moves from the ward for incurables at
the *Mater* to the maternity ward at Holles street ("From one extreme to the other," 97); and Bloom rewrites the Prayer for the
Dead: "In the midst of death we are in life. Both ends meet" (108).
Even the Botanic Gardens thrive in the shadow of the cemetery:
"It's the blood sinking in the earth gives new life" (108). "Read
your own obituary notice they say you live longer. Gives you second
wind. New lease of life" (109).

In the *Odyssey* the shade of Odysseus' mother tells her son that
he is not meant for the nether regions, he must soon crave the sunlight. The Mediterranean sun is revivifying. When Odysseus continues to gather shades, he sees first the ghosts of immensely fertile
women: Tyro, Antiope, Alcmene, Chloris. Bloom, too, sees the
articulation of life in death. He turns from the memories of his
dead son to his live daughter: "Soon be a woman. Mullingar. Dearest
Papli. Young student. Yes, yes: a woman too. Life. Life" (89).
When Bloom finally leaves the cemetery in *Hades*, his eye is cast
to the light: "Back to the world again. Enough of this place" (114).

> Plenty to see and hear and feel yet. Feel live warm beings near
> you. Let them sleep in the maggoty beds. They are not going to
> get me this innings. Warm beds: warm fullblooded life.   (115)

"How grand we are this morning," Bloom concludes: let no man
write his epitaph. The death chapter in *Ulysses* is, in a way, its chapter of reincarnations. Only *Cyclops, Oxen of the Sun,* and *Circe*
outdo *Hades* in reviving the dead, the first two for predominantly
parodic reasons, the last for potentially sinister ones. Reincarnation
offers a hint of mythic things to come. From Paddy Dignam shooting out of his coffin, like Finnegan, asking "what's up now" (98) to
the mystery man in the macintosh, that "lankylooking galoot"
(109),[5] Ireland's luck and unluck, unresolved and undying, reincarnation is the civilization's hope. Parnell will return, Odysseus will

---

[5] Phillip F. Herring sees Joyce's Zürich notebook entry: "Tarnkappe"
(VIII.A.5, p. 307) as signifying Hades' invisible cloak: hence, M'Intosh's macintosh.

return, all God's ghosts will return from the grave. "If we were all suddenly somebody else" (110), thinks Bloom, but all *are* in the novel's Dantesque continuum: "As you are now so once were we" (113). The clue to the comic life in *Ulysses* is that nothing ends, it simply changes form: "Kay ee double ell. Become invisible. Good Lord, what became of him?" (112).

AEOLUS

If the opening chapter of *Ulysses, Telemachus*, was all circumference, *Aeolus* is all center. Bérard sees the island as the Semitic *Aiolie*, or high, pointed isle (II, 189), and the Greek *Strongulè* (Stromboli), the round isle. Stromboli, the isle of Aiolus Hippotades, is topographically at the center of the Odyssean, or western, Mediterranean in the Tyrrhenian sea off the northern coast of Sicily. Stromboli is in the Lipari island group, and over the years has vied with the naming island, Lipari itself, as the prominent member of the archipelago.[6] For mariners, at least, the pointed height and circular volcanic rock walls of Stromboli make it a central landmark in the hub of commerce around the Italian boot.

The setting of Joyce's *Aeolus*, the offices of the *Freeman's Journal* and *Evening Telegraph* near the high-pointing Nelson's Pillar, is "IN THE HEART OF THE HIBERNIAN METROPOLIS" (116). For *Ulysses* this is a chapter of second starts, and Bloom's eastward move to the center of the city from Glasnevin reorients the day: graveyard to metropolis; from death to a new lease on life. In the *Odyssey* there is a month's worth of activity on the home isle of the wind king, but the seas (and wind) around Aeolus are finicky, to say the least. The sirocco alternates with the zephyr, and, as the *Odyssey* graphically illustrates in its parable of greed, either wind is likely to start or stop blowing at any time. The tramlines at the beginning and end of Joyce's *Aeolus*, a later addition to the text of the chapter, tell the directional and frustrating story of Odysseus' second near-homecoming, blown south and southeast around the

---

[6] In his Princeton dissertation, *The Growth of James Joyce's Ulysses* (1975), Michael Groden speculates that the relative locations of Stromboli and Lipari are picked up by Joyce in his placement of *Aeolus* around Nelson's Pillar and the Prince street newspaper offices (p. 109). Groden's chapter on *Aeolus* provides ample evidence that Joyce adapts a significant amount of Bérard material for this episode.

tip of Italy. At the beginning of *Aeolus* the trams all move from Nelson's Pillar to points in the south and southeast of Dublin. At the end of the chapter the trams are paralyzed, halted in their tracks. *Aeolus* at the pillar is a circulatory joke in Dublin. Early on, the United Tramway Company's timekeeper "bawled off" (116) trams leading to various "homing" destinations. On the way back, the call is silenced as the trams, with the addition of two more southern lines, Rathfarnham and Donnybrook, stop dead.

> At various points along the eight lines tramcars with motion-less trolleys stood in their tracks, bound for or from Rathmines, Rathfarhham, Blackrock, Kingstown and Dalkey, Sandymount Green, Ringsend and Sandymount Tower, Donnybrook, Palmer-ston Park and Upper Rathmines, all still, becalmed in short circuit. (149)

The direction of the trams, superimposed on a Mediterranean map of the *Odyssey*, clearly parallels the homeward route of Odysseus from Stromboli. Michael Groden, who has looked at the fabric of this chapter closely in his study, *The Growth of James Joyce's Ulysses*, suggests that the tracks and the routes of both Dedalus and Brayden to the newspaper offices mark the Phoenician route of the thalassocrats to Sicily from Levantine seas. From Bérard's point of view, of course, this is precisely why Odysseus follows the same route away from Stromboli and back again. But here is an instance in which a Dublin location is doing double narrative work, not merely double in the sense that Joyce adapts a Homeric map, but double in that *Aeolus*, in placing Dedalus and Bloom near each other, be-gins to combine aspects of the two plots of the *Odyssey*. If Dedalus, like Telemachus, were returning home from the southeast, from the Peloponnese, he would approach the Ithacan (Dublin) center risking ambush by the suitors (Mulligan and Haines) at the Ship pub, slightly northeast of the newspaper offices and just northeast of Stephen's ultimate destination, Mooney's pub, where Stephen "lands" at the end of the episode.[7] In the *Odyssey* the ambush point is on the island of Asteris (Daskalio, according to Bérard), just northeast of the Odyssean palace-port. Since Telemachus never appears with his father in the western Mediterranean, many of his adventures in the Dublin of *Ulysses* usurp what would seem to be

---

[7] Mooney's is at 1 Abbey street and the Ship pub at 5 Abbey street.

Odyssean spaces. But if we adjust the map, Joyce can accommodate the range of the host epic. In this instance, the timing is off for the ambush, but with no one in Joyce's city actually leaving it, the epic timing is always off. Dedalus, arriving from the southeast strand, avoids the ambush. In the *Odyssey*, when the suitors realize what has happened, they consider calling off the ambush with a message, but quickly reconsider: "Too late for messages" (Book XVI, Fitzgerald, p. 301). In *Ulysses*, Dedalus, passing by College Green post office on his way to the newspaper offices of *Aeolus* (Hart and Knuth, p. 24), reverses the procedure. He sends Mulligan a message, a telegram about the Victorian refinement of mockery.

When Odysseus arrives in Aeolus' archipelago kingdom from the land of the Cyclopes farther up the Italian coast below the Bay of Cumae, he is detained by the king of winds. Since in the Joycean sequence *Hades* is a replacement for *Cyclops*, Bloom arrives in *Aeolus* from the cemetery in Glasnevin, northwest Dublin. Later we will see that Joyce sets *Cyclops* in another northwest location, at Barney Kiernan's pub near the law courts. Bérard, of course, places *Hades* and *Cyclops* in the same Cumaean area. In mythic geography Hades is a northwest boundary-land, and Aeolus' isle is in the center of the Italian Mediterranean. For Odysseus to get another chance at home from Stromboli, if Bérard is correct, means that he travels from a mythic border first to a new Mediterranean center, then to an older Mediterranean center. Like many centers in migrational history, the Lipari group divides eastern and western seas. It does so at Sicily, just as Ithaca does at the Ionian extension of the Peloponnese.

The isle of the wind king, although well centered, still has its dangers. Bérard explains that the volcanic activity on Stromboli casts huge rocks afloat in the sea, giving approaching navigators the illusion of floating islands. Moreover, the volcanic ash, blown by the south wind, poses its own threat to seamen in the navigational lanes down from Cumae. Michael Groden suspects that Stephen's brief vampire lyric, composed in *Proteus* and versified in *Aeolus*, owes something to Bérard's discussion of the sirocco and volcanic ash: "*On swift sail flaming / From storm and south / He comes, pale vampire, / Mouth to my mouth*" (132). Joyce could make use of the merest scrap of geographical material. In his Zürich notebook he enters for the cliffs of Stromboli, flecked with volcanic deposits: "brazen walls (solidified lava) fer spéculaire" (VIII.A.5, p. 302).

Stuart Gilbert links Lenehan's riddle in *Aeolus* ("rows of cast steel")
to these bronzed island walls, but Joyce might also have those
frustrating tramtracks in mind, tracks, like the wind, moving
south.

Odysseus remains on Aeolus' island for a month. There is a clear
suggestion of time wasted, of little accomplished. Joyce mirrors the
scene in *Aeolus*. Talk is action for Dublin. The meaning of *Aeolus* in
Joyce's *schema* is the mockery of victory. At one point in the previous episode, *Hades*, Bloom thinks of Robert Emmet, an eighteenth-
century Irish patriot whose epitaph reads: "When my country takes
her place among the nations of the earth then and not till then, let
my epitaph be written. I have done." Robert Emmet died in 1803.
He still waits. The second headline of *Aeolus*, "THE WEARER
OF THE CROWN" (116), explains why. An Irish parodic voice,
coming from an as yet untapped stylistic source in *Ulysses*, understands part of Ireland's problem in her domination by an English
"CROWN." The headlines of *Aeolus* are a mockery of even the
possibility of Irish action. Joyce realized the importance of initiating
his urban parody when he added the headlines in revising the episode. *Aeolus* is at the center of Dublin; it marks not only a new
start for Bloom, but a new stage in his purely urban *Wanderings*.
The city's parodic voices will unsettle the epic day in *Ulysses* from
Aeolus through *Nostos*.

Aeolus teaches Bloom something about urban circumstance, just
as it teaches Dedalus, who has much to learn from his city, something about comic indulgence. In bondage, victims are likely, at any
moment, to be reduced to the indignity of getting their royal Irish
arses kissed. And when this happens, it is potentially a headline
event: "K.M.R.I.A." (147).[8] By the *Sirens* episode, still in fine
parodic voice, *Ulysses* and Dublin teach Bloom another variation
on indignity. While Boylan goes "home" to Molly, Bloom sits and
farts to the tune of Robert Emmet's epitaph. There are no crowns
to wear in the middle of Joyce's Irish city.

[8] J. G. Keogh, "*Ulysses* 'Parable of the Plums' as Parable and Periplum,"
JJQ, 7 (1970), pp. 377-378, suggests that Bérard's rendering of the Kim-
merian death region, "*k.m.r.* désigne *l'obscurité*" [Bérard, 11, 319] in its
Semitic root, may stand for K.M.R.I.A. or "kiss my royal Irish arse" (147)
from *Aeolus*. This may be over-ingenious, but Joyce was heavily steeped in
Bérard at this point in *Ulysses*. It is not beyond him to have exercised his
wit on his own source material.

In the *Odyssey*, Odysseus gets one chance to escape the deadened center. Homer once again miniaturizes the entire *Wanderings*, as Odysseus sails for nine days only to have his crew let the wind out of the bag on the tenth, blowing him back just as he sights home. Bloom is similarly cut off from an opportunity. "Begone!" says Myles Crawford, the editor, "The world is before you" (129): "Back in no time, Mr Bloom said, hurrying out" (129). Bloom just misses working out the details of his "innuendo of homerule" advertisement renewal for Alexander Keyes, wine and spirit merchant, and he is cast out once again into the squalls of Dublin with the same indignity Odysseus experiences at the hands of Aiolus Hippotades. Bloom's prospects and retrospects for home-rule are buffeted by the winds blowing south off of Prince street.

The *Aeolus* adventure in the *Odyssey* is the least heroic of all the *Wanderings*. The situation is almost admonitory. It is not odd that Joyce should sense its Old Testament flavor (Moses and the promised land) in his adaptation for *Ulysses*.[9] Odysseus receives instructions from a surrogate, but powerful god-king. Disobedience and inattention subvert law. The patriarchal Aeolus calls Odysseus, upon his humbling return, a creeping thing when god-given opportunity turns to contempt. Joyce parallels the Odyssean and Biblical homecomings with Stephen's comic parable, *A Pisgah Sight of Palestine or The Parable of the Plums*. Stephen's invention combines parable with a local vision of a paralyzed space near Nelson's Pillar. "*Parable of the Plums*" is a good pun, one of Joyce's best, on the seemingly endless *periploi* (singular: *periplous*) that Bérard discovers in the movements plotted by the *Odyssey*.[10] *Aeolus*, particularly, is filled with *periploi*: the trams provide a series of their own, the circuitous route southeast and northeast taken by the Invincibles from Phoenix Park in Crawford's frenzied reconstruction is another, and the *periplous* of the plum-spitting old ladies from Fumbally's lane circling north of their destination, Nelson's Pillar, is a third. The "two Dublin vestals" (145) of the *Parable* move circuitously across the Liffey from the Liberties, progress northeast to Marlborough street (fittingly, another English commander's name), and sneak up on the naval commander, the "onehandled adulterer,"

[9] See Irene Orgel Briskin, "Some New Light on 'The Parable of the Plums.'" *JJQ*, 3 (1966), pp. 248-251, for a discussion of its Old Testament debts.

[10] Keogh, "*Ulysses'* 'Parable of the Plums' as Parable and Periplum," can take credit for uncovering this pun on the Greek *periplous*.

Lord Nelson, only to neutralize themselves in front of him. All action is up and down—all suspended *nostoi* a joke. Stephen's is a city vision fitting for a city chapter: mocked victories, defeated hopes, too-early arrivals like Moses' on Pisgah, too-late arrivals like Matthew's foolish virgins at the bridechamber. Florence Mac-Cabe, one of the two old ladies, actually has an address in the Liberties on Bride street or Blackpitts. These are an odd set of names for the same street, but they fit Stephen's parodic version of the brides of Christ and the fallen plum pits of the day's escapade up the Pillar.

To be Irish is to be a born loser, a plunger, "loyal to lost causes" (133). The Irish "haven't got the chance of a snowball in hell" (131). If they do not see to "the death of the intellect and of the imagination" (133) themselves, the English, cloacally obsessed, see to the necessary political repression. Parody is perhaps the only action, the only plot, available from the top of another nation's pillar, dead center in a dying city. But Stephen's very act in recording the condition of his land, even if in the voice of his joking vision, begins the rite of release, the creator's and the artist's. Creation is from nothing: "On now. Dare it. Let there be life" (145). *The Parable of the Plums* in *Aeolus* animates a sterile world with a laugh at its own center and at its own expanse.

LESTRYGONIANS

Bloom has good reason to be wary after *Aeolus*. He had suspected that justice is "everybody eating everyone else. That's what life is after all" (122). In Bérard's chapter on the Lestrygonians of the *Odyssey,* Joyce may have learned that the original inhabitants of the Straits of Sardinia, where the Odyssean episode is presumably set, were the rude northern Corsicans. Bérard explains that these mountain men were dangerous murderers who, as the Semitic etymology of their name suggests, kill with their teeth: "couper et broyer avec les dents" (cut and grind with the teeth) [Bérard, II, 245]. The Semitic original for the tribal Corsicans derives from the phrase, which appears in other contexts in the Bible, *eḳal ḳeres* (k.r.s.). Metaphorically, the phrase signifies an attack with one's mouth: to speak against. *Lestrygonians* in *Ulysses* proves Bérard's and Bloom's case literally and metaphorically. The proof condemns Irish masticators and backbiters.

In the *Odyssey* the sleek black ships of Odysseus put in at the narrow straits off Port Pozzo in Sardinian waters. Bérard recognizes the fountain of Artaki as a place name wandered from Asia Minor. The axis of transmission, as is so often the case in the *Odyssey*, is southeast to northwest. Bloom, moving south and east for most of the *Lestrygonian* episode toward the library, never establishes a "firm" place, but he does, at least, keep to the day's axis. Odysseus, too, is never fully localized on Lamos, the land of the Lestrygonians. He moors so that he can bolt seaward at any moment. There is an uneasy and jittery quality to this northern land. Odysseus prepares his ship beforehand for the quick cut and run—he is even willing to sacrifice the bulk of his fleet to escape.

Odysseus' men, his national companions at arms, as Joyce calls them, have already caused him anguish. Their raid at Ismarus initiated godly retribution, their disinclination to return from Lotusland stymied movement, their mutiny over the tied bags of wind defied the authority of two kings. Odysseus approaches Lamos on the *qui vive*. In *Lestrygonians* Bloom, too, is especially cautious. He avoids the cannibal trap of Burton's for the calm of Davy Byrne's. He thinks of James Carey "that blew the gaff on the invincibles" (163), and sides with the wilier ways: "James Stephens' idea was the best. He knew them. Circles of ten so that a fellow couldn't round on more than his own ring. Sinn Fein" (163). "Sinn Fein" means ourselves alone. The cautious do not walk into Irish traps. As an acquaintance says of Bloom, "God Almighty couldn't make him drunk, Nosey Flynn said firmly. Slips off when the fun gets too hot" (178). Bloom proceeds alone while Irishmen talk behind his back: *ekal keres*.

Lestrygonians takes Bloom from the *Freeman's Journal* and *Evening Telegraph* offices "riverward" down Sackville street and across the Liffey, south. On Westmoreland street he continues to walk past Trinity College to Grafton street, turns east at Duke street to pop in and out of Burton's, decides on Davy Byrne's a few addresses back, after a bite continues southeast to Dawson, Molesworth, and Kildare streets, reaching the National Museum after a quick duck south to avoid Blazes Boylan, the Antiphates or chief Lestrygonian of the episode. Dublin's turns are turns for or from the worse. The city digests itself in this chapter of peristalsis: "This is the very worst hour of the day. Vitality. Dull, gloomy: hate this hour. Feel as if I had been eaten and spewed" (164).

In the *Odyssey*, Odysseus sailed six days and nights north from Aeolus' island to Lamos. Homer's description has led some to believe that the land of the Lestrygonians is even farther north than Bérard's placement in the Straits of Boniface off the northern coasts of Sardinia. The *Odyssey* tells us that Odysseus sails to where "the low night path of the sun is near the sun's path by day" (Book x, Fitzgerald, p. 168). Bérard thinks this a reference to the "Cape de la Nuit," or Midnight Cape, at the extreme northwest point of Sardinia. When Odysseus cuts anchor and makes for the open seas, Homer tells us that the land of death fell behind. In his flight, Odysseus heads toward the dawn—that is, toward the east away from the regions of gloom.

Bérard points out that the Sardinian straits were treacherous not only because of their narrow inlets and high rock formations, but because the island archipelagos nearby were the haunts of pirates and sea raiders. The Phoenicians entered these waters with caution, and from traces of Semitic names along the straits and on island coasts, it is understandable why they might have done so. Etymology reconstructs terrain: "Bandits' Cape" and "Fugitive's Point." Bérard writes that the *Lestrygonian* adventure is about the will to protect and escape: "Le poète n'imaginera que fuites. C'est d'abord la fuite des hommes envoyés pour explorer le pays. . . . C'est ensuite la fuite d'Ulysse lui-même qui ne tire sa vaillante épée que pour couper ses amarres et s'enfuir en abandonnant le gros de sa flotte" (The poet imagines only flights. First it is the flight of the men sent to explore the country. . . . Next it is the flight of Odysseus himself who only draws his valiant sword to cut the cables and take flight, abandoning the greater part of his fleet) [Bérard, II, 244].

In *Lestrygonians*, Bloom stands and marks the Dubliners with whom he lives. Druids, he thinks, were cannibals, fond of an occasional "kidney burntoffering" (151). We remember his own breakfast. He crosses the O'Connell bridge, and from the Liffey he sees "a puffball of smoke" (152). He is as alone as Odysseus—he is even as alone as the English Ulysses, Robinson Crusoe, whom he thinks about in this jittery episode (153). Bloom moves across Dublin, first in a southerly direction and then, as Odysseus, almost due east. When he sights the devilish Blazes Boylan, he darts south to the Kildare street museum and the safety of the Greek goddesses carved in stone. Odysseus had turned to the land of a real Greek goddess, a minor goddess, Circe, daughter of Helios, the sun.

Bérard speaks of the *Lestrygonian* adventure in the *Odyssey* as an unrecorded *periplous*. It should not take six days to reach Sardinia from Stromboli unless the route were indirect. But it was not a Phoenician habit to sail directly to any destination in Tyrrhenian waters. Mariners kept putting in at ports and capes: "ne suivaient pas cette route droite" (they never followed this [the] straight route) [Bérard, II, 230]. Since we see nothing in the *Odyssey* of what must have been Odysseus' leisurely six-day voyage up the Italian coast, Joyce, like Bérard, gives us an added attraction. He lets Bloom roam at leisure over Dublin's trade lanes. He even adds his typically urban axis—the parodic plunge. In *Lestrygonians* the prophet Elijah falls at "thirtytwo feet per sec" (152) into the Liffey. Dennis Breen ("Meshuggah. Off his chump," 159) has no horizontal control whatever: "U.P.: up" (158). Bérard writes that the land of the Lestrygonians is filled with birds of all sorts, even pelicans, appropriate in this chapter of gorging and diving: "La Sardaigne est, entre toutes les îles, une terre d'oiseaux" (Sardinia is, amongst all the isles, a land of birds) [Bérard, II, 223]. Doves and pigeons are especially numerous: "Les colombes et pigeons remplissent les grottes" (The doves and pigeons fill the grottoes) [Bérard, II, 224]. In the vertical spaces of *Ulysses* the city pigeons perform their "little frolic" above the Irish house of parliament: "Must be thrilling from the air" (162). Joyce enters a Sardinian place name in his Zürich notebook: "Ais trugonié (Cape of Pigeons)" (VIII.A.5, p. 301). The vertical joke continues. If Breen plans to sue to get "it" down, Bloom bristles at the question of Molly's tour of the north with the Lestrygonian, Boylan: "Who's getting it up?" (172), asks Nosey Flynn. Bloom responds, "Getting it up?" (172). All Dublin's giants, who bend to "feed" in the gloom, suspect that Boylan is up to more than Bloom.

Like Odysseus cutting his moorings, *Lestrygonians* ends with Bloom's making a quick flight at the last moment, swerving "to the right." In a way, he had been reconnoitering the escape route throughout: turn toward the sun—the east or southeast. His memories alone take the chapter back to happier times—the picnic on Howth (176), which Molly will later move along her own southeast axis back to Gibraltar, the Glencree dinner in the south years before in county Wicklow, the night of Godwin's concert in the

Mansion House on Dawson street in Bloom's favorite southeast quadrant of Dublin: "Happy. Happy" (156). The worst thought of all for Bloom involves the projected misery of Boylan's impending visit to 7 Eccles: "Today. Today. Not think" (180). He empties his mind of the thought of Boylan by countering the proposed northern singing tour with Molly. Bloom turns in another direction: "Tour the south then. What about English watering places?" (180). When Boylan, in effect, chases Bloom to the museum, the Mediterranean hero meets his dream, statues of the south: "Shapely goddesses, Venus, Juno: curves the world admires" (176).

SCYLLA AND CHARYBDIS

Obstacles abound in *Ulysses* even when the action stands stock-still. *Scylla and Charybdis* is set in the National Library adjacent to the National Museum, 7-10 Kildare street. Only at the end of the chapter does anyone leave the library in the reader's view. Geography has less to do with movement on a stage than movement between literature's metaphoric rocks and whirlpools, smiles and yawps, Stephen's virgin Dublin and decadent Paris, Shakespeare's Stratford and London, Telemachus' Ithaca and Peloponnese, Odysseus' Mediterranean and Aegean seas. The general axis of the epic and the epic novel is maintained: southeast-northwest. Joyce makes interchangeability a keynote of the chapter, and it is clear from a later notesheet entry for *Eumaeus* that the ancient and modern axes were the same. Heroes and places cut across time: "Eum. laments Telemachus off to Paris" (Herring, p. 403). For Dedalus, these movements away from and back toward home are Viconian and, ultimately, enclosed: "Every life is many days, day after day. We walk through ourselves, meeting robbers, ghosts, giants, old men, young men, wives, widows, brothers-in-love. But always meeting ourselves" (213). Personal aesthetics for Stephen are spatial aesthetics: "space which I in time must come to, ineluctably" (217).

In the episode, Scylla is one of the novel's hard rocks. Bérard thinks its name derived from the overhanging cliff off the Straits of Messina, the Semitic *skeula*: s.k.l., the rock (Bérard, II, 350). Joyce's novel is scattered with hard rocks from Molly's Gibraltar to Sinbad the Sailor's "roc's auk's egg" (737) in *Ithaca*. Dangerous, but at least substantial, rocks are preferable to Charybdis-like whirlpools: "Hole of Loss" (VIII.A.5, p. 300), as Joyce transcribes Bérard's etymology in his Zürich notebook. Charybdis not only halts movement, but renders men impotent. Bérard reports an account of a very large boat in the Straits of Messina suddenly stopped in the counter-currents whirling in coastal waters: "ils s'y trouvent arrêtés tout à coup et restent comme immobiles; ni le vent ni les voiles ne les peuvent tirer de là" (they find themselves stopped there all of a sudden to remain as if they had been immobilized; neither the wind nor the sails were able to pull them out) [Bérard, II, 362].

Scylla and Charybdis is another of the adventures that Joyce has worked into his novel out of sequence. But whether coming from Lamos of Lestrygonian territory or from Circe's double-isle Aiaia, Odysseus would come from the same direction as does Bloom in Dublin. In the *Odyssey*, Circe, who is not to appear in *Ulysses* until midnight, instructs Odysseus upon his return from Hades of the pitfalls of the lower Italian peninsula. He must avoid the enchantment of the Sirens' song, which Bérard thinks issues from the sirocco at Capri, he must bypass the Wandering Rocks in the Lipari group, and chance the many-legged monster, Scylla, in the Straits of Messina. Odysseus has Charybdis all to himself on the return pass after his men kill the herds of Helios on Trinacria. Joyce builds both passes, going and coming, into his one chapter. In *Ulysses*, *Scylla and Charybdis* is a much more complex episode than its set of Odyssean parallels. Artists as well as heroes leave the rock of their homeland or home city, test themselves in the whirlpool of exile, and return home in substance or in vision.[11] First there is a sundering—the betrayal discovered at home (and if it is not discovered, it is invented) becomes a betrayal revenged quite literally in a roundabout way. Time and space are on the side of the artist: "See this. Remember" (192), thinks Dedalus when as an Irish poet he feels spurned by his peers. The *Nostos* of life and art is the resolution of narrative movement, an elliptical path on *terra firma*, an elliptical orbit if read in the stars. When the exile returns, whether Odysseus, Shakespeare, or Joyce, "The motion is ended" (213). Artists are returned ghosts who damn the mocking quick and revive the grateful dead.

[11] S. L. Goldberg's *Classical Temper: A Study of James Joyce's Ulysses* (London, 1961) is thorough and clear when treating Stephen's (and Joyce's) aesthetic. See also Richard Ellmann's treatment of *Scylla and Charybdis* in *Ulysses on the Liffey*, pp. 81-89, and Robert Kellog's "Scylla and Charybdis" in Hart and Hayman, pp. 147-179.

Joyce establishes the meaning of the chapter in the *schema* as
two-edged dilemma. Sailing through aesthetic variables as dangerous
as jutting cliffs and ocean *trous* is tricky. Scylla, the rock of "hard
facts" (184), knows little of idealized visions, and Charybdis, the
whirlpool, spouts and chews debris from below into mere foam
above. Stephen's antagonists in the episode come from both sides.
Mulligan is everyone's hard rocks—he even takes Shakespeare
through a quick life and ignominious death: "He died dead drunk"
(204). Stephen, for Mulligan, is a young Shakespearean pretender.
He, too, lay in his own "mulberrycoloured, multicoloured, multi-
tudinous vomit!" (217). Russell and the Theosophists, on the other
side, spout formless forms: "Art has to reveal to us ideas, formless
spiritual essences. The supreme question about a work of art is out
of how deep a life does it spring" (185). Form is a sacrificial con-
cession for the Theosophic or mystical "allfather": "Formless spiritual" (185), Stephen mocks. Charybdis spouts up, but ultimately draws
down. What finally holds the two monsters, Scylla and Charybdis,
at bay is Stephen's theoretical middle way, the idea that drama or
narrative is factual and form-filled at base but visionary in process.
Art, finally, requires belief before proof. Stephen is the visionary
Aristotelian in his own limited way.

> Unsheathe your dagger definitions. Horseness is the whatness of
> allhorse. Streams of tendency and eons they worship. God: noise
> in the street: very peripatetic. Space: what you damn well have
> to see. Through spaces smaller than red globules of man's blood
> they creepycrawl after Blake's buttocks into eternity of which this
> vegetable world is but a shadow. Hold to the now, the here,
> through which all future plunges to the past.   (186)

Vision without substance is Blakean parody, a sundering without
a reconciliation. Substance without vision has no future sense of
past. In *Nestor* Stephen describes himself as a learner. In *Aeolus*
he looks to his city and admits that despite its sterility he has much
to learn from it. In *Scylla and Charybdis* he asks, "What have I
learned? Of them? Of me?" (215). He poses himself a fair question.
What he has to say of Shakespeare and aesthetic form is part of a
fair answer. Movement becomes personality becomes aesthetic design. His own action, antecedent to the action of *Ulysses*, provides a
clue to Shakespeare's ghost story, a clue to the ghost story of all

plots: Dublin to Paris, the southeast mission; Paris to Dublin, the northwest trial.

Stephen is not without his troubles on this day. As was apparent in *Telemachus*, as Mulligan's double he is a self-mocker. His relation to Mulligan is uneasy—something between symbiotic and parasitic. Belief is necessary in a substance-transforming vision, but Stephen can barely believe his own theory: "I believe, O Lord, help my unbelief" (214). He exposes himself amidst a brood of mockers—he talks aloud and silently to himself, and sometimes his listeners overhear. Mulligan offers the subplot of mockery all the while; the processes of the debaser's art are epic-stunting. Stephen and Bloom are Mulligan's butts. *Everyman His own Wife or A Honeymoon in the Hand*, Mulligan's "*national immorality*" (216), is a libel on the sterile father and the "unliving son" (194). But Stephen can bear up, as we have seen earlier: "They mock to try you. Act. Be acted on" (211). He had used these very phrases for Shakespeare.

In the background of the chapter, the ghost walks. Bloom, the crafty Ancient Mariner, the "pale Galilean" (201), *Leo panthera*, steers his course undaunted. He sails the straits between two potential obstacles, Dedalus and Mulligan, just as earlier in the museum he sailed close to two curved shores, the "Venus Kallipyge" (201). The older hero's mission is to seek form's original substance in its shapely "ends," a pleasant task in this comic epic of the human body. Bloom's mission at the orifice of Aphrodite makes sense in this chapter of aesthetic theory. All journeys, biological or epic, are restorative. Mulligan thinks Bloom perverse because he enjoys pure substance. Joyce thinks him part of a comic novel because he sees process in form.

CALYPSO

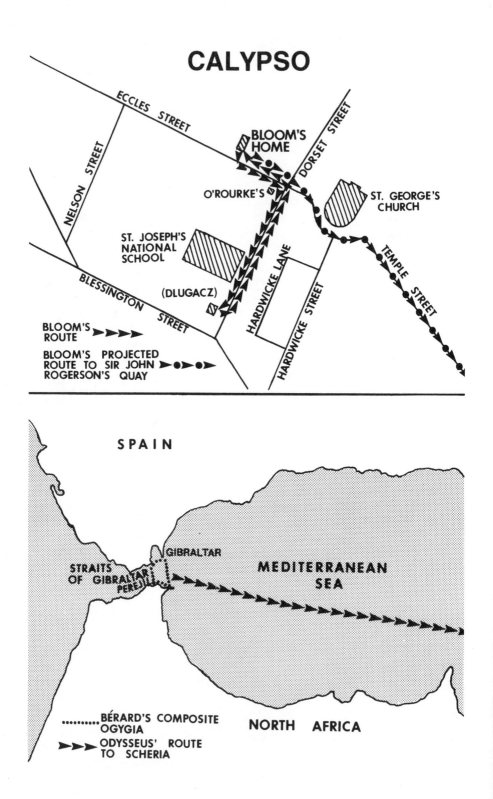

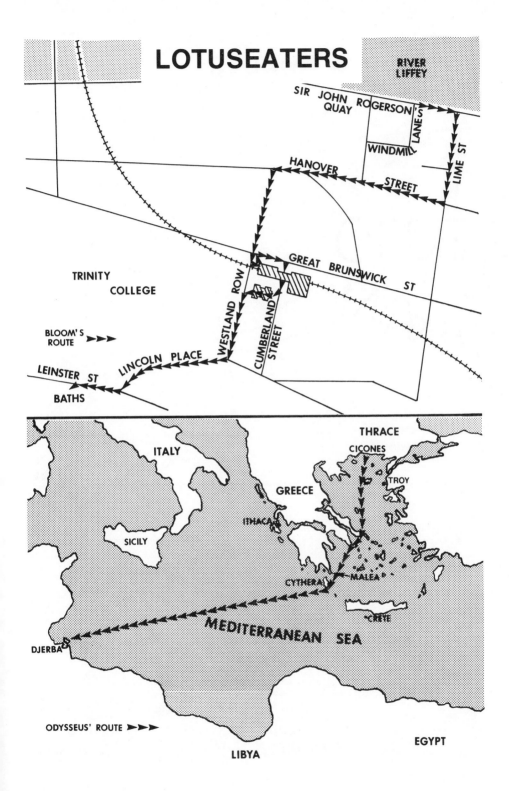

LOTUSEATERS

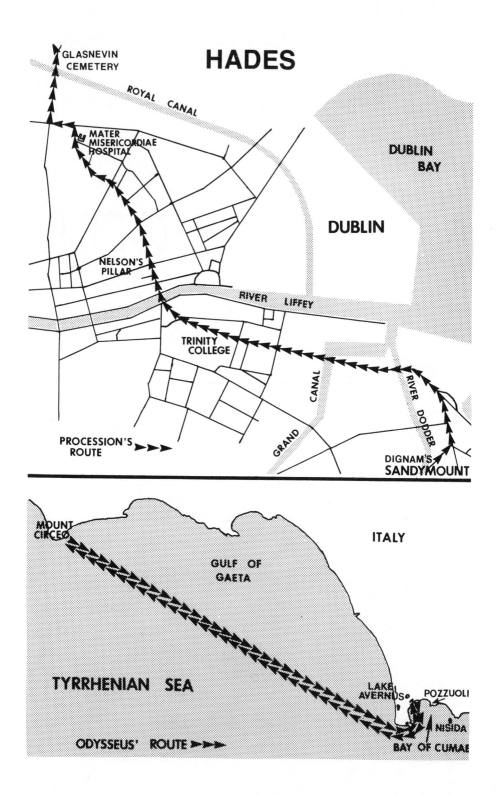

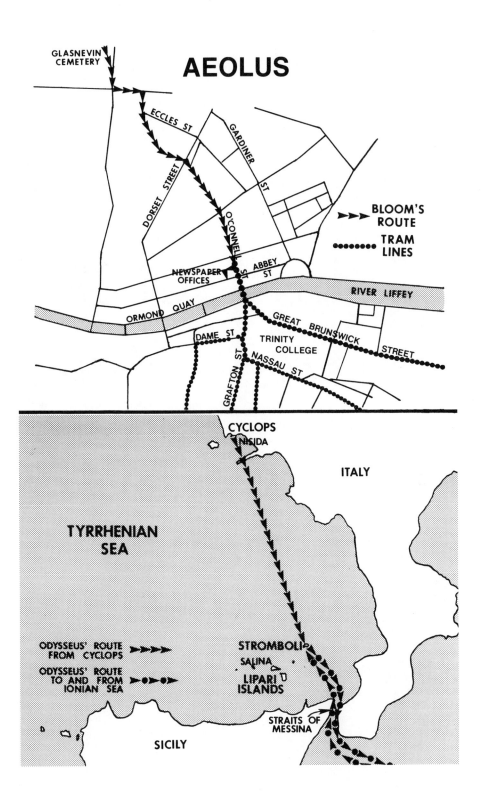

AEOLUS

GLASNEVIN CEMETERY

ECCLES ST

GARDINER ST

DORSET STREET

O'CONNELL ST

▶▶▶ BLOOM'S ROUTE

•••••••• TRAM LINES

NEWSPAPER OFFICES

ABBEY ST

ORMOND QUAY

RIVER LIFFEY

DAME ST

GREAT BRUNSWICK STREET

TRINITY COLLEGE

GRAFTON ST

NASSAU ST

CYCLOPS NISIDA

ITALY

TYRRHENIAN SEA

ODYSSEUS' ROUTE FROM CYCLOPS ▶▶▶

ODYSSEUS' ROUTE TO AND FROM IONIAN SEA ▶•▶•▶

STROMBOLI

SALINA

LIPARI ISLANDS

STRAITS OF MESSINA

SICILY

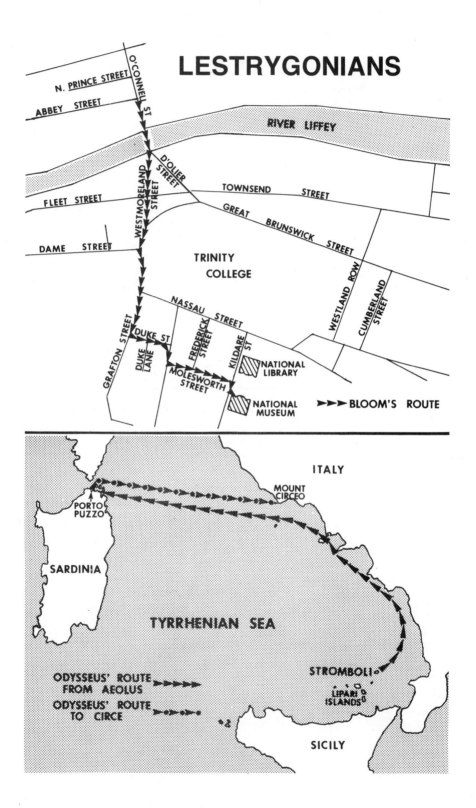

LESTRYGONIANS

O'CONNELL ST

N. PRINCE STREET

ABBEY STREET

RIVER LIFFEY

D'OLIER STREET

WESTMORELAND STREET

TOWNSEND STREET

FLEET STREET

GREAT BRUNSWICK STREET

DAME STREET

TRINITY COLLEGE

WESTLAND ROW

CUMBERLAND STREET

NASSAU STREET

GRAFTON STREET

DUKE ST

DUKE LANE

FREDERICK STREET

KILDARE ST

MOLESWORTH STREET

NATIONAL LIBRARY

NATIONAL MUSEUM

►►► BLOOM'S ROUTE

ITALY

MOUNT CIRCEO

PORTO PUZZO

SARDINIA

TYRRHENIAN SEA

STROMBOLI

LIPARI ISLANDS

ODYSSEUS' ROUTE FROM AEOLUS ►►►

ODYSSEUS' ROUTE TO CIRCE ►•►

SICILY

SCYLLA AND CHARYBDIS

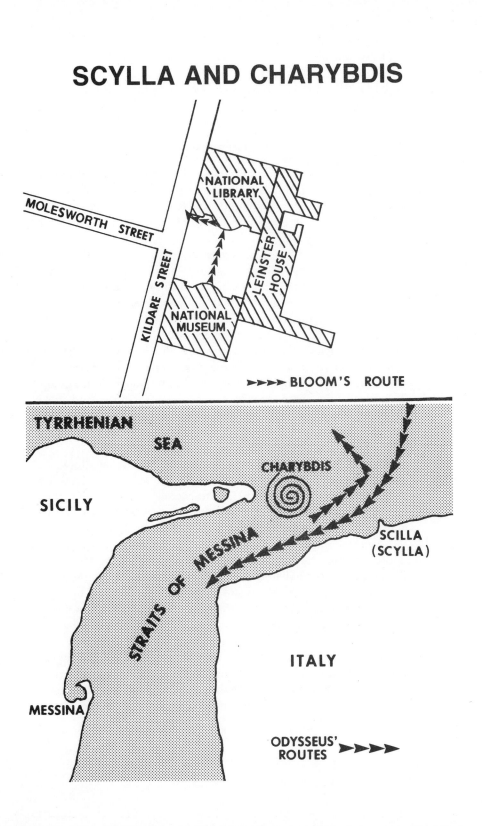

NATIONAL
LIBRARY

MOLESWORTH STREET

KILDARE STREET

LEINSTER HOUSE

NATIONAL
MUSEUM

►►►► BLOOM'S ROUTE

TYRRHENIAN SEA

CHARYBDIS

SICILY

SCILLA
(SCYLLA)

STRAITS OF MESSINA

ITALY

MESSINA

ODYSSEUS' ►►►►
ROUTES

THE WANDERINGS OF ODYSSEUS: II

WANDERING ROCKS

ACCORDING to Victor Bérard, Odysseus' *Wanderings* render, anthropomorphically, several of the major navigational hazards of the seas known to the Greeks. The Wandering Rocks or *planktai* are mentioned very briefly in the epic as one of the possible obstacles facing Odysseus on his passage to the island of Helios after his visit to Hades. In Circe's preview of adventures, she describes the Wandering Rocks as impassable, adding that only Jason and his Argonauts, with the aid of Hera, managed to slip between the crashing obstacles. The hazard is such that no living creature escapes it— even the doves of the region, as Circe tells it, crash against the smooth surfaces of the deadly *planktai*. Bérard seizes upon Circe's ill-fated doves as his first clue in placing this adventure. He argues that the *planktai* (derived from the Semitic p.l.k., rounded or conical) are two conical volcanic mountains on Salina in the Lipari island group. The island, like the archipelago, is a haven for doves and other varieties of birds, but massive land or subterranean ocean eruptions can clear the area of every living creature fast enough to escape [Bérard, II, 348].

Odysseus has the option of avoiding the Wandering Rocks by sailing between Scylla and Charybdis in the Straits of Messina a little to the west. He chooses the treacherous channel rather than attempt that which only Jason survived. Somewhat pained by the allusion to Jason in the *Odyssey*, Bérard insists that at least part of the *planktai* warning is an interpolation. Bérard's puzzlement is understandable. He has Odysseus placed squarely in the Mediterranean off the lower Italian boot. The Wandering Rocks, in the Jason legend, appear at the northern end of the Bosporus Straits at the gateway to the Euxine. Jason and his ship, the *Argos*, barely squeeze through the Symplegades, a point marking the dividing line of Europe from Asia, west from east. Just as Bérard links the Elysian Fields at the world's western end with the Hades of Avernus in the Cumaean Bay, he allows the Wandering Rocks to have two mythic identities. But he is troubled with the actual geography. Almost reluctantly, he chooses Salina of the same island group as Aeolus' Stromboli, although farther west. Coincidentally, Salina is the closest point in Bérard's Homeric scheme to the city of Trapani on the western coast of Sicily, where Samuel Butler places most of the *Odyssey*'s action in his version of the epic, *The Authoress of the Odyssey*. Joyce chooses as his only apocryphal episode in *Ulysses* an adventure placed by his one reliable source closest to the territory of the most apocryphal, although witty, piece of blarney in the Homeric tradition. The convergence here is no doubt a three-way accident, but it is the sort of accident that Joyce enjoys.

When Joyce provided the *schema* for *Wandering Rocks*, he, like Homer, alluded to the Argonaut adventure: "Bosporus-Liffey." Ireland's legendary migratory settlers, of course, were originally inhabitants of the Euxine region: the Milesians. A hint of Joyce's design appears in a notesheet entry for *Cyclops*, a chapter versed in appropriate Irish history: "Milesians (Argos) exp. Euxine, America" (Herring, p. 106). The Milesian-Euxine connection evidently means more to Joyce than to Homer (or Bérard), and the fact that he includes *Wandering Rocks* in *Ulysses* as an adventure that did not occur in the *Odyssey* accommodates a more purely Irish axis of migration. Joyce follows through to the American extension in the episode with the reference to the catastrophic explosion of the steamship *General Slocum* in New York's East River near Hell Gate (221).

Whatever reasons Joyce may have had for his lengthy treatment in his own epic of an adventure bypassed by Homer, he still draws heavily from Bérard's diligent search for a Mediterranean place for the *planktai*. Bérard's sub-chapter on the Wandering Rocks is replete with material that works its way into Joyce's episode. In its active state, the Lipari volcanic archipelago is as hostile an environment as a navigator might dread encountering. The sea is alive with floating debris, the air is filled with smoke and ash, and the straits between the islands are extremely turbulent. Commentators on *Ulysses* see Joyce's *Wandering Rocks* as a city of traps, a city of irresolution, *cul de sacs*, accidents, missed connections and missed streetcars, misread signs, wrong turns, indignities, and sheer labyrinthine terror, a Minoan as much as a Greek adventure. No doubt it is, to an extent. But Joyce also describes his city by adapting details from Bérard's search for the Mediterranean *planktai*.

Joyce begins *Wandering Rocks* with "The superior, the very reverend John Conmee, S. J." (219), and Bérard begins with the volcanic valley on Salina, a valley called, coincidentally, "Val de l'Église" (Valley of the Church) [Bérard, II, 343]. The valley also had another name which the Italians misunderstood as Valley of Happiness (*Fossa Felice*). According to Bérard, the real derivation, from ancient time, is more accurately represented in the Italian *Fossa Felci* (ditch of ferns). Fossa also means grave, and the second section of Joyce's *Wandering Rocks* finds Corny Kelleher examining "a pine coffinlid" and "chewing his blade of hay" (224 and 225).

Bérard's Lipari group, and Salina in particular, is actively volcanic. He cites Diodorus: "Toutes ces îles eurent de grands épanchements de feu, dont les cratères et les bouches subsistent, visibles jusqu'à ce jour" (All the isles displayed grand bursts of fire, whose craters and mouths subsist, visible today) [Bérard, II, 347]. Don John Conmee watches his letters deposited in the "mouth of the bright red letterbox" (220); in another *Val de l'Église*, Mary's abbey, a vesta "consumed itself in a long soft flame and was let fall" (230); Katey and Boody Dedalus's peasoup is a miniature volcano when a "heavy fume gushed in answer" (226) or when Boody breaks "big chunks of bread into the yellow soup" (227); Stephen thinks of "cold specks of fire" (241); Long John Fanning "blew a plume of smoke from his lips" (247); and even Mulligan "slit a steaming scone in two and plastered butter over its smoking pith" (249).

Bérard details several accounts of disasters in Tyrrhenian waters near the Lipari group. One in particular from the geographer Strabo is a "phénomène aussi terrifiant" (a phenomenon just as terrifying) as anything that might happen in the wider oceans. Two Lipari isles, Hiera and Euonymos, which Bérard thinks are possibly Panaria and Vulcano today, erupted while a barque filled with passengers was sailing between. Lives were lost in the holocaust, passengers burned in the sea, and even several days later "on put voir la mer couverte d'une sorte de boue flottante, d'où montaient des flammes, des fumées et d'épaisses vapeurs" (one could see the sea covered with a kind of floating ooze, from where flames, fumes, and thick vapors rose) [Bérard, II, 347]. We remember once again the *General Slocum* from *Ulysses*, the "dreadful catastrophe in New York."

> Terrible affair that General Slocum explosion. Terrible, terrible! A thousand casualties. And heartrending scenes. Men trampling down women and children. Most brutal thing. What do they say was the cause? Spontaneous combustion: most scandalous revelation. Not a single lifeboat would float and the firehose all burst.
>
> (239)

In Bérard's version of *Wandering Rocks*, and in Joyce's, the services of the episode's "Ocean Accident and Guarantee Corporation" (236) are not merely precautionary. Even Tom Rochford, who dips into "manholes like a bloody gas pipe" to rescue "the poor devil stuck down in it half choked with sewer gas" (233), braves a version of the Lipari volcanic mouths. Like Stephen in his own city, Dubliners move between "two roaring worlds where they swirl" (242). For Joyce, some fictional spaces are neither land-locked nor sea-locked. They are, in fact, errant. And the action in *Wandering Rocks* is as much a mock-epic joke on the nautical idea of "errantry" as it is an urban labyrinth. Perhaps the best joke of all is on Bérard, a joke Joyce may well have never known about. When in 1929 Bérard went back to Salina because he still was uncertain that he had the identification of the land of the *planktai* correctly marked, he had occasion to change his mind. It was not Salina, after all, that Circe warned against. Rather, the straits between Lipari and Vulcano islands were more likely. Even Bérard must have been aware of the irony. The Wandering Rocks had gotten up and moved.[1]

Joyce's orchestration of Dublin locations and movements in *Wandering Rocks* contains some generally realized patterns, some framing and orienting schemes, and some sure-fire traps (Hart and Knuth, pp. 27-31). Events in the episode divide along the Liffey's northern and southern banks, and along a turned Euxine grid, European and Asiatic. Joyce lets the chapter range the compass points. The Viceregent's stately procession, *imperio in imperium*, moves, for the most part, south of the Liffey as it follows a southeast route to the Mirus Bazaar in Ballsbridge. Bloom had already associated the Viceregal mission with the Mercer's street hospital charity, originally supported by the famous performance of Handel's *Messiah* (183). This procession to Ballsbridge near Sandymount is hardly that of a Semitic savior. The Viceregent represents the eastern usurper whose empire Stephen and Mulligan disparaged earlier when they looked out southeast over Dublin Bay in *Telemachus*. Father Conmee, who moves north of the Liffey toward Artane, is another Dubliner with eyes in his head who cannot see. He unintentionally rousts Lynch from his love-nest near Artane while repeating the Hebrew letter *sin* from his breviary (224). Lynch makes the same mistake as Bérard's early travelers on Salina who mistook the *Val de l'Église* for the Valley of Happiness.

[1] Victor Bérard, *Les Navigations d'Ulysse* (Paris, 1929), IV, 463-466.

As the black hole at the center of *Ulysses*, *Wandering Rocks* draws the matter of Dublin to it. The episode has always invited speculation as the adventure that at once miniaturizes all the others and goes the Homeric tradition one better.[2] Many epics of great scope contain scaled-down versions of themselves within their larger structure. In *Wandering Rocks* there is a strong temptation to connect its nineteen subsections, with some adjustments, to the eighteen chapters of *Ulysses*. Many have tried.[3] The most ingenious scheme I know of is the linking of the novel's first nine episodes with the first nine subsections of *Wandering Rocks*. The tenth subsection of Joyce's apocryphal adventure depicts Bloom in the middle of Dublin, a *trou* or hole in the center just as Wandering Rocks is a *trou* in the *Wanderings* of the Odyssean hero. After the apocryphal middle subsection of the novel's super-added center, the connections pick up again with the second nine episodes of *Ulysses* and the remaining subsections of *Wandering Rocks*. If this works, and I am committed neither to proving that it does nor to the belief that it ought to, the wittiest parallel in the complex scheme is to the *Nausicaa* episode of *Ulysses*. In the appropriate subsection of *Wandering Rocks*, Ben Dollard stands north of the Liffey on Ormond Quay next to Reddy's and Daughters. Ten minutes later, Gerty MacDowell, the heroine of *Nausicaa*, puts in a brief appearance in the processional section of *Wandering Rocks*. She stands next to Dollard's printing house (a different Dollard) on Wellington Quay directly across the Liffey from Ben Dollard, but very close to where Bloom had been for most of the hour. Dollard, who years before had worn Bloom's pants badly "with all his belongings on show" (270) is now wearing a "blue cutaway" (244): "Hold that fellow with the bad trousers" (244), says Simon Dedalus as Dollard comes into view. Gerty, whom we will see later in *Nausicaa* with all *her* belongings on show for Bloom, is wearing blue lace panties.[4]

Clever as some of these parallels may be, their discovery is more a test of endurance than a measure of insight. The episodes in *Ulysses*

---

[2] See Gilbert, pp. 233 and 235.

[3] William York Tindall, *Reader's Guide to James Joyce* (New York, 1959) gives up his search, admitting its folly, after suggesting correspondences for several of the novel's early chapters and the early subsections of *Wandering Rocks* (p. 182).

[4] I am indebted to James Nohrnberg for this example and for a much larger set of parallels that he has worked out.

store up information about each other as the day progresses. Parallels can be found in any subsection of *Wandering Rocks* for any chapter in the novel. To work with the idea of an interior epic is part of a deliberately frustrated pattern in *Ulysses*. On the other hand, the very attempt to seek out patterns, even comic ones, recognizes the novel's sense of recapitulative design. In *Wandering Rocks* it is not merely the episode's relation to the rest of the novel that invites speculation, but the relation of one subsection to another. Here, too, we can proceed with some confidence up to a point, and then we grow suspicious. The clues are there, but they usually fall short of a fully consistent pattern. Bloom, for instance, spends the hour at the center of the chapter and the center of his city near the book stalls at Merchant's Arch Quay. As an "allroundman," like Odysseus, perhaps Bloom is center and circumference. If so, *Wandering Rocks* might exfoliate around the Bloom or flower in the center. Conmee and the Lord Lieutenant are contraries at the extremes of the sub-sections (1, 19). The one-legged sailor, a physical cripple, pairs with Cashel Boyle O'Connor Fitzmaurice Tisdall Farrell, a mental cripple (2, 18). The two Dedalus sisters are an appropriate match for the current Dedalus tower-mates, Mulligan and Haines (3, 17). Boylan, Bloom's enemy, pairs with Cunnigham, Bloom's friend (4, 16). Stephen and Artifoni talk of artistic sacrifice while Dollard and Cowley talk of economic sacrifices (5, 15). Unfortunately, any further contraries in the pairings, if there are any, elude me. Possibly the positionings in the chapter might offer yet another way into its design. Again, we can look to a spatial pattern of exfoliation around Bloom at the center. The flanking subsections take place north and south of the Liffey. We can get as far with this scheme as we could with the other. It works for 1, 19; 2, 18; 3, 17; 4, 16; then it breaks down. Joyce's indication in the *schema* is, finally, a puzzle-solver's comfort. The chapter is labyrinthine, its environment hostile, its paths errant. Clive Hart and Leo Knuth, in *A Topographical Guide to James Joyce's Ulysses*, seem committed to tracing the detailed spatial intricacies of the episode, but, ultimately, even they recognize that only the prophetic Elijah leaflet escapes down the Liffey into the bay. Bloom, the hero, marks the dangers of the *trou* in the middle of the novel by standing nearly still for most of the hour at the center of the labyrinth. As a Taurus by birth, Bloom is both the bull-god and the sacrificial victim, as is fitting for the epic and urban proportions of Joyce's *Wandering Rocks*.

In a perverse way, orientation in Dublin is disorienting. The course of the Liffey shifts 90 degrees to accommodate a European and Asiatic bank. Father Conmee walks from his parish off Mountjoy Square to Artane in the direction of Howth Head. But he thinks of Clongowes, southwest. Joyce has the Viceregal procession cross the Royal Canal in Pembroke, a physical impossibility, as any Dubliner would know, and a mistake that puts the Lord Lieutenant back on Conmee's side of the Liffey.[5] Dublin's citizens suffer from urban "chaosmos." Artifoni misses his tram, the bicycle racers chase their tails, Master Dignam wanders the streets and misreads posters, Tisdall Farrell walks east on Leinster and Clare streets to North Merrion Square and then turns on his heels and, for no apparent reason, repeats the walk back. The H.E.L.Y.'S. sandwichboard men make their way up Grafton street and down Grafton street. Gerty MacDowell, standing near her future mystery man, Bloom, misses the Viceregal procession near Wellington Quay because her view is blocked by a tram. *Wandering Rocks* concludes with an epiphany of indifference. The Viceregal cavalcade, viewed, misviewed, unviewed, makes its way southeast, but as with almost everything else in the chapter, we never quite see it reach its destination. If Dublin's citizens are frustrated in their own domain, and if the chapter's *loci* are intentionally confused, as Joyce hints in the *schema*, the confusion replicates the gist of the novel's innovation upon the epic's form. Wandering Rocks, like epic spaces, are by their nature moveable.

SIRENS

Sirens is one of the most irreverent attacks on Irish paralysis in *Ulysses*, although some see in the chapter the suggestion that, as in the overture to the episode, the only way to begin is to be done.[6] In the *Odyssey*, Odysseus has to learn moderation—the Sirens are a lure to distraction, another false homecoming. If Bloom needs anything in his own land, it is not moderation. In a curious way, the *Sirens* chapter of *Ulysses* plays to Bloom's strengths—not to his weaknesses—and that is why the episode produces a paralytic lull. In the Dublin of *Sirens*, the "real classical" (263) force, the blind piano-tuner, is

[5] See Clive Hart, "Wandering Rocks," Hart and Hayman, p. 199.
[6] See Jackson I. Cope, "Sirens," in Hart and Hayman, pp. 217-242, for an affirmative and very good reading of this chapter.

gone. He has left his tuning fork in the bar for a land deprived of an epic ear. The sentiment of musical Dublin is an excuse to sit and drink. Only the themes of songs touch on action: love, war, and rebellion. At the Ormond Hotel bar, the Odyssean parallel is "sweat cheat" enchantment. Bloom makes short shrift of music's rigorous affinities ("Musemathematics," 278): "it's what's behind" (274) that counts. And from the Greek goddesses of the National Museum to Molly's plump, melonous hemispheres, *behind* means sex. In *Sirens* Bloom is bound apart from what he might want, a victim like Orpheus in the *schema*, not because he looks behind, but because there is no Molly's behind in front of him. In the midst of Boylan's seduction of his wife, the best Bloom can do is generate a fundamental fart at the end of the episode—well-tuned, liberated: "Pprrpffrrpppff. *Done*" (291).

The *Sirens* episode takes place mainly in the Ormond bar and grill, Upper Ormond Quay near the Essex (Grattan) bridge over the Liffey. Bloom's path from the pornography racks of Merchant's Arch across the Liffey is plotted, contrapuntally, in the chapter's opening pages. He moves from east to west, but at one point Joyce inverts the sequence of establishments that Bloom passes along Wellington Quay (Hart and Knuth, p. 32).[7] Bloom walks past Moulang's (31 Wellington Quay), appears to turn west to Wine's (35 Wellington Quay), and then heads on again past Carroll's (29 Wellington Quay). Perhaps "bearing in his breast the sweets of sin" (258) he is distracted. He moves from one sort of pornography at the book racks toward another at the Ormond.

In the *Odyssey* the Sirens appeal to Odysseus' wandering weary Greek warriors not yet rid of the agonies attendant upon their return from the wars. The crew of Odysseus' ship is bewaxed, Odysseus himself bound, and the Sirens sing of an enchanting "way out," which, like that of Lotusland, renders men impotent. Bérard places the Sirens at the Straits of Capri in the Tyrrhenian Sea, south of the Gulf of Naples, off the Sorrentian peninsula. The placement in *Ulysses* is to the west on the Liffey (as Capri is west of Sorrento) in proximity to the Cyclopes' territory (Barney Kiernan's in Dublin, further northwest). In Bérard's scheme the closest geographical point to the Sirens is also the Cyclopes' territory slightly northwest in the Bay of Naples. Joyce has taken the episodes out of sequence

[7] See Fritz Senn, "Symbolic Juxtaposition," *JJQ*, 5 (1968), 276-278.

and adjusted directions of approach, but, again, he holds to a map and to an axis line.

Odysseus resists the unnerving strains of the Sirens, perhaps the sirocco, the south wind whistling for days on end against the cavernous rock facade of the cliffs at Capri. Bérard cites a passage from De Borch's *Lettres sur la Sicilie*: "Le *schiroc*, qui souffle avec violence, relâche nos fibres et nos nerfs au point qu'on se sent une espèce de dégoût général pour toute espèce de travail" (The sirocco, which blows with violence, slackens our fibers and our nerves to the point that one senses a sort of general disgust for all kind of work) [Bérard, II, 340]. The sounds of the Ormond are difficult for Bloom, too: "Music. Gets on your nerves" (288). Sirens may be beckoning, but they soon cloy. Writing *Sirens* seems to have had a somewhat similar effect on Joyce. He complained to Harriet Weaver: "Since I wrote the *Sirens*, I find it impossible to listen to music of any kind" (*Letters*, I, 129).

Bérard points to the Semitic origin of the Sirens' name as magical "holders" or "binders" (*Aben-sir-en* or plains of enchantment) [Bérard, II, 336]. He argues that the descriptive word for the episode's action is *enchaînement* or fettering: "Si l'épisode des Lestrygons dans le pays des Sardes, des *Fuyards*, est la *Fuite* d'Ulysse, si l'épisode de Kirkè dans le sanctuaire de l'affranchissement est la *Libération*, on voit que l'épisode des Sirènes est, avant tout, l'*Enchaînement*" (If the *Lestrygonian* episode in the country of the Sardinians, the *Fuyards*, is Odysseus' flight, if the *Circe* episode in the sanctuary of freedom is liberation, one sees that the *Sirens* episode is above all, the binding up [shackling]) [Bérard, II, 335]. The term is fitting for the scene literally portrayed in the *Odyssey* and figuratively portrayed in *Ulysses*. Odysseus bound and Bloom tied to Richie Goulding are versions of impotence, the former in the throes of desire, the latter peculiarly self-willed and passive. When Budgen suggested to Joyce something of Bloom's wish to cast himself in the role of cuckold, to share the Sirens' call with other men, Joyce explained to Budgen that Bloom acts from a severe form of passive jealousy where inaction is vicarious desire (Budgen, p. 315). In the *Sirens*' fugal arrangement Blazes Boylan, "the conquering hero" (264), walks and rides from the Ormond to Bloom's home while Bloom, psychologically conquered, sits immobile. Good devil that he is, Boylan "plunged a bit" (265) on the filly, Sceptre, and he has the same in mind for Molly Bloom. Dublin's Sirens sing the seaside songs of plaintive separation, pain, loss, and betrayal.

In the Ormond grill, adjacent to the bar, Bloom, if we take Joyce's analysis seriously, is bound by circumstances partly of his own arranging. He listens to the chapter's strains: Miss Douce as Floridora, "Idolores of the Eastern Sea"; the tenor-baritone duet, *Love and War*; Goulding's *All is lost now*; Simon Dedalus' *M'appari* from Flotow's *Martha*; the base barreltone Ben Dollard's *Croppy Boy*. Miss Douce, an ersatz Siren having returned sunburned "raw" from the strand at Rosevor, north, provides the fugal *sonnez la cloche* with her snapping garter. Irish sentiment is but a chord away from Irish vulgarity. For Bloom, music is untapped sexual warmth, a hope and a threat.

> Words? Music? No: it's what's behind.
> Bloom looped, unlooped, noded, disnoded.
> Bloom. Flood of warm jimjam lickitup secretness flowed to flow in music out, in desire, dark to lick flow, invading. Tipping her tepping her tapping her topping her. Tup. Pores to dilate dilating. Tup. The joy the feel the warm the. Tup. To pour o'er sluices pouring gushes. Flood, gush, flow, joygush, tupthrop. Now! Language of love. (274)

Simon Dedalus' "flight" through the air of *M'appari* fulfills what Artifoni had spoken of to Stephen in *Wandering Rocks* as music's *cespite di rendita*, the cornucopia of return (228). Simon's voice soars to a consummate return after a lyric exile, a wandering and homecoming, "dominant to love to return" (275). Bloom thinks of his own rechanneled desire.

> —*To me!*
> Siopold!
> Consumed.
> Come. Well sung. All clapped. She ought to. Come. To me, to him, to her, you too, me, us. (276)

If Bloom's jealousy is inclusive and consuming, love's language, music, is a mockery. In *Sirens* only Boylan returns from the dominant to the tonic of Molly's bed. He "jingles" along the Lower Ormond Quay, Bachelor's Walk (appropriately), north on Sackville street by horse-drawn cab, past Dlugacz's on Dorset, past Larry O'Rourke's on Upper Dorset, and finally to a stop at 7 Eccles. Boylan's route replicates part of Bloom's in the earlier *Calypso* episode. But Molly is no longer a nymph loyal to Odysseus. She is the variant Penelope, the queen of legend, unlike Homer's, who takes lovers by the dozens. Meanwhile, the blind tuner comes back to get what he forgot: his tuning fork. Bloom writes a dissonant epitaph, a fart.

CYCLOPS

The *Cyclops* episode of *Ulysses* is set at Barney Kiernan's pub on Little Britain street or, in this most nationalistic of chapters, *Brian O'Ciarnain's* in *Sraid na Bretaine Bheag* (316). The range of the episode, from Arbour Hill to Kiernan's, is as far due west, with the exception of the northwest Glasnevin cemetery, as the day's action will extend. Dublin's western grid is appropriate for Irish nationalism, a political phenomenon itself out of the west of the country. Bérard sees the Homeric Cyclopes as barbaric mountain men of the Cumaean coastal plains of western Italy, living in caverns projected southwest over the ocean for protection from the bitter northern winds [Bérard, II, 171]. Bérard speaks of the reaction to the inhabitants of these regions: "Les navigateurs du temps se plaignent de leurs violences, de leur manque de justice" (The navigators of those times complained of their violence, of their lack of law) [Bérard, II, 175]. The inhabitants of *Ulysses* in Kiernan's pub are mostly ex-members of the Dublin Metropolitan Police, but the pub itself pays homage to criminality with its collection of murderers' weapons and hangmen's glasses.[8]

Cyclops is the novel's showcase for epic wit and epic violence, from the shot-putting citizen to the British hangman, "barbarous bloody barbarian" (303). Battles are fought around and beneath the review stands at an execution: "All the delegates without exception expressed themselves in the strongest possible heterogeneous terms concerning the nameless barbarity which they had been called upon to witness. An animated altercation (in which all took part) ensued" (307). But Cyclopean parody has unheard of urban innovations on epic form: pickpockets.

Commendatore Beninobenone having been extricated from underneath the presidential armchair, it was explained by his legal

[8] For a description of Kiernan's pub, see Gilbert, p. 258.

advisor Avvocato Pagamimi that the various articles secreted in his thirtytwo pockets had been abstracted by him during the affray from the pockets of his junior colleagues in the hope of bringing them to their senses. The objects (which included several hundred ladies' and gentlemen's gold and silver watches) were promptly restored to their rightful owners and general harmony reigned supreme. (308)

General harmony is comedy's domain, but it arrives with a sleight of epic hand and a preposterous lie. In a notesheet entry for *Cyclops* Joyce remarked on the technique of his parody: "Compare: Giant: giant: :giant: dwarf" (Herring, p. 101). The hint could be from Rabelais or Swift or Lewis Carroll. In parody, to make a local space look big it is necessary to shrink its subjects to midgets. To make a local space look ridiculous it is necessary to inflate its subjects to giants. The parodic voice of *Cyclops* marks, in one of its epic catalogues, yet another migration from the Holy Lands to the British Isles; we hear of Goliath in one breath and Jack the Giantkiller in the next. *Cyclops* approaches the sheer weight of mock-heroism, so heavy that only parodic indulgence can support the "broadshouldered deepchested stronglimbed frankeyed redhaired freely freckled shaggybearded widemouthed largenosed longheaded deepvoiced barekneed brawnyhanded hairylegged ruddyfaced sinewyarmed hero" (296).

In the *Odyssey* the adventure with Polyphemus was the first really violent test for the guileful hero, a naming of epic names: "Noman is my name," Odysseus' punning ruse, is more fully articulated in the Homeric identification, "I am Laertes' son, Odysseus." In *Ulysses* the test is more confusing for the hero. Bloom faces yet another test against Dubliners who "couper et broyer avec les dents," who cut, grind (and backbite) with their teeth. Bérard notes that the Cyclopes are like the mountain-dwelling Lestrygonians, cousins almost. In the *Lestrygonians* episode of *Ulysses*, Bloom's ears ring from the Dublin Metropolitan Police whistle (163). Joyce's Zürich notebook enters: "King cries (DMP whistle)" (VIII.A.5, p. 301). This refers to Antiphates, the chief Lestrygonian, who beckoned his tribe of giants to the cliffs to hurl rocks at a swiftly departing Odysseus. Polyphemus had done the same thing. In *Ulysses*, the citizen-Cyclops, associated with the DMP, is equally hostile. Joyce enters in his notesheets for *Cyclops*: "puissant chieftain" (Herring, p. 115).

Bloom, the eastern interloper, is in a strange western land. His Jewish race is suspected by an Irish antagonist who forgets that the cherished Milesians at one time followed the Jews out of Egypt. Instead he blames an ancient race: "coming over here to Ireland filling the country with bugs" (323). The citizen, by all rights, should value a connection: "Jews & Irish remember past," Joyce writes in a notesheet entry (Herring, p. 82).

In the Homeric version of the *Cyclops* adventure, Odysseus' curiosity gets him into difficulty. His men want Polyphemus' cheese, and Odysseus wants a look at the big fellow himself. As is typical of much of the action in Joyce's parody, Bloom finds himself in trouble even without the questionable reward of seeing a freak. He receives only insults. At one point in *Cyclops* the citizen refers to Breen and it is clear that he intends Bloom as well.

> —Pity about her, says the citizen. Or any other woman marries a half and half.
> —How half and half? says Bloom. Do you mean he . . .
> —Half and half I mean, says the citizen. A fellow that's neither fish nor flesh. (321)

In a sense, an exchange like this is the price Bloom pays as Joyce's modern hero. It is not so much his nationality or sexuality that we worry about, but the half-life he leads inside and beneath Homer's *Odyssey*. Just after this exchange between Bloom and the citizen, the narrator of *Cyclops* comments, "Begob I saw there was trouble coming" (321). The trouble is the chapter's crisis. Heroism in the *Odyssey* is the blinding of the giant Polyphemus. In *Ulysses* the climax is reduced to an altercation in a seedy pub where the victorious hero is as much in the dark as his stout-blinded antagonist. Bloom has no idea what the violence is about.

The parallels in *Ulysses* to the action of the *Odyssey* have, to this point in the novel, been miniaturizations to fit the time and space of the day. Something of this continues in *Cyclops*, but Joyce refines another parodic technique which inflates heroism far beyond its proportions in the Homeric epic.[9] At the same time the goings-on at Kiernan's bring the novel much lower than most other chapters in

[9] Hugh Kenner, "Homer's Sticks and Stones," *JJQ*, 6 (1969), 285-298, suggests that some of the inflated language in *Cyclops* parodies the Butcher and Lang prose translation of the *Odyssey*, from which Joyce worked, but of which he could not possibly have thought much. Joyce's friend, Ezra Pound, despised the Butcher and Lang translation.

Ulysses care to go. The giant or egocidal terror, as Joyce labeled the meaning of the episode, is the violence of the citizen-hero, but it is also the debased narration of the "I" who sees everything and values nothing. Even Mulligan's mockery cannot approach the debasing talents of *Cyclops'* narrative voice. In the *Ithaca* episode of *Ulysses* Joyce will see an ordinary, if earthy, Dublin wife from Gibraltar as Gaea-Tellus. The narrator of *Cyclops* sees in Molly a "fat heap . . . a nice old phenomenon with a back on her like a ballalley" (305). This is not giganticism—it is not even realism. The "I" narrator as he tells us was "just passing the time of day" (292). Joyce does much the same thing in *Ulysses*, a book whose very structure counts on "just" passing the time of day. But there are ways to pass it. For the "I" narrator time has no significance beyond its literalness. The antithesis of giganticism is absolute demythification, and that is what *Cyclops* sets up in its narrative voices.

Once removed from the "I" narrator, Ireland is a land of super-forms. It can mark its avatars in its landscape from Ben Howth to Slieve Bloom, Moses on the Mountain. Its people are the oldest people, Druids and Celts. Its migrations are the oldest migrations, Milesian and Phoenician. On the other side, Ireland is a land of ridiculous, decaying Sir Louts. It has been nowhere for hundreds of years and has nowhere to go. It is the land of pubs, bad debts, hangman gods, empty harbors, bardic dogs, and former police. All Ireland appears in *Cyclops*—even the citizen's modest handkerchief illuminates Inisfail the fair from Fingal's Cave to the Henry street Warehouse. The land's geography—its flora, fauna, fish-life, raw materials, manufactured goods, provinces, seaports, mountains, and rivers—is catalogued by the epic and mock-epic gazetteer. Harbors, from the flourishing Queenstown to the wind-exposed Blackshod Bay, are ports in the episode's verbal storm. We move from splendor to the invective of talking dogs curious "to know who to bite and when" (324). Ireland has its patriots, its men of moderation, and its xenophobes. The boorish citizen, we discover in the next chapter, *Nausicaa*, may well be the grandfather of Gerty MacDowell, a gentle Odyssean Phaeacian. In the *Odyssey* the Cyclopes and the Phaeacians were former neighbors, but the refined Phaeacians moved east when they could no longer bear up under the strain. In Dublin, the citizen is brute to Gerty's delicacy. They are at proper geographical removes—the citizen in the northwest of the city, and Gerty in the southeast at Sandymount strand.

Bérard places the land of the Cyclopes in the Bay of Cumae at the northern peninsula of the larger Gulf of Naples. The *Odyssey* makes it clear that the Phaeacians lived in Hypereia before their long eastern migration. Bérard's etymology makes it clear that Hypereia is the Greek version of the Semitic Cumae or highland [Bérard, II, 114]. The Homeric locale is fairly well narrowed in the *Cyclops* adventure to the bay near the islet of Nisida along the volcano-dotted Cumaean shore. After voyaging from Libya, a southern land of ease, Odysseus moors his ships and proceeds to explore the Cyclopean coasts. Bloom is up from the musical delirium of the southern Ormond and now on point duty outside Kiernan's. He is waiting for Martin Cunningham to work out Dignam's immediate finances. Bérard sees the little island where Odysseus moors as a volcanic rock's throw from the dangerous coastal hills and caves of the mountain men. Nisida, unlike the inhabited mainland, was a place of Phoenician commerce, a traditional jumping-off point for various markets. Even Nisida itself served as a market for the early navigators: "cette île offre aux premiers navigateurs le site d'un grand *emporium*" (this isle offered the first navigators the site of a great emporium) [Bérard, II, 154].

For Bérard, the territory of the Cyclopes is keyed by their name: one-eyed, round-eyed [Bérard, II, 115]. They are not only the mountain men of the highlands, but anthropomorphic representations of the volcanic features of the plains. In *Ulysses* the volcanic "eye" parallels are amusingly literal, from the "I" of the opening retrospective narration to the "mote in others' eye" and "the beam in their own" (326) to Bloom's lucky escape with the sun in the citizen's eye (colloquial for dead drunk). But there is a sense in Joyce's parody that he was not working with material that in itself was fully serious. In his *Authoress of the Odyssey*, Samuel Butler compares the *Cyclops* episode to an ancient Sicilian ceremonial picnic where the doltish mountain men are mocked by the plains folk as they come down from the highlands leading flocks of goats. Joyce surely sees even the Homeric episode as a bit of a farce. His reference in the *schema* to Galatea suggests that he had in mind Ovid's *Metamorphoses*, a work that treats Polyphemus like the burlesque hero he is. Ovid displays the giant combing his beard to attract what must have seemed to him a lovely midget, Galatea.

In his own distracted way, Bloom in *Cyclops* mimics Odysseus as closely as he will all day. The episode mingles confusion, farce, comedy, guile, and finally bravado. Bérard tells the story, which

he records from Dionysus of Halicarnassus, of several Greek merce-
naries who devised a stratagem to capture the Cumaean territory
from its ancient inhabitants by disguising themselves in animal
skins and hiding their swords in heaps of dry sticks. They took their
befuddled victims by surprise [Bérard, II, 129]. The first time we see
Polyphemus in the *Odyssey* he is carrying a load of dry sticks. Part
of Odysseus' stratagem is to escape from the cave by clinging to
the skin of animals. There is something of the local folk tale in all
this—and everything, except a kind of thematic reading, militates
against our taking even the Odyssean version too seriously. Bérard
describes another local angle to the story: "Pour se concilier l'hu-
meur de ces Barbares, les navigateurs grecs ou romains leur ap-
portent d'excellents vins . . . et ces vins servent non pas aux échanges,
mais simplement aux cadeaux" (In order to placate the humor of
these barbarians, the Greek or Roman navigators brought them excellent wines . . . and these wines did not serve for trade, but simply
as gifts) [Bérard, II, 176]. That Odysseus plies Polyphemus with
drink is obvious, and in our first sight of the citizen in *Ulysses* he
is perched on his bar stool "waiting for what the sky would drop
in the way of drink" (295). Northern giants drain the land: "Want
a small fortune to keep him in drinks" (314), says the narrator.

In *Cyclops* the west of Dublin around the nearby courts on Little
Green and Halston streets is hardly the bastion of justice. The
barbarians need to be placated. But Bloom's tentative probings into
the pub while waiting for Cunningham enrages the xenophobic
citizen. In the *Odyssey*, at a fairly early stage in the hero's *Wanderings*, the *Cyclops* episode disturbs the balance between prudence and
confrontation, between inventive guile and dangerous slip-ups. The
Cyclops episode of *Ulysses* occurs much later in Bloom's daily trials,
and is more important in developing his spirit than in curbing his
curiosity. *Cyclops* provides Bloom with a chance to announce himself to Dublin. That he brings too much light to the gentiles is an
accident of the day's racing results more than a flaw in his character.
Bloom confronts his own citizenship and his own racial heritage,
and he reduces the Irish citizen to flustered rage. Odysseus' confrontation with Polyphemus is part of an important lesson in readjustment to a more tempered and human ethic. Violence cannot
be a norm, and the further Odysseus gets into his adventures the
more he seeks moderation. In the single day of *Ulysses* Bloom has
moderation to spare—he needs his moment of assertion. Later, in

Eumaeus, he takes considerable pride in the outcome of the events at Kiernan's. His heroism is small, and it can only really be measured in the context of the boisterous absurdity of the mock-heroic. But what Bloom does for his land, the bulk of the Irish merely discuss. John Wyse Nolan informs the Nationalists at the pub that Bloom "gave the idea for Sinn Fein to Griffith to put in his paper all kinds of jerrymandering, packed juries and swindling the taxes off of the Government and appointing consuls all over the world to walk about selling Irish industries" (335-336).

Just as in the *Odyssey* there is more to the probing quality of the adventure than the eye-searing denouement, there is more to Bloom than his antagonists, confusing hegemony with abrasiveness, are willing to admit. By the end of the chapter Bloom takes on full prophetic dimensions. The tone, clearly, is still parodic, but Joyce has been inviting his readers all day to see substance in his Odyssean adaptations. At 5:00 P.M. the metaphoric home-rule sun rises in Ireland, the land of gloom, to shine in the eye of a drunken giant: "Mercy of God the sun was in his eyes or he'd have left him for dead" (343). His aim skewed, the citizen's biscuit tin misses Bloom and hurtles down the street southwest by west. The almost crucified eastern Jew ascends like Elijah from the depths of the episode's parodic vertical axis, and, like Odysseus under swift southern sail to Aeolia, gloriously and ingloriously sails away, south down Little Green street.

Elijah! Elijah! And he answered with a main cry: *Abba! Adonai!* And they beheld Him even Him, ben Bloom Elijah, amid clouds of angels ascend to the glory of the brightness at an angle of fortyfive degrees over Donohoe's in Little Green Street like a shot off a shovel. (345)

It occurs to Polyphemus in the *Odyssey*, as he stands on his high land begging Odysseus—son of Laertes, no longer noman—to return so that he might wreak vengeance, that his own miserable blinded plight was foretold. All his present grief was described to him, but Polyphemus guessed that only an equal in size could harm him. In *Ulysses* the citizen is all Irish brawn, a true Norseman, a shot-put champion, but he is incapacitated by the little man with the prophetic mission. Perhaps he expected a rival in Balor of the Evil Eye. Perhaps he *is* Balor of the Evil Eye and Bloom arrived instead: "How the mighty are fallen!" (292)

NAUSICAA

Cyclops parodies the apotheosis of the moderate hero in the presence of gigantism itself, but parody for Joyce can be elevating. In *Nausicaa* Bloom is more modest still, and more compromised by the Homeric parallel than he could ever have been in *Cyclops*. The "foreign gentleman that was sitting on the rocks looking was . . . *Cuckoo*" (382). For the second time in the day Bloom appears in Sandymount: "History repeats itself" (377). Like the "nobleman" he sees "Blown in from the bay" (375), he is his own "*Mystery Man on the Beach*" (376). After his semi-vertical departure from Kiernan's pub, he presumably makes his way to Dignam's residence by public transportation. Two hours have passed since *Cyclops* and we are told nothing of Bloom's visit to 9 Newbridge street, Sandymount. The lost time is Joyce's partial acknowledgment of disturbed Homeric sequence—his usual way of reorienting the directions of the day.

For Odysseus the land of the Phaeacians was his last adventure before *Nostos*. For Homer the Phaeacian sequence follows the return from *Calypso* at the very beginning of the narrative version of the *Wanderings* (Book VI). After seventeen days at sea from Ogygia, Odysseus drifted to the land of Nausicaa from the extremes of the Mediterranean, keeping the northern constellations on his left and sailing around the Italian boot that had given him so much trouble in the earlier years of his *Wanderings*. He landed, according to Bérard, north of his own home island at the Grecian isle of Corfu off the Corinthian coast. The Phaeacian land, Scheria, is the last half of an epithet. Corfu means ship, and Scheria, black: hence, black ship for a nation of swift mariners [Bérard, 1, 500]. Bérard has Odysseus put up on the western side of the snake-shaped isle, possibly in the cove of Alipa in the Bay of Liapides. Alcinous' city is nearby off Mount St. George.

The brine-soaked Odysseus is reborn on the shores of a river inlet and, after a night's rest and a titillating confrontation with the young Nausicaa, he is given the gift of divine presence by Athena. Bloom's plight is different—his wife at home is unfaithful and the prelude to his homecoming is onanistic retreat. Masturbation is partly a metaphor for Bloom's forced eroticism—his habitually delayed homecoming. In itself, masturbation is too slight an epic event for a chapter's worth of literary laughter. It signals a desire in Bloom for an "immanence," as Lukács would put it—that is, partly a wish to make the possible actual.

In Joyce's *schema* the narrative technique of the chapter is retrogression and progression. The pattern works for more than Gerty's and Bloom's narrative voice or for Bloom's sexual doldrums and release. In the *Odyssey* the Phaeacians retrogressed east from the land of the Cyclopes, Hypereia. The Phaeacian retrogression becomes the last stop on Odysseus' progression to *Nostos*. For Odysseus, as for Bloom, it is the "new I want" (377). The motif of the foreigner's restoring the land—almost a fairy tale motif—is central to the *Nausicaa* episode in the *Odyssey*, and, in a more ambiguous way, central to *Ulysses*. "Why me?" Bloom wonders of Molly's original interest in him: "Because you were so foreign from the others" (380). Virgil plays on this motif when his Trojan Aeneas appears as the mysterious stranger in Italy in the prelude to a new revival of an old land and an old empire. In *Nausicaa* Bloom is the wearied wanderer from the east watching the day catch up to western evening lands.

Bérard's treatment of the Phaeacians is one of his most fascinating chapters. He points out that Corfu and Ithaca are on the same line of demarcation between the known world of the east and the unknown marvels of the west and northwest. Joyce's notesheets for *Nausicaa* pick up the hint.

W. kingdom of souls: Poseidon, Nicolo (della? Ma) Odyssey— struggles v unknown (Herring, p. 152)

Corfu, for Bérard, is an anomaly in western Greece, and not merely because the *Odyssey* describes it as a kingdom that seems more in keeping with the Levant. Bérard actually traces the Phaeacian culture back through the trading routes of the eastern Mediterranean, through the Greek western isles to the mainland Peloponnese, to Crete, Rhodes, and even Egypt. The habits and the clothes of the Phaeacians belong to times and places past.

Par quelques détails de leur costume et de leurs moeurs, les Phéaciens semblent se distinguer des Achéens et se rapprocher des nations de l'Extrême-Levant: "Les Égyptiens, dit Hérodote, portent des vêtements de lin qu'ils veulent toujours fraîchement lavés; ils y attachent le plus grand soin, car ils vont jusqu'à préférer la propreté a l'élégance."

(By several details of their clothing and their customs, the Phaeacians seem to distinguish themselves from the Greeks and to approach the nations of the Levant: "The Egyptians," said Herodotus, "wear linens that they always want freshly washed; they attach great care to them, for they go so far as to prefer propriety to elegance.")   [Bérard, 1, 574]

Joyce alludes to Nausicaa's preoccupation with clean linen in a short note for the episode: "Nausicaa & clothesline" (VIII.A.5, p. 296). Perhaps with Bérard in mind, Joyce also has Bloom observe that fashions always change, "Except the east" (368). In the *Odyssey* Telemachus and Odysseus will converge on Ithaca from two directions. Bérard's theory, at this juncture, is that they both move along the prominent east-west Phoenician-Greek axis. *Nostos* is a joining of east and west: "La Phéacie est pourtant en rapports avec la Patras de ce temps, je veux dire avec la Pylos de Nestor . . . Ithaque, à mi-chemin" (Phaeacia is still lined up with Patras of this time, that is with Nestor's Pylos . . . Ithaca is mid-way between) [Bérard, 1, 581]. Two heroes, one tempered by the west, the other nurtured in the east, sail from two points equidistant from the same mid-point. Odysseus' return is like Telemachus' departure, but when the son comes home he sails the same way back from Pylos.

Il faut compter que la Phéacie est séparée d'Ithaque par une nuit de navigation. Pour venir aux îles achéennes, les vaisseaux phéaciens mettent environ une nuit. La navigation d'Ulysse sur le vaisseau phéacien sera semblable de tous points à la navigation de Télémaque vers Pylos. Tout ce que nous avons dit de celle-ci peut s'appliquer à celle-là. Comme le vaisseau de Télémaque, le vaisseau phéacien d'Ulysse partira le soir, pour profiter de la brise de terre qui se lève trois heures après le coucher du soleil.

(It can be calculated that Phaeacia is separated from Ithaca by a night of navigation. In order to reach the Greek isles, the Phaeacian ships put out for a night. The voyage of Ulysses on the Phaeacian vessel would be comparable at all points to the voyage of Telemachus to Pylos. All that we have said about that voyage can be applied to this one. Like the ship of Telemachus, the Phaeacian ship of Ulysses leaves at night to profit from the breeze that arises three hours after sunset.)   [Bérard, 1, 487]

This is an extremely important spatial parallel in terms of the significance of the approaching *Nostos*. All homegoings are nocturnes, as Joyce observes. In the *Odyssey* the Phaeacians provide

Odysseus respite and reintroduction to civilized ways before his return to Ithaca. In Argos and Pylos, Telemachus witnesses civilizations that have adjusted to *nostoi* of their own. When Odysseus "talks out" the barbarities of the past in his Phaeacian narrative, and when Telemachus avoids the ambush of the suitors by beaching on the southeast side of his island, both return ready. Odysseus awakes on Nausicaa's isle to watch the princess at the shore playing ball with her handmaidens after they have done the palace's laundry. The chore is appropriate. Odysseus will return to his own shores and, with Telemachus' help, wash out the dirty laundry of Ithaca once and for all.

The mood of Joyce's *Nausicaa* is climactic in parody but restorative in its preparation for homecoming. Bloom's mirage, unlike Gerty's, has national dimension: "Mirage. Land of the setting sun this. Homerule sun setting in the southeast. My native land, goodnight" (376). The evening land has found itself, as Stephen predicted it would in *Proteus*: "Where? To evening lands. Evening will find itself" (50). Place, of course, is not the only connection between *Proteus* and *Nausicaa* in *Ulysses*. In *Proteus* Stephen wrestled with the processes of change and stability, center and limits, origins and ends, birth and death. The signatures Bloom reads on the sands of Sandymount in *Nausicaa* interpret the same "stuff" of nature: "Nature. Washing child, washing corpse" (373). The myth from which the story of Proteus derives in the *Odyssey* treats of expansion across the known and the unknown to the western extremes and back. Gerty MacDowell's opening lines in *Nausicaa* set the 8:00 P.M. Dublin expanse: "The summer evening had begun to fold the world in its mysterious embrace. Far away in the west the sun was setting and the last glow of all too fleeting day lingered lovingly on sea and strand" (346). If Gerty's "namby-pamby," as Joyce calls it, dulls the ear, Bloom sets the same mythic expanse in layman's "scientific" language: "Back of everything magnetism. Earth for instance pulling this and being pulled. That causes movement. And time? Well that's the time the movement takes" (374). Even prophetic extension over stellar expanse is explicable for Bloom's factual mind: "Magnetic needle tells you what's going on in the sun, the stars" (374). As for the return, the epic *Nostos*, Bloom compliments birds on their heroic nerve over Odyssean spaces: "Nerve? they have to fly over the ocean and back" (378). For the renewing hero in the post-Renaissance world, the earth has no "ends really because it's round" (378).

Bloom's thoughts on the strand, although different in tone from the anguished musings of Dedalus and the saccharine projections of Gerty MacDowell, touch on the same theme: what constitutes fulfillment? Gerty had thought of Bloom as a nobleman from the land of song, from the southern Mediterranean. And Molly had conjured up a nobleman, Don Miguel (Poldo) de la Flora, to stay the advances of Mulvey on Gibraltar. Bloom's detumescent thoughts of Gerty's flirtatious imagination remind him of Molly.

> She must have been thinking of someone else all the time. What harm? Must since she came to the use of reason, he and he. First kiss does the trick. The propitious moment. Something inside them goes pop. Mushy like, tell by their eye, on the sly. First thoughts are best. Remember that till their dying day. Molly, lieutenant Mulvey that kissed her under the Moorish wall beside the gardens. (371)

Bloom's translation back in time takes him to the Mediterranean. He is the man of song. The renewal on the strand "Makes you want to sing after" (370). This is Bloom's more active voice, not his passive one of *Sirens* (an episode, by the way, which had a musical false homecoming of its own, but, like the imitative arts in Plato, a step further removed from reality). Bloom's masturbatory act is, in its way, restorative: "Did me good all the same. Off colour after Kiernan's, Dignam's. For this relief much thanks" (372). *Nausicaa* sends us back to "the blood of the south" (373). Bloom's watch, his waterworks, may have stopped at 4:30 P.M., the hour of Molly's infidelity, and the clock at the end of the chapter may echo the "*Cuckoo*" of Bloom's marital bed, but on Sandymount strand Bloom reorients himself for homecoming. The spirit of *Nausicaa* has only to deposit him on his native shores, northwest.

Nausicaa in *Ulysses* is out of sequence from the Homeric original. Joyce labeled only the last three chapters of *Ulysses* his *Nostos*, but in the *Odyssey* over half the action of the poem is set on Ithaca. It is not surprising that Joyce is getting a bit anxious to bring his characters together (and home) in this thirteenth episode, approximately half way (in bulk) through his novel. Book XVIII is the very book of the *Odyssey* in which Odysseus sets foot on his own land. From this point in *Ulysses*, Dublin, in effect, again performs a double service. Joyce lets his city remain the western Mediterranean as Bloom rounds out the *Wanderings*, but at the same time he readies the map of Dublin as the home island, Ithaca. *Ulysses* enters its nocturnal, homegoing phase.

OXEN OF THE SUN

In *Oxen of the Sun* Bloom returns to the womb of the maternity hospital. Nine years before he had lived on Holles street near the lying-in ward, and, like Odysseus, had been wandering ever since, often in the trying northwest. "Deshil Holles Eamus" (383) at the beginning of the episode announces another homecoming. J. S. Atherton explains "Deshil" as a pun on the Gaelic *deiseal*, to go right or sunward. The Latin rounds out the phrase: "Let us go south to Holles street."[10] Holles street is in Dublin's southeast quadrant. Odysseus and his remaining crew risk Scylla and pass through the Straits of Messina to Trinacria, also southeast to the isle of the sun king, Helios.

In the *Odyssey* the slaughter of the kine of Helios is the most terrifying episode in the *Wanderings* because it is the only adventure in which the motive for barbarism is starvation. The medicals at the Holles street hospital have no such excuse. According to Bérard, Odysseus and his men, having escaped total destruction at the many hands of Scylla, arrive through the straits and moor near Cape Schiso on the trident or triangular isle (Sicily). To the north is the sickle-like port of Messina. Joyce enters in his Zürich notebook: "Messina Sickle" (VIII.A.5, p. 300). Farther down the straits but still north of Cape Schiso was what was to become the early settlement of Tauromenium, with its obvious reference to Sicily's abundant cattle. The site became an Apollonian shrine and one of the renowned *omphaloi* of the Greek geographical system. Joyce enters a simple "Taormina" in his notesheets (Herring, p. 191). Joyce's many notebook and notesheet entries, in addition to dozens of references in the chapter to things bullish, mark the episode's topographical correspondence with the land of Helios' cattle.

The Homeric epithet for Trinacria is "island of the world's delight." Helios' land is portrayed by the *Odyssey* as visibly and audibly ineluctable: through Helios all things are seen, all speech is known. Joyce adapts the Homeric conceit in the opening pages of *Oxen of the Sun*. The hospital itself is matrix, "quickening" and "sunbright wellbuilt" (384). In his Zürich notebook Joyce calls the "Sun's oxen bright radiant ox" (VIII.A.5, p. 300). Bérard refers to the island as another of the narrative's versions of paradise for sailors approaching from all directions.

[10] J. S. Atherton, "Oxen of the Sun," in Hart and Hayman, p. 313.

Pour les navigateurs qui viennent de la trop chaude Afrique ou de la Grèce rocailleuse, ces grands boeufs, ces beaux boeufs siciliens semblent plus admirables encore. Les navigateurs qui viennent du Nord en descendant le détroit sont aussi frappés du contraste, quand ils rencontrent ces pâturages verdoyants et fleuris de l'Etna après les pentes arides, brûlées, des montagnes côtières.

(For navigators coming from the great African heat or from rocky Greece, these large, beautiful Sicilian cattle seem still more admirable. Navigators arriving from the north by descending through the straits are also struck by the contrast when they encounter these flourishing green pastures of Etna after the arid, parched slopes of the coastal mountains.)   [Bérard, ii, 389]

Bérard himself seems a little "struck" with the beauty of the place. In the Odyssean scheme the attractions of Trinacria equal those of Lotusland, Circe's Aiaia after liberation, or Calypso's Ogygia: "Fleuves ou rivières, cours d'eau constants ou torrents capricieux, sources chaudes ou froides, cette région bien arrosée présente aux navigateurs un pays riant, une terre de bucolique, une suite de vallées fleuries, de petites embouchures, de deltas verdoyants, de villages et de villes" (Rivers or streams, constant running water or capricious torrents, hot or cold springs, this watery region presents to navigators a cheerful countryside, a bucolic land, a succession of flowering valleys, of small river basins, of green deltas, of villages and towns) [Bérard, ii, 390].

The Mediterranean place for *Oxen of the Sun* makes Joyce's sterile Dublin seem a sorry site. But perhaps Joyce has something else in mind. There is another way to look at the chapter that accounts not only for the presence of Bloom-Odysseus on Joyce's version of Trinacria, but of Stephen-Telemachus on Ithaca. *Oxen of the Sun* in *Ulysses* assists in accommodating the *Wanderings* to the *Nostos*. Telemachus is told to beach southeast on his island at homecoming to avoid the western ambuscade on Asteris, which, if we view this episode keeping in mind Dedalus' presence in it, occurs at the Westland Row station after the action of the chapter proper. In the *Odyssey* the ethic of the suitors awaiting Telemachus' ambush on Asteris is little different from the piratical ways of older Achaean days or the antithetical fervor of Odysseus' Trinacrian crew. It is significant that the suitors' one substantive plan in the *Odyssey* is for an ambush by sea. Antinous and the other "king's sons" live without vision—they merely accumulate—actively disbelieving in the process that is behind the reinvigorative myth of the *Odyssey*, the return of the king. Joyce's *Oxen of the Sun* unites a modest king and an embryonic king's son in one Dublin birth ward.

In *Ulysses*, except for the degenerate confusion of the afterbirth on Holles and Denzille streets at the end of the episode, *Oxen of the Sun* records the vigil in the maternity hospital awaiting the birth of Mina Purefoy's child. The thematic and parodic counter-structure of the episode involves the positive and negative sense of proliferation, birth or slaughter, "wombfruit" or "*Mort aux vaches*" (398). Within its complicated, and variously amusing, gestational imitations of English prose styles, *Oxen of the Sun* records the processes of fertilization (the "life essence essential"), parturition, fructification, virgin birth, and normal birth. The drunken medicals, murderers of the sun and mockers of the son in the Odyssean and Telemachian versions, concentrate on counter-issues of sterilization, abortion, and infanticide.

In Dublin, the delight of the sun's life as a daily return can be nullified or, at least, abrogated. The perverse path of the sun, the left or "widdershins" turn, is a death-stopped darkness. Joyce's home-land is no Mediterranean paradise, abundant in its stock, and Mina Purefoy's child is a stiff birth among the votaries of levity. Mockery and sacrilege force Joyce's and Homer's heroes to proceed alone. Bérard, who characterized the *Lestrygonian* episode as flight and the *Sirens* as fettering, characterizes the Helios adventure as isolation: "la terre du Soleil, la rive sicilienne, voit son *Isolement*, son *Abandon*" (the land of the sun, the Sicilian riverbank, sees his isolation his abandonment) [Bérard, II, 386]. Bérard points to the Semitic root for Sicily, which signifies exile or orphanage (*s.k.l., sekoul, Sikelia*). Joyce jots down the etymology in his Zürich notebook: "Sekoul (Heb) orphanos alone" (VIII.A.5, p. 300). Homer weaves this motif into the fabric of his adventure. Not only is Odysseus alone in wishing to avoid the island, but he is alone, wandering off by himself, once he is talked into landing. Odysseus pleads with Eurylokos to avoid this paradisaical lure, but to no avail: "they are with you to a man. / I am alone, outmatched" (Book XII, Fitzgerald, p. 219). For a good part of Joyce's *Oxen of the Sun* Bloom seems given to bouts of wandering vision—it is as if he is barely there. And at the end of the chapter, of course, the scheme is afoot for real abandonment as the betraying Mulligan plans the desertion of Dedalus with the urban exile, Bloom, in suspicious pursuit. Another loner, M'Intosh from *Hades*, now a fallen vagabond, walks by, all tattered and torn: "Walking Mackintosh of lonely canyon" (427). Joyce hinted to Gilbert that one of M'Intosh's avatars was the mystery man from Pylos, Theoclymenos, whom Telemachus picks up on his return journey to Ithaca (Gilbert, pp. 171-173). If so, M'Intosh (Mackintosh), the exile, appears at the right time in the right place —when the map of Dublin joins the adventures of the *Odysseia* and *Telemachia* at *Nostos*.

In *Proteus* Stephen refers to Ireland as "the isle of dreadful thirst" (41). It is the medicals' thirst for drink in *Oxen of the Sun* that counters articulation. Casting another event in the shadow that comes before, Dedalus wonders in the morning whether the black clouds would produce a thunderstorm when "Evening will find itself" (50). *Oxen of the Sun*'s evening has found itself—the islanders still thirst dreadfully, and the thunder does, in fact, drown the mocking medicals in a different kind of drink. In the *Odyssey* when the thunder comes all the Greek crew go under and Odysseus is the sole survivor. His sense of abandonment and isolation is given an intricate symbolic analogue as he is blown north past Scylla and Charybdis. Odysseus can proceed farther only if he revitalizes himself. He is forced to drape his body over the branch of a fig tree until the Charybdian whirlpool subsides. His crew had taken life, and the biological processes of the Mediterranean now give it back to him. Odysseus, forced like Bloom into a state of androgyny, bears himself another chance as he hangs from the fig tree for the cycle of a day. Joyce sets about the process of refertilization in *Oxen of the Sun* by making gestation the progressive substance of his narrative voice. He writes to Budgen that the episode connects with events earlier in the day and mimics "the natural stages of development in the embryo and the periods of faunal evolution in general" (Letters, I, 139).[11] After his rebirth in the Mediterranean, Odysseus moves west to Calypso. After the full gestation of *Oxen of the Sun* Joyce moves his cast of characters (Bloom in pursuit of a "son") to Westland Row.

Joyce comes as close in *Oxen of the Sun* as he will in all *Ulysses* to voicing his views on the substance of the land he writes about. Cattle are important in migrational myths, as we have seen. To kill them is to put a stop to sustenance and movement. From the hoof and mouth disease in Ireland, to the drought, to drunkenness, it is clear that the nation has little to offer its living. Sterility and

[11] See A. M. Klein, "The Oxen of the Sun," *Here and Now*, I (1949), 28-48, for a full analysis of the episode's embryonic technique.

debilitation run counter to the intricate gestational metaphor that Joyce works into the episode. It is here that irony dominates the action of the chapter. Even in a maternity ward, the forces of life still have to search for allies. Joyce had complained ever since his 1907 lecture on Ireland that the loss in population was the nation's greatest concern. Through famine and emigration in the nineteenth century, Ireland was the only significant European country to decline in population. Its citizens and its resources were deserting to America—continuing the westward migration across the Atlantic. Joyce enters in his notesheets: "Irish Amer capitalists" (Herring, p. 119). In this episode Joyce is as severe as was Jonathan Swift in his *Irish Tracts* at calling ironic attention to the land's most wasted resource, life itself. Mulligan, the infertile fertilizer from Lambay Island, gives voice to the decline of the country. Urban pathology is the bleak answer to gestational form.

> Mr M. Mulligan (Hyg. et Eug. Doc.) blames the sanitary conditions in which our greylunged citizens contract adenoids, pulmonary complaints etc. by inhaling the bacteria which lurk in dust. These facts, he alleges, and the revolting spectacles offered by our streets, hideous publicity posters, religious ministers of all denominations, mutilated soldiers and sailors, exposed scorbutic cardrivers, the suspended carcasses of dead animals, paranoic bachelors and unfructified duennas—these, he said, were accountable for any and every fallingoff in the calibre of the race.
>
> (418)

Dedalus, as usual, is caught between the regenerative and degenerative drifts of the episode. He is the "most drunken" of those present, and his voice is an ambiguous one for fertility. He offers an Oedipal reading for the incarnation myth: the son jostles with the father in avoiding the mother. Stephen is confused. The Virgin Mary, "our mighty Mother," bears the Homeric analogue, the "Healer and Herd" (391). For the artist fertility is not merely an issue of emigration and birth control: "In woman's womb word is made flesh" (391). For Stephen the virgin mother has some relation to the act of creation. Exactly what is another question. Either Mary is impregnated by knowing the Creator or she is not. If not, there is something insubstantial about the act. If so, there is something debasing, at least in Stephen's current state of mind, about it. Stephen wants the form of art for himself, and presumably others. That is, he wants the "Hoopsa . . . boyaboy" (383) of his own making, but he is uneasy about the vehicle of its transmission. He lies about his teaching wages, saying that he was paid "for a song which he writ" (391), and when he dares crown himself with laurel and pronounce himself Helios, "I, Bous Stephanoumenos, bullockbe-friending bard, am lord and giver of their life" (415), Vincent responds: "That answer and those leaves, Vincent said to him, will adorn you more fitly when something more, and greatly more, than a capful of light odes can call your genius father" (415). Always, Stephen wavers between extremes. At one moment he "murdered his goods" (391) with whores, an indulgence that places him in the camp of the slaughtering crew, and at the next he is "the eternal son and ever virgin" (392). Fertility and sterility are mixed in Stephen's Bunyanesque allegory of Hamlet's speech on marriage.

> Then wotted he nought of that other land which is called Believe-on-Me, that is the land of promise which behoves to the king Delightful and shall be for ever where there is no death and no birth neither wiving nor mothering at which all shall come as many as believe on it? (395)

Stephen has a fear of gestation and a fear of sterility. Land of Delight may be the epithet for Helios' Trinacria, but Stephen's earthly paradise is spent in the Liberties or in Mecklenburg: "Copulation without population" (423). When it thunders during the chapter, Dedalus turns ashen. He fears the thunder that brings the rain because he fears the thunder that brings revenge on the infertile.

In the *schema*, Joyce lists matrix as the "organ" of the chapter, and Joyce in a letter to Budgen marks Stephen as embryo and Bloom as spermatozoon. The developing seed does not know where it has been, nor is it certain where it is going. But the spermatozoon has an impulse of its own. Bloom is the one figure in the episode who recognizes the fullness of life. He has a "plentitude of sufferance" (407). Alone in the chapter, he is an intruder from the east, "an exotic tree" whose roots have dried in the last ten years. Bloom is without population or copulation in Dublin, but he still carries the Mediterranean warmth with him. Like Odysseus, Bloom is under constant threat from his environment and his associates. But he makes it through on sympathy ("Stark ruth of man," 385) and endurance while the Irish crew blaspheme life in the riot of a short-ranging feast. Odysseus acts in the *Odyssey* to protect the sacred cattle because he knows, or has been forced to learn, what kind of action is in his best interest. Bloom, "that had of his body no manchild for an heir" (390), senses at first hand that, whatever his current condition, the promise of fertility is his life's primary hope. Intuiting that somehow it is in his best interest, he protects Dedalus the son. The movement continues: northwest.

CIRCE

The visit to Nighttown in *Ulysses* is the beginning of another of those miniaturized attempts to square the epic circle "and win that million" (515). Even before the time of the novel many of the street names in Nighttown had been changed to protect the none too innocent. Monto (for Montgomery street) or Mecklenburg was a notorious mecca for whoredom known throughout the British Isles. The literal movement in the *Circe* episode through this district near the center of Dublin involves reconnoitering, pursuit, and, finally, circling back. Stephen and Lynch have made their way from Amiens Station to Nighttown after taking the loopline from Westland Row where there was a suspicious mix up with Haines and Mulligan in another version of the Asteris showdown on the home island.[12] Bloom, as we later learn, missed the tram stop and had to double back from the northeast. If Joyce has rearranged his episodes to allow *Circe* to partake of homecoming, it is significant that Odysseus approaches his home, according to Bérard, by sailing from the northeast around the protruding bulk of Ithaca to the inland port of Vathi at center island.

Stephen (Telemachus), of course, keeps to the right path, and, just as his prototype in the *Odyssey*, he avoids the more dire straits of *Nostos*. Lynch and Stephen approach the district: first they move southwest on Talbot street. They then turn northwest on Mabbot street (Corporation street), and northeast on Mecklenburg street (also called Tyrone at the time and now Railway). The chapter may be "sinister" (436), but the bulk of the turns in the episode are, indeed, "right" ones. Stephen and Lynch finally recede into the bowels of Nighttown—"You might go farther and fare worse" (475), says

[12] Hugh Kenner, "Circe," in Hart and Hayman, thinks that Stephen's sore hand in *Circe* leads back to the Westland Row confusion where Dedalus may have taken a swing at Mulligan. If so, we have more reason to see the narratives at this point in *Ulysses* partaking of both the *Wanderings* and the homecoming. Kenner sees a certain consistency in Stephen's lashing out: "That Joyce's Hamlet should become the man of action comports with the principle by which Joyce's Ulysses becomes the man of acquiescence" (p. 353).

the whore, Zoe, to Bloom who is in pursuit of Dedalus. All end up at Bella Cohen's brothel, 82 Mecklenburg. At the end of *Circe*, after Stephen's quickly resolved altercation with the British soldier, Bloom and Dedalus find themselves together at Tyrone and Beaver streets. In *Eumaeus* they complete the square by walking down Beaver, turning at Foley, passing the Amiens Station where the circuit began, and heading beyond the Custom House to the Cabman's shelter. Joyce is consistent with his model in this episode of circles and descents. Odysseus loops back to Circe's isle, the double isle, Aiaia, after his journey to the realm of Hades.

In the Homeric epic *Circe* is a middle adventure, but its range is thematically greater than that of all others. The episode is a micro-cosmic wandering and homecoming. Not only does Odysseus touch down on the enchantress' isle twice, but he scouts the island (really a cape) from shore to interior before he later takes the interior route to Circe's lair. The panorama is analogous to the many journeys around capes or islands in the *Odyssey*. Just before he sends his men to explore Circe's territory, Odysseus kills a stag and feasts his companions, saying that it is not meet that they should starve before their otherworldly descent: "we'll not go down into the House of Death before our time" (Book x, Fitzgerald, p. 170). The irony is extreme because that is precisely what will happen, both on Circe's isle and, later, in Odysseus' voyage to the underworld. But the episode is as extreme as the irony. Odysseus' men are transformed into pigs. When Odysseus and his men are transformed back, those of his crew who remained near the shore compare the event to home-coming and Aiaia to Ithaca. It is "as if they saw their homeland, and the crags of Ithaka" (Book x, Fitzgerald, p. 178). There is no doubt that the *Circe* adventure in the *Odyssey* has something of all the other adventures, including homecoming, in it. Even Odysseus is not eager to leave this island once he masters its mistress. Joyce, in saving his *Circe* episode for last in Bloom's *Wanderings*, sees its full potential. The last false homecoming in *Ulysses* is the fully antip-odal world from the sty of the brothel, a circus animal's delight, to the expanded dream of a paradisaical universe: New Bloom-usalem.

Throughout the day Stephen and Bloom experience material and visionary transformations, but Joyce marks *Circe* in his *schema* as vision animated to the bursting point. The *Odyssey*'s Circe is magical like Proteus, to whom she has often been compared. Circe is a minor goddess-magician—she has in her possession the secrets of proliferate and controlled form. She is the daughter of the sun god Helios and Perse, child of the ocean stream. In other words, her heritage is oriental and occidental. Bérard explains that her name and her island mean hawk. *Kirķe* is the rare feminine form of the Greek masculine *ķirķos* which usually serves both genders. Aiaia is a feminine form of hawk (Semitic: *ai'a*) which also serves both genders. Masculine and feminine—this transforming goddess doubles up. She is a bird of light and darkness. Joyce transcribes material from Bérard in his notesheets: "the hawk. Sun of living. Sun of dead" (Herring, p. 281).

As a magician of nature, Circe has the capacity to tame ferocious beasts and unman men. Versed in the deepest mysteries, Circe, like the double-sexed Tiresias of the Theban legend, possesses the female and generic qualities that her name and island suggest. In *Ulysses*, of course, Bella Cohen is both a woman and a man. Bloom himself is caught up in the episode's transforming sexuality—he is the "new womanly man" of *Circe*. As a weaver like Penelope and a nymph like Calypso, Circe plays all the roles to Odysseus: adversary, ally, surrogate wife, mistress, patron. Circe's island, Aiaia, according to Bérard's study of local myths, was associated with magic and enchantment, and had been so for ages. Bérard places Aiaia at the extension of the northern peninsula of the Gulf of Gaeta. Mariners approaching from sea often view points as islands because they are unsure of land formations and the extent of surrounding ocean [Bérard, ii, 267]. And islands or points of peninsulas are traditionally connected with magical lore [Bérard, ii, 290]. The lush coastal growth of Circe's cape, especially when contrasted with the dry lands of the plains, add to the mythology of Gaeta's magical places. Bérard argues that along with the doublet *Kirķe-Aiaia* the Phoenicians had a name for a nearby point meaning enchantment (*Axour, Anxour*, Bérard, ii, 290). Both capes were later used as prisons [Bérard, ii, 298]. The idea of capturing and releasing is a long, and literal, association with Cape Circeo. Joyce enters Bérard's notation of a kind of ritual formula for the release of enslaved beings at the point: "servi sedeant, liberi surgant" (Herring, p. 281). The simple result: "Freeman" (Herring, p. 281). We see here a primary organizational principle of *Circe* in *Ulysses*: restraint and release.

Joyce's rotogravure description of Bella Cohen's lair in *Ulysses* plays upon Circe's lush Odyssean habitat, and a related masculine cape toward the dawn (orient) that Bérard derives from vulture-eagles: "*Kaieta-Aiétés*" or Gaetae [Bérard, ii, 297].

(Gazelles are leaping, feeding on the mountains. Near are lakes. Round their shores file shadows black of cedargroves. Aroma rises, a strong hairgrowth of resin. It burns, the orient, a sky of sapphire, cleft by the bronze flight of eagles. Under it lies the womancity, nude, white, still, cool, in luxury. A fountain murmurs among damask roses. Mammoth roses murmur of scarlet winegrapes. A wine of shame, lust, blood exudes, strangely murmuring.)

(477)

The version of Aiaia in *Ulysses* is an exotic whorehouse, doubling as the place of beasts, a circus. Bella Cohen keeps the animals tamed just as Circe does. Bérard discusses the Odyssean adventure as a variant of a local Gaetan legend of Feronia, goddess of wild beasts. A young Jupiter knows the proper herbs with which to charm beasts and snakes, hence is on to Feronia's secrets. Feronia and young Jupiter become Circe and Hermes in Bérard's reading. Joyce's Zürich notebook includes a reference to Circe as "goddess of fauves" (VIII.A.5, p. 303), and to "Hermes = Jupiter puer–son" (VIII.A.5, p. 304). Joyce, perhaps, sees here a variant adversary-ally pairing that informs a large part of the mythic encounters and a large part of the personal encounters in *Ulysses*. It is also possible that Joyce picked up a hint for Bella Cohen's name from Bérard, who, trying to seize upon an example of transference of generic to proper names, comes up with: "*fer-i*, ont *Fer-onia*, comme *Bell-um* a *Bell-ona*" [Bérard, II, 286]. In any case, Feronia and Jupiter become Circe and Hermes in the Homeric version, and Bella Cohen and Bloom in Joyce's. Moreover, Joyce's notesheet entries: "Jūpītēr īs añi-mal" and "King of beasts" (Herring, p. 268), suggest the transformations in the brothel, a place of bestial desires and heavenly attractions. God-beast is the extreme transformation either way. Punning on several of the episode's mythic connections, Joyce comments on the Circean heritage: "Circe draws Sun from ?herd" (Herring, p. 303). The full range is here: god (Helios) to beasts (herd), sun to son, temptress to protectress.

Joyce sees in the Circean legend of magic, transformation, and shapelessness the *verstiegenheit* or extravagance of vision symptomatic of mental-epic interiors, especially those in the century preceding his own. He absorbs in *Circe* the traumatizing and fantasizing spaces of the mind, and he adapts not only classical and Renaissance models, but the prominent spatial self-histories of Romantic tradition. The outrageous explosion of an interior world is characteristic of dramatic and narrative forms from Goethe's "Walpurgisnacht" in *Faust* to Blake's *Milton*, Shelley's *Prometheus Unbound*, Flaubert's *La Tentation de Saint Antoine*, Lewis Carroll's *Through the Looking Glass* and Ibsen's *Peer Gynt*. In the nineteenth century the predisposition for gigantism is both visionary and Tartarian.[13] Chaos is the proliferate protean condition gone awry, transformation without the promise of form. Joyce owes much in *Circe* to the *Odyssey*'s graceful witch, something to Ovid's *Metamorphoses*, and something to Dante's *Inferno*, but his great literary debt is to a tradition haunting his youth and threatening his maturity—the Romantic epic of inner spaces: "From the sublime to the ridiculous is but a step," says Virag in *Circe* (515). *Circe* is the parodic companion to James Thomson's seriously tortured poem, *The City of Dreadful Night*, a mind-night and mid-night finale to Romantic vision.

Circe is the enchanted space of *Ulysses*, the night dream dump of the novel. Hugh Kenner describes Joyce's strategy: "as *Ulysses* is the *Odyssey* transposed and rearranged, 'Circe' is *Ulysses* transposed and rearranged" ("Circe," in Hart and Hayman, p. 356). In a way this makes it possible, as in *Oxen of the Sun*, for the episode to accommodate both the *Wanderings* and the homecoming. When Odysseus first beaches at a point in Ithaca near the middle of his island (Bérard's Port Vathi), he is in a geographical position *vis à vis* Eumaeus' hut and the palace up-island comparable to Bloom's in Nighttown, as he moves toward the cabman's shelter in *Eumaeus* and then toward his home at 7 Eccles street in *Ithaca*. Furthermore, when Odysseus beaches and wakes, he does not know that he is home—his land is distorted for him, misted over. He considers that he has yet another western adventure to experience.

> Meanwhile, on his island,
> his father's shore, that kingly man, Odysseus,
> awoke, but could not tell what land it was
> after so many years away; moreover,
> Pallas Athena, Zeus's daughter, poured
> a grey mist all around him, hiding him
> from common sight. . . .
> The landscape then looked strange, unearthly strange
> to the Lord Odysseus: paths by hill and shore,

[13] Richard K. Cross, *Flaubert and Joyce* (Princeton, 1971), entitles his chapter on *Circe* appropriately: "The Nethermost Abyss" (pp. 125-149).

glimpses of harbors, cliffs, and summer trees.
He stood up, rubbed his eyes, gazed at his homeland,
and swore, slapping his thighs with both his palms,
then cried aloud:

> "What am I in for now?
> Whose country have I come to this time? Rough
> savages and outlaws, are they, or
> godfearing people, friendly to castaways? . . ."

(Book XIII, Fitzgerald, pp. 235-236)

This is as phantasmagoric as the technique of *Circe*. And it *is* partly the technique of *Circe* to make Bloom think he is somewhere else, in another world. The unsteadiness of the episode in *Ulysses* produces the novel's most bizarre deformations and its most grotesque guilt-ridden fears. Homes in Dublin's hell, its *"city and urban district,"* have wallpapered walls with *"scenes truly rural of happiness of the better land"* (462). Only outside the center does paradise open up. Inside, the world shares the wildest delights with egregious debasements. The sunburst *"in the northwest"* (482) reawakens the land of King Leopold I, but Bloom, the notorious fire-raiser, is at the next moment a filament "from the roots of hell" (492). It is year I Paradisaical Era until Elijah returns to ask the world if it has "cold feet about the cosmos" (507).

Joyce's sense of interior spaces in *Circe* is not limited to any one source. The chapter is recapitulative of the novel and of a good many occurrences in the history of the human race. It borrows from the geography of Ithaca and from the geography of the Odyssean adventures in the Gulf of Gaeta. The Gulf of Gaeta is an important place in the *Odyssey*. Bérard sees it as the hub of a set of episodes, rivaled only by the grouping around the Straits of Messina. Most of the adventures near Messina (*Aeolus, Scylla* and *Charybdis, Oxen of the Sun*) are passageway episodes—if Odysseus passes through, he returns home. The Gaetaen adventures, on the other hand, are probing adventures. Odysseus metaphorically turns inward—he learns something about his own nature. On the southern border of the larger Gulf of Gaeta is the Bay of Cumae. Cumae is one of the first important western Greek settlements. It is also one of the centers, or *omphaloi*, of an extended civilization marked by Apollonian shrines at Delos, Delphi, Leucas, and, on the same axis, Cumae. Joyce was aware enough of the general connection between this area of Italy and the older *omphaloi* to jot down in his *Circe* notesheets: "Pythian Apollo of Delphos" (Herring, p. 309). For

Bérard, Circe's Aiaia is at the tip of the northern peninsula near Mount Circeo, Hades is off the middle of the interior gulf near Avernus, and the Cyclopes inhabit the southern extension of the Cumaean Bay near Pozzuoli. Like Ithaca itself, at the western extension of Greece, the Gaetaen region is at once the boundary and the last center. *Cyclops, Circe*, and *Hades* are the longest episodes of the *Wanderings*, and each leads Odysseus through some form of transformation, self-knowledge, or self-control.

In the geographical layout of the Gaetaen adventures, the *Odyssey* makes it clear that all three episodes deal with interiors. Not only does Odysseus go into Polyphemus' cave, but he has to explore inland from where the rest of his company has moored in order to locate the Cyclops in the first place. In *Hades* he must first go inland from the Gulf of Lucrino, and then dig a votive pit in which to conjure up the shades. And Hermes stops Odysseus on his way to Circe's lair and asks why he is taking the "inland" path alone. Interior landscapes, the insides or depths of places, are the grounds of literature's most outrageous lies—myths of descent, enchanted forests, caves of despair, wonderful holes—but the lies of interior spaces are designed to reveal in-depth truths. It is not until the Knight of la Mancha descends into the Cave of Montesinos in *Don Quixote* that we learn the full and fantastic extent of his sterile life "above ground." Similarly, it is not until Bloom takes the Nighttown plunge in *Ulysses* that we learn of the full range of abuses and fantasies available to him for the asking in Dublin.

In the episodes set near or in the *Odyssey*'s Gaetaen region, Bérard sees the beginnings of a pattern of cyclic renewal. The "noman" of *Cyclops* enters Hades as *no man* has, and drinks of Circe's potion as *no man* can. But more important, Bérard sees a connection in the original of Circe, Feronia, and the myth of Proserpina. One of the variants of the Feronia legend involves the seasonal progression and is related to the abduction myth of Proserpina to Hades: "*Feronia* fut assimilée à Proserpine" (Feronia was assimilated into Proserpina) [Bérard, ii, 285]. Joyce records: "Proserpina" and "Feronia" (VIII.A.5, p. 303). Odysseus and his men stay on Circe's island for a year, and the seasonal cycle is described with precision. The year is time renewed—Odysseus leaves in the long days of summer to journey to the land of Hades and return to Circe's island once again. In his Zürich notebook Joyce enters the Proserpina myth for his *Hades* section: "4 black deathless horses to rob Persephone" (VIII.A.5, p.

307). The descent is still seasonal—death is renewable. For the *Circe* notesheets, Joyce adapts part of the myth of Dedalus, and connects it to the summoning of Stephen's mother as a Shakespearean ghost: "SD's mother drag him to hell" (Herring, p. 303). His notesheets also connect Circe and Hell's tour-guide, Tiresias: "Circe's Tiresias, her tipster" (Herring, p. 320). In the episode itself Joyce provides the common touch to the myth. Zoe says of her whoremistress, Bella Cohen: "She's on the job herself tonight with the vet, her tipster, that gives her all the winners and pays for her son in Oxford" (475). Bella, of course, like Circe for Odysseus and like Proteus for Menelaus, has the power to send Bloom "skipping to hell and back" (544).

In linking the *Circe* and *Hades* episodes as it does, *Ulysses* shares in the process of cyclic renewal. Corny Kelleher, the transporter of bodies to the underworld, arrives at the conclusion of *Circe* to oversee the disposition of Stephen's lifeless-seeming form. Subsequently, as he leans over Stephen's fallen body, Bloom sees a vision of Rudy, one of the chapter's many ghosts. Rudy had died an infant in the middle of winter. Stephen is a long summer day's replacement for a life lost. In the middle of the episode Stephen confuses himself by mixing up Circe, the daughter of Helios, and Ceres, the mother of Persephone. He discusses cyclic form and the musical octave: "Circe's or what am I saying Ceres' altar" (504). Later, a revivified, youthful Bloom explains how he "sacrificed to the god of the forest. The flowers that bloom in the spring" (549). *Circe* in *Ulysses* is not only the descent, the calling up of the day's ghosts, but the right turn toward renewal. In his own sense of it, Bloom has a mission worthy of the abuse he undergoes to complete it. "Still, he's the best of that lot" (452), Bloom thinks of Dedalus, whom he pursues, protects, and, in his fashion, renews.

Circe is, indeed, the interior of *Ulysses*. It is in the interior of the city, the interior of the mind, and the interior of the novel. And it reveals truths that encompass the lives of its characters and the shape of *Ulysses*. Stephen Dedalus may fall in the none too "metaphysical" battle of Mecklenburg, but Bloom, in *Circe*, is on hand to help. And the hand he offers is an experienced one in Joyce's version of epic action. Bloom is said to belong to a family having experienced cases of shipwreck and somnambulism. Surely, this is fitting for the modern Odysseus. Through the interiors of the episode, the ghost of a hero walks backward in time and forward in space.

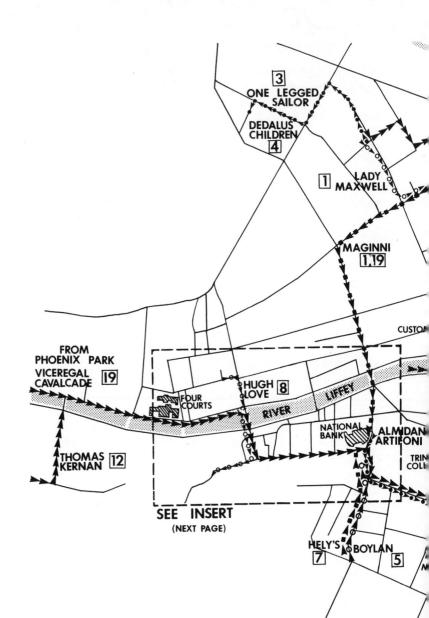

ONE LEGGED
SAILOR `3`

DEDALUS
CHILDREN
`4`

`1` LADY
MAXWELL

MAGINNI
`1,19`

CUSTO...

FROM
PHOENIX PARK
VICEREGAL
CAVALCADE `19`

FOUR
COURTS

HUGH
LOVE `8`

RIVER

LIFFEY

NATIONAL
BANK

ALMIDAN
ARTIFONI

THOMAS
KERNAN `12`

TRIN
COLL

SEE INSERT
(NEXT PAGE)

HELY'S
`7`

BOYLAN
`5`

BOXED NUMBERS DENOTE
SUB-SECTIONS OF CHAPTER

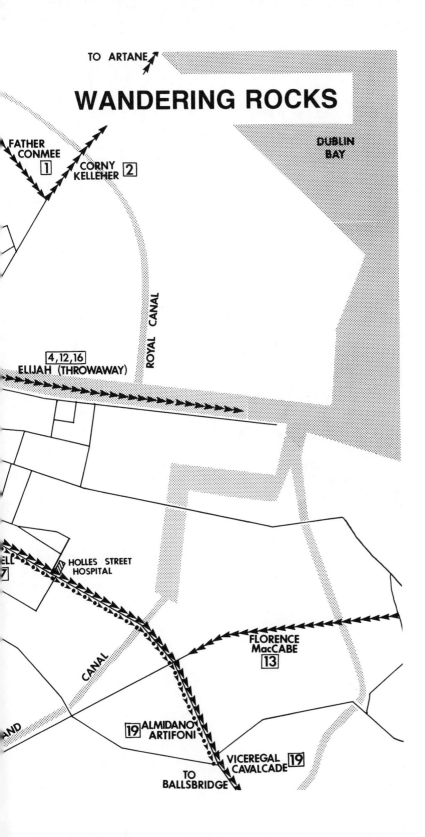

TO ARTANE

WANDERING ROCKS

FATHER
CONMEE
1

CORNY
KELLEHER 2

DUBLIN
BAY

ROYAL CANAL

4,12,16
ELIJAH (THROWAWAY)

HOLLES STREET
HOSPITAL

ELL
7

CANAL

FLORENCE
MacCABE
13

AND

19 ALMIDANO
ARTIFONI

VICEREGAL 19
CAVALCADE

TO
BALLSBRIDGE

WANDERING ROCKS
(Insert)

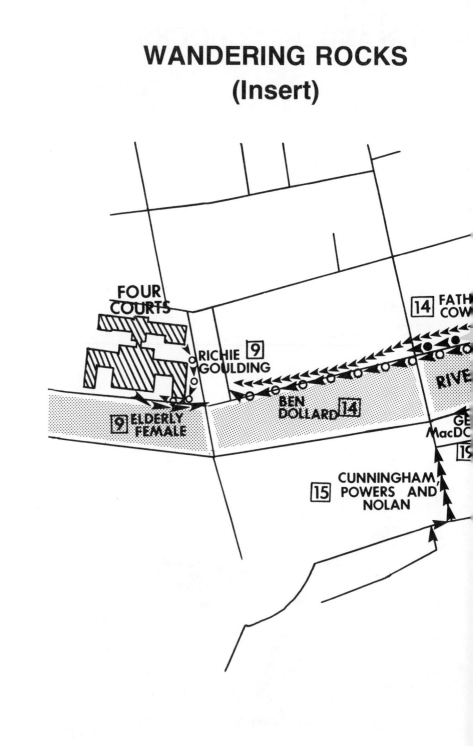

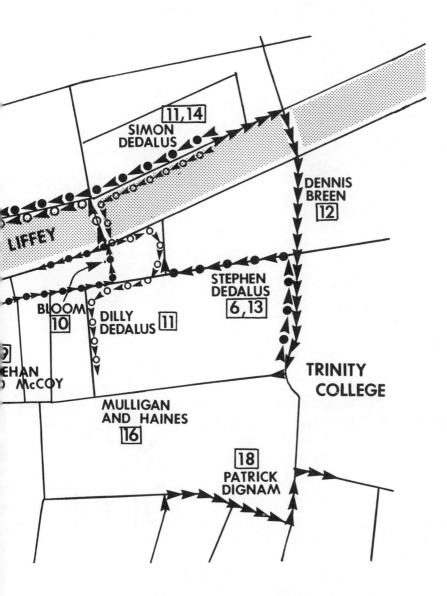

11,14
SIMON
DEDALUS

DENNIS
BREEN
12

LIFFEY

STEPHEN
DEDALUS
6,13

BLOOM
10

DILLY
DEDALUS 11

TRINITY
COLLEGE

EHAN
McCOY

MULLIGAN
AND HAINES
16

18
PATRICK
DIGNAM

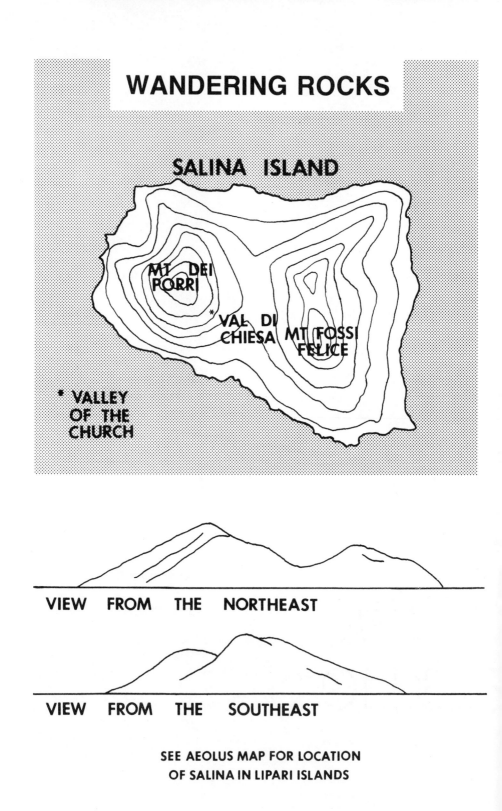

WANDERING ROCKS

SALINA ISLAND

MT DEI PORRI

* VAL DI CHIESA   MT FOSSI FELICE

* VALLEY OF THE CHURCH

VIEW   FROM   THE   NORTHEAST

VIEW   FROM   THE   SOUTHEAST

SEE AEOLUS MAP FOR LOCATION
OF SALINA IN LIPARI ISLANDS

SIRENS

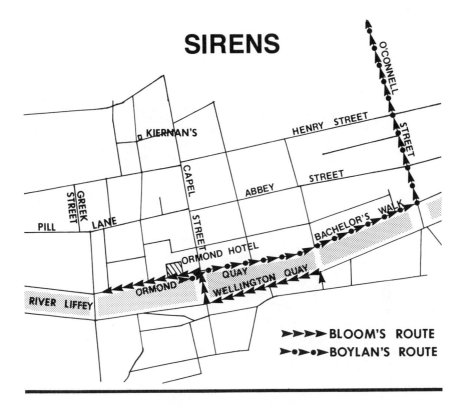

►►►► BLOOM'S ROUTE
►•►•► BOYLAN'S ROUTE

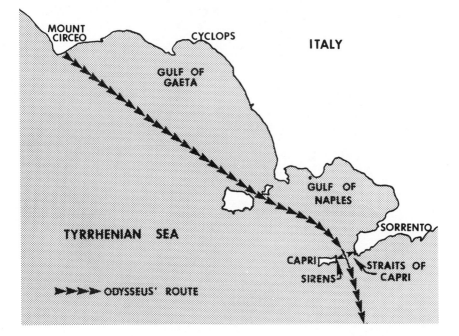

►►►► ODYSSEUS' ROUTE

CYCLOPS

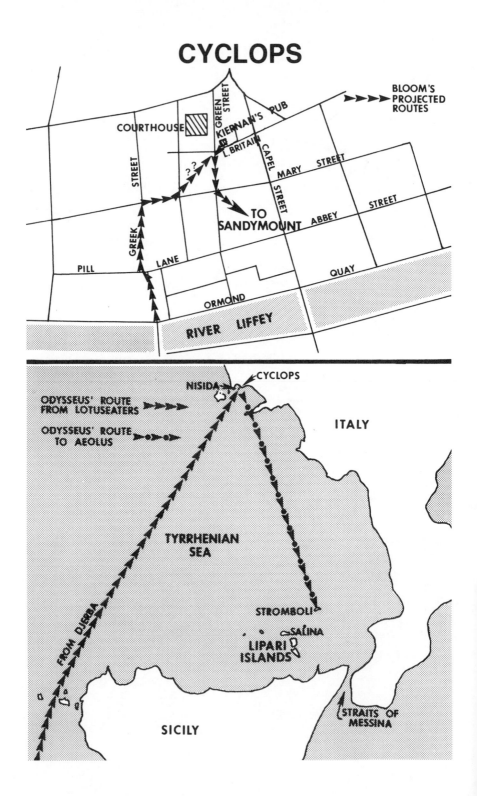

BLOOM'S PROJECTED ROUTES

COURTHOUSE

GREEN STREET

KIERNAN'S PUB

L. BRITAIN

CAPEL STREET

MARY STREET

STREET

STREET

ABBEY STREET

TO SANDYMOUNT

STREET

GREEK

PILL LANE

QUAY

ORMOND

RIVER LIFFEY

NISIDA

CYCLOPS

ODYSSEUS' ROUTE FROM LOTUSEATERS

ODYSSEUS' ROUTE TO AEOLUS

ITALY

TYRRHENIAN SEA

FROM DJERBA

STROMBOLI

SALINA

LIPARI ISLANDS

STRAITS OF MESSINA

SICILY

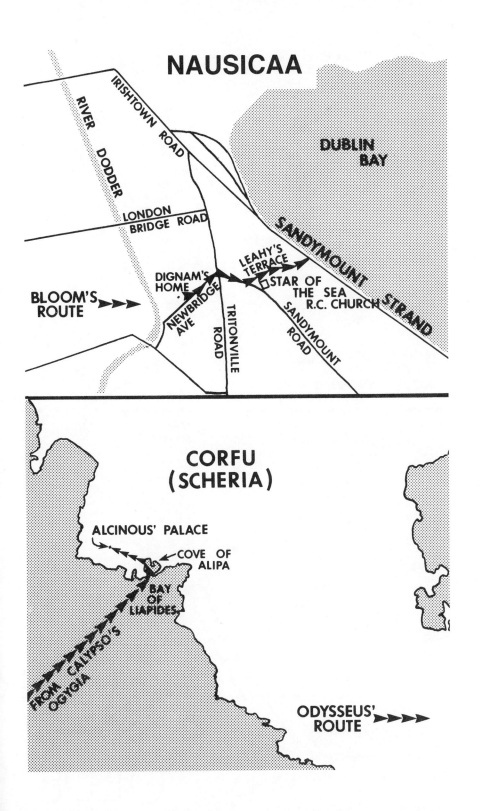

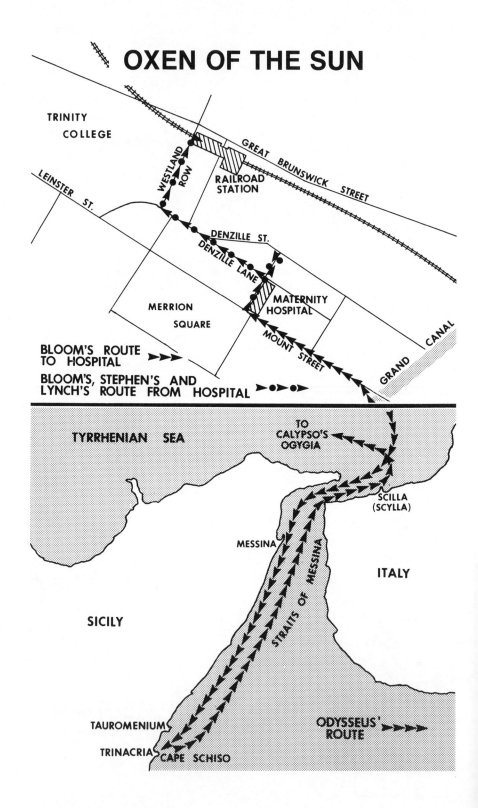

OXEN OF THE SUN

TRINITY COLLEGE

GREAT BRUNSWICK STREET

WESTLAND ROW

RAILROAD STATION

LEINSTER ST.

DENZILLE ST.

DENZILLE LANE

MERRION SQUARE

MATERNITY HOSPITAL

MOUNT STREET

GRAND CANAL

BLOOM'S ROUTE TO HOSPITAL ▶▶▶

BLOOM'S, STEPHEN'S AND LYNCH'S ROUTE FROM HOSPITAL ▶●▶●▶

TYRRHENIAN SEA

TO CALYPSO'S OGYGIA

SCILLA (SCYLLA)

MESSINA

STRAITS OF MESSINA

ITALY

SICILY

TAUROMENIUM

TRINACRIA

CAPE SCHISO

ODYSSEUS' ROUTE ▶▶▶

CIRCE

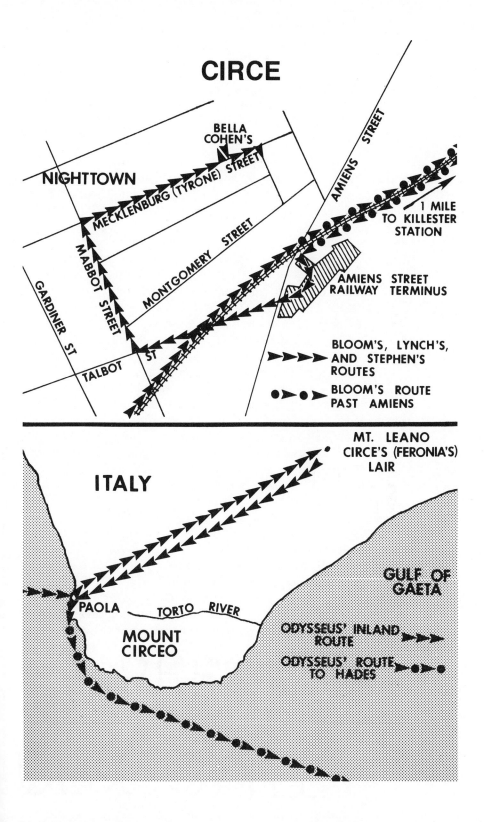

NIGHTTOWN

BELLA COHEN'S

MECKLENBURG (TYRONE) STREET

MONTGOMERY STREET

AMIENS STREET

MABBOT STREET

GARDINER ST

TALBOT ST

1 MILE TO KILLESTER STATION

AMIENS STREET RAILWAY TERMINUS

BLOOM'S, LYNCH'S, AND STEPHEN'S ROUTES

BLOOM'S ROUTE PAST AMIENS

ITALY

MT. LEANO CIRCE'S (FERONIA'S) LAIR

GULF OF GAETA

PAOLA

TORTO RIVER

MOUNT CIRCEO

ODYSSEUS' INLAND ROUTE

ODYSSEUS' ROUTE TO HADES

NOSTOS

EUMAEUS

IN the *Odyssey* the geography of the *Nostos* surveys the home island. Bérard states simply: "C'est un périple sémitique, en effect,
qu'il faut supposer comme source originelle du Nostos" (It is a
Semitic *periplous* in effect, that one necessarily supposes as the original source of the *Nostos*) [Bérard, II, 557]. Odysseus is dropped off
at the cave of Phorcys, proceeds on foot to Eumaeus' hut after his
meeting with Athena, and later walks the longer footpath down the
rocky countryside to his palace up-island. Bérard places the cave
in the inlet off Port Vathi, approximately mid-island [Bérard, II,
462]. Eumaeus' hut is southwest of the Phorcys cave and the grotto
of the Naiades near Raven's Rock and the fount of Arethusa
[Bérard, II, 461]. This is slightly northwest of Telemachus' dis-
embarkation point before he lets his ship continue without him for
the loop into the bay past the suitors. The walk to the palace from
the hut is northeasterly, back in the direction of Port Vathi following the lay of the land, and then northwesterly to the region near
Port Polis and Stavros [Bérard, II, 469]. Even a cursory look at the
Dublin map suggests that Joyce has reconstructed the Ithaca grid
with some exactness in his own *Nostos*. The Cabman's shelter is
southwest from Nighttown, and Stephen and Bloom trace almost
the same route toward home that they would have traced had they
been Telemachus and Odysseus moving toward the palace. In *Ulysses* the movement takes two chapters. *Eumaeus* handles the plotting,
Ithaca fulfills the northwest return.

At the beginning of *Eumaeus* Stephen and Bloom move out of
Nighttown down Beaver street, "or, more properly, lane" (613), as
the run-on narrative voice of the episode insists. Bloom does most
of the talking while his not yet perfectly sober companion, "not
to put too fine a point on it" (614), distrusts everything he hears and
sees. In comparison to the following *Ithaca* episode, *Eumaeus* proceeds by refusing to put too fine a point on anything. From Beaver
street (lane), Stephen and Bloom turn north on Montgomery (now
Foley) and immediately southwest, make a hairpin turn down
Amiens, bee-lining behind the Custom House and under the Loop

Line bridge to Beresford place and the Cabman's shelter near Butt bridge.

Bérard's *Les Phéniciens* generally has a chapter for each adventure of the Homeric epic. Joyce's naming of his episodes in *Ulysses* corresponds to Bérard's three-part division of the *Odyssey* into the *Telemachia*, the *Odysseia*, and the *Nostos*. Joyce names each episode as Bérard names his chapters. But Bérard has no direct equivalent for Joyce's *Eumaeus*. Instead, the circumstances detailing Odysseus' landing at the cave of Phorcys and his movement overland to the swineherd's hut are treated toward the middle of a later chapter in Bérard, *Le Royaume d'Ulysse*, a chapter that would correspond to Joyce's *Ithaca*. But in his first volume, long before he treats the Odyssean adventures narrated from the court of the Phaeacians, Bérard includes a long section called *Les Navigations Phéniciens* in which he begins with the life story of Eumaeus, his kidnapping, his wanderings, his exile as a servant in Ithaca, and continues with a survey of the Mediterranean based loosely on the lies Odysseus tells of his own voyaging while in Eumaeus' hut. Interestingly, Odysseus earns the right to hear Eumaeus' "true" story only after he constructs an enormous lie about his own piratical life. The Homeric poet knows that a culture expects what it is used to. To buy time for revenge, Odysseus fulfills the expectations of an older set of east-to-west fables.

Eumaeus' adventure first takes Bérard to the triangular island group of Syra, Delos, and Mykinos in the Aegean Cyclades. Syra is toward the gloom, relative to the other two islands, and in Eumaeus' story we have another miniature geographical system that conforms to the larger structure of the poem. Bérard follows the Phoenician navigations of Eumaeus, and then of Odysseus, along the coasts of Asia Minor, Ethiopia, Libya, North Africa, the Straits of Gibraltar, over sea and land routes back to familiar waters, to the Peloponnese, to the Ionian Isles, to Thesprotia, to the Euxine. If Joyce read this chapter for his own *Eumaeus*, the old Phoenician sea-dog of the episode, Murphy, provides *Ulysses* with interludes similar to those of the *Odyssey*'s tales at *Nostos*. Murphy, too, goes everywhere—believably or not—and his part in the episode justifies the chapter's art in Joyce's *schema*: navigation. I think that Joyce borrowed the tag from the title of Bérard's digression on Phoenician "Navigations." One of Joyce's longest notes in the entire collection of notesheets (the other is a transcribed advertisement for Wonder Workers' remedy for rectal complaints) is the itinerary of Odysseus' lie to Eumaeus. He puts this to very little use in *Ulysses*, but the gist of it may have given him the clue for Murphy. Joyce jots down the specifics.

> went to Troy, came back Egypt, crew outrage Egyptians, these set on them, he implores king, 7 yrs. there, Phenician lures Ul. away, 1 year, to sell him in Libya, shipwreck borne on mast to Thesprotis, Pheidon king helps, shows him Ul's treasure, Ul gone to Dodana oracle, Ph. sends him to Dulicium grain, crews strip him swims off.   (Herring, p. 407)

This is an east-to-west journey, and, like that of Menelaus' *Nostos*, it lasts seven years in the Levant before the return to Greece. The movement of the wandering fulfills the range of the eastern seas: Troy to Egypt to Libya to Thesprotia, or, simply, northeast to southeast to southwest to northwest. Odysseus boxes the compass. We remember Bloom's remark about Murphy: "assuming he was the person he represented himself to be and not sailing under false colours after having boxed the compass on the strict q.t. somewhere" (626). Joyce makes the connection between Murphy and Odysseus explicit in his notesheets: "Ps Ul's tale resembles Ul's" (Herring, p. 404), where "Ps Ul" stands for Ulysses' Pseudoangelos, or Murphy. At least in his disguise as beggared liar, Odysseus shares roles with Murphy: "Odys & Pseudo = 2 imposters" (Herring, p. 396). Murphy's blarney is marvelous.

> —You must have seen a fair share of the world, the keeper remarked, leaning on the counter.
> —Why, the sailor answered, upon reflection upon it, I've circumnavigated a bit since I first joined on. I was in the Red Sea. I was in China and North America and South America. I seen icebergs plenty, growlers. I was in Stockholm and the Black Sea, the Dardanelles, under Captain Dalton the best bloody man that ever scuttled a ship. I seen Russia. *Gospodi pomilooy.* That's how the Russians prays.   (625)

Phoenicians are sea-dogs, but like all sea-dogs they lie on the waters. Bloom speaks to Stephen.

> —Our mutual friend's stories are like himself, Mr Bloom, *apropos* of knives, remarked to his *confidente sotto voce.* Do you

think they are genuine? He could spin those yarns for hours on end all night long and lie like old boots. Look at him.

Yet still, though his eyes were thick with sleep and sea air, life was full of a host of things and coincidences of a terrible nature and it was quite within the bounds of possibility that it was not an entire fabrication though at first blush there was not much inherent probability in all the spoof he got off his chest being strictly accurate gospel. (635)

We are not meant to treat Murphy's tales as integral to *Ulysses*. But, just as in Bérard's freewheeling account of the Phoenicians in the Mediterranean (in comparison to the very deliberate narrative uses Homer makes of space in the individual Odyssean adventures), Joyce uses Murphy to emphasize the difference between range and purpose in narrative movement. Lying and truth-telling are less important than that place and direction contribute to an *ethos* in the epic or to a meaning in the novel. Murphy is the modern outcast before he is the returned voyager. He has a Greek figure tattooed on his chest that can do funny things with its face—Murphy is a puppet Odysseus, Ancient Mariner, Flying Dutchman, Sinbad the Sailor. There is "something spurious in the cut of his jib" (636) and not merely because he lies: he is displaced. And there is something odd about the sailor who reads his own seven years at sea in his favorite book of adventures, *The Arabian Nights* (659).

Joyce's Pseudoangelos is not so much an attack on the concept of a commonplace Odysseus as he is a foil for the mock-heroic accoutrements of Bloom. As long as Murphy is around Bloom can take on the substance of the hero at home without the baggage of the epic navigations he has unknowingly carried all day. Joyce will not let Murphy touch the real Mediterranean axis in the world of *Ulysses*. When asked by Bloom if he has seen the Rock of Gibraltar, Murphy suddenly gets tired of talking. Instead, he "grimaced, chewing, in a way that might be read as yes, ay, or no" (629). Of course, Molly Bloom's mumbled no at the beginning of *Ulysses* and her yesses at the end of it pass directly through that very Gibraltar axis to the hero of the hill on Howth, Don Poldo de la Flora.

Odysseus will invent stories in the *Nostos* of the *Odyssey*. Bloom is not beyond telling a lie or two to suit his own immediate ends. But the difference between Murphy and Odysseus or Murphy and

Bloom is that with Odysseus and Bloom the real story is eventually revealed. It is in *Eumaeus* that Bloom begins recapitulating his day consciously.

> Added to which was the coincidence of meeting, discussion, dance, row, old salt, of the here today and gone tomorrow type, night loafers, the whole galaxy of events, all went to make up a minia- ture cameo of the world we live in, especially as the lives of the submerged tenth, viz., coalminers, divers, scavengers, etc., were very much under the microscope lately. To improve the shining hour he wondered whether he might meet with anything ap- proaching the same luck as Mr Philip Beaufoy if taken down in writing. Suppose he were to pen something out of the common groove (as he fully intended doing) at the rate of one guinea per column, *My Experiences*, let us say, *in a Cabman's Shelter*.
>
> (646-647)

When Odysseus first arrives on Ithaca, the king of the land is just another democrat—he does not even know he is on his own territory: "What am I in for now?" he thinks (Book XIII, Fitzgerald, p. 236). Athena, in disguise, greets him and observes ironically, "Stranger, you must come from the other end of nowhere" (Book XIII, Fitzgerald, p. 237). In the geographical mythic structure of the poem, he certainly has. After the western extension but before the actual revenge upon the suitors, most of the time on the home island is taken up with two kinds of narrative movement—forward with stratagems, identifications, recognitions, trials, and purges; backward buying time with fabricated yarns of eastern origins. The double movement adds to the tension of the revenge plot and releases the tension of the years at sea. The *Eumaeus* se- quence in the *Odyssey* is clearly transitional. Not only does the action translate the sphere of the epic to the home island, but Odys- seus translates himself into the various roles of his land: beggar-king, guest-host, itinerant-husband. The ease with which roles are changed and stories of wealth and beggary relayed suggests that the values of the epic must cut deeply into the structure of the land. No dis- tinction between men holds that has been imposed recklessly and without the assent of the gods. The democracy of the *Eumaeus* se- quence in the *Odyssey* contrasts with the abuse of aristocratic privi- lege in the court at Ithaca.

The scene at the Cabman's shelter in *Ulysses* is not unlike the scene on Ithaca in the early stages of *Nostos*. Dublin is an island city that seems to have gathered an equally "miscellaneous collection of waifs and strays and other nondescript specimens of the genus *homo*" (621). Odysseus on Ithaca is little more than a beggar. Theoclymenos, who had seen better days, hitches a sail with Telemachus from Pylos. Even a real beggar shows up at the palace and unwisely tries to edge the disguised Odysseus out of the doorway, a prime spot for receiving scraps from the table. This luckless fellow, named Iros by the suitors because of his willingness to carry messages, is lucky to escape with a smashed jawbone when Odysseus has done with him. A suitor sets the tone for inhospitality after Odysseus dispenses with Iros: another "walking famine out of business."

The slow and deliberate preparation in the *Odyssey*, the mingling of classes, the sorting out of loyalties, works in the poem because the build-up leads eventually to the violent purge and slaughter at the palace. Violence is not Joyce's way. The winding down of *Eumaeus* in *Ulysses* provides a problem of a different nature from that in the *Odyssey*. A calm before another calm is unlike a calm in the eye of a storm. But this is no reason to see *Eumaeus*, as many have, as either a failure in suspense or an experiment in the reproduction of boredom. Joyce is working with more subtle transitions. The resolution of *Ulysses*, at least as far as Stephen and Bloom are concerned, is a matter of verbal connection, not epic revenge. In *Eumaeus* for the first time in sixteen chapters the two important male characters of the novel talk at leisure. There is some blarney on Bloom's part and some rudeness on Stephen's, but the usual open hostility of the Dublin day is not so manifest here. The heroes are among *"hoi polloi"* (622). Bloom expresses distaste for the local police because they look after the wealthy and desert the poor. The downs of *Eumaeus* are the real outs of Dublin. Lord John Corley and Gumley are another set of tattered and torn vagabonds. Bloom and Stephen, for that matter, are not in the best of financial or spiritual conditions. But Bloom is not a deserter. He belongs neither in Nighttown, from where he has just come, nor at the Cabman's shelter, where he now is. He is there only to help—to voice some of the same values of human hospitality that appear in the *Eumaeus* sequence in the *Odyssey*. Corley mistakenly thinks Bloom a perpetual down-and-outer—a habitué of the Bleeding Horse in Camden street, a seedy establishment in which Bloom has probably never set foot. Perhaps Corley makes the habitual Dublin mistake of linking Bloom with Boylan, who, as Robert Martin Adams guesses, probably spends time at the Bleeding Horse. Or, seeing Bloom at the Cabman's shelter, itself a none too elegant haunt, Corley imagines Bloom at rock-bottom in the Liberties of south central Dublin as well. Odysseus, of course, also spends time, for reasons necessary to him, in seedy haunts of Ithaca. Despite the tired low-life setting of *Eumaeus*, Bloom's good will shines through the weariness of the night. He may be a bit puzzled by Dedalus, but his thoughts are decent, even fatherly.

> The queer suddenly things he popped out with attracted the elder man who was several years the other's senior or like his father. But something substantial he certainly ought to eat, were it only an eggflip made on unadulterated maternal nutriment or, failing that, the homely Humpty Dumpty boiled. (656)

Substance and "maternal nutriment" are what the *Nostos* holds in store, whether Stephen or Bloom know it at the time or ever know it. For Joyce it is the ability to transform the almost mystical epiphanies of domestic life into the fabric of fiction that makes for narrative resolution. The future artist, Dedalus, is, at this time, too morose to project. He can barely pay attention, and he seems as un-interested in resolution as he is in action. *Eumaeus* thrusts all the burden on Bloom even though he is often "poles apart" (634) from Dedalus. Some of Bloom's restorative drivel is absurd and slight. He backs off from ideas when he cannot understand Stephen's re-sponse or when he thinks his moderate socialism, appropriate to the episode, is offensive to Stephen's *Übermensch* pretensions. Often, Bloom intentionally misunderstands Stephen just to keep the con-versation going. His demurrer on Stephen's definition of the soul as simple substance, "you do knock across a simple soul once in a blue moon" (634), is not so much stupidity as chatter. At times he simply prefers not to understand. When, for instance, Stephen suspects that Ireland must be important because it belongs to him, Bloom allows Stephen to sidestep the issue: "—What belongs? queried Mr Bloom, bending, fancying he was perhaps under some misapprehension. Excuse me. Unfortunately I didn't catch the latter portion . . ." (645). At times he really has no idea where Stephen's mind ranges. Bloom suggests that Stephen eat some solid food; Stephen thinks of Mediterranean treachery.

—Liquids I can eat, Stephen said. But oblige me by taking away
that knife. I can't look at the point of it. It reminds me of Roman
history.

Mr Bloom promptly did as suggested and removed the incrimi-
nated article, a blunt hornhandled ordinary knife with nothing
particularly Roman or antique about it to the lay eye. . . .

(635)

Bloom, a simple substance in *Eumaeus*, acts to bridge a few of the
human gaps that the extended *Wanderings* of the day have brought
about. *Eumaeus* is part of *Nostos*. It is recuperative. Just as Odysseus
as wanderer experiences a change of pace before a final exertion in
Eumaeus' hut, Bloom the exile enjoys the prospect of a friend in
Dublin's Cabman's shelter. Erin's King, Parnell, is expected home
at any moment from the grave—even if in the Irish parodic twist he
had previously come home for another man's wife rather than voyage "across the world" for his own. The more modest king in Dublin, who claims once to have restored Parnell's hat to him, is already
home. Ever since *Oxen of the Sun* Bloom has been helpful to the
son of another man. His is a small gesture, but Bloom seems the
only citizen of his land capable of such small gestures.

Ithaca

At one point in his chapter on Odysseus' home island archipelago,
Le Royaume d'Ithaque, Bérard discusses the tiny, tree-denuded isle
of Daskalio where he thinks the suitors lay in ambush for Telemachus [Bérard, ii, 491]. Joyce is so eager to make what identifications he can between Ithaca and Ireland that he jots down in his
Zürich notebook: "unwooded isles now (cf. Ireland)" (VIII.A.5, p.
296). If Daskalio can be all Ireland, surely Ithaca could be Dublin
of the *Nostos*. Joyce's *Ithaca* begins with the walk home from Beresford place, Stephen and Bloom following a parallel route northwest
to Eccles with a slight detour and a slight extension to Temple
Hill when they might earlier have turned off Gardiner place. The
path of the *Odyssey* is duplicated. Odysseus tells Telemachus what
he already knows, that the palace is a long way from Eumaeus'
hut. Just as Stephen and Bloom have moved back near Nighttown
from the Cabman's shelter before they swing toward 7 Eccles street,

235

the island path from the swineherd's hut on Ithaca leads slightly northeast until past the inlet at the Gulf of Molo. From that point the route is steadily northwest, perhaps with a slight jog around the Bay of Port Polis.

Stephen's and Bloom's parallel walk is not only absorbed in the objective catechismic parallel structure of the episode, but given a recapitulative mythic variation in the elliptical extension and return of all space in the tracks of the Great Northern Railway.

> Retreating, at the terminus of the Great Northern Railway, Amiens street, with constant uniform acceleration, along parallel lines meeting at infinity, if produced: along parallel lines, reproduced from infinity, with constant uniform retardation, at the terminus of the Great Northern Railway. Amiens street, returning.
>
> (730)

Out and back: wandering is an exile and a return even from local neighborhoods. In *Ithaca*, the planets enter the novel's recapitulative finale. The *Ithaca* notesheets record: "Planets—they ?wanderers" (Herring, p. 482). One particular heavenly configuration, Cassiopeia, associated all day with Shakespeare, Stephen, and Bloom, is very much a part of the Odyssean wanderings. Joyce notes: "9 years wander (Cassiopeia)" (Herring, p. 428). In the episode itself the nine years refer cryptically to Bloom's return to Cassiopeia in his cometery orbit as a comic-epic wanderer, "an estranged avenger, a wreaker of justice on malefactors, a dark crusader, a sleeper awakened, with financial resources (by supposition) surpassing those of Rothchild or of the silver king" (728). The daily journey of the earth in the novel is easier—it takes only twenty-four hours "through everchanging tracks of neverchanging space" (737).

Ithaca moves the epic into its modern domain—the positivist universe. Leopold Bloom lists his desired intellectual pursuits at Flowerville, his dream home of southerly aspect: "Snapshot photography, comparative study of religions, folklore relative to various amatory and superstitious practices, contemplation of the celestial constellations" (715). The snapshot is recorded realism—the constellations, the myth of the galaxies. *Ithaca* works with the basic ingredients of the novel's material world, the circumstantiating array of "facts."[1]

---

[1] See A. Walton Litz, "Ithaca," in Hart and Hayman, pp. 385-405. Litz discusses the episode's mythic and factual fictional bias, crediting Arnold Goldman's descriptive phrase, "myth/fact paradox" (Goldman, *The Joyce Paradox* [Evanston, Ill., 1966], p. 105).

Even the parodic axis of *Ulysses* aligns facts and their mundane-mythic elaborations. Having forgotten his key to the front door, Bloom climbs the railing and drops a short flight down to the area door. His fall is determined by his weight, which he knows because he weighed himself on the appropriately mythic Ascension day (668). A joke such as this is clever, but not so radical a departure from the *Odyssey* as it might seem. The Homeric poem is intricately worked out in its last twelve books—placed and planned to the last detail. But when Odysseus finally meets his own father in Book XXIV, he transforms his adventures into a brief allegory of all mankind. In effect, he offers a generalized reading of the narrative he has just resolved: "I come from Rover's Passage where my home is, and I'm King Allwoes' only son. My name is Quarrelman" (Book XXIV, Fitzgerald, p. 454). And, of course, amidst all the precision and localization of the *Nostos*, in the last book of the *Odyssey* yet one more journey is made, this one long and elliptical and mythic, as Hermes leads the shades of the slaughtered suitors to the wastes of Asphodel at the world's end.

Ithaca's style in *Ulysses* is as measured as the comic pinprick and as expanded as "Meditations of evolution increasingly vaster" (698). Bloom and Stephen talk about most things under the sun—Bloom is questioned on the rest. Toward the end of the episode Bloom contemplates a journey to the extreme boundary of space, but does not trust the laws of the universe to return him. The sun-compelled hero prefers the comforts of *Nostos*.

> What play of forces, inducing inertia, rendered departure undesirable?
>
> The lateness of the hour, rendering procrastinatory: the obscurity of the night, rendering invisible: the uncertainty of thoroughfares, rendering perilous: the necessity for repose, obviating movement: the proximity of an occupied bed, obviating research: the anticipation of warmth (human) tempered with coolness (linen), obviating desire and rendering desirable: the statue of Narcissus, sound without echo, desired desire. (728)

Home is a world of stuff and full of small renewals. Bloom can stand in his yard and think of the apparition of a new solar disk without worrying about the inevitability of its rising. He returns inside to sleep at the center. As far as the geographical day of Ulysses is concerned, Bloom rests easy. His elegiac pantomime squares the solar circle.

237

Going to a dark bed there was a square round Sinbad the Sailor roc's auk's egg in the night of the bed of the auks of the rocs of Darkinbad the Brightdayler. (737)

We know from typescripts of *Ithaca* that Joyce organized the chapter under the headings: street, kitchen, garden, parlour, and bedroom.[2] In a fine essay on *Ithaca*, A. Walton Litz pauses to compare the location headings to the narrative progress of Dante and Virgil out of the *Inferno* to the light of day and the stars of night. Joyce uses Dante's own narrative *and* exegetical phrase, "*In exitu Israël de Egypto*" (698), in his parallel passage from the kitchen to the garden. Litz insists that we read this section of *Ithaca*, and countless other sections of *Ulysses*, as a kind of narrative *tertium quid*, a text that both incorporates and mocks epic values.[3]

The objectifications of banality in epic proportions are, no doubt, obsessive; so, too, are the sublimities of mythic extension. Facts are reductive; myths are hyperbolic. But Joyce's fictional range, his absorption of all plots into one plot, allows him to draw significance from various textures. He can debase the epic—make it look meager —or he can outdo even the *Odyssey*'s allegory of Quarrelman-Odysseus at the end. But to have these options Joyce feels that he must first build upon a bedrock of facts. For the *Nostos* of the *Odyssey* he takes detailed notes on the Homeric original. Although he may not use the bulk of his notes in the actual text of *Ulysses*, he refreshes his memory on the movements and actions of the poem.[4] In approaching the palace Odysseus moves from path to anterior chambers to courtyard to hall to bedroom. If this sounds familiar, it recalls Joyce's own typescript headings for *Ithaca*. The street in *Ulysses* is obviously the path to the Ithacan palace. Once arrived, Odysseus conducts a strategy session near the main hall. He decides that the arms have to be moved to a location in the palace that will make it impossible for the suitors to lay hands on them as they have done with all else. At the moment, the arms happen to be in a "hot" place, near the hearth, presumably against the wall near where the massive

[2] See Peter Spielberg, *James Joyce's Manuscripts and Letters at the University of Buffalo: A Catalogue* (Buffalo, 1962), V.B. 15.a and V.B. 15.b.

[3] Litz writes: "But the genius of Joyce and of *Ulysses* lies in the indisputable fact that the form is both epic and ironic, Bloom both heroic and commonplace" ("Ithaca," in Hart and Hayman, p. 391).

[4] See especially his entries for *Eumaeus* in the notesheets, Herring, pp. 403-407.

amounts of food were prepared for the suitors. The excuse to move the arms is reasonable enough—they were being tarnished by the smoke. Joyce sees the witty connection with Bloom's kitchen and with Dante's *Inferno*—another hot place.

The scene set in Bloom's garden corresponds to the action in the Homeric courtyard. Homer's outside space is the setting for the bow test, and the initial setting for the slaughter to follow. The Homeric climax is purgative. For Joyce it seems to be an act of perfect micturition. Old sly-boots, not keen on violence, has his heroes relieve themselves on the usurped and now restored native ground. Of course, the garden scene in *Ulysses* does not end with the bodily purge. A shooting star connects the Lyre (Dedalus, the Hermes poet) to Leo (Bloom) through Berenice (Molly). The heavenly family purifies the skies. We remember Dedalus' remark in *Proteus*: "walking beneath a reign of uncouth stars" (48). The allusion, as mentioned earlier, is to Giordano Bruno's *Spaccio della bestia trionfante*, an allegorical work in which the polluted heavens are cleansed by the forces of triumphant justice. Joyce adds a favorite hermeticist to the purging plot of the *Odyssey* and the redemptive plot of the *Divine Comedy*.

After the slaughter of the suitors, Odysseus returns to his great hall and issues orders that the interior and exterior be cleansed of the carnage. When Bloom reenters his parlor, he does not clean— he merely discovers "by knocking his sconce against them sure" that his furniture has been rearranged. Symbolically, Boylan and Molly are the ones who have rearranged it.[5] In *Ithaca* the furniture stays where it is for the time being, but the domestic contents of the house are, at least, fictionally reorganized. The parlor section of *Ithaca* sets out the stock of Bloom's life at home—his library is cata-logued, his mantel described, his pockets emptied, the contents of two drawers itemized. Odysseus, before he returns to the bedroom of his wife, sees to domestic details; Joyce, before he returns Bloom to Molly's bedroom, lets his readers see all the household's domestic details. Finally, Odysseus goes to rediscover his bed, and Bloom goes to discover who else has been in his bed. Street, kitchen, garden, parlor, and bedroom: the progression is literal enough from the

---

[5] Hugh Kenner sees the connection and the irony in the Aristotelian "sconce knocking" of *Proteus* and the furniture rearranging in *Ithaca*. See Kenner's essay, "Molly's Masterstroke," in *Ulysses: Fifty Years*, ed. Thomas F. Staley (Bloomington, Ind., 1972), pp. 19-28.

Odyssey—Joyce makes it figurative for Dublin's epic comedy, rounding into the geodetic form of *Penelope* and the new day.

The *Odyssey*, especially its resolution, is a problem for Joyce, who is determined neither to protect Penelope nor to slaughter the suitors. Resolution in *Ulysses* is very much a part of the circumstantial fictional universe. Bloom knows that life has its local traumas when he cracks his head against the walnut sideboard in the dark. His response to that indignity is immediate—his response to the larger disorders of the day are progressively ameliorative: "Envy, jealousy, abnegation, equanimity" (732). In the world of *Ulysses* the violation of another's bed is reconstitutive—adultery is not the worst calamity. Surely it is not

> as calamitous as a cataclysmic annihilation of the planet in consequence of collision with a dark sun. As less reprehensible than theft, highway robbery, cruelty to children and animals, obtaining money under false pretences, forgery, embezzlement, misappropriation of public money, betrayal of public trust, malingering, mayhem, corruption of minors, criminal libel, blackmail, contempt of court, arson, treason, felony, mutiny on the high seas, trespass, burglary, jailbreaking, practice of unnatural vice, desertion from armed forces in the field, perjury, poaching, usury, intelligence with the king's enemies, impersonation, criminal assault, manslaughter, wilful and premeditated murder. As not more abnormal than all other altered processes of adaptation to altered conditions of existence, resulting in a reciprocal equilibrium between the bodily organism and its attendant circumstances, foods, beverages, acquired habits, indulged inclinations, significant disease. As more than inevitable, irreparable. (733)

For Bloom the apathy of the stars in the interstellar world tell him to adapt to the altered conditions of existence. "The preordained frangibility of the hymen" (734) is less important than the return at the end of the day. Bloom lies in bed next to Molly, joining the west and east in the novel's actual and epic geography. As voyager and homebody, they lie northwest and southeast respectively.

In what final satisfaction did these antagonistic sentiments and reflections, reduced to their simplest forms, converge?

Satisfaction at the ubiquity in eastern and western terrestrial hemispheres, in all habitable lands and islands explored or unexplored (the land of the midnight sun, the islands of the blessed, the isles of Greece, the land of promise) of adipose posterior female hemispheres, redolent of milk and honey and of excretory sanguine and seminal warmth, reminiscent of secular families of curves of amplitude, insusceptible of moods of impression or of contrarieties of expression, expressive of mute immutable mature animality. (734)

The plot of *Ulysses* does not resolve with its characters particularly aware of its resolution. That is beside the point. And to prove his point, Joyce ends *Ithaca* with a little round dot: micro and macrocosm.

Where? (737)

•

PENELOPE

Joyce has written in his notesheets for *Oxen of the Sun* that "imagination has a body to it" (Herring, p. 256). The carousing medicals of that chapter ended up with the corpse of their native language. *Penelope* reproduces the risen body in the shape of the earth entire while Molly Bloom attacks the demythifiers, calling upon the fullness of nature to do so.

God of heaven theres nothing like nature the wild mountains then the sea and the waves rushing then the beautiful country with fields of oats and wheat and all kinds of things and all the fine cattle going about that would do your heart good to see rivers and lakes and flowers all sorts of shapes and smells and colours springing up even out of the ditches primroses and violets nature it is as for them saying theres no God I wouldnt give a snap of my two fingers for all their learning why dont they go and create something I often asked him atheists or whatever they call themselves . . . (781-782)

Molly is a believer in creation from nothing. She answers the questions Stephen had mocked earlier, questions of substance and form. With the return to Eccles street, *Ulysses* returns to itself— "Penelope" is the muse of the first chapter in the novel's *schema*. Joyce conceives of *Ithaca* as "in reality the end as *Penelope* has no beginning, middle or end" (*Letters*, i, 172). The novel begins for Dedalus with the surrounding country and awakening mountains, and it concludes with the curvilinear spaces of the day readying to reawaken—still very much outside in the open air. The night is for rest, recumbent, "the manchild in the womb" (737). Locally, Bloom's *Calypso* address is the same as his *Penelope* address, but structurally, the day follows the sun northwest from Gibraltar to Dublin. So, too, does Molly's narration. If Joyce borrows the migrational line in Shelley's *Hellas* for the progression to Ireland's evening lands, he may also borrow the encompassing feminine fiction of another daughter of the pillars at Gibraltar, Shelley's *Witch of Atlas*, for the concluding chapter of *Ulysses*. Shelley's Witch, localized in her cave at the Straits, is an insomniac, a weaver like Penelope, Circe, and Marion "Tweedy," a transformer, a tour-guide for the denizens of sleep from the Nile to the Arctic. She is a goddess of substanced forms.

In the Egyptian *Book of the Dead*, which Joyce used liberally in *Finnegans Wake* and from which Victor Bérard derived a Mediterranean system of geography, yet another goddess of Gibraltar is described: the Egyptian Nut. Nut's bowed body formed the dome of the universe, head and arms facing east and legs west. Ra, the sun god, made his way across the dome daily from east to west. The arms and legs of Nut formed the four pillars of the earth, resting in Asia and at the Straits of Gibraltar. Joyce copied down a variant of this scheme, complete with diagrams, from Bérard's *Les Phéniciens* [Bérard, II, 261-263].[6] For *Penelope* Joyce has to rearrange the metaphor in accord with the earth's revolving around the sun, but the conceit is the same: Molly is "gynotropic"—she is an earth goddess. Joyce's description of the last chapter of his novel in a letter to Frank Budgen is well known. I repeat it here in its entirety because it substantiates what seem to me the two most important qualities of the geographical structure of *Ulysses*: direction and extension.

> *Penelope* is the clou of the book. The first sentence contains 2500 words. There are eight sentences in the episode. It begins and ends with the female word *Yes*. It turns like the huge earthball slowly surely and evenly round and round spinning. Its four cardinal points being the female breasts, arse, womb and cunt expressed by the words *because, bottom* (in all senses, bottom button, bottom of the glass, bottom of the sea, bottom of his heart) *woman, yes*. Though probably more obscene than any preceding episode

it seems to me to be perfectly sane full amoral fertilisable un-
trustworthy engaging shrewd limited prudent indifferent *Weib.*
Ich bin das Fleisch das stets bejaht. (*Letters*, I, 170)

Whatever the eight sentences of Molly's monologue represent—
her eighth of September birthday, her side-on view of two plump
melonous hemispheres, the symbol of infinity, the progression
through the octave, the full set of compass points—they make up the
web of movement in the *schema*. The relationships among the
sentences offer some of the same problems as do the relationships
among the subsections of *Wandering Rocks*, but Joyce offers better
clues for *Penelope*. Molly's mind oscillates as it turns from sex to
adornment to love along the Gibraltar-Dublin axis. Diane Tolemeo
has argued credibly in an essay, "The Final Octagon of *Ulysses*,"
that Molly's eight sentences fall and rise as their subject matter replicates in mirror images (1, 8; 2, 7; 3, 6; 4, 5).[7] Without repeating her
conclusions, which are detailed, I would simply look briefly at the
sentences as they spin around on the episode's gynotropic axis.

The four cardinal points, north, south, east, and west, recur in
patterned ways in *Penelope*. Adjustments must be made for the
shape of the human body, but the breasts of Joyce's earth goddess as
she lies, we might speculate, with her navel at Gibraltar, may point
north, her arse south, her womb east, and her cunt west. The com-
posite image makes sense. Joyce never deserts the body as a beginning and ending form. The breasts are the upward expanse (north);
the arse southerly (the fundament); the womb east (origin); and
the cunt western extension (egress and return). With the exception
of "because," the descriptive words of the letter also make sense:
bottom-arse, woman-womb, yes-cunt. (In *Finnegans Wake*, Joyce
even calls the west "yest," *FW*, 597). "Because" seems a neutral
word, but it occurs almost exclusively in the first sentence of Molly's
monologue, a sentence taken up entirely with Ireland, and opposite

---

[7] See Diane Tolemeo, "The Final Octagon of *Ulysses*," *JJQ*, 10 (1973),
439-453. The *Ithaca* notesheets give Ms. Tolemeo the clue for her scheme:

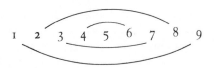

$$1 \quad 2 \quad 3 \quad 4 \quad 5 \quad 6 \quad 7 \quad 8 \quad 9$$

(Herring, p. 450).

in tone from the eighth, or resolving, sentence. "Because" occurs
in the first sentence at a ratio of over 10:1 in comparison with its
occurrences in the other sentences of *Penelope*. Molly is out of place
in northern domains among Ireland's "homemade beauties" or "sparrowfarts" (762). She points out that "youve no chances at all in this
place like you used long ago" (758). As a conjunction, "because"
offers reasons or qualifying explanations. And that is precisely what
Molly does in the first sentence. Over and again she contrasts herself to her domain. "Because" separates the Rose of Castille from
Irish Molly, O. Its occurrences mark the Spanish-Irish disjunction,
Molly's sterile northern life. Bloom's asking for breakfast generates
a "because"—it reminds Molly of the deserted, pious, childless Mrs.
Riordan at the northern City Arms Hotel. Men, "weak and puling"
(738), Bloom's pathetic correspondence with Martha Clifford, Mary
Driscoll's false "bottom," aging men, sex with a bishop, the grey
matter of soulless brains, Boylan's "tremendous big red brute of a
thing" (742), Boylan's Stallion, and jealousy all merit one of Molly's
"becauses." The only "because" in the first sentence not related to a
distinctly negative association is Molly's pleasant weariness after
eating "potted meat" (741), Dublin's corpse and corpus.

"Yes" is the affirmation to Molly's qualifying voice. Appearing
most often in the eighth sentence, "yes" signals the northwest passage. Molly in her final sentence renews the ancient Phoenician-
Irish connection through the Straits of Gibraltar by conflating the
two great moments of her life, with Mulvey under the Moorish
wall and with Bloom on the slope of Howth Hill. Molly need not
distinguish the personal and geographical transitions. Gibraltar is
Howth as "yes" begins and ends the episode: egress and re-entrance.

Molly begins her eighth sentence by rejecting the ill manners and
brutishness of Boylan. She continues by refusing to think any more
of her infant son's death: "O Im not going to think myself into
the glooms about that any more" (778). And she confronts the
strange habits of Bloom with her full sexuality, her fundamental
nature.

> if I am an adulteress as the thing in the gallery said O much
> about it if thats all the harm ever we did in this vale of tears
> God knows its not much doesnt everybody only they hide it I
> suppose thats what a woman is supposed to be there for or He
> wouldnt have made us the way He did so attractive to men then

if he wants to kiss my bottom Ill drag open my drawers and bulge it right out in his face as large as life he can stick his tongue 7 miles up my hole ... (780)

From this point Molly draws the last sentence to Gibraltar and back to Howth where Bloom warms the Irish mountain: "the sun shines for you he said the day we were lying among the rhododendrons on Howth head" (782). That was the day "I got him to propose to me ... he said I was a flower of the mountain yes so we are flowers all a womans body yes that was one true thing he said in his life and the sun shines for you today yes" (782).

"Bottom" and "woman" work as key words in more obvious and consistent ways—and it is needless to rehearse them. What is important to Joyce in the spinning arrangement of his sentences are the alternating impulses, positive and negative, fertile and sterile, of memory and of place. The sentences are carefully orchestrated and they range from Gibraltar to Dublin (Dublin getting the edge in sheer bulk because Molly's memories are not as equally divided as the years she spent in each place). Molly's Gibraltar is a special challenge to Joyce. He never set foot on the peninsula or on the Rock. Molly's memories belong to material he cribbed from Gibraltar guidebooks—he even sketched a map of the island in his notesheets (Herring, p. 511). As always, it was important to Joyce that he get local textures right. James Van Dyck Card and Phillip F. Herring have uncovered some of the Gibraltar material Joyce relied upon, and several passages Card cites from Henry Field's *Gibraltar* (New York, 1888) clearly reveal a debt to that book.[8]

Early in *Gibraltar* Field writes: "Few places have seen more history" (p. 4). Gibraltar is a migrational hub, and that was part of Joyce's interest in it. Settlers come from the Levant and exit into the Atlantic. Field writes.

> Here Spaniards and Moors, who fought for Gibraltar a thousand years ago, are at peace and good friends, at least so far as to be willing to cheat each other as readily as if they were of the same religion. Here are long-bearded Jews in their gabardines; and Turks with their baggy trousers, taking up more space than is allowed to Christian legs; with a mongrel race from the Eastern part of the mediterranean known as Levantines; and another like

[8] James Van Dyck Card, "A Gibraltar Sourcebook for 'Penelope,'" *JJQ*, 8 (1971), 163-174.

245

unto them, the Maltese; and a choice variety of natives of Gibraltar, called "Rock scorpions," with Africans blacker than Moors,
who have perhaps crossed the desert, and hail from Timbuctoo.
All these make a Babel of races and languages as they jostle each
other in these narrow streets, and bargain with each other, and
I am afraid sometimes swear at each other, in all the Languages
of the East. (pp. 33-34)

When Joyce adapts this passage for Molly in *Ulysses*, he recreates
the same racial riot.

and the auctions in the morning the Greeks and the jews and
the Arabs and the devil knows who else from all the ends of Europe and Duke street and the fowl market all clucking outside
Larby Sharons and the poor donkeys slipping half asleep and the
vague fellows in the cloaks asleep in the shade on the steps and the
big wheels of the carts of the bulls and the old castle thousands of
years old yes and those handsome Moors all in white and turbans
like kings asking you to sit down in their little bit of a shop . . .
(782)

Gibraltar appears at the end of *Ulysses* to provide Dublin a connecting, Mediterranean axis. One passage from Henry Field's *Gibraltar* that James Van Dyck Card does not cite in his essay offers Joyce
one of those coincidences of which he was fond. As Christian sailors
leave the Straits, passing by the highest point of the Rock, O'Hara's
Tower, they salute a shrine to the Virgin Mary, Molly's namesake
and an *extremely* faithful Penelope.

Here the old Phoenicians sacrificed to Hercules, as they were
approaching what was to them the end of the habitable globe;
and here, in later ages, a lamp was always hung before the shrine
of the Virgin, and the devout sailor crossed himself and repeated
his Ave Maria as he floated by. (p. 133)

We recall the Dantesque light of the Virgin in the Blooms' window in *Ithaca*, but Joyce is capable of providing a variety of homages
to a number of Marions. Earlier in *Ulysses*, when Molly appears as
the nymph of the Gibraltar Straits in *Calypso*, we learn that Bloom
thinks her brass bed had travelled. "All the way from Gibraltar"
(56). This is only fitting for a Mediterranean nymph who, as Simon
Dedalus tells us in *Sirens*, arrived along the same route: "From the

rock of Gibraltar . . . all the way" (269). But in *Penelope* Molly reveals that she lied to Bloom: "the lumpy old jingly bed always reminds me of Old Cohen I suppose he scratched himself in it often enough and he thinks father bought it from Lord Napier that I used to admire when I was a little girl" (772). Old Cohen may be a relic of Gibraltar or Dublin, but like his namesake in *Ulysses*—*Circe*'s Bella Cohen—he sells beds of infidelity. The irony of moveable (and saleable) beds is extreme. Odysseus knows at *Nostos* that his famous bed cannot move. It is rooted in the ground, carved out of the trunk of an olive tree around which the bedroom was constructed. The olive tree, so important a symbol in the Homeric epic of domestication, is Athena's civilizing gift to the city of Athens. Penelope accepts Odysseus fully only when he identifies the structural rootedness of the bed—it cannot be otherwise in an epic of fidelity. But Joyce wants direction more than he wants rootedness. The bed moves. So has the epic. The northwest axis offers Joyce the opportunity to translate what the *Odyssey* originated.

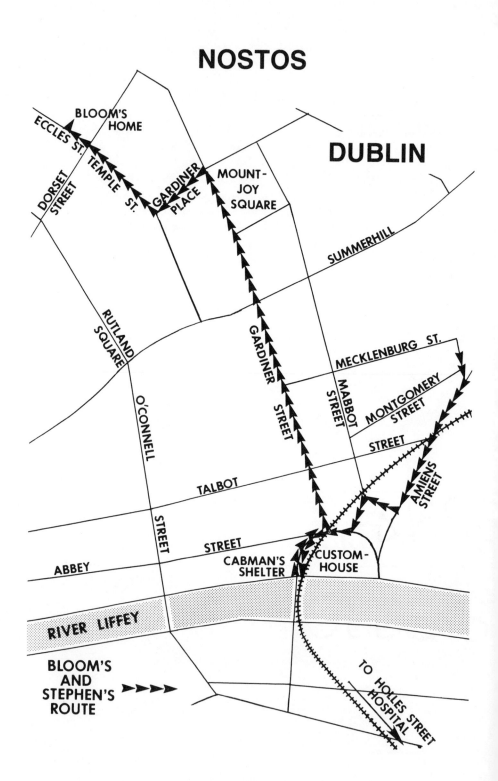

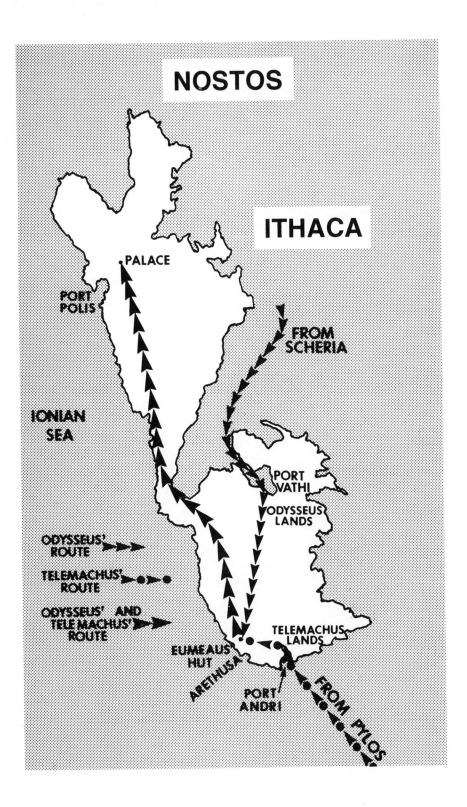

NOSTOS

ITHACA

PALACE

PORT POLIS

FROM SCHERIA

IONIAN SEA

PORT VATHI

ODYSSEUS LANDS

ODYSSEUS' ROUTE

TELEMACHUS' ROUTE

ODYSSEUS' AND TELEMACHUS' ROUTE

TELEMACHUS LANDS

EUMEAUS HUT

ARETHUSA

PORT ANDRI

FROM PILOS

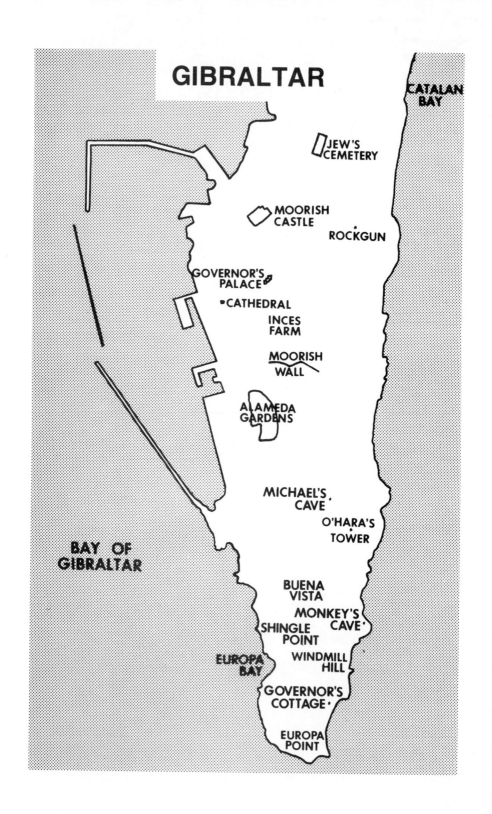

GIBRALTAR

CATALAN BAY

JEW'S CEMETERY

MOORISH CASTLE

ROCKGUN

GOVERNOR'S PALACE

CATHEDRAL

INCES FARM

MOORISH WALL

ALAMEDA GARDENS

MICHAEL'S CAVE

O'HARA'S TOWER

BAY OF GIBRALTAR

BUENA VISTA

MONKEY'S CAVE

SHINGLE POINT

EUROPA BAY

WINDMILL HILL

GOVERNOR'S COTTAGE

EUROPA POINT

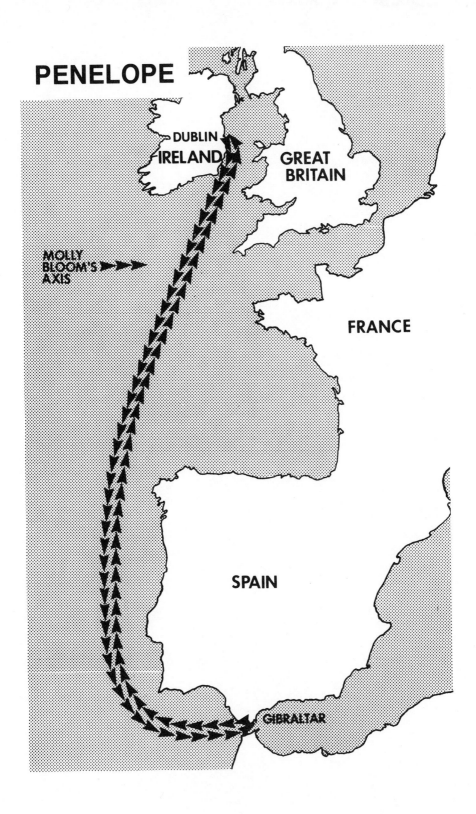

THE MOTION IS ENDED

MIDWAY through the second volume of *Les Phéniciens et l'Odyssée*, Victor Bérard tells the story of a misadventure in the Straits of Boniface off the northern coast of Sardinia. Having set sail in his own yacht, Bérard had traced Odysseus to the supposed Corsican-Sardinian haunts of the man-eating giants of Lamos, first cousins to the equally brutal Cyclopes. Preparing to round Cape Maddelena toward the harbor of the Odyssean Lestrygonians, Bérard and his small crew were surprised by a sudden and violent squall. His yacht was hailed by the warning blasts of a small fleet of Sardinian coast guard *vaporetti*. The naval officer in command, whom Bérard immediately named Antiphates, the chief Lestrygonian, guided the yacht to harbor in the storm. Upon a cursory investigation, he suspected that the expedition was up to something fishy in Sardinian waters. The "Lestrygonian" impounded the yacht and its equipment. Bérard protested that he was an epic toponymist seeking to prove that the *Odyssey* reproduces the voyages of Semitic navigators. He retrieved what he considered exculpatory evidence: a Greek text of the *Odyssey*, an *Atlas antiquus*, and a Hebrew dictionary by a man with the fortuitous name of F. Leopold.

Much as Joyce admired Bérard, he admired coincidences even more. This one must have pleased him. His own Leopold, a migratory Hebrew, a translated Greek hero, and a modest Irishman, spends most of the day under one or another sort of suspicion in a land plagued by the ghosts of epic movements. But in *Ulysses* the heroic has its mundane resolution. When Bloom returns home, his travels are but a memory. He seeks the domestic ritual. The great wanderer of Homeric legend, the conqueror of giants, takes off his shoes at 7 Eccles street.

> Did the process of divestiture continue?
> Sensible of a benignant persistent ache in his footsoles he extended his foot to one side and observed the creases, protuberances and salient points caused by foot pressure in the course of walking repeatedly in several different directions. (711)

As Dedalus says of Shakespeare, the motion is ended.

INDEX

(extension), xii, 7, 18, 19, 24, 25, 28-9, 34, 47, 52-3, 68, 70-1, 92, 98, 139, 143, 146, 242, 243; and Theosophy, 61

Fitzgerald, Robert, his *Odyssey* translation, 25, 30, 87, 118, 152, 157, 165, 206, 211, 215, 232, 237

Flaubert, Gustave, xv n, 214

Fletcher, Phineas, *Purple Island*, 40

Flotow, Friedrich von, *Martha*, 77, 191

Fludd, Robert, 54n

Freeman's Journal, 100, 163, 169

Frye, Northrop, 48n, 64

Gaea-Tellus, 38, 195

Gaeta, 159, 212, 215-16; *map of*, 227

Galatea, 196

Galway, xiv, 7, 17, 28n, 29, 68

General Slocum (ship disaster), 183, 184

geography, *see* Bérard, climate theory, Egyptian geographical systems, epic, Greek migrations, *Odyssey*, Phoenician navigations, *Ulysses*

Giamatti, A. Bartlett, 108, 119n

Gibraltar, xi, 9-10, 17, 27, 28, 34, 35, 38, 41, 63, 65, 72-3, 83, 85, 98, 105, 124, 138-39, 150-51, 160, 171, 172, 195, 203, 229, 231, 242-47; *map of*, 250

Gifford, Don, 59

Gilbert, Stuart, xvi, 3-4, 17, 50, 61n, 71n, 138, 151, 159, 166, 186n, 192n, 207

Gillet, Louis, 19

Givens, Seon, 7n, 62n

Glasheen, Adaline, 36n, 130

Glasnevin (Prospect cemetery, Dublin), 6, 34-5, 36, 71, 81, 128, 156, 161, 163, 165, 192

Goethe, Johann Wolfgang von, 30, 214

Gogarty, Oliver St. John, 73-4, 138; *see also* Mulligan

Goldberg, S. L., xvi, 88n, 173n

Goldman, Arnold, 236n

Gorman, Herbert, 151, 159

Goulding, Richie, 190, 191

Greece, and climate theory, 67-8; and mockery, 139-40; and Proteus, 106-08, 112; *see also Odyssey*

Greek migrations (settlements), x-xi, xiv-xv, 3-5, 7-12, 16-23, 25, 27-30, 31-4, 45-7, 53, 127-28, 141, 143, 145, 159-60, 200-01, 204-05, 215, 230, 241; *see also* Cumae, Italy, Ithaca, *Odyssey*, Peloponnese, Phoenician navigations

Greene, Thomas, 13n, 108n

Griggs, Earl Leslie, 61n

Groden, Michael, 20n, 95n, 163n, 164, 165

Grotten, Frank, Jr., 107n

Güntert, Hermann, 160n

Hades, 13, 15, 34, 106, 128, 158, 159, 161, 162n, 165, 173, 182, 211, 216

Hades (episode), 20, 35, 36, 48, 57, 71, 81, 91, 128, *156-63*, 165, 166, 206, 216-17; *map of*, 178

Haines, 87, 119, 164, 187, 210

Hamlet, 102n, 114, 119, 139, 209, 210n

Hamlet, 56, 88

Handel, George Fredrick, 185

Haroun al Raschid, 90, 108, 118-19, 148

Hart, Clive, 6, 35n, 36n, 52, 58n, 60n, 93n, 123, 126, 129, 130, 142n, 154, 165, 173n, 185, 187, 188n, 189, 204n, 210n, 214, 236n, 238n

Hartman, Geoffrey, 29n

Hastings, James, 53n

Hayman, David, 36n, 52, 58n, 60n, 93n, 123n, 130, 142n, 173n, 188n, 204n, 210n, 214, 236n, 238n

H.C.E. (Earwicker), xv-xvi, 21, 47-8, 53, 80, 108, 151

Helen of Troy, 30, 107

Heliodorus, 69

Helios (sun king), 34, 57, 67, 130, 157, 171, 173, 182, 204, 206, 209, 212, 213, 217; *see also* Oxen of the Sun, Sicily, Trinacria

Hercules (Heracles), xii, 57, 142, 246

Ogygia (Calypso's isle), 27-8, 35, 83, 105, 126-27, 130, 138, 151, 160n, 199, 205
omphalos (navel), 25, 28, 53-4, 127, 138-39, 141, 204, 215
Orinoco River, 70, 98, 103
Orpheus, 189
Ortygia, 25
Osiris, 9, 26, 110
Ovid, *Metamorphoses*, 196, 214
Oxen of the Sun, 15, 34; *see* Helios
Oxen of the Sun (episode), 34, 49, 56, 58, 92, 119, 128-29, 162, *204-10*, 214, 215, 235, 241; *map of*, 226

Paige, D. D., 112n
Paracelsus, 51
Paris (city), 7, 107, 144, 146, 172, 175
Paris (of Troy), 107
Parnell, Charles Stuart, 162, 235
parody, of astrology, 54-60; of epic structure, xi, 16, 87-8; of Ireland, 193-95, 198-99; of literary structure, 206, 213-15; of Theosophy, 114-15; of urban world, 93-7, 166-68, 171
Patch, Howard Rollin, 156n
Pater, Walter, 117n
Peloponnese, 4-5, 8, 11, 30, 87, 105, 126, 139, 141-42, 144-45, 159, 164, 165, 172, 200, 229; *map of*, 149
Penelope, 12, 13, 35, 58, 59, 86, 130, 139, 151, 192, 212, 240, 241, 242, 246-47
Penelope (episode), 38, 41, 49, 68, 91, 139, 144, 151, 240, *241-47*; *maps of*, 250-51
Perejil, 150
Perse (daughter of Ocean stream), 130, 212
Persephone, 158, 216-17
Phaecia (Phaecians), 6, 10, 13-14, 15, 19, 127, 128-30, 153-54, 157, 195-96, 199-202, 229; *see also* Nausicaa
Pharaohs, 106-07, 109-10
Pharos isle, 11, 106, 145-46, 148; *see also* Proteus
Phidias, 108
Phoenician navigations, x, xii, xiv,

3-5, 7, 8, 11, 13, 16-18, 21-3, 25, 32, 98, 127, 146, 150-51, 154, 164, 170-71, 195, 196, 201, 212, 229-31, 244, 246; *see also* Bérard, *Odyssey*
Phoenix Park (Dublin), 7, 29, 167
Pico della Mirandola, 117
Pillars of Hercules, xi, 19, 27, 150
Pillot, Gilbert, xiv, 28n
Pisgah Sight of Palestine or the Parable of the Plums, 16, 125, 141, 167-68; *see also* Dedalus
Pisistratus, 86
Plato, 46, 117n, 203
Plutarch, 28, 138
Polyphemus, *see* Cyclops
Pomeranz, Victory, 155n
Ponchielli, Amilcare, 24
Pope, Alexander, 42
Portrait of the Artist as a Young Man, 7, 52, 73, 109, 117
Pound, Ezra, x, xv, 39n, 112, 194n
Pozzuoli, 159, 216
Prescott, Joseph, 60n
Proserpina (Persephone), 216
Prospero, 99
Proteus (sea-god), xiii, 5, 11, 15, 83, 87, 88, 90, 105-20, 140, 144-48, 161, 202, 211, 217; king, 107, 110
Proteus (episode), 33, 52, 55-6, 90, 106-09, 115, 117, 125, 126, *144-48*, 151, 160, 161, 165, 202, 207, 239
Pryse, J. M., 70
Poseidon, 8, 13-14, 15, 31, 46, 105-06, 116, 143, 152, 156, 200
Purchas, Samuel, 29
Purefoy, Mina, 37, 56, 97, 206
Pylos, 6, 15, 87, 105, 116, 126, 141-44, 201-02, 207, 233; *map of*, 149
Pyrrhus, 20, 141, 144
Pythagoras, 51

Quillian, William H., 102n

Ra (Egyptian god), 242
Rabelais, 51, 193
Raleigh, John Henry, 35n
Read, Forrest, xv n
Rhadamanthys, 117, 160

Library of Congress Cataloging in Publication Data

Seidel, Michael A   1943-
  Epic geography.

  Includes index.
  1. Joyce, James, 1882-1941. Ulysses. I. Title.
PR6019.09U694 1976   823'.9'12   75-30207
ISBN 0-691-06303-6